The decorations are up, the presents are
finally wrapped — so now it's time to curl up
with these three classic yuletide stories.

Brought to you by three of our all-time
favourite authors to make this a...

Christmas to Remember

The Fifth Day of Christmas — Betty Neels
Christmas Masquerade — Debbie Macomber
Unexpected Engagement — Jessica Steele

*MILLS & BOON and MILLS & BOON with the Rose Device
are registered trademarks of the publisher.*
Harlequin Mills & Boon Limited,
Eton House, 18-24 Paradise Road, Richmond, Surrey, TW9 1SR

CHRISTMAS TO REMEMBER
© by Harlequin Enterprises II B.V., 2004

The publisher acknowledges the copyright holders of the
individual works as follows:

The Fifth Day of Christmas © Betty Neels 1971
Christmas Masquerade © Debbie Macomber 1985
Unexpected Engagement © Jessica Steele 1996

ISBN 0 263 84506 0

059-1104

*Printed and bound in Spain
by Litografia Rosés S.A., Barcelona*

The Fifth Day of Christmas

by
Betty Neels

MILLS & BOON®

CHAPTER ONE

VIEWED FROM the comparative comfort of the ambulance's interior, the M1 looked uninviting. Miss Julia Pennyfeather, too occupied with her patient to have bothered overmuch with the passing scenery, now realised that the motorway was becoming more and more shrouded in fog, which, coupled with the fast darkening sky of a December afternoon, boded ill for their chances of reaching their destination as early as they had hoped. She pulled her cloak closely around her, cast a quick look at her dozing patient and peered out once more. There seemed to be a lot of traffic surging past, at great speed and in a confusion of lights, a sight which made her thankful that she wasn't called upon to drive the ambulance. She frowned in thought, then, moving cautiously, opened the little glass window behind the driving seat and said softly to the man sitting beside the driver, 'Willy—the fog, it's getting worse, isn't it?'

The man the back of whose neck she had addressed turned a cheerful face to answer her. 'Proper thick, Nurse, but it's not all that far. We're coming up to Newcastle now; it's about sixty miles to the Border and another twelve to the crossroads where we turn off—and the house is another ten miles or so.'

'It's nearly four o'clock,' said Julia. 'We shan't get there much before nine...'

'Just in nice time for a bit o' supper, Nurse, before we 'ands over the patient and goes to our warm beds.'

They were off the motorway now and almost clear of Newcastle; two hours' steady driving would bring them to the Border, and once they were in Scotland... She broke off her speculations as the girl on the stretcher asked, 'Where are we, Nurse?'

Julia told her, adding in a determinedly cheerful voice, 'We shan't be long now—three hours at the most, perhaps less. I expect you'd like a drink, wouldn't you?' She unscrewed a vacuum flask and poured the milkless tea into a mug. 'As soon as we arrive, you shall have your insulin and your supper— I'm sure they'll have it ready for you, for your nurse will have arrived some time this afternoon.'

'I hope I like her.'

Julia glanced at her patient. 'I'm sure you will,' she replied in a soothing voice, and privately hoped that she was right. Miss Mary MacGall hadn't been the easiest of patients—eighteen years old, pretty and spoilt and a diabetic who somehow never managed to achieve stabilisation, she had been a handful the Private Wing of St Clare's Hospital had been glad to see go. In the two short weeks she had been there, having an acute appendix removed, and then, unfortunately, peritonitis, which naturally played havoc with the diabetes, she had been rude to the Matron, flirted outrageously with the young housemen, and exasperated the consultant staff; only with Julia was she amenable, and that was something neither Julia nor her fellow workers could fathom, unless it was that Julia's dark and striking beauty was such a magnificent foil to her own blonde prettiness. And Julia didn't fuss, but

treated her with the pleasant calm that a well-trained
nanny might have shown to a recalcitrant child. Not
that Julia looked in the least like a nanny—indeed,
just the opposite, with her almost black hair and great
brown eyes with their preposterously long lashes. Her
mouth was a little large perhaps, but beautifully
shaped and her nose was straight, with the merest hint
of a tilt at its tip. She was well above average height,
nicely rounded and refreshingly and completely natural. She was just twenty-two and had achieved State
Registration only a few months previously. And only
the day before she had left the hospital where she had
spent several happy, busy years, not because she had
particularly wanted to, but to look after her sister-in-
law who had just had a second child and was suffering from depression. It had been, therefore, a happy
chance that Mary MacGall should have demanded to
be sent home by ambulance, and also demanded, at
the same time, that Julia should go with her on the
journey. Julia was due to leave anyway, and it would
give her a couple of days' respite before she went
home.

When next Julia looked out of the window it was
snowing hard and the fog had become dense. The
ambulance was travelling slowly now, with its blue
light flashing, and Julia was uneasily aware that they
were skidding from time to time. She opened the little
window once more and said softly into Willy's ear,
'Is it freezing as well?'

He nodded without looking round.

'Are we lost?'

She heard his chuckle and took comfort from the

sound. 'Not a bit of it, Nurse. We're over the Border—we'll be at the crossroads soon.'

'Is Bert all right? Does he want to stop?'

She peered ahead, the visibility was down to about ten yards and that was obscured by driving snow.

Bert answered for himself. 'I'm OK, Nurse. It's not far now and I think we'd do better to keep going. It might clear.'

She agreed softly, knowing that he had said that to reassure her, and closed the window, observing for the benefit of her patient,

'We've a dozen miles or so to go. Are you very hungry? I've some cream crackers here and there's plenty of tea.'

But Mary was disposed to be difficult. She said rather peevishly,

'I want a huge steak with lots of duchesse potatoes and creamed cauliflower and lashings of gravy and sauce, then Charlotte Russe with masses of whipped cream and a plate of petits fours—the gooey ones, and a huge whisky and soda—oh, and Kummel with my coffee.'

Julia felt sympathy with her patient. After all, she was very young; she would be on a fixed diet for the rest of her life. It was a pity that she was so spoiled that she refused to accept the fact, and anyway, once she was stabilised, the diet wouldn't be too awful, for her parents were wealthy enough to give it the variety those in more straitened circumstances couldn't afford. She said kindly, 'You make me feel quite hungry too, but you'd pay for it afterwards, you know.'

The girl beside her scowled. 'Who cares? That's what you're for—to see that I don't die in a coma.'

Julia looked at her reflectively. 'There's always the possibility that someone might not be there...'

'Oh, yes, there will,' declared Mary, and sat up suddenly. 'I suppose you wouldn't like to stay with me—for ever, I mean.'

Julia smiled, feeling a little touched. 'How nice of you to ask me. But I have to go home and look after my sister-in-law for a bit, then I thought I'd get a job abroad for a year or two—and I've still got my midwifery to do.'

'Marry a rich man instead.'

'Why rich? As long as he's the right one, the money doesn't matter very much, does it? You need enough to live on and educate the children.'

'And pretty clothes and the hairdresser and jewellery and going to the theatre and out to dine, and a decent holiday at least twice a year.'

Julia said soberly, 'Perhaps I'm not ambitious,' and turned away to look out of the window again—a pointless act, for it had been quite dark for some time now.

When the ambulance at last stopped, Julia couldn't believe they had arrived, for the last hour had been a nightmare of skidding and crawling through the blanket of fog and snow and now there was a gale blowing as well. She stepped out of the ambulance into several inches of snow and then clutched at her cap as a gust of wind tossed her backwards as though she had been a leaf. It was pitch dark too, but in the ambulance lights she could just see the beginning of steps leading upwards. She stood aside to let Bert and Willy get into the ambulance and asked, 'Shall I ring the bell?' and thought how ridiculous it sounded in this black waste of snow and fog and howling wind. But Bert said cheerfully enough,

'OK, Nurse—up them steps, and look out for the ice.'

She advanced cautiously with the beam of her powerful torch guiding her: it wasn't so bad after all—the steps ended at a great door upon whose knocker she beat a brisk tattoo, and when she saw the brass bell in the wall, she rang that for good measure. But there were no lights—she peered around her, unable to see anything but the reassuring solidarity of the door before her, and that hadn't opened. She was about to go down the steps again to relay her doubts to her companions when the door swung open, revealing a very old man holding a hurricane lantern. She was still getting her breath when he spoke testily.

'Ye didna' need to make all that noise. I heard ye the fust time.'

Julia, who had nice manners, apologised. 'Is this Drumlochie House?' she asked through teeth which were beginning to chatter with the cold.

'Aye—ye'll be the nurse with Miss Mary?'

'That's right—could you turn on the lights, please, so that the ambulance men can bring her indoors?'

'No lights,' said the old man without annoyance. 'Wind's taken the electric—can't think how ye got here.'

Julia couldn't either, but it hardly seemed the right moment to discuss it. She said instead, 'Then would you leave the door open and we'll bring Miss Mary in.'

She didn't wait to hear his reply but went carefully down the steps again.

She followed the two men, with the carrying chair and Mary in it, between them, back up again, shuddering at the possibility of a broken ankle or two added to Mary's diabetes. But they achieved the entrance without mishap and went inside where the old man was waiting for them, his lamp held high. 'So ye're back, Miss Mary,' he was, it seemed, a man of few words, 'your room's ready.'

He turned and started to walk across the hall towards the staircase discernible in the gloom, and the ambulance men, still with Mary between them, followed him with Julia bringing up the rear, shivering a little partly because she had got cold waiting at the front door and partly because her surroundings were, inadequately lighted as they were, a trifle forbidding. They seemed to walk a great distance before the old man at length opened a door and they entered Mary's bedroom—a large apartment with a fire burning in its open fireplace and most pleasantly furnished. Julia, looking round her, heaved a sigh of relief. If their rooms were half as comfortable they would have nothing to grumble about.

'Where's the nurse?' she asked the old man.

He stood and thought, his head on one side, for an aggravating moment. 'The nurse? Weel, she's to come from Edinburgh, but it's been snowing a blizzard since daybreak hereabouts. There'll be no nurse.'

'No nurse!' Julia looked at him with something like horror. 'But I'm going back to London with the ambulance in the morning—I can't leave my patient. Where's the telephone?'

'The wind's had it.'

The wind, thought Julia bitterly, was answerable for a lot.

'There must be some way of getting a message— to the village or a doctor—or the police.'

He didn't even bother to say no, just shook his head. 'Snow's deep,' he observed without emotion. 'There's Jane the cook and Madge the maid gone to Hawick yesterday to shop for Miss Mary's return. They'll not be back for twa days, maybe.'

Julia's dismay was smothered in a flood of practical thoughts.

'Food?' she asked. 'Hot water, candles?'

'Food's enough—candles and lamps we've got— hot water, now, that's another matter. I've no call for hot water, stove's gone out.'

'If you could possibly light it for us again? Miss Mary—all of us, we need to wash at least. Are there any rooms ready for us?'

He shook his head. 'No. Madge was to have done that, and me thinking ye'd not get here in this weather—I didna' light the fire...'

'Never mind—could the ambulance men come and help you? They're tired and hungry—they must have a meal and a good sleep. If you'd give them the bed-linen I'm sure they'll make up the beds, and I'll come down to the kitchen and cook something.'

He looked at her with a glimmer of respect. 'Aye, do that if ye will. Miss Mary—she's all right?'

'Once she has had her supper she will be.' Julia smiled at him and went to fetch Bert and Willy.

There was food enough once she could find it in the vast semi-basement kitchen. She pottered about, still wrapped in her cloak, while the men made up beds and lighted fires, making Mary's supper as attractive as possible.

It was getting on for midnight when Julia removed the supper tray, and Mary, still grumbling, had consented to go to bed. Julia left an oil lamp the old man had produced in the room, wished her patient a good night and went in search of Willy and Bert. She found them, after a great deal of tramping up and down draughty corridors, very snug in a little room on the floor above.

'Nothing but fourposters downstairs,' Willy explained. 'We've found you a nice room below, Nurse, got a fire going an' all. First left at the bottom of the stairs.'

She thanked them, warned them that she was about to cook supper and went in search of her sleeping quarters. The room was reasonably near her patient's, she was glad to find, and at the head of the stairs, and although there was a piercing draught whistling round the hall below, the room itself looked pleasant enough. She sighed with relief, went to look at Mary, who was already asleep, and made her way downstairs once more. The old man had disappeared; to bed probably, having considered that he had done enough for them. She set about frying eggs and bacon and boiling the kettle for tea, and presently the three of them sat down to a supper, which, while not being quite what they had expected, was ample and hot.

The three of them washed up, wished each other good night, and crept upstairs, bearing a variety of candlesticks and yawning their heads off. Julia, with a longing eye on the comfort of the bed, undressed with the speed of lightning, unpinned her hair, brushed it perfunctorily and went to find a bathroom. There were several, none supplying more than tepid water, so she cleaned her teeth, washed her face and hands with the same speed with which she had brushed her hair and, after a quick look at the sleeping Mary, retired to her room, where, without daring to take off her dressing gown, she jumped into bed. And as she closed her eyes the front door bell rang.

She waited a moment, pretending to herself that she hadn't heard it, but when it pealed again she got out of bed, picked up her torch, thrust her feet into slippers and started downstairs. The wind was fiercer now and the draughts eddied around her, chilling her to the bone. Only the thought of the unfortunate person on the doorstep urged her on. It would be the nurse, arrived by some miracle Julia was far too tired to investigate, or perhaps the cook and the maid from Hawick, although she fancied that the town was a good many miles away. She undid the bolts of the front door, slid the chain back and opened its creaking weight on to the fog and wind and snow outside.

There was a man on the top step, a very large man, who stood wordless and patient while she allowed her torch to travel his considerable length. She knew that he was staring at her from the gloom and when she said impatiently, 'Oh, do come in—we'll both catch our deaths of cold…' he stepped into the hall without uttering a word, only when he had locked the door behind her did he say without heat,

'Of all the damn fool things to do—opening a door to a complete stranger in the dead of night!'

Julia's beautiful eyes opened wide. 'But you rang the bell.'

'And have you never heard of opening a door on its chain? I might have been armed with a shotgun.'

Julia interrupted him in a matter-of-fact voice, 'Don't be absurd—who'd be out on a night like this with a shotgun?'

He laughed then. 'Since you're kind enough to trust me, could I beg shelter until the morning? I'm on my way down from Edinburgh and quite obviously I've taken the wrong road.'

He gave himself a shake and the snow tumbled off him, to lie unmelting on the floor. 'You're not alone in this place?'

'No,' said Julia with calm, 'I'm not—there are two ambulance men asleep upstairs, so tired they won't hear a sound—and my patient—oh, and there's a kind of ancient family retainer, but I haven't seen him for several hours.'

He took the torch from her hand and shone it deliberately on her.

'You are a fool,' he remarked mildly. 'Here you are, a very beautiful girl unless my eyes deceive me, with two men sleeping like the dead upstairs, an old retainer who's probably deaf and a patient chained to his bed...'

'Look,' said Julia patiently, 'I'm very tired—you're welcome to a bed,' she waved a vague arm towards the staircase. 'There are plenty of empty rooms if you like to choose one. Are you hungry?'

She had taken the torch once more from his grasp and shone it briefly on him. 'Take off that coat,' she advised. 'I'll go and put the kettle on—will bacon and eggs do?'

'Not only beautiful but kind too,' he murmured.

'Thank you, I'm famished. Where's the kitchen? Go back to bed and I'll look after myself.'

She was already on her way kitchenwards. 'It's warmer there than anywhere else. Come along.'

Ten minutes later he was sitting at the kitchen table devouring the food she had cooked, while she made the tea. 'Thank heaven there's a gas stove,' Julia commented as she fetched two cups. 'The wind took the electric and the telephone.'

'How very whimsical!'

Julia poured him another cup of tea and then filled her own cup. In the little silence which followed a clock wheezed dryly and struck twice, and the wind, taking on a new strength, howled like a banshee round the house. Julia looked up to see the stranger's eyes fastened on her. He smiled and said, 'If you trust me, go to bed—I'll clear up and find myself a room.'

She got to her feet and picked up her torch, yawning as she did so. 'There's your candle,' she indicted a brass candlestick with its snuffer which she had put ready for him. 'Don't come into my room, will you? It's at the top of the stairs—nor the third one on the right—that's my patient's. Good night.'

She wondered why he looked amused as he wished her good night, getting politely to his feet as he did so, which small action somehow reassured her.

Not that she needed reassuring, she told herself, lying curled up in her chilly bed; the fire had died down and the warmth it had engendered had already been swallowed up by the icy air. She shivered and decided that she liked him, even though she knew nothing about him, neither his name nor his business, but she liked his face—a face she felt she could trust, with strong features and steady blue eyes and a mouth that was firm and kind. And even though he had called her a fool—which she was bound to admit was the truth—he had also called her beautiful. She fell uneasily asleep, smiling a little.

Something wakened her in the pitch darkness, a sound, not repeated. She switched on the torch to find that it was just after six o'clock, and sat up in bed, the better to listen. The sound came again—a hoarse croak. She was out of bed, thrusting her feet into her slippers as the list of post-operative complications liable to follow an appendicectomy on a diabetic patient unfolded itself in her still tired mind. Carbuncles, gangrene, broncho-pneumonia…the croak came again which effectively ruled out the first two, and when she reached her patient's bedroom and saw Mary's flushed face as she lay shivering in bed, she was almost sure that it was the third.

As she approached the bed Mary said irritably, 'I feel so ill, and I can't stop coughing—it hurts.'

'I'll sit you up a bit,' said Julia with a calm she didn't feel. Sudden illness on a hospital ward was one thing, but in an isolated house cut off from the outside world, it was quite a different matter. She fetched more pillows and propped the girl up, took her temperature which was as high as she had expected it to be, and gave her a drink, while all the time she was deciding what to do. Presently, when Mary was as comfortable as she could be made, Julia said,

'I'm going to send someone for the doctor—once we've got you on an antibiotic you'll feel better within hours. Will you stay quietly until I come back?'

She found the stranger in the third room she looked into, lying on his back on a vast fourposter bed, fast asleep. She put out an urgent hand and tapped a massive shoulder and he opened his eyes at once, staring at her with a calm which she found most comforting.

Before she could speak he said reflectively, 'The hair's a little wild, but I still think you're a beautiful girl. What's the matter?'

Julia swept her long black hair impatiently on one side the better to see him. 'My patient—she's ill. I'm afraid I must ask you to go and find a doctor or a telephone or—or something. I can't ask the ambulance men to go; they've got to go back to London today and they must have a night's sleep.'

He had sat up and swung his legs over the side of the bed. 'And I, being a man of leisure, am the obvious one to sacrifice on the altar of frostbite and exposure.'

Julia just stopped herself in time from wringing her hands. 'I'd go myself, but who's to look after Mary if I do?'

'A moot point,' he conceded, and stood up, reassuringly large. 'And before I detect the first rising note of hysteria in your very delightful voice, I must tell you that I am a doctor.'

Julia's first reaction was one of rage. 'You beast,' she said roundly, 'letting me get all worried!'

He smiled at her and lifted her neatly to sit on the bed and then sat down beside her. 'I am of the opinion that if I were not a doctor I should even now be meekly dressing myself, preparatory to tramping miles in search of aid, while you coped with great competence with whatever crisis has arisen. Now, let's have the bad news.'

She shivered, and was glad when he put an arm around her shoulders.

'My patient's a diabetic—an unstabilised one. She had appendicectomy followed by peritonitis two weeks ago. She made a good recovery although she isn't very co-operative and has had several slight comas. She wanted—insisted on coming home and it was arranged that she should travel from St Clare's in London by ambulance. We had a job getting here, but on the whole she had a comfortable journey and her usual diet and insulin. Her TPR was normal last night. She's loaded with sugar and acetone now and her temp's a hundred and three.'

He got off the bed, taking her with him. 'Well, you pop back to the patient and make soothing sounds while I put on some clothes and fetch my case—it's locked in the car just outside the door.' He gave her a gentle push. 'Go along now, there's a good girl.'

Mary was restless when Julia got back to her. She said as soon as she caught sight of her, 'I'm going to die, and there isn't a doctor.'

Julia gave her another drink of water and then went to build up the fire. 'Yes, there is.' She explained about his arrival during the night in a few brief words because Mary was too feverish to concentrate on anything. 'He'll be here in a moment,' went on Julia soothingly, 'he'll take a look at you and then prescribe something which will have you feeling better in no time.'

She went and got the case history notes and the charts and diets she had prepared so carefully for the nurse who was to have taken over from her, laid them neatly on a table and then hastily plaited her hair. She had just finished doing that when the doctor knocked on the door and came in.

Not only had he donned his clothes, but a faultless professional manner with them, which somehow made the whole situation seem normal and not in the least worrying. He knew what he was about, for he dealt with his patient gently and with a calm air of assurance which convinced her that she was already getting better, and then went to bend over Julia's papers, lying ready for them. When he had finished reading them he looked up and asked,

'Is there a doctor's letter?'

'Yes,' said Julia, 'it's in my room.' She didn't offer to fetch it.

'I think I should see it—I'll take full responsibility for opening it, Nurse. Would you fetch it?'

She did so without a word, not sure as to the ethics of the case, and stood quietly by while he read it. Which he did, refolding it into its envelope when he had finished and adding some writing of his own before handing it back to her.

'Penicillin, I think, Nurse. Shall we give her a shot now and repeat it six-hourly? And the insulin—she's been on Semilente, I see. We'd better increase it this morning and test every two hours until this evening. Now, diet...'

He went away when he had given Mary her penicillin and told her cheerfully that she would be out of bed in a couple of days, leaving Julia to reiterate all he had said before she went to dress. Once more in uniform and intent on perching her cap on her neatly arranged hair, she turned in surprise when there was a tap on her door.

'Tea,' said the stranger, 'and if you'll tell me where the ambulance men are I'll wake them for you.'

Julia took the proffered cup. 'How kind,' she said with surprise, and felt suddenly downcast when he answered carelessly,

'Oh, I'm handy about the house,' for it made him sound as though he were married. She said hastily because she wanted to change the trend of her thoughts, 'Is the weather better?'

He sat down on the end of the bed and started to drink the ambulance men's tea. 'No—the snow's in drifts—the car's almost covered and so is the ambulance. There's no snow at present, but there's more to come as far as I can see in this light. The fog has lifted, but the ground's like glass.'

She sipped her tea. It looked as though they would be there for another day at least and she was surprised to find that she didn't mind in the least. When he asked, 'What's your name?' she answered without hesitation. 'Pennyfeather, Julia Pennyfeather.'

'Miss Pennyfeather—it is Miss?'

She nodded. 'You're drinking Willy's and Bert's teas,' she pointed out.

'I'm thirsty. Don't you want to know my name?'

She nodded again.

'Van den Werff—Ivo. Very nearly thirty years old and until now, a confirmed bachelor.'

She ignored her sudden delight. 'Dutch?' she hazarded. 'Do you work in England—no, Scotland?'

'I've been on a course at the Royal Infirmary in

Edinburgh. I'm on my way back to Holland, but I intend to spend a day or so in London before I cross.'

Julia drank her tea, conscious of a sense of loss because presently he would be gone and she would never see him again. He got up off the bed and picked up the tray with the two empty cups and went off.

Julia went downstairs herself a few minutes later and found the old man sitting by the gas stove, drinking tea. She said good morning pleasantly and was told there was nothing good about it, so she busied herself getting her patient's diet and went back upstairs with it. It was another ten minutes by the time she had given the insulin and arranged Mary more comfortably to have her tea and bread and butter, and when she got back to the kitchen the old man had gone. She set about laying the table and got out the frying pan once more; lucky that there were plenty of eggs and a quantity of bacon, she thought, peering into the old-fashioned, roomy larder. She was making the tea when the three men came in, Willy and Bert very apologetic at having slept through the night's calamities. They looked well rested though, and volunteered cheerfully to do any chores she might choose to set them.

Bert looked at Julia an asked worriedly, 'And what's to be done about you, Nurse? We'll 'ave to go the minute we can—will you be able to come with us? You can't stay here alone.'

'She won't be alone.' The doctor's quiet voice sounded quite certain about that. 'I'll stay until the patient's own doctor can take over and the nurse can get here.'

'That's quite unnecessary,' said Julia quickly, 'I'm

perfectly able to manage…' she remembered how she had awakened him that morning and went faintly pink, and before she could finish what she was going to say, Bert observed with obvious relief, 'Ah, well, if the doc's going to be 'ere, that's OK, ain't it, Willy? Can't do better than that.'

'Then that's settled,' said Dr van den Werff, ignoring the light of battle in Julia's fine eyes. 'In any case, we can do nothing today except get this mausoleum warm. If the snow holds off we might reconnoitre later on…in the meantime shall we share out the chores?'

Something which he did with a pleasant authority which neither Willy nor Bert disputed, and which Julia, even if she had wished to do so, was unable to argue against because she had to go back to her patient, leaving him to explain to the old retainer, who had appeared from nowhere to join them at breakfast, just why they were forced to remain at Drumlochie House for at least another day.

CHAPTER TWO

JULIA HAD PLENTY to do, for not only did she have to see Mary comfortably settled and work out her diet for the day; there were meals to cook for the five of them as well. Fortunately she was a good cook; at one o'clock she was able to call them into a solid meal of soup, followed by bacon omelettes with jacket potatoes done in the Aga, and a baked rice pudding to follow, and when she would have apologised for the plainness of the fare they looked at her with astonishment, declaring that it was one of the best meals they had eaten for a very long time.

It was after this warming meal that Julia found herself with the doctor while he went over Mary's tests and wrote up the insulin. Mary had responded very well to the penicillin; her chest condition had already improved, although she was sorry enough for herself, but she was too listless to complain about her diet, and for once there seemed no danger of her going into another coma. Julia had given her another penicillin injection at noon and rather to her surprise, her patient had made very little fuss about it and had even laughed a little at the doctor's jokes when he came to see her. Julia stood by him while he wrote up the insulin chart for the rest of the day and as he was putting his pen away, said,

'I—we are very grateful to you, doctor. Mary's better, isn't she?'

'Yes.' He gave her a thoughtful glance. 'Are you in a hurry to be gone?'

'If you mean do I have a job to go to, no. I left St Clare's three days ago—I came here with Mary to oblige her parents—they're abroad, and Matron...'

'You're going on holiday?' He put the question so gently that she answered him without hesitation.

'No, I'm going home to my brother's—his wife—that is, he thinks it would be nice if I stayed with them for a bit and...' She stopped, for she really had no intention of telling him anything about herself. 'Oh, well,' she finished airily, 'it's all arranged,' and if she had expected him to press for more of an answer than that she was disappointed, for all he said was, 'We've dug out the car and ambulance. If it doesn't snow any more today Bert and Willy might get away in the morning.'

Julia was examining what he had written with unnecessary interest.

'Did you mean what you said?' she asked, not looking at him, 'I mean about staying? Don't you have to get home?'

'I can't very well leave my patient, can I?' he wanted to know with an air of reasonableness which she found infuriating. 'I can't deny it's most inconvenient, but then we're all being inconvenienced, aren't we?' He gave her a sideways look. 'Would you like to go for a walk?'

Julia gave him a surprised look and then said sensibly, 'Yes, but I can't—I haven't any boots and I can't leave Mary.'

'We'll get the old retainer to fit you out, and Bert

and Willy can mount guard over Mary for an hour. You've got to get some fresh air some time.'

She was given no more chance to protest but caught firmly by the arm and walked back to the kitchen, where Bert and Willy immediately agreed to look after their patient and the old man, winkled out of some cosy haunt of his own, produced rubber boots which more or less fitted and a great hooded cape which reached her ankles and had obviously been cut to fit someone of majestic proportions. The doctor fastened the hood under her chin with a large safety pin Bert obligingly produced, got into his own out-door clothes and opened the back door.

They made their way through the snow and, pres-ently, out of the gate at the back of the garden. It led on to moorland, which, in the right kind of weather, must have contained magnificent views. Now only the nearest of the foot-hills could be seen. The Cheviots, she knew, were close but shrouded in the still linger-ing mist into which the trees ahead of them marched, to disappear into its gloom. 'Do we know where we're going?' Julia asked with interest.

'Vaguely. We're quite safe as long as it doesn't snow, and I don't think it will.' He took her arm to help her along and at the touch of his hand she felt a little glow of warmth deep inside her.

'It's only three weeks to Christmas,' she observed, trying to ignore the glow. She would be with her brother and his family and his friend James would come over for Christmas dinner. She frowned at the thought and the doctor said, 'And you're not looking forward to it.' It was a statement, not a question.

'Well, no, not very. I've spent my last few Christ-mases in hospital and it was rather fun…'

'But that's not the reason.'

He was far too perceptive. Julia stood still and looked around her. 'How quiet it is,' she almost whispered. She looked up at the lowering sky too and her hood fell back. The doctor undid the safety pin and pulled it back over her black hair, then fastened the pin again and before she could turn her head away, bent down and kissed her.

'Only a seasonal greeting,' he explained gravely, and Julia striving to behave as she felt a sophisticated young woman should, said a little breathlessly, 'Yes—well, should we be going back?'

He took no notice of this remark but tucked her hand in his and continued walking through the snow, while she, hampered by the boots which were a little on the large side, plodded beside him.

'Tell me about yourself,' he invited, and for a moment she was tempted to do just that—to tell him how she disliked the idea of going back to Stoke-cum-Muchelney, because she was afraid that she would never get away again, only if she married James. She looked sideways at the man beside her, comparing him with James, who came off very second best. James was already getting thin on top, while her companion had plenty of hair on his handsome head, of a pleasing fairness and elegantly cut; James hadn't a square chin and his mouth was small and a little thick in the lip. The doctor had a firm, well-shaped mouth and his voice was pleasant too, deep and unhurried, and he didn't say H'm each time he spoke. The thought that Doctor van den Werff would make the splendid husband of her vague dreams crossed her mind, to be dismissed immediately. He was a complete stranger—well, almost complete; she knew nothing about him, and, she told herself firmly, she didn't intend to. In a couple of days' time, when the nurse arrived and he could contact the doctor, he would go, and so would she, both to their respective worlds.

'There's nothing to tell,' she replied with a cool politeness which wasn't lost on him, for he said instantly, 'Ah, yes—not my business, eh?'

He let go of her arm and stopped to scoop some snow into his gloved hand, looking at her and laughing as he did so, and she, guessing that the snowball was meant for her, made haste to dodge it, a difficult task with the boots hampering her every step. It would have been silly not to have defended herself, which she did with some success, for he was a large target and although quick on his feet, not quick enough. She tossed the snow at him with all the pleasure of a small child, laughing and shouting and momentarily forgetful of her prosaic future. Presently, still laughing and panting from their exercise, they turned back to the house.

The rest of the day seemed a little dull after that. Julia, her hair tidied once more and crowned with its nurse's cap, returned to her patient, her pink cheeks and sparkling eyes belying the extreme neatness of her person, a fact which Bert and Willy duly remarked upon when she saw them. They had been discussing her, she sensed, as she entered the room, and they made no attempt to hide the fact from her, for Bert said at once,

'We were wondering, Willy and me, if we ought ter go—it don't seem right, leaving you alone. Yer don't mind staying—just with the doc, I mean?'

Julia smiled very nicely at him. 'No,' she said gently, 'I don't mind, Bert. In fact I shall feel quite safe.'

''E seems a nice sort of fellow,' said Willy, 'even though 'e is a foreigner.' He got up and went to the door. 'If yer're quite happy about it, Nurse?'

She answered him seriously. 'If I weren't, Willy, I should have asked you both to stay. What time do you expect to leave in the morning?' She frowned. 'I must write to Sister…'

'Eight o'clock or thereabouts. We'll go back the way we came, though the Carlisle road isn't all that far, but it wouldn't be easy to reach. The doc says he'll come a bit of the way with us, just in case we get stuck. We're going to ring Miss Mary's doctor for him too, so's 'e can come over just as soon as the road's clear. Doc's written it all down for us. I'm to tell 'im you're 'ere as well.'

Julia said uncertainly, 'Oh, are you? I never thought of that.' Nor had she. It seemed Doctor van den Werff had taken the welfare of his fellows very much to heart; she felt pretty certain that when the time came, he would arrange for her departure, buy her ticket and see that she had enough money for necessities on the journey back. Which reminded her, she had a little money with her, but not nearly enough to take her back to London. She would have to borrow, and from the doctor, for it was unthinkable to ask her patient for it and the old retainer was equally impossible. The family doctor might be of help, but she disliked asking for a loan from a stranger. That Doctor van den Werff was a stranger too had for the moment escaped her.

Mary woke up and Julia, who had been standing idly by the window, went to draw up the penicillin before getting her patient's tea and then, when the doctor obligingly said the he would sit with Mary, went down to the vast kitchen to get supper for the rest of them.

She was up early the next morning making sandwiches for the two ambulance men and filling the thermos and then cooking as generous a breakfast as she dared for them. The food was getting a bit low by now, although she would be able to go on making bread for some time, and there were plenty of potatoes, but there was Mary to think of, for as soon as she had recovered from her broncho-pneumonia she would want to eat again. Julia had set aside as much as possible for her, which meant that she and the doctor and Hamish would have to make do with a restricted though ample enough diet.

The morning was a mere glimmer at the end of the long night when she went to the door to see the men off. They wrung her hand, took the letter she had written and trudged through the frozen snow towards the stable. The doctor followed them. He had hardly spoken during breakfast, but now he paused at the door. 'I'll be back as soon as I can,' he said cheerfully, 'but don't worry if I don't turn up until later in the day—we might get held up with the drifts and have to dig ourselves out. If I can get as far as the main road I'll try and find out what's happening about the telephone, or get a message into Hawick. The men will telephone there from Newcastle anyway, but I don't think we should leave any stones unturned, do you?'

Julia asked, 'Will you be able to telephone your family in Holland? Won't they be worrying?' and went faintly pink when he said coolly, 'Time enough for that, Miss Pennyfeather—we have to get you settled first, don't we?'

He grinned suddenly, turned on his heel and set out into the icy morning.

The house was very quiet when they had gone. She had listened to them starting up the ambulance and then the car and, minutes later, their horns blaring a goodbye to her as the noise of the engines became fainter and fainter and then ceased altogether, leaving her lonely.

But there wasn't much time for loneliness; there was Mary to see to and the rooms to tidy and the food cupboard to be frowned over once more. Hamish had brought in some more eggs, but everything else was getting on the low side, though there was plenty if someone arrived that evening and brought food with them, but Julia had looked out of the window as soon as it was light and had been disquieted by the grey sky with its ominous yellow tinges streaking the horizon, and the wind was getting up again as well. She went back to Mary's room and built up a magnificent fire as though by so doing she could ward off the bad weather she guessed was coming.

The wind began to whine in real earnest about three o'clock and the first snowflakes whirled down, slowly and daintily at first and then in real earnest. It didn't look as though the nurse would arrive that day, nor the cook and the maid, nor, for that matter, thought Julia gloomily, Doctor van den Werff. He was probably stuck in some drift miles from anywhere; she was thankful that she had made him take some sandwiches and a thermos too.

She took Mary's tea up presently, to find her awake and more cheerful, and she was still with her when she heard the car return. It was dark outside and the fast falling snow almost obliterated its headlights as it went past the house in the direction of the stables. Julia left Mary to finish her tea and went downstairs, her cape held close against the draughts, and reached the kitchen as the doctor came in from outside, bringing a rush of cold air in with him.

Julia went to the stove and opened one of the plates so that the singing kettle could boil. 'I thought you'd never get here,' she said, trying to make her voice light.

The doctor took off his coat and shook a quantity of snow from it on to the floor, then hung it on the back of a chair where it began to steam. Only then did he speak, and the extreme placidity of his voice annoyed her.

'My dear Miss Pennyfeather,' he remarked, 'I told you that I should come,' which calm and brief speech caused her to burst out, 'Well, I know you did, but sitting here waiting for you isn't the same...'

'Waiting for me, were you? I'm flattered—at least I should have been in any other circumstances. Unfortunately the telephone wires are still down—I wasted a great deal of time. Still, the snow ploughs have been out on the main road.' He sat down at the table and she realised that this meagre information was all she was going to get about his day. She poured him some tea from the pot she had just made and offered him bread and jam.

'Is the weather very bad?' she wanted to know.

'Quite nasty, but I don't fancy it's going to last. Has everything been all right here?' He glanced at Hamish, who nodded before Julia could answer. 'Aye, the fires are lit, and there's plenty of wood. I'll kill a chicken tomorrow.'

The doctor nodded. 'Good idea—otherwise I'll have to go out with a gun.'

'What,' said Julia indignantly, 'and shoot any small creature, half-starved and frozen?'

He didn't laugh at her. 'I shouldn't enjoy it,' he said gently, 'but we have to eat. But don't worry, if Hamish here lets us have a chicken we'll do very well for a couple of days—Mary can have it too.'

Julia agreed, wondering the while what Mary's mother would say when she arrived home and found no food in the cupboards and several beds in use. But of course they would all be gone by then and she herself would never know, she would be in Somerset and this strange adventure would be a dream—so would the doctor. She sighed and got up to refill the teapot.

She had tucked Mary up for the night and had gone to her room to sit by the fire before beginning the chilly business of undressing when there was a knock on the door and the doctor came in.

'Mary?' asked Julia as she started to her feet.

'No—she's asleep, I've just been to look. I want to talk to you and your room is warmer than mine—do you mind if I come in?'

Julia felt surprise, pleasure and finally a faint excitement which she firmly suppressed. She sat down again. 'There's a chair in that corner, it's larger than the others,' she said sensibly.

His lips twitched, but he went obediently and fetched it, sat down opposite her and began without preamble.

'The reason I was going to London before returning to Holland was in order that I might engage a nurse to take back with me. There is a young lady staying with my family—an English girl who contracted polio just before I came over to Edinburgh. She went to hospital, of course, but now she is back with us, but I hear that she is very bored with only my sister to talk to, for she doesn't care to learn Dutch. She's convalescent and has made a splendid recovery which I feel could be hastened even more by having someone with her to whom she could talk freely.'

He paused and looked across at Julia, his eyebrows lifted in an unspoken question.

'Me?' asked Julia, and felt a pleasant tingle of excitement.

'Yes—it would save me hunting around in London, and I think that you may suit admirably. You are very much of an age and capable with it. If you could see your way to coming for a few weeks? I know it is sudden, but I fancy you wouldn't mind overmuch if you didn't go to your brother's. Am I right?'

'Yes—I don't want to go in the least,' she said bluntly, 'but I really should.'

'Forgive me, but is your brother not able to afford a nurse for his wife, or help of some sort?'

She flushed. 'Yes, of course he can, only I expect

he feels it's a waste of money to pay someone when there's me.'

'So you would have no feeling of—er—guilt if you were not to go?'

Julia was a little surprised to find that she didn't feel in the least guilty. She said briefly, 'No.'

'Then, Miss Pennyfeather, will you come? I know this is a most irregular way of offering a job, but in the rather peculiar circumstances in which we find ourselves…you trust me?'

Julia looked startled. 'Trust you? Of course I trust you.' Her voice sounded as startled as her face. 'I hope I shall suit your patient.'

She hoped that he might give her a few more details, but it seemed that he didn't intend doing so, not at that moment anyway, for he went on to ask her if she had a passport and would she mind being out of England for Christmas.

She said a little breathlessly, for she was still surprised at herself for her rash acceptance of a job she knew nothing about, 'Yes—I've a passport, it's with my things in London. I've never been out of England at Christmas time, but I don't suppose I shall mind.'

'No? I daresay you'll find it much the same as in England. We have the same family gatherings, but I don't think we put quite such emphasis on presents. We have St Nikolaas, you see, earlier in the month.'

She nodded, having only a slight inkling of what he was talking about. She had heard of St Nikolaas, naturally, and she knew all about his white horse and Black Peter, but that was already over and done with; it was almost Christmas. A Christmas she might enjoy much more than if she went to her brother's.

His voice cut through her thoughts with a gentle persistence she couldn't ignore. 'If I might have your attention, Miss Pennyfeather? We shall have to stay here until such time as the nurse, the doctor and the servants arrive, then I propose to drive down to London where you can collect your clothes and whatever else you want. We can cross from Harwich when it suits us and drive home from there.'

Julia watched him put another log on the fire. 'I don't know where you live.'

'Near Tilburg, a small town called Oisterwijk. I work at the hospital in Tilburg—I'm an anaesthetist. I also go once a week to Breda and s'Hertogenbosch and occasionally to Eindhoven. My father has a practice in which I am a partner and when he retires I shall take it over. My sister runs the household and I have two brothers younger than I—one is married, the youngest is still finishing his post-graduate course at a Utrecht hospital.'

'And my patient?'

He gave her a sharp glance and took so long in replying that she thought that probably he was deciding what to tell her. 'Miss Marcia Jason,' he said at length, 'who was staying with us when she was taken ill. We are all very fond of her, and to get her completely well again is our dearest wish.'

Julia ignored the pang she felt at his words, for she suspected that it had something to do with the doctor being fond of his patient... It was extremely foolish of her to get interested in him. She told herself that it was only because they had been thrown together in trying circumstances that she felt...she decided not to pursue her train of thought and looked up to see the doctor regarding her steadily. 'And now,' he invited, 'tell me something of yourself.'

To her surprise she did, although she hadn't really meant to. Out it all came, her brother and Maureen and her home and how lovely the garden was in the summer and how awful London was if you hadn't anywhere to go—and James. He didn't speak, just sat and listened as she enlarged upon James and his tedious perfections. 'He's s-so right always,' she ended, 'and so dreadfully patient and good when I lose my temper. He says I'll be better when we settle down: But I don't want to settle down—not with him.'

'Have you anyone in mind?' queried her companion mildly.

She said uncertainly, 'No—oh, no,' and knew in her heart that it wasn't quite true. James and Maureen and her brother too had told her a great many times that there was no such thing as love at first sight; love came gradually, they had explained patiently, and Julia, an unwilling listener, had considered that it all sounded rather dull. She had said so, passionately, and they had smiled at her with pitying coolness. She said now, 'I shouldn't have said all that about James.' She gave the doctor a direct look. 'It was disloyal.'

He smiled nicely. 'No. As far as I can judge, you owe this James nothing, and you can be sure that I'll forget everything about the tiresome fellow, and I suggest that you do too, otherwise you'll find yourself living in a semi-detached with a great deal to do and a string of babies.'

'But I like babies!'

He closed his eyes. 'So do I, Miss Pennyfeather. How delightful that we agree upon such an important aspect of life. If we persevere we shall undoubtedly find other things just as important.'

Julia stared at him, her lovely eyes wide. As though it mattered if they agreed about anything! The fewer things the better, she was inclined to think, bearing in mind Miss Marcia Jason...

'Is she pretty?' she asked suddenly. The doctor looked as though he was laughing silently, but he had that sort of face, anyway.

'Very,' he answered without hesitation, 'small and fair, with large blue eyes. She has an extremely intelligent brain.'

'Has the polio affected her badly?'

'Luckily the damage is slight. It's a question of constant encouragement, that's why I thought a nurse, someone sensible and her own age, would give her the stimulus she needs for the last few weeks of convalescence.'

Julia nodded while she seethed. She had had her share of men friends, none of whom had ever called her sensible in that matter-of-fact voice. She gave him a cross look and went scarlet when he added, 'Not that being sensible is your only attribute, my dear young lady, but it is the only one which applies in this case, I think.' He got up, taking his time, and at the door he said, 'Let us pray for good weather so that we may get away from here as soon as possible; I have never suffered so many draughts. Goodnight, Miss Pennyfeather.'

It snowed again the next day, but late in the afternoon the weathered cleared and at teatime Hamish offered the information that the worst was over, and neither Julia nor Doctor van den Werff thought to question his pronouncement, for after all, he had lived in the Border country all his life, and he should know. As if to bear him out the radio in the doctor's car proclaimed exactly the same state of affairs, if in somewhat more elaborate language, adding a rider to the effect that telephone communications were being reinstated as quickly as possible. But the telephone at Drumlochie House remained silent and no one arrived, which wasn't surprising, for the snow plough hadn't got so far.

The snow plough, however, came the next morning and Doctor van den Werff went up to the road and brought the driver back for coffee. The road was clear, the man told them, at least a narrow lane of it, and once on the main road the going wasn't too bad, although he warned them about skidding and went on to relate, to the delight of old Hamish, several unfortunate incidents which had occurred owing to the bad weather; he would have gone on for some time in like vein had not the doctor reminded him that he still had the stretch of road to Hawick to clear. When he had gone the doctor looked at his watch and remarked. 'He should be there by midday or a little after. I should think we might expect someone by this evening. It is to be hoped that the telephone will be working again before then so that I can talk to Mary's doctor—he should have had my message by now, that is, if Bert managed to get it to him.'

The doctor didn't telephone, but came in his car with Jane and Madge sitting inside it. By the look on their faces, Julia thought that perhaps the journey hadn't been all that smooth, a supposition the doctor bore out with forceful language when he got out of the car. 'But I got your message,' he said as he looked round the hall for Doctor van den Werff, who wasn't there, 'and I came as soon as I could—I had no idea…is Mary all right?'

Julia, easing him out of his duffle coat, said that yes, she believed so and that Doctor van den Werff would have heard the car and would be in to tell him all he wished to know. She then offered everyone tea, introduced herself to Jane and Madge, begged them to go and get warm in the kitchen and then inquired of the doctor if he had brought any food with him.

'In the boot, I'll bring it in presently, Nurse.' He turned away as Doctor van den Werff walked in and Julia made her escape, leaving them to introduce themselves, for she had no idea of the doctor's name.

They were drinking tea while Julia apologised for the amount of food they had eaten during their stay, when the two men came in with the air of people who were quite satisfied with each other. She poured them each a cup, offered a plate of scones and murmuring something about seeing to Mary, went upstairs, followed almost immediately by Jane and Madge, who made much of the invalid and listened with patience to her highly coloured version of her journey home. They rose to go at length, promising supper within a couple of hours, and went away, discussing the merits of a nice toad-in-the-hole as opposed to Quiche Lorraine. Scarcely had they gone when the two doctors presented themselves at the door and spent half an hour examining their patient and studying charts after which her own doctor pronounced himself well satisfied as to her condition and promised to be out the following morning. 'And the nurse,' he observed, 'I fancy she'll be here very shortly,' he smiled at Julia. 'You'll be free to go, Nurse, with my grateful thanks.'

Julia murmured a reply, thankful that she had made up the bed in the room next to hers. She would get someone to light a fire there as soon as possible. The doctor shook her hand in a powerful grip, thanked her once more and went downstairs. Presently she heard his car making its careful way back to the road.

When she went downstairs presently the doctor was nowhere to be seen, but when she went into the hall she heard his voice in the sitting room, an icy apartment which housed the telephone which she was pleased to see he was using. He looked up as she went in and said cheerfully,

'We're on again, and the wind has brought back the electric too.' He got up and came towards her. 'What do you think of Doctor MacIntory?'

Julia looked at him, her head a little on one side. 'He seemed very nice—so that's his name. Do you plan to go tomorrow if the nurse comes tonight?'

He nodded. 'If you have no objection, I'm anxious to get home.' He smiled suddenly and because his smile gave her a faintly lightheaded sensation, she said the first thing which came into her head. 'What sort of car have you got?' she wanted to know.

'Come and see,' he invited, and went to fetch the cloak hanging behind the kitchen door and wrapped her in it and gave her his hand to hold because the steps were ice-covered again. The stable was gloomy and cold and could have housed half a dozen motor cars; there was only one there now—the doctor's and well worth housing. It was a Jensen Interceptor, gleaming and sleek and powerful. She walked round it exclaiming, 'What a lovely car—how fast does she go?'

He laughed. 'Just over a hundred and thirty miles an hour, but we'll be lucky if we manage fifty in this weather.'

Julia withdrew her head from the interior of the car and turned to look at him. She said politely, 'Look, I'm sure you're anxious to be gone. Would you like to go now? There's nothing to keep you, you've seen the doctor and done more than you need...the nurse might not come...I can go back by train.'

She got no further, for the doctor had her by the shoulders and was shaking her gently. 'I have no patience with you,' he said a trifle testily. 'Of course I'm anxious to get home, but you don't really think that I would go just like that and leave you here? Besides, I like company on a long journey and I should have to wait for you in London.' His hands tightened on her shoulders as he bent his head to kiss her. 'Have you forgotten, Julia, that I've engaged you to look after Marcia?'

Being kissed like that had made her forget everything, but it didn't seem very wise to say so. She withdrew a little from him and said in a commendably sensible voice, 'No, of course I hadn't.' A very large image of the beautiful Miss Jason floated before her eyes. She said firmly, 'I think I must go and see how Mary...' then paused, frowning. 'I can hear...there's a cat here,' she said quickly. 'Oh, the poor thing!'

The doctor went past her to a corner of the stable. 'Yes, there is,' he said casually. 'At least, there are five—mother and kittens—look!'

Julia peered down into the apple box filled with

straw which he indicated, and the mother cat, with the kittens crawling around her, peered back. Julia said in a voice soft with pity, 'Oh, please can't we take them inside and feed them?'

'She's the stable cat and won't stay in the house. I found the box for her before the kittens arrived and I've fed her regularly. She's fine. I'll tell Jane or Madge to keep an eye on them when we go.'

Julia stooped and put out a finger, and the cat licked it politely and then turned to the more urgent business of washing her kittens. Julia stood up and looked at her companion. 'You're very kind. A lot of men wouldn't have bothered,' she said. 'Why didn't you tell me? I could have fed her.'

'You had enough to do. You're a practical young woman, aren't you, Julia?'

Part of her mind registered the pleasing fact that he had called her Julia twice within a few minutes while she replied, 'I don't know—I suppose being in hospital makes one practical.' She started walking towards the door. 'Do you think the nurse will come today? It's already five o'clock and very dark.'

The doctor opened the stable door before he replied. The wind was slight but icy cold and Julia shivered and wrapped her voluminous cape more closely round her as they made their way back to the house.

'I should think the trains are running,' said the doctor. 'She's coming straight from Edinburgh to Hawick and if the doctor could get through so can a taxi.'

It seemed his words were to be ratified. Barely an hour later a car rolled to a halt at the front door. Julia heard it from Mary's room where she was doing the evening chores, and hurried downstairs to welcome the arrival, but Doctor van den Werff had heard the taxi too and was already there, talking to a small woman, who could have been any age from forty to fifty, and whose pleasant face lighted up with a smile when she saw Julia. The doctor performed the introductions smoothly, giving them barely time to utter the most commonplace civilities before suggesting that the kitchen might be a warmer place than the draughty hall.

'Oh, how thoughtless of me,' cried Julia, 'you and the driver must be frozen!' She led the way to the kitchen. 'I'm sure Jane won't mind if I make you some tea.' She arranged Miss MacBonar on one side of the stove and the driver on the other and went to where Jane was making pastry at the table.

'You don't mind,' she begged that lady, 'if they sit here get warm, and would you mind very much if I made them some tea? I'm afraid we've used the kitchen to live in while you've been away.'

Jane smiled. 'Aye, it's a cold house, Nurse—it's been none too easy for you, I daresay. And don't worry about the tea. Madge made it when she heard the taxi. Should I keep the driver here for his supper, do you think? It'll be easier going on the way home if he's got something hot inside him.'

'What a good idea. I'm going back to Miss Mary now and then I'll come back and take Miss MacBonar up to meet her. I expect you know that the doctor and I are leaving tomorrow?'

Madge gave her a quick glance. 'Aye, he told me. A kind gentleman he is, ye'll have a safe journey with him.'

Julia said a little shyly, 'Yes, I'm sure I shall,' and

made her way through the icy hall and up the stairs
to Mary, who was sitting up in her chair by the fire,
demanding to know exactly what the new nurse was
like.

'Nice,' said Julia promptly. 'If I were ill I should
like her to nurse me—I'm going to fetch her in a few
minutes and then I'll get your supper and take her
down to have supper with us.' She picked up the insulin syringe. 'Now roll up your sleeve, Mary—it's
time for your injection.'

Nurse MacBonar and Mary took to each other on
sight; Julia left them together while she went down
for Mary's tray and having settled that young lady to
her satisfaction, took her colleague along to her own
room to give her the details of her patient. 'And your
room's next door,' she explained, 'and I'm sure if you
don't like it no one will mind if you change. I'm
afraid we just took the first ones we saw when we
arrived. There's a fire going and I've put a hot water
bottle in the bed. I wondered if you would like half
an hour to yourself until supper? I'll come and fetch
you.'

They went downstairs together a little later to find
that the table had been laid in the dining room, a
forbidding apartment with a great many hunting tro-
phies on its walls and a quantity of heavy mahogany
furniture arranged very stiffly beneath them. But there
was a fire in the hearth and the supper was ample and
well cooked. The three of them sat at one end of the
large oval table and Nurse MacBonar told them at
some length and a good deal of dry humour of her
difficulties in reaching them.

'But I hear from Doctor MacIntory that you had

your ups and downs too,' she remarked cheerfully. 'I can imagine how you felt when you arrived,' she looked at them in turn. 'Did you get here to together?'

It was the doctor who answered. 'No, for I am on my way to London from Edinburgh—I got hopelessly lost, and how I got here I have no idea, but Miss Pennyfeather was kind enough to take me in...'

'Weren't you scared?' inquired Miss MacBonar of Julia. 'A strange man coming to the door like that?'

Julia avoided the doctor's eyes. 'I was so cold and tired I didn't think about it,' she confessed, 'otherwise I daresay I should have been frightened.'

'Oh well,' said Miss MacBonar comfortably, 'it was only the doctor here, so there was no need.'

This time Julia glanced up to find him watching her and although his face showed nothing of it, she knew that he was laughing silently. He said pleasantly, 'You invest me with a character I fear I cannot lay claim to. Miss Pennyfeather, who has had to put up with me these last few days, could tell you how tiresome I can be at times.'

Nurse MacBonar chuckled. 'Aren't all men tiresome at some time or another?' she wanted to know. 'Not that the world would be much of a place without them, and I should know—I've buried two husbands. Are either of you married?'

Julia shook her head and the doctor murmured in a negative manner.

'Ah, well, your turn will come. Do you plan to leave early?'

Doctor van den Werff picked up his fork preparatory to demolishing the portion of bread and butter pudding Julia had just handed to him.

'Eight o'clock—that will allow for any small hold-ups on the way.' He looked at Julia with lifted brows. 'That is if our Miss Pennyfeather is agreeable?'

Julia, smouldering inwardly at being addressed as our Miss Pennyfeather, said coolly, 'Yes, quite, thank you,' and then addressed herself to Miss MacBonar. 'I'll call you before I go, shall I? Mary sleeps until eight or thereabouts, so you'll have plenty of time to dress.'

They separated to go their various ways after supper. Julia to get Mary into bed and settled for the night.

She was a little silent as she went quiet-footed about the room putting everything to rights. Her patient lay watching her and then asked, 'Aren't you excited about tomorrow? Lucky you—all day with Ivo.'

'Ivo?' asked Julia.

'Doctor van den Werff, silly. Isn't it a nice name? I like him, don't you?'

Julia, looking for a clean nightie for her patient, agreed. 'Oh, yes, and you have cause to be grateful to him too.'

'Well, I am. I told him so. I'm grateful to you too. Have I been a good patient?'

Julia looked across the room at her charge, a little wan still but pretty for all that. She said generously, 'Yes, you have. It hasn't been much fun for you, has it, but you've stuck to your diet like a brick and not fussed over your injections. Go on being good, won't you? Nurse MacBonar is nice, don't you think? We both like her very much and she'll look after you splendidly, and if you keep to your diet and do as

you're told you'll be able to lead the same life as any
of your friends.'

'Yes, Ivo told me that too. I'll try. I like you, Nurse
Pennyfeather—I like Ivo too. You'd make a hand-
some pair.' She narrowed her blue eyes and stared at
Julia, who stared back, mouth agape.

'We'd what?' Julia reiterated.

'Make an awfully handsome pair. I can just see you
coming down the aisle together, you with your eyes
sparkling like they do when you're pleased and happy
and your cheeks all pink, and him, proud and smiling.'

Julia contrived a laugh, a very natural one consid-
ering her heart leapt into her throat and was choking
her. She said with admirable calm, 'Go on with you,
Mary, it's your own wedding you should be thinking
about, not anyone else's. Now go to sleep, because I
shall wake you early to say goodbye in the morning.'

They wished each other goodnight and Julia, as it
was still early, went along to Miss MacBonar's room,
trying to dismiss Mary's words from her mind and
failing utterly.

Her colleague had finished unpacking and had arranged her small possessions around her so that the
room looked almost cosy. She looked up as Julia
knocked and went in and said, 'There you are, dear.
Should we go down and have a last word with the
doctor? I think he expects it.'

Julia ran a finger along the carved back of the
rather uncomfortable chair she was leaning against.
'He doesn't expect me,' she said positively, 'but I'm
sure he'd like to see you—last-minute things,' she
added vaguely. 'Doctor MacIntory said he'd be along

tomorrow if we've forgotten anything. The charts are in the table drawer in Mary's room, and I've brought the insulin and syringe with me—I keep them in my room, here they are.'

She handed them over and Nurse MacBonar nodded understandingly and got to her feet. 'Then I'll pop along then and see that nice doctor of yours.' She beamed at Julia as they went out of the room together. 'You won't come too?'

'No, I don't think so. I'm tired,' said Julia mendaciously. They wished each other goodnight and she went along to her room and started to undress slowly, oblivious of the room's chill. She wasn't tired at all. There was no reason at all why she shouldn't have gone downstairs with Nurse MacBonar, at least no reason she was prepared to admit, even to herself.

CHAPTER THREE

IT WAS COLD and dark when they left the next morning after the ample breakfast Madge had insisted upon them eating. And the road was like a skating rink. Julia clutched her hands tightly together under her cloak, sitting very stiff and upright beside the doctor, expecting every minute to go off the road or land upside down in a ditch.

'Sit back,' commanded her companion quietly, 'nothing's going to happen. You aren't frightened?'

'I'm terrified!' declared Julia.

'You must have realised that it would be like this?'

'Yes, of course I did.' She spoke crossly.

'And yet you came with me?'

'Well, I—I'm sure you're a good driver,' she answered lamely.

'So you trust me as a driver as well. Good. Go on trusting me, Julia. Lean your head back and relax—I shan't take any risks.'

She did as she was told and found to her surprise that after a little while she was actually enjoying the nightmare journey in an apprehensive sort of way, and when presently the doctor asked her if she was warm enough and then went on to talk about a hundred and one unimportant things, his quiet voice never altering its placid tones, flowing on through even the most hair-raising skids, she found herself answering him in a quite natural voice, and if her lovely face was a little paler than usual, there was no one to remark upon it.

Once on the main road the going was easier, although woefully slow in places so that when they reached Newcastle the doctor judged it wise to order sandwiches with their coffee in case it might prove difficult to stop later on.

The M1, when they got to it, was almost clear of snow, however, although lumps of it, frozen solid, added to the hazards of the already icy surface, but traffic was sparse at first and there was no fog so that they made good progress; so much so that south of Doncaster the doctor suggested that they should stop for lunch.

'There's a place I've been to before,' he said, 'a mile or two off the motorway. I think it's called Bawtry.'

It was pleasant to get off the monotonous highway for just a little while, and the old coaching inn where he stopped looked inviting.

'I'm sorry about my uniform,' said Julia as they went inside. 'I don't look very glamorous.'

He gave her a sideways glance. 'And what makes you think that I like a glamorous companion?'

She said in a prosaic voice, 'I thought men did.'

He took her arm because the pavement was still slippery. 'Not always,' he said, half laughing, 'in any case you've no need to worry; with your looks you could get away with anything you choose to put on.'

He said it so carelessly that she felt doubtful if he meant it as a compliment. She sighed and he said at once, 'You're tired, you need a meal.'

The food was good and the dining room pleasantly

warm. They ate roast beef with all its traditional accompaniments washed down with burgundy, and while the doctor contented himself with the cheese board, Julia, who had a sweet tooth, applied herself to a chocolate soufflé. She ate with relish and as she put down her fork, remarked, 'You know, food you haven't cooked yourself always tastes different—besides, we had rather a monotonous diet at Drumlochie House, didn't we?'

'But excellently cooked. We were all glad there was no bread, yours was so delicious.'

'I enjoyed baking it,' said Julia simply. 'What time shall we get to London?'

'Almost a hundred and sixty miles—it's hard to say. Three hours normally, but I should think we might double that allowing for slow going and hold-ups. Getting bored?' he asked with a smile.

Julia shook her head, wishing very much to tell him that she was enjoying every minute of his company. Instead she remarked, 'Not in the least. I like motoring, though I don't do so much of it.'

'Hasn't James got a car?'

She pinkened. 'Yes—a Morris, but he doesn't believe that you should travel fast on the roads nor that you should use a car solely for pleasure.'

The doctor choked. 'Good God—what kind of pleasure?'

'Well, short trips to the sea, somewhere where we could do the shopping at the same time, and—and picnics…'

'Sandwiches and a thermos flask?' he wanted to know.

'Yes. James considers eating out is a great waste

of money.' Her already pink cheeks went a little pinker. 'Oh, I beg your pardon, that sounds rude and ungrateful just after you've given me such a gorgeous lunch. I—I didn't mean that at all; I love eating out and driving miles. I'd forgotten what fun it was.' She sounded wistful.

'I can see that I shall have to rescue you from James.'

'How?'

'By a method which will prove quite infallible.' The doctor's voice was light. Julia decided that he was joking. She asked equally lightly,

'Do tell me.'

He shook his head, 'No—not yet, but I promise it will work.'

They got up to go and Julia, still persisting, asked, 'You mean if I take a job away from home for a long time he might forget me?'

'Something like that.'

The short winter's day was already dimming although it was barely two o'clock. Julia looked anxiously at the sky as they got into the car. 'It's not going to snow again, is it?' she asked worriedly.

'I shouldn't think so. If it does and it gets too bad we'll just have to stay the night somewhere, but I don't think that will be necessary.'

She settled down as he started the car, drawing her cloak around her, thankful for the warmth and comfort. Presently she closed her eyes; they were back on the M1 once more and there was nothing to see, only the road running ahead of them and the traffic weaving in and out of the lanes in a never-ending, tiring pattern. The doctor was doing a steady fifty, overtaking whenever he had the opportunity; he didn't seem disposed to talk. She opened her eyes and peeped at him once; his good-looking profile looked stern and thoughtful. Immersed in dreams of Miss Marcia Jason, thought Julia pettishly, and closed her eyes again, sternly dismissing her own dreams. She opened them a few moments later, aware of something wrong, although the man beside her had made no sound. They were on the point of passing an articulated lorry and as she looked behind her the doctor accelerated to a sudden breathtaking speed, sliding ahead of it with seconds to spare as a car, roaring down the motorway, passed them within inches. Julia caught a glimpse of its occupants laughing and waving. 'That was a bit near,' she said in a voice which quavered just a little. 'I'm glad you're a good driver.'

The doctor sounded grim. 'Yes, so am I—they're the sort who cause a pile-up. He passed us at over a hundred and twenty.'

'What were we doing when you overtook?' Julia wanted to know.

He grinned. 'Never you mind,' he replied, 'but it was either that or being pushed into the next world...' He broke off and said something harsh and sudden in his own language, and Julia watched with silent horror as the car, careering madly half a mile ahead of them, tried to pass a huge transport which was on the point of crossing into the fast lane, and even as she watched she was aware that the doctor had slowed and was edging back on to the slow lane and on to the hard shoulder of the road, to stop close to the appalling chaos.

The transport driver, in a last-minute attempt to

avert disaster, had slewed to his left, but the oncoming car had been too fast for him. It was wedged, no longer recognisable as a car, under the huge back wheels, its recent occupants lying untidily around it. Even as they were looking, two more cars crashed into it.

The doctor reached across Julia, locked the door and undid her safety belt. 'When I get out,' he commanded, 'get into my seat and don't put a foot outside the door until I say so.'

He took his bag from the back seat and got out himself, and then after a quick look around, turned to help her. The traffic, for the most part, was still moving south down the slow lane, Julia could hear the urgent squeak of brakes behind them as they made their way to the wrecked cars. There was already a small crowd of people—the doctor tapped the nearest man on the shoulder and said with mild authority,

'Would you go to the side of the motorway and find the telephone? One shouldn't be too far away—tell the police and say we shall want several ambulances.' He didn't wait to see if the man would do as he asked but shouldered his way through the little group, propelling Julia along beside him. The first victim lay very quietly, which was only to be expected of someone with a compound fracture of skull and a badly torn leg. Doctor van den Werff examined her swiftly, grunted gently and said, 'Get a tourniquet on that leg, Julia, and try and get a pad and some sort of bandage on her head, then come to me.' He opened his case, gave her a handful of slings and a packet of gauze and went away.

Once she had something to do, it wasn't so bad.

Julia forgot the horror of it all in the urgency of her work. She begged a tie off a man standing nearby, tightened her home-made tourniquet with her pen and then turned her attention to the woman's head. There wasn't a great deal which could be done. She covered the wounds carefully with gauze and slid a cotton sling carefully around the woman's head and fastened it loosely, then enlisted the tieless man's help, explaining what he had to do about the tourniquet, and went to find the doctor.

He was sprawled across the wreckage of the first car, his head and shoulders out of sight in the tangle of twisted steel; she worked her way to his side and looked inside too. Her almost soundless 'Oh' was full of horror and she closed her eyes, willing herself not to be sick. She opened them again as the doctor pulled her out to stand beside him. He said in a perfectly ordinary voice, 'Very nasty, but I doubt if he knew anything about it. Who's next?'

Julia, her face very white, spoke with a mouth which shook a little.

'That woman—I left a man with her, he seemed sensible. There's someone screaming...'

'Hysterics,' said the doctor briefly. 'Let's have a look at this one.' A man this time, conscious and miraculously only slightly injured. The doctor sent him to the side of the road, accompanied by two willing helpers, who, now that they had got over the initial shock, had offered, as had several others, to help in any way they could. The next one was a man too, with a leg twisted at a strange angle and a pale, unconscious face. The doctor felt the man's head with gentle fingers and said,

'I think we'll leave him as he is until the ambulances get here. But we'll splint that leg.'

Which he did, with the aid of two planks of wood torn from a packing case and two more ties. Two children came next, both sadly dead. Julia turned away from them with a heavy heart to join the doctor at the side of the last victim—a woman, and conscious. Her pale lips sketched a smile as they knelt down beside her. 'It's my back,' she whispered, 'it feels funny.'

The doctor said with gentle decisiveness, 'They'll put that right in hospital. Stay exactly as you are, will you, my dear? You'll not have to wait long, I can hear the ambulance now.'

He stayed where he was, a gentle hand on her shoulder, and said to Julia, 'Tell the ambulance men to come to this patient first and fast. Then find the driver of the transport—he's not amongst this lot, probably he's all right, just shocked, and if I'm not about see if anyone was hurt in the other two cars. I don't think so, they'd all better be examined in hospital.'

Julia sped away, glad to have something to do. The driver was still sitting in his cab, dazed with shock and but for a few bruises, unhurt. All the same, she persuaded him to go with her in search of the doctor, whom she found helping to load the woman with the broken back on to an ambulance. He gave her a hasty glance. 'He's all right? Leave him here, I'll have a quick look before he goes for a check-up. See about the others?'

She saw about them; bruises and a cut or two and some nasty grazes, nothing that half an hour in hospital casualty wouldn't put right. She led them, unnaturally quiet with shock, over to the ambulances too and sat them on the blankets someone had spread on the grass at the side of the road, then looked for the doctor. He was with the group of police and ambulance men and a breakdown lorry gang, bending over the wreckage where the dead man lay. She looked away as they began to draw something covered in a blanket out of the tangled mess, her stomach turning over, and most fortunately had her attention immediately distracted by the arrival of another ambulance, complete with doctor and nurse. By the time she had answered their immediate questions, the little group had dispersed from around the wrecked car and Doctor van den Werff was wiping his hands on a towel produced by one of the ambulance men, and while he talked to the doctor Julia went with the nurse to see what help they might give the ambulance men in stowing the remainder of the slightly injured passengers into the last two ambulances, but she had only been with them a very few minutes when the doctor tapped her on the shoulder, picked up his car coat from the ground where he had tossed it earlier and instead of putting it on, draped it around her shoulders; it was only as he did so that she discovered that she was shivering violently. They had reached the car when she said in a surprised, tight little voice, 'I think I'm going to faint,' and did so.

She came round in the car, with her cap off and her head against the doctor's shoulder, as she opened her eyes he said mildly,

'Stay as you are,' and she was glad to do so; his shoulder felt comfortably solid under her swimming head and the weight of his arm round her shoulders was reassuring.

'I've never done that before,' she said in a surprised apologetic voice. 'That man in the car…'

His arm tightened. 'Forget him,' his voice was calm and matter-of-fact and very kind. 'Think instead of the help you were able to give to the others.'

'I didn't do much,' she said forlornly, almost on the verge of tears. 'You did all the work…those two children…'

He ignored her last muttered words and said briskly, 'If you hadn't helped me I should have wasted a great deal of time bandaging and tying splints and so forth, and while I was doing that someone else might have died.'

'The man in the car, and the children…do you think they…?'

If he felt impatience at her insistence he gave no sign but said in his calm way, 'None of them knew anything about it, and that's the truth, Julia; you're too nice a person to lie to.'

For some reason Julia couldn't even guess at, she began to cry then. She cried and snivelled and sniffed while the doctor sat silent, and when at last she fumbled for her handkerchief, he offered her his own, still without speaking.

Her face mopped, she sat up, feeling a great deal better, and made shift to repair the damage to her face and tidy her hair, still sniffing from time to time. When she had finished her eyes still looked red and so did the tip of her nose, but neither of these things could dim her vivid good looks. She said soberly, 'If you want to change your mind about employing me to look after Miss Jason, I shall quite understand.'

He looked completely taken aback. 'But I don't want to change my mind. Whatever put the idea into your head? I want only the best for Marcia, and I think you are exactly what I hoped to find.' His voice was very decided and Julia heaved a sigh of relief.

'Oh, thank you—I thought I'd better ask after making such a fool of myself. Have you a very deep regard for her?'

She heard him sigh, but all he said was: 'I haven't seen her for six months.' Which didn't quite answer her question. He had sighed very deeply, though; Julia, who had a romantic nature, thought that it was probably with longing. She quelled a fresh desire to burst into tears once more, although for quite a different reason this time, and when he suggested that they should stop for tea at the earliest opportunity, she was able to agree in a calm little voice which was, nevertheless, quite unlike her usual tones.

The accident had occurred a few miles north of Nottingham. The doctor started the car and drove past the chaos. He was going faster now despite the icy road, but there was no fault to find with his driving; Julia sat back relaxed in a friendly silence until a sudden thought struck her and she asked,

'Have you somewhere to go tonight? Will it be a little late for you to go to a hotel?'

She could not see his face, but she was sure that he was smiling.

'I think I shall be all right—I usually go to the same hotel when I'm in London—they know me there. What about you? Your friend will be home?'

'I'm sure she will, and even if she isn't I know where the second key is hidden.' She added shyly, 'I'm sure she'll be glad to give you a meal.'

'That's kind, but I believe I'll go straight to the hotel when I've seen you safely there. I want to telephone to Holland.'

Miss Jason, thought Julia sadly. How he must dote on her to telephone her all that way at that time of night! She wondered what it would feel like to be loved like that and was unable to pursue the thought further because he was speaking again. 'I'll come round and see you some time tomorrow if I may. Do you suppose you could be ready to catch the night boat from Harwich?'

'Yes, of course, I've only to pack a few things.' She stared ahead of her into the dark night, made darker by the car's powerful lights, aware that if he had asked her to go with him to the other side of the world she would have given him the same reply because she loved him; she admitted the fact to herself without surprise and with the unhappy satisfaction of knowing that her brother and Maureen and James had all been wrong—love for her, at least, hadn't come gradually. It had come when she had opened a door to a stranger on a bitter cold night.

They reached Connie's flat just after ten o'clock and as the doctor stopped the car outside the tall terraced house he put his head out of the car window and looked upwards. 'There are lights on the top floor,' he announced.

'Good,' said Julia, 'that's Connie's.' She started to open the door, but he put a large gloved hand over hers and said mildly, 'Not so fast—I'll get your case. Wait there until I open the door.'

Julia did as she was told meekly, not that she was a meek girl by any means, but she had discovered in the last few days that sometimes it was nice to be told what to do. At the door she put her hand out for her case, but he shook his head. 'Lead the way up, I'll see you safely indoors.'

Connie came to the door, in her dressing gown and with her head crowned with a complexity of rollers tied into a pink hair-net. She flung her arms round Julia and exclaimed, 'Where have you been? Come in at once…' She caught sight of the doctor and asked instantly, 'Who's that?'

Julia performed the introduction with a certain amount of haste, not because she didn't want Connie to meet her companion, but because he had said that he wanted to go to his hotel as quickly as possible.

'Come in,' invited Connie, 'I'll knock up a meal and some tea,' and added as an afterthought, 'Sorry about the hair, I've just washed it.'

The doctor smiled charmingly at her, but shook his head. 'I should have liked that, but I really must go.' He turned to Julia. 'You'll have a lot to do tomorrow, I expect, so I won't bother you, but may I call for you about six? We could have a meal before we leave and iron out any problems.'

'That will do very well,' stated Julia calmly, wondering how she could bear to see him go. But he did, almost at once, and Connie closed the door and pulled her into the little sitting room and sat her down in one of the shabby armchairs by the gas fire. 'Tell me at once,' she breathed, 'where are you going?'

Julia told her while they got supper together; she told Connie about her stay in Drumlochie House too—at least, she told her most of it. It was when they were parting for the night that Connie asked, 'What about James?'

'And what about James?' asked Julia in her turn, a little coldly. 'He doesn't own me. I've never encouraged him to think that I would marry him, you know; he's conceited enough to take it for granted—and George and Maureen have egged him on...' Her beautiful black brows drew together in a frown, she looked flushed and angry and quite strikingly lovely as she stood in the doorway of Connie's spare bedroom. 'James,' she said with vehemence, 'makes me sick!'

She slept the deep sleep of the young and healthy and got up in time to cook breakfast for them both while Connie got ready to go to St Clare's. She tidied the little flat after her friend had gone, washed up and got dressed herself and went out. First to the bank for some money, then to purchase a suitable number of white uniforms and caps and a number of articles she felt it necessary to take with her. She was on her way back when her eye was caught by a wool dress with a narrow, ankle-length skirt and full sleeves caught into long tight cuffs. It had a high neck and she knew that the deep rose of its colour would suit her. She bought it recklessly and without a pang for the hole its price had made in her savings. Savings at that moment didn't matter in the least.

She had a sketchy lunch and went round to St Clare's to see Private Wing Sister, who listened to Julia's somewhat expurgated account of her journey with Miss Mary MacGall, expressed pleasure that she had got another patient so quickly and wished her luck, adding,

'So you won't be going home yet, Nurse Penny-feather?'

Julia hedged. 'Well, not for a short time—I don't imagine that this job will last more than a week or two—probably I shall bring Miss Jason back to her home.'

She hadn't imagined anything of the sort until that moment, but it satisfied Sister, a stickler for having everything cut and dried long before it was done. 'Splendid,' she said now, 'and remember, Nurse, when you feel free to leave your sister-in-law we shall be glad to have you back with us. Matron was only saying so this morning on her round.'

Julia thanked her and got up to go; there was still George to telephone and the afternoon was advancing. She rang his office in Frome, where he had a flour-ishing solicitor's practice, and told him, with the brev-ity he always required on the telephone, what she was about to do. He wasted no words on recriminations but plunged into a reproachful speech of such tenor that if she had been listening she would have felt a complete heel; but she heard hardly a word of it; she was thinking that in two hours she would see the doc-tor again. When George paused for breath, she said kindly, 'I'm sure you can get a nurse from that agency in the High Street, George. I'll write from Holland. Be good. 'Bye!'

She smiled as she hung up; George hated being told to be good.

The doctor arrived punctually, but Julia was ready

and waiting for him. She was wearing her Jaeger coat and skirt of a pleasing turquoise and brown check with its matching turquoise jersey and a fur bonnet on her black hair, and had completed this outfit with brown boots and gloves and a shoulder bag. She was aware that she looked rather nice; nevertheless it was gratifying when he said quietly,

'How charming you look, Julia,' and although that was all he gave her a look of admiration which warmed a mind chilled by thoughts of Miss Marcia Jason.

They were in the car and already moving when he observed, 'It's early to dine in any of the restaurants, I thought we might go back to my hotel—there's a grill room there.'

Julia, thinking of her sandwich and cocoa lunch, felt relieved, for she was hungry. She murmured suitably and wondered which hotel it was. Something smallish, she decided, where he would be treated as a person and not a room number, because he was that sort of a man. He drove westward away from the city and presently turned into Dover Street and stopped outside Brown's Hotel.

'Is this it?' inquired Julia, a little taken aback. She didn't know much about London hotels, but she thought that this one was amongst the best of them in a quiet way. Certainly they were treated with an old-fashioned courtesy which she imagined no longer existed—probably, she reminded herself wryly, because she wasn't in the habit of frequenting such places. When they were seated the doctor said,

'I hope you're hungry—I am. I've had so much to do all day I didn't stop for a decent meal and I don't suppose you did either. Shall we have some sherry while we decide what to eat?'

They settled for Crabe à la Diable followed by baked gammon and peaches. It was while Julia was choosing a sweet that she looked up to ask apprehensively, 'Will it be rough?—the crossing, I mean. Should I not have any more?'

The doctor said on a laugh, 'I should think it will be very rough, but don't let that worry you now—I don't fancy you're the sort to be bowled over by a mere storm at sea,' and when she still looked uncertain: 'Try a water ice, that's harmless enough.'

She took his advice and as she was eating it asked, 'Are you in a hurry to be gone?'

He was sitting back in his chair, watching her. 'No,' he said slowly, 'I'm in no hurry at all—we have all the time in the world.'

Ordinary words enough, but somehow she had the impression that they had another meaning. She finished her ice, accepted his offer of coffee and sat back too.

'May I know something about my patient?' she asked in a businesslike voice.

'Your duties?' he queried smoothly. 'Would you agree to looking after her in the mornings—she needs a good deal of help still and there are exercises and so on—after lunch perhaps you would take an hour or two off, and return to duty after five o'clock until bedtime. Would a half day when it could be arranged suit you and any other reasonable time off you may wish to have? I'm sorry if it sounds a little vague, but I am a little out of touch with Marcia's progress. I'm sure no one will object to you arranging times to suit yourself.'

Very vague, Julia agreed silently, no mention of days off, and half days when they could be arranged sounded ominous; it was surprising what one did when one was in love. If he had said no off duty at all she would still have gone.

'We haven't discussed your salary,' he added, and mentioned a sum which made her raise her eyebrows. 'That's too much,' she said sharply, 'a great deal more than I could earn in England.'

'You won't be in England,' he pointed out smoothly, 'and remember you may have to alter your working hours to get up at night. My father agreed with me that it was a fair sum to offer you.'

Julia looked at him thoughtfully. 'If your father…!' she began. 'Very well, but if I don't find I have enough to do to justify all that money, I shall say so.'

He stretched a hand across the table and they solemnly shook hands. 'Done,' said the doctor, 'and there's another thing. I should much prefer you to call me Ivo—I feel distinctly elderly each time you address me so severely as Doctor.'

'All right, Ivo,' she answered, 'you still have to tell me about my patient.'

He frowned very slightly. 'I'll tell you all I know, but as I said, I haven't seen Marcia for more than six months, although I have had frequent reports and in her letters she told me that she has been making progress.' The frown deepened. 'Slow progress, I'm afraid; she should have been walking…however…!' He plunged into the details of the case and Julia, listening with eyes on his face, thought how lucky

Miss Marcia Jason was, even if she had had polio.

They started their journey soon after that and when they reached Harwich and were on board, Ivo said, 'Go to bed, Julia, it will be a rough crossing. I'll ask the stewardess to come to you presently with a bedtime drink. If you don't feel like breakfast in the morning, have something in your cabin.'

Julia, who had had ideas about staying up until the boat sailed, meekly agreed and went to her cabin. Probably Ivo didn't want her company and anyway, she was tired and her cabin, although small, seemed the height of comfort. She was undressed and in her bunk when the stewardess came in with a little tray of tea and biscuits and the strong advice to ring for her immediately she was needed. 'And I'll bring you your tea just after six, miss, and if you wish you can order breakfast then.' And when Julia thanked her and offered to pay for her tea, she was told that all that had been taken care of by the doctor. So she sipped her tea and ate a biscuit and presently, despite the uneasy movement of the boat, fell asleep. She wakened several times during the night, to feel the violent tossing of the boat and hear a multitude of creaks and groans, but she went to sleep again and only awoke when the stewardess arrived with her morning tea, and when that good lady wanted to know if she would like her breakfast in her cabin, Julia replied that no, she felt marvellous and would breakfast with the doctor and could someone tell him.

She found him waiting for her and as she sat down and wished him good morning he said, 'I hear you slept well—I'm glad, for it was a rough night. You feel like breakfast?'

'I'm hungry,' stated Julia simply, and went on to eat everything he ordered with an appetite unimpaired by the boat's sidlings. The doctor ate heartily too while they held a lively conversation upon a variety of topics until he suggested that she might like to go up on deck. The Hoek van Holland was very near now, its lights twinkling through the still dark morning, and on either side of it the dark outline of the flat coast melted away into the wild blackness. The wind was still blowing half a gale; it whipped a fine colour into her cheeks and put a sparkle into her dark eyes; she looked vividly alive and very attractive as they went below and the doctor stared at her with appreciation.

They reached Tilburg by eleven o'clock, the doctor having driven most of the way without haste. True, he had raced along the highway to Rotterdam from the Hoek, where he had been caught up in the morning traffic of that thriving city, allowing Julia time to gaze out of the window and wonder how he could ever find his way out of the maze of the crowded streets.

They ran out of the sprawling city at last, crossed a bridge over water again, and still on the *autobaan*, took the road south, past Dordrecht, over the Moeredijk bridge, towards Breda, but just as they were within sight of that city, Ivo had turned off the main road, and skirting Breda, had taken the road to Tilburg, a town, which when they reached it, Julia liked. It was surprisingly modern and looked prosperous too and was, explained Ivo as they drove through its heart, owing to its thriving woollen industry. It was also, he added, full of schools of every kind and there was a university as well.

They had left Tilburg on a quiet country road which presently ran between green fields and increasingly large clumps of trees. Now, thought Julia, it began to look more like the Holland she had imagined; even in the bare greyness of a winter's morning, the countryside had charm. But it was when Ivo turned the car into a long avenue of tall trees, their branches meeting overhead, that she exclaimed, 'Oh, this is lovely! I didn't expect it.'

The trees edged wooded land on either side, dark and still frost-covered from the night's cold, and presently she noticed that there were occasional gates barring narrow lanes leading from the road and winding away into the trees.

When she glimpsed a house, well back from the road, she asked, 'Are there people living in the woods? How quiet and peaceful it is, and how beautiful.'

Ivo looked pleased. 'You like it? My home is almost at the end of this road, close to Oisterwijk. It is quiet, but we like it like that, and even in the summer when the visitors come, we are quite undisturbed.'

He turned off the road as he spoke, through an open wooden gate and along a short sanded lane between larch trees; the lane turned abruptly and the house came into view—a pleasant house of red brick, flat-faced with big windows and a front door which looked a little too large for it. It was fair sized and Julia, looking at its solid front, thought that it might be a lot larger than it appeared. It had a neat lawn, now heavily covered with frost, and a pleasant backing of trees. As they got out of the car, the front door was opened by an elderly woman who stood back to allow a much younger woman to run out to them. She was tall and well built and Julia would have recognised her as Ivo's sister Jorina anywhere, for her features were a softer, feminine version of his and her eyes were of the same penetrating blue; only her hair, short and inclined to curl, was corn-coloured, whereas Ivo's was straight and pale. The girl ran to the car and flung herself into the doctor's arms, crying excitedly, 'Ivo—how lovely to have you home again—how I've missed you!'

She threw her arms around his neck and hugged him, then drew away a little to say to Julia, 'Forgive me—I'm so pleased to see my brother again.' Her English was fluent, but with much more of an accent than Ivo, who introduced the two girls, and waiting only long enough for them to sake hands and smile at each other, said, 'Let's get indoors—it's cold and I'm sure Julia would like to get settled in.'

They all went into the house, where Ivo paused at the door to introduce Bep, the elderly woman who had opened the door in the first place, before sweeping the two girls through the hall and into a large front room, behind whose door Julia had heard a dog barking furiously. As they entered this pleasant room a large Old English sheepdog launched himself upon the doctor, who greeted him with every sign of pleasure if slightly more calmly. 'This is Ben,' he explained, 'and you must forgive his boisterous manners, but he hasn't seen me for six months.' He fended off the dog goodnaturedly and went on, 'Let me take your coat, Julia, and do go and sit by the fire.'

Jorina said quickly, 'Yes, do, you must be cold. Bep's bringing the coffee.' She took a chair near Julia and smiled at her with friendly eyes and then turned to look at her brother when he spoke.

'I'll go up and see Marcia—is she still in the same room?'

'Yes—we wanted her to have a room downstairs now that she is at last beginning to get around a little, but she said that you would be coming home and could carry her up and down.'

She had her face turned away from Julia as she spoke and there was something in her voice which made Julia long to see her face. She looked at the doctor instead and saw an expression she couldn't make out cross his handsome features, but it had gone at once, too swiftly for her to guess at.

'Will you take Nurse Pennyfeather with you?' Jorina wanted to know, and he, without looking at Julia, said at once, 'No—time enough for that when we've had our coffee and a little talk,' and left the room.

Julia stared at the fire, telling herself that it was a relief that he hadn't wanted her to go with him, for to have had to stand by and watch their meeting after so long an absence would have been more than she could have borne. Her lively imagination was following him upstairs when it was halted by Jorina saying, 'Ivo calls you Julia, would you mind very much if I do too? And perhaps you will call me Jorina.'

She smiled again and looked so like her brother that Julia's heart bounced, but she said quietly enough, 'I'd like that very much, thank you,' and broke off as Bep came in with a big silver tray loaded with coffee cups and a plate of little sugary biscuits. She set the tray down by Jorina, lit the little spirit stove under the silver coffee pot and went away again without a word, and Jorina said as she poured the coffee,

'Old-fashioned, is it not? But my father likes it and so does Ivo, but when I marry I shall have a modern percolator which makes no work.'

'You're going to be married?' asked Julia with interest.

'Yes—in six months, perhaps sooner. My fiancé is a—how do you say—lawyer in Arnhem.'

'So your father will have to get someone to run the house?' interposed Julia, trying not to be curious but failing lamentably.

'Well, yes—to work with Bep, you know. But if Ivo marries then there may be no need, but I do not know.'

Julia bit into a biscuit because it was something to do and then had great difficulty in swallowing it, her throat was so dry. Even now Ivo was upstairs with Marcia, probably discussing the wedding date. She had been a fool to come. She closed her eyes for a brief moment, afraid that she might burst into tears, then opened them again as the door opened and Ivo came in.

He looked at her sharply as he sat down opposite her and asked,

'Do you feel all right? You look,' he hesitated, 'tired.'

Julia guessed that wasn't the word he had intended to say. She said steadily, 'Perhaps I am, but only for a minute. I think I'm excited,' and then wished she hadn't said it because she was sure that was the last thing she looked.

He must have agreed with her secret thought, for he raised an eyebrow and half smiled as he turned to Jorina. 'Marcia has progressed very well, but I'm glad I brought Julia with me, for she needs a great deal of encouragement after being an invalid for so many months.' He took the coffee cup he was offered and asked, 'How's Father?'

'Very well, but working too hard; he talks of retiring now that you are back. If you took Theo as a partner later on, you could still do your work at the hospitals and keep the practice going. Is that possible?'

'Of course—if Father will give me time to put my affairs in order first.' They began to talk about Edinburgh and the course he had been following there and became so absorbed in their talk that Julia was surprised to hear the lovely old painted clock on the wall strike twelve, and so it seemed was Ivo, for he paused in what he was saying and exclaimed, 'Julia, how thoughtless I am—you shall go to your room and then I'll take you to meet Marcia.'

Julia followed Jorina upstairs, stifling the idea that the last thing she wanted to do was to see Marcia. She would be with her for most of the day from now on and might not see Ivo at all, and even if she did, never alone. She sighed inwardly and crossed the landing behind Jorina and into a long passage leading to the back of the house. She had been right; the house had a sizeable wing behind as well as a floor

above the one they were now on. Jorina opened the
first door they came to.

'Marcia's room is in the front of the house—' she
waved an arm vaguely. 'We've had a bell fixed so
that if she should want you she can ring, but she's so
good I don't expect she will ever use it.'

Julia heard faint mockery behind the words and
wondered about it, then forgot it in the pleasure of
seeing her room. It was furnished most elegantly and
with great comfort in the Adam period, with curtains
and bedspread of pink striped silk, a pale echo of the
deeper pink of the carpeted floor. There was a small
buttonbacked chair too with a small table beside it
and a writing desk in the window. There were even
books piled on a dainty little wall table. Jorina asked,
'You like it? The bathroom is across the passage and
is for you alone. Now I leave you and presently Ivo
will come.' She went to the door. 'I am glad that you
are here,' she said with a sincerity which was heart-
warming.

Left to herself, Julia spent a few minutes exploring
her room. It was indeed comfortable, almost luxurious. She unpacked a few things and went to find the
bathroom—pale pink to match the bedroom and furnished with an abundance of towels and soaps and
bath salts. Julia heaved a sigh of pleasure at the sight
of them. Even if she was going to be lonely here, it
would all be most comfortable.

She had tidied herself and was standing by the window looking out upon the wintry scene outside when
Ivo knocked and came in. He said rather shortly
'Ready?' and stood aside as she went through the
door, then led her across the landing where he opened

a beautifully carved door and said, 'Come in, won't you?'

The room was beautiful, with a high ceiling like the sitting room and just as beautifully decorated with plaster work. The walls were hung with striped silk in a very pale blue and there was a fire burning in the steel grate and a great many pictures about the walls. The bed was a little ornate for Julia's taste; she didn't like French furniture herself, although she had to admit that it was beautiful enough. There were several easy chairs and a daybed upon which her patient was lying. Julia walked across to it and stood looking down at its occupant while the doctor introduced her. As she shook the languid hand held out to her she took stock of Miss Marcia Jason and instantly disliked what she saw. Miss Jason was a pale blonde with a long face, rendered thin by illness, no doubt, but possessing a kind of beaky, austere beauty which Julia found distinctly chilling. She had pale blue eyes framed in long colourless lashes and a mouth that was too thin and which was now turned down at its corners in a sweetly sad way which made Julia quite out of patience. It was impossible to see how tall Miss Jason was as she was lying down, but all that was visible of her looked ethereal, even if flat-chested. She said now in a sweetly gracious voice, 'Dear Ivo, to bring me my very own nurse. I know you'll help me to bear my burdens—I've done my best, but sometimes I have felt that I needed someone—robust upon whom to lean.'

Julia said 'Oh, yes?' politely. No one had ever called her robust before. She became aware that her junoesque curves might strike someone of Marcia's meagre proportions in that light, and probably the doctor, loving the tiresome creature before her, shared her views. Julia blushed at the thought and blushed anew when her patient said, 'There—have I been too outspoken? I've always considered that the truth is all-important, but I have no wish to offend you.'

Julia managed to smile quite nicely. 'I'm not offended,' she said serenely. 'I hope that before I go, I shall be able to give you some of my robustness so that you can get out and about and enjoy life again.'

'But I enjoy myself now—I've forced myself to bow to circumstance and I'm aware that I shall never be as others are. All the same—' she cast what Julia could only describe as a melting look at the doctor, 'I still have a number of attributes, I believe, and am not altogether wanting in intellect. Ivo will tell you of our conversations when we first met and of the letters I've written. I'm a good letter writer.'

Julia said a trifle woodenly, 'That's an accomplishment these days.' She had never before met anyone so conceited and self-complacent; moreover, she suspected that Miss Jason, in other circumstances, would have been on her feet by now and struggling back to a normal way of living. She had a tussle ahead of her, and for what? she asked herself bitterly: so that this pale creature should become the doctor's wife? She said bracingly,

'I'll come back after lunch and we can talk a little and perhaps you will tell me how far you've progressed, then we can work out a routine.'

Miss Jason gave a silvery laugh. 'Routine? My dear nurse, I have no routine—how is that possible with my state of health? You find it difficult, a jolly, buxom girl like yourself, to understand how we frailer women feel. But we'll have our little talk by all means, for I'm sure you mean it for the best.'

She smiled, the same sweet smile, and Julia smiled back over gritted teeth. It had been bad enough to be called robust; now she was jolly and—unforgivable—buxom. The girl was detestable!

She went out of the room without looking at the doctor. He seemed like a stranger now; not the resourceful friendly man she had spent those days at Drumlochie House with, or the calm man telling her what to do at the accident on the M1 and then holding her close while she cried. This man beside her was calm, but withdrawn too, as though everything they had done together had been forgotten. Perhaps it had.

She went downstairs beside him without speaking and sat soberly throughout lunch, which they ate in a small bright room at the back of the house. The conversation, sustained easily enough by Ivo and his sister, was lively enough and covered a whole range of subjects, but Miss Jason wasn't mentioned once.

It was after they had left the dining room that Ivo asked her to go with him to his study—a large room, Julia discovered, lined with books and surprisingly tidy. He waved her to a chair and sat down at his desk.

'Marcia has made great progress,' he began, 'though I had hoped that she would have been more active, but you can see that she needs encouragement—she has the idea that she will never be quite well again, which indeed she will be if only she will make the effort.' He gave Julia a fierce, daunted look and went on harshly, 'I have a great regard for her, Julia, I hope that you will help her.'

Julia nodded, wondering why it was he found it necessary to remind her so frequently that he had a great regard for Marcia. Once was enough—too much, she thought. 'Of course I will,' she said cheerfully. 'I'll start slowly, don't worry, but I'll persist. Can I have precise instructions?'

'You will have to ask my father for those. Marcia is not of course my patient. I do know that she is capable of walking with support. She needs other interests.'

'Well, she's got them now you're back.' Julia's voice was very even. She got up and walked to the door. 'I'll get into uniform and go to her now,' and Ivo who had gone to the door with her said suddenly, 'Julia, it's impossible...' She gave him a kind smile, for of course he was worrying about his Marcia. 'No, Ivo, it's not—nothing's impossible if you set your heart on it!' She walked past him and crossed the hall and went slowly up the stairs, her lovely head held high.

CHAPTER FOUR

THE ELDER Doctor van den Werff came home after tea. Julia was in her room unpacking and when Bep knocked on the door and signed to her to go downstairs, she did so. She had changed into her new white uniform and made up a muslin cap, and so attired went quickly down to the hall, rather uncertain as to where she was to go. She need not have worried, for Ivo was waiting for her. He said at once,

'I hope we don't disturb you, but my father is anxious to meet you and evening surgery is in half an hour. His study is over here.'

He led the way across the hall and opened a door on the opposite side to the sitting room and motioned her inside. The man who stood waiting for her was as tall as his son and just as big. His hair, not yet wholly grey, receded from the same wide forehead, his eyes were just as blue and his mouth just as kind. Julia, who had been rather dreading this moment, smiled radiantly at him, for after all, he was only Ivo in thirty years' time and therefore no stranger. She said, 'How do you do, doctor,' in a quiet voice and took the seat he offered her as he took his own chair behind his desk. Ivo, who had followed her in, perched on its side, one long leg swinging. Julia looked around her; the room was obviously used as a consulting room as well as a study—there was a couch along one wall and a glass case with instruments tidily arranged inside it and a hand basin on one corner, half hidden by a screen. She finished her survey and turned her gaze on the older man, who smiled in his turn.

'We're very glad indeed to have you with us, Miss Pennyfeather,' he began. 'I hope that you will be happy while you are here—I assure you we shall do our best to make you so.' He shifted his chair a little so that he could get a better view of her face and went on, 'And what do you think of your patient?'

Julia hesitated. It really wouldn't do to tell him her opinion of Miss Jason; she might get sent back to England by the next train if she did. She had spent a couple of hours with Marcia during the afternoon and had to admit to herself that her hastily formed opinion hadn't been changed in the least. It had, if anything, become firmer. She had, after a polite, exhausting argument, got her patient to her feet and walked her a few steps about the room, an act which had served to strengthen her suspicion that her companion could do a good deal more than she would have everyone else suppose. Julia, remembering her promise to Ivo, encouraged her gently and assured her that within a very short time she would find herself walking normally— even going downstairs. They would start tomorrow, said Julia in her kind, firm voice, but this evening Doctor van den Werff had said that he would carry Miss Jason down to a family dinner party.

She had left the room, the memory of the smug little smile on her patient's face very vivid in her memory. She said now, weighing her words, 'Miss Jason seems to have reached a period of inactivity, but that often happens, doesn't it? I think that now

Ivo has returned it will give her the encouragement she needs to make the final effort to return to a normal life. It must be difficult after months of doing nothing much. How many months is it?'

'Ten. You're right, nurse, and I applaud my son's happy idea of bringing you back with him. This is a fairly quiet household; perhaps Marcia has been too much on her own.'

Julia pinkened. 'I didn't mean that,' she protested. 'I sound as though I'm criticising my patient. I'm not, but I promised Ivo that I would get her well and I will, only I think I should tell you what I think.'

She paused after this speech, drew breath, and sat silently waiting for someone to say something. It was Ivo who broke the silence, and he spoke in a silky voice she had never heard before. 'And are you sure that you are not overestimating your powers, Julia? I am aware that you are a capable and efficient nurse, but surely not such a very experienced one?'

Julia's bosom heaved as she got to her feet and stood facing him, her head very erect, her eyes flashing. 'If you feel,' she said in austere tones, 'that you've made a mistake in bringing me here, I'll pack my things and go back on the next train.'

Ivo had risen too, and they stared at each other for a long a moment until he said, 'Julia, I beg your pardon—I'm behaving like a pompous ass and I don't mean a word of it—put it down to worry if you will. The last thing I want you to do is to go away.'

Julia's heart somersaulted under her white uniform. She said with admirable calm, 'Then I won't,' and sat down again, and Ivo's father, who had sat silently watching them, gave a dry little cough and remarked,

'Very well, now that the air is cleared, shall we put our heads together?' He smiled at Julia, 'And may I call you Julia, young lady? My son appears to do so and I can see no reason why I should not if you have no objection.'

Julia beamed at him. 'I'd like you to,' she said, and he nodded and went on, 'Now I will tell you all I can about Marcia, for we are as anxious as you are to get her fit again. She was in Holland on a short study tour—probably Ivo has already told you that she is a highly qualified teacher of marked intelligence. She and Ivo met at a reception in Tilburg,' he paused and looked at Julia from hooded eyes. 'They had much in common and she visited us frequently. It wasn't until the day she came to say goodbye and arrange to see Ivo in England that she became ill. She had been feeling poorly for a day or two—headache, sore throat— you know all the symptoms, of course—she was actually with us when the paralysis set in. She was in hospital for three months and then returned here where she has been ever since. She—er—bore her illness with almost saintlike fortitude and when she asked if she might come here until she was strong enough to travel home, we were only too glad to offer her hospitality. As I am sure you have gathered from Ivo, he and Marcia…' He left the sentence in the air for Julia to finish as she thought best and went 'Marcia's serious mind is a great attraction to him, you understand.'

He sat back and looked at Julia and she looked back at him and could have sworn that behind those half closed lids, his eyes were alight with laughter.

She asked herself silently why and commented soberly,

'A terrible thing to happen…'

'Yes. Now as to her drugs and treatment—' He became all at once professional and remained so until Julia finally rose to her feet when he got up too, saying, 'I hope you will come to me with any difficulty however small, Julia, and if I am not here, Ivo will be, I daresay. I shall see you at dinner and I look forward to that.'

Julia went back to her patient and helped her change into a dark red velvet dress which drained all the colour from her already pale face and was cut far too tight. Julia, zipping it up the back, remarked cheerfully that the dress was a little close-fitting—a good sign because it meant that her patient was putting on weight, whereupon Miss Jason replied indignantly that she had put on too much weight over the past months and was anxious to lose a few pounds. 'For,' she said with what Julia chose to call a simper, 'we slim girls owe it to ourselves to keep our figures, don't you agree?' She gave her high clear laugh. 'Though of course, Nurse Pennyfeather, I expect you find that a piece of nonsense.' She added, 'Do you never diet?'

'Never,' said Julia goodnaturedly.

'Should you not?' persisted Miss Jason. 'You are a little—if you'll forgive me—plump, are you not?'

Julia refused to get annoyed. 'I feel like Juno,' she said with a chuckle. 'Thank you for the compliment.' Which silenced Miss Jason most effectively.

They dined in a small panelled room behind the doctor's study, the five of them sitting round an oval

Empire table covered with a fine white linen cloth and set with heavy silver and a quantity of cut glass. After dinner Marcia begged, with a great deal of unnecessary charm, to be allowed to stay up, managing to imply at the same time that she was a little afraid of what Julia might say if she did. Julia, listening to her and feeling like a tyrant, asked, 'Did I really order you to bed after dinner? I don't remember doing so—I must have been out of my mind if I did. Why on earth shouldn't you stay up until a reasonable hour if you wish? There's no reason why you shouldn't.' And had the satisfaction of seeing her patient frown and disclaim any pretensions to enough strength to remain up late.

Half an hour later Doctor van den Werff was called out to a case, but before he could get to his feet, Ivo was already at the door.

'Let me, Vader,' he said decisively. 'You've had a long day—I know the Bakker children well enough, and I daresay it's nothing serious; you know how nervous Mevrouw Bakker is.' He looked round the room, saying, 'You'll all forgive me, I know.'

He stared at Julia and then past her to Marcia who was speaking in a tiresomely reasonable voice which somehow conveyed that her feelings were hurt. 'Your first night back,' she said gently, 'and I had so much to tell you about my studies of Vondel's work—your father was kind enough to get me the English translation…'

Ivo interrupted her gently and with carefully hidden irritation.

'I'm sorry, Marcia, there will be time later on for

us to talk. I'm home for good, you know. I'll see you in the morning.'

He was almost through the door when Marcia said plaintively, 'I'm sure I don't know who is to get me upstairs. Must I spend the night here?'

Her words fell upon her companions' ears, but not upon Ivo's, for he had gone. Before anyone else could speak, Julia said briskly,

'Just the opportunity we need, Miss Jason—imagine what a triumph for you when you tell Ivo that you went upstairs on your own two legs!'

Her patient gave her a fixed look. 'Why do you call Doctor van den Werff Ivo?' she wanted to know.

'He asked me to. You see, when we were at Drumlochie House it was rather—rather like make-believe, if you know what I mean, and it would have been ridiculous if we had been formal with each other. I expect you've heard him call me Julia, haven't you?' She smiled at Marcia's cross face. 'I expect you would have done the same in those circumstances.'

'I doubt it. I hope you don't expect me to call you Julia. I shall address you as Nurse. Is that not correct?'

'Quite,' said Julia dryly. She turned to Doctor van den Werff, who had been sitting quietly listening to every word.

'What do you think, doctor?' she asked. 'May I help Miss Jason to her room? We have a stick here and the stairs are shallow and the balustrade strong. It would be a marvellous surprise for Ivo, wouldn't it?'

'Indeed, yes, Julia. Do so by all means.' He turned to Marcia. 'My dear,' he said mildly, 'think how pleased he is going to be—your first positive step to a normal life.' His voice was serious, but Julia felt sure that if only she could have seen his eyes, they would have been twinkling at some joke of his own.

There was a great deal of fuss getting Marcia on to her feet, for she didn't want to, which made it twice as hard. But eventually Julia, by sheer stubbornness, had her standing, and after more fuss, walking slowly, leaning heavily on Julia's arm and wielding the stick with unnecessary clumsiness. Going upstairs was a lengthy business, punctuated by Marcia's dignified protests and audible sighs; she even so far forgot herself at one point to observe that Julia was a hard young woman, devoid of all sympathy, to which Julia replied,

'Yes, I'm sure I must seem so to you, and I do sympathise, but I want to help you to get quite well, you know, and once you've done this, you'll find it will get easier and easier. Sit on the stairs a minute and get your second wind.'

Thus cheerfully admonished, Miss Jason allowed herself to be gently lowered on to the staircase and Julia sat down beside her, 'For,' she said in her friendly voice, 'we might as well be comfortable.'

'Comfortable?' echoed Marcia bitterly. 'I shall never…' She broke off as Jorina and her father came out of the sitting room to gaze up at them from the hall.

'I knew you could do it if you tried, Marcia,' said the doctor. 'I can see you'll soon be getting around like the rest of us.'

Marcia allowed her long face to break into a wistful smile.

'You have no idea of the struggle I've had, Doctor van den Werff, but I will not give in—I should have been in my room by now if Nurse hadn't commanded me to take a rest—though I own I'm quite exhausted.'

Julia saw the faint frown on the doctor's face. 'You must not do too much,' he began. 'Nurse, perhaps we had better carry Miss Jason to her room.'

Julia presented him with an untroubled face, although her thoughts were the reverse. She was as certain as she could be that Marcia was far stronger in the legs than she would have them believe. But she had, after all, only just arrived and the fact that she disliked her patient could be influencing her judgement, though she felt that unlikely; she was too well trained for that. She said now, 'If Ivo isn't going to be too long, shall we stay here? Then he can see for himself how well she has managed and carry her the rest of the way.'

The doctor was about to debate this when the front door opened and Ivo joined them. He began. 'Hello, Vader, a false alarm—the baby...' and then he stopped and stared up the staircase to where Marcia and Julia, looking a very ill-assorted pair, were sitting.

'What on earth are you doing?' he demanded. 'Marcia, don't tell me you got there on your own legs?'

Julia had known that Marcia would take full advantage of the situation, and she proceeded to do so now. 'Are you surprised, Ivo? Nurse insisted that I walked upstairs to my room, and I've been absolutely terrified, but I've managed to get as far as this, and now you're back and I'll go on again so that you can see for yourself, though I confess I'm ready to drop.'

She gave a trill of laughter, a combination of courage and weariness and gentle resignation to the great bully of a nurse beside her. 'Isn't it lucky that Nurse is such a strong girl? If I'm to be forced to walk everywhere, she will need to pick me up a dozen times a day.'

He was halfway up the stairs. 'What a wonderful surprise for my first day home,' he said lightly, and bent and lifted her and carried her into her room, put her gently on the bed, said goodnight equally gently and went away, standing aside for Julia as she followed them, without looking at her. Only as he turned to go did he catch her eye and she knew that he was holding his anger in check. Later on, she judged, she would be told off.

But first there was Miss Jason to get to bed—a slow business because she had known that Julia had been shown in a bad light and she wanted to extract as much pleasure from the fact as possible by making sly references to the episode whenever she could turn the conversation to her liking. But Julia parried her oblique remarks easily enough, talking about anything which came into her head and refusing to rise to any of her patient's barbed remarks. At length she said goodnight and went downstairs again; if there was going to be a row, she might just as well get it over.

Apparently Ivo felt the same way, for he opened his study door as she reached the foot of the stairs and requested her in a quiet voice to join him. He bade her sit down, still very quiet, and asked in a beautifully controlled rage, 'And what in the name of thunder have you been doing?'

Julia, during the slow half hour of putting Marcia to bed, had had time to think. She said reasonably, 'It seemed to be a good idea to start Miss Jason off in the way she must go. She has to make the effort, you know—what better moment to start, with the incentive of your delighted surprise when you returned?'

He said, in low-voiced fury, 'I can conceive of nothing less likely to give me delight—Marcia is a very delicate woman.'

'Fiddlesticks,' said Julia, who hadn't meant to say that at all but hadn't been able to restrain herself. 'Miss Jason has been very ill; she's better, admit it. If you were checking a patient in hospital in as good a physical condition as hers, wouldn't you prescribe as much exercise as she could manage within reason? She should have been doing far more than she is.'

He came and stood over her. 'Aren't you presuming a little too much, nurse?' His voice was dangerous. 'And how could you know what I would prescribe for my patients?'

'Oh, I don't,' said Julia, 'I only guessed,' and he made an exasperated sound which she ignored. 'I'm trying to help you and Miss Jason—I said I would, if you remember.' She went on in a reasonable voice, 'But if you want her to stay bedbound, please tell me and I'll nurse her exactly as you wish—blanket baths, meals in bed, pressure points—the lot.'

She drew breath after this outrageous speech and looked at him to see what he would say. He looked so forbidding that she let it out very slowly so that he shouldn't see that she was just a little frightened of him. He said through clenched teeth, 'You take too much upon yourself, Miss Pennyfeather. I should very much like to…' He closed his lips and to her regret, didn't finish the sentence.

She said, her dark eyes very bright, 'I seem to remember you saying not a couple of hours since that you didn't wish me to go. And,' she added for good measure, 'do you have to be quite so bad-tempered?'

He was suddenly bland, his fine rage nicely under control. 'Don't tell me, my dear girl, that anything I should say or do could affect your actions in any way. It is unfortunate that you move me to anger rather more than most people.'

'You're quite right,' said Julia disconcertingly. 'You were angry with me the first time we met because I opened that door.' She added indignantly, 'And if I hadn't you'd still be standing there, frozen to death!'

To her surprise he gave a shout of laughter. 'Julia, you're impossible! I began by being furious with you and now...' He caught her round the waist and when she looked up at him, kissed her quite roughly on the mouth. Julia made no attempt to free herself from his arms, but stood stiffly within them, her eyes on his shirt front. She said quietly while her heart rocked under her neat uniform,

'I quite understand that you're happy to be home again doctor, but wouldn't it be better if you kissed the right girl?'

He showed no sign of penitence and made no effort to loosen his hold, but said idly, 'What a little waist you have. And who is the right girl?'

She gave him an open-mouthed look. 'Why, Miss Jason, of course. She was telling me about—about you this afternoon.' She took a deep breath and went on, 'I'm sorry that I annoy you so much—I'll keep out of your way as much as I can.'

He ignored this. 'What did Marcia have to say?' he asked in a mild voice which lulled her into answering, 'That you were a brilliantly clever man with a great future and that you needed a—a helpmate with a similar brain and that she was glad to have at last found a man who disliked levity unless it was relevant to the occasion and...'

He asked with interest, 'Are you making all this up?'

'No—I wouldn't know how to. But it must be nice for you, and for her, of course.' She gently disengaged his arms from about her person and he dropped them to his side and took a step or so away from her.

When he spoke his voice was quiet. 'There's no need to keep out of my way. Even when you annoy me I enjoy your company.' His eyes searched her face. 'I must explain if I can—at Drumlochie it was as if we lived in another world—it seemed more real than this one. I forgot for the time the obligations which I had. They didn't seem to matter—when you opened the door, you opened it on to make believe, although I'm not sure now if it wasn't real.' He stopped. 'I'm not explaining very well.'

'No,' agreed Julia in a wooden voice, 'you're not, but I understand very well what you mean. You forgot all about Miss Jason waiting for you. It's a pity you didn't remember—you might not have asked me to come back with you.'

It surprised her when he smiled. 'No, I think it will turn out to be a very good thing that you came. You'll get Marcia fit.'

Julia walked over to the stove and held out her hands to its warmth.

'Will you marry her when she's well?' she asked coolly.

Her voice had been cool, his was suddenly icy. 'That, Miss Pennyfeather, is entirely my own business.'

There was a little devil inside Julia, egging her on. She walked to the door. 'Well, of course it is, but I like to know how much time I have—can you wait until she's absolutely fit or are you so eager to marry her that you'll be content with a semi-invalid?'

He covered the room in a couple of strides and took her by the shoulders, shook her until the teeth rattled in her head and then let her go and stood staring at her with a set face. She stared back, appalled at what she had said. At length she spoke from a throat gone dry. 'That was dreadful of me—I'm sorry, I didn't mean a word of it. I don't know why…please forgive me.'

She left him abruptly and went up to her room, to sit on her bed going over and over the scene in his study and wondering what had possessed her to behave so badly. Presently she undressed, had a bath and then, ready for bed, went along to see if there was anything more she could do for Miss Jason.

'Nothing, thank you,' stated Miss Jason firmly. 'I'm relaxed both in mind and body, despite your rough treatment of the latter, Nurse,' this with a little laugh to indicate that she was joking. 'I shan't need you until the morning. Good-night.'

Julia, still meek, went back to her own room and got into bed, where she lay warm and comfortable, reading the same page of a book she had picked up from the table, and wishing with all her heart that she was back at Drumlochie House, huddled in bed in her ice-cold bedroom, knowing that just down the corridor Ivo was stretched out on his fourposter ready to come at once if she should want him—not the Ivo she had been talking to an hour ago, but the Ivo she had first met in that other, happier world.

She saw only Jorina and Bep when she went downstairs in the morning. Marcia was still asleep; it seemed a good idea to have breakfast before she wakened. Jorina greeted her warmly, inquired as to whether she had slept well and been warm enough and went on:

'Father and I thought you would be down again later in the evening, but Ivo said he had had a talk with you and you had gone to bed. I expect you were tired.' She gave Julia a smiling glance. 'Or was Ivo cross about something? I thought I heard his voice…something's worrying, though I don't know what, he'd only been in the house for ten minutes for me to see that. Have some more coffee? I hope you don't find our breakfasts too strange after your eggs and bacon.' She handed Julia her cup and passed her a dish of cheese. 'Try some of this on your bread, it tastes good. Are you going to get Marcia down today?'

Julia was soothed by Jorina's pleasant acceptance of her company. She said readily, 'Yes, going down will be much easier. Is—will Ivo be in to lunch? If not, I'll wait until the afternoon and Miss Jason can be down waiting for him and he can help her in the evening—that should encourage her.'

'I'm sure it will.' Jorina's voice was dry. 'He won't be back until about five—he's in Tilburg today, but he'll be helping with the surgery this evening. If you bring her down about three o'clock we could have a cup of tea together. When are you to be free?'

Julia gave her a grateful look. No one had mentioned off duty and she had forgotten to ask about it; anyway, the opportunity hadn't presented itself. 'I don't know. Ivo said something about one or two half days each week and a day off when it could be arranged. He didn't say anything definite about off duty.'

'Well, how about this afternoon? If you bring Marcia downstairs about three and go off until six?' She slipped an arm into Julia's. 'I hope you will be happy with us—it will be nice to have someone to talk to. There's Marcia, of course,' she added hastily, 'but I'm not clever, you see, and I bore her.'

It was an hour later, while Julia was supervising Marcia's exercises, that a visitor was announced to see that young lady.

'Mijnheer August de Winter,' said Bep stolidly from the door, and Julia was surprised to see the delight in Marcia's long face—much more delight than she had shown towards Ivo, for all her gentle speeches to him. Julia, on her way to the door with a murmured, 'I'll leave you,' was stopped long enough to be introduced as 'my nurse Ivo brought back with him in the hope of getting me strong again,' and then Marcia turned her pale eyes on her and explained, 'This is Mijnheer de Winter, a schoolmaster in Tilburg, who has been good enough to keep me company whenever he has had the time to spare.'

Julia watched her patient simper—really, the woman was fifty years behind the times! She belonged in a Victorian novel. She didn't think much of Mijnheer de Winter either; his face was even longer than Marcia's and his eyes pale. He had mousy hair, brushed neatly across the baldness on top of his head, and a mean little mouth. Julia went out of the room, closing the door softly behind her, thinking that the pair of them were exactly right for each other. Hard on that thought came another. Did Ivo know about her patient's visitor?

She went along to her room and wrote a letter, and when she went back after a little while with her patient's lunch tray, it was to find her alone once more.

Marcia held up a massive tome for her to see and cried in her wispy voice, 'You see, nurse, how kind Mijnheer de Winter is. He came especially to bring me this volume of Virgil—I happened to mention that I should like to read it once more.' She smiled and said almost playfully, 'Don't mention his visit to Doctor van den Werff—I mean Ivo, of course, I don't want to make him jealous and I've not had the time to tell him about August's visits yet.'

Julia lifted the lid off the omelette she had borne upstairs. 'I don't tell tales,' she remarked briefly. 'I hope you enjoy your lunch.'

She didn't enjoy her own, although she pretended to for Jorina's sake. The more she saw of her patient the less she liked her. She was reasonably sure that Marcia had the full use of her arms and legs and for some reason didn't want anyone to know, not for the moment—and now she was sly as well. And there was really nothing that Julia could do about it.

After several false starts and a great deal of shillyshallying on the stairs, Marcia got down them rather

well, probably, thought Julia nastily, because there
was no one to see except herself. It was already past
three o'clock, for her patient, although she knew that
Julia was to be free at that hour, had contrived a number of last-minute hindrances, Julia drank a hasty cup
of tea and went to change out of her uniform. A quarter of an hour later she was walking down the road,
thinking to herself that if she disliked her patient, the
feeling was reciprocated, although she doubted if either of them would admit it. It was already dusk, for
it had been a dull cold day, with grey cloud overhead
and a blustery wind—it would be dark by the time
she had walked the mile or so into Oisterwijk, but it
was a main road and she couldn't very well miss her
way back.

By the time she had looked round the little town it
was five o'clock and almost dark, so she headed for
home again. She had walked for ten minutes or more
when she discovered that she was on the wrong road.
She retraced her steps, found the right way, and
started off once more.

A car raced past her towards the town, its lights
blazing so that when it had gone by the dark seemed
even darker; she heard its brakes squeal as it stopped
and turned and came back towards her, its powerful
headlamps pinpointing her in the night. She didn't
change her pace, nor did she look round. Even when
the car dropped to a crawl beside her she looked
steadily ahead. It went past her and drew up and Ivo's
voice, very quiet, said, 'Get in, Julia.'

She did as she was told, not in the least deceived
by his tone. As she slid into the seat beside him, she
could almost feel his anger. But she wasn't going to

allow herself to be intimidated. 'How nice,' she said chattily as he leaned over her to shut the door. 'Are you on your way home?'

'I've been home.' He started the car, driving slowly, and her heart began to hammer because she was so very conscious of him close beside her. She edged away carefully to stop rigid as he said, still quiet,

'You don't need to do that. I'm not going to hit you, tough heaven knows—what possessed you to go out in the dark?'

She could hear by his voice that he was still holding back rage and made haste to say in mollifying tones, 'Well, there wasn't time during the day and I wanted to go for a walk and I thought it would be nice to see Oisterwijk. It's pretty, isn't it? and the shops are nice, only I couldn't buy anything.'

He made a sound which might have been a laugh. 'Why not? Don't tell me you allowed the language to stand in your way.'

'No, I don't think I would have done, but I had no money—Dutch money.'

He turned the car into the short lane leading to the house and stopped and turned to peer at her through the dark. He said evenly,

'You shall have money tomorrow. I'm sorry about that, I should have thought of it.'

Julia stirred, a little uneasy; he was being so very calm. She was mistaken, for when next he spoke his voice was very nearly a snarl.

'Don't dare to do this again, Julia. What a little fool you are—good God, anything might have happened to you! Supposing you had been given a lift…!'

She interrupted him a little indignantly, 'Two cars stopped, but I didn't go with them because I wasn't quite sure where the house was in the dark and it might have been difficult to make the driver understand.'

'You are not to accept lifts…!'

'But I just have,' she pointed out calmly, 'from you.'

She heard his sharp indrawn breath. 'Don't be frivolous,' he said violently. 'I came to look for you.'

Her heart bounced against her ribs, but her voice was still coolly calm. 'I didn't know—thank you. I hope I haven't spoiled your evening.' She thought him most unreasonable when he answered abruptly, 'You might have thought of that sooner.'

Julia protested, 'How could I? I wasn't to know that you would come and look for me. I think you're being unreasonable, and I'm twenty-two, you know, and quite capable of looking after myself. Thank you all the same,' she added politely.

She heard him sigh. 'Perhaps you will be good enough to go walking in daylight—and if you must go to Oisterwijk, or anywhere else, after dark, please ask one of us to run you there in a car.' His hand came down on hers, linked in her lap. 'Please, Julia.'

She wanted to take his hand in hers. It was an effort to keep her hands resting quietly under his touch. She said at once, 'Yes, of course I'll do what you ask. I hope you're not—not angry any more.'

His hand tightened for a moment and slid away. He said in a very quiet voice, 'Oh, my dear girl,' and then in a normal voice, 'Have you had a busy day with Marcia? I hear she walked downstairs.'

Julia gave him a cheerful account of the day's doings, omitting the small frictions between herself and her patient. They were unimportant; the important thing was to get Marcia well so that this man beside her could marry her, since he wanted to. She sighed soundlessly.

After dinner Doctor van den Werff declared that he had letters to write and within a few minutes Jorina got up too, saying that she was going to telephone Klaas, which left Marcia lying gracefully on one of the sofas by the fire, Ivo sitting opposite her in a great armchair with Ben at his feet, listening with apparent interest to her opinion of Goethe's works, and Julia, sitting a little apart.

When Marcia paused for breath Julia got to her feet with the fictitious statement that she had letters to write. 'And I'll get your room ready for you, Miss Jason, and come back presently, and we'll try walking upstairs. Shall we say two hours?'

Ivo raised his eyes briefly from the contemplation of his well-shod feet. 'If you intend walking upstairs, Marcia, I shouldn't make it too late—it would never do to overdo things.' He glanced at Julia. 'Would you come back in an hour, Julia?' His voice held mild authority and although Marcia pouted prettily, he took no notice. As Julia went from the room she heard him ask,

'And what do you think of Vondel—not much known...'

She had expected her patient to make a great fuss about going upstairs, but as she reached their foot,

leaning on Ivo's arm, Doctor van den Werff flung
open his study door to say that Ivo was wanted on
the telephone at once, and without him for an audience there was no point in drooping and sighing. Julia
got her to bed, said goodnight and went along to her
room; she might as well go to bed too. She had taken
off her cap when Jorina appeared. 'I've made some
coffee,' she said persuasively, 'come on down and
have a cup.'

They went together to the empty sitting room and
over their coffee talked about Jorina's wedding. They
were deep in the bridesmaids' outfits when the two
men came in and their chat became the pleasant end-
of-day talk Julia remembered so clearly at Drumlochie House. And when after a little while she got up
to go to bed it was Ivo who said,

'Not yet, Julia, unless you're very tired.' He put
down his coffee cup. 'Jorina, I haven't had time to
tell you about the delicious bread Julia baked…'

It was when she at length got up to go that Ivo said
at the door,

'There's something I want to know. Why do you
call Marcia Miss Jason?'

'She prefers it—some patients do, you know, just
as they prefer to call the nurse by her full name. It
doesn't mean anything.' She looked anxiously at him.
'We get on famously,' she lied, and smiled, 'She's
been simply wonderful today.'

'Has she? It must have been very lonely for her all
these months—she has no friends here and no visitors, only Jorina and her girl friends, and they…
You'll be good company for her. She told me this
evening how very empty her days have been.'

Julia nodded, said goodnight and went upstairs. So Marcia hadn't told him about Mijnheer de Winter after all.

CHAPTER FIVE

A WEEK WENT BY, one day slipping without haste into the next, and Marcia, whether she liked it or not, showed marked improvement. Julia had managed to get some sort of routine into the days, and now her patient was coming down before lunch instead of after—something she didn't seem to like very much, and it wasn't until Mijnheer de Winter called again and Marcia was forced to entertain him in the sitting room with Jorina and Julia there that Julia realised why—her patient's caller had looked decidedly taken aback when he had been shown in and had stayed, making rather self-conscious conversation, for a bare ten minutes.

Later that day, when Julia had been alone with Jorina, she had asked about him and Jorina had laughed and said, 'Oh, him. Isn't he a pompous little man? Marcia told me that Ivo finds him agreeable, though, and is grateful to him for visiting her all the while he's been in Scotland. All I can say is that Ivo must have changed a great deal if he likes him.' She eyed Julia, placidly making up a muslin cap, with a thoughtful look. 'He has changed.'

Julia didn't look up. 'Well,' she said reasonably, 'he does bring her the kind of book she enjoys.'

'Homer, Virgil,' said Jorina with something like disgust. 'I'd rather browse through *Elle*.' She put down the sweater she was knitting. 'Julia, do you think she's a bit too clever?'

Julia clasped her hands round her knees and thought. Determined to be quite fair, she said at length, 'It depends on whom she marries, doesn't it? I expect some men admire a good brain—if they're clever themselves.'

'Well, Klaas is clever, and I don't know one end of the Greek alphabet from the other,' Jorina smiled, 'but he admires me.'

It was when the question of Julia's half days came up that Marcia suggested that Jorina should take her into Tilburg one afternoon.

'I'm quite able to amuse myself for an hour or so,' she said with her habitual gravity, and smiled bravely when, Ivo said,

'That's very kind of you, Marcia, but will you be quite all right on your own?' Whereupon she had leaned forward and pressed his hand and murmured, 'You forget, Ivo, that I've had many months alone and in pain.'

Julia squirmed in embarrassment and looked away so as not to see Ivo's face, and met his father's stare instead. She saw the gleam of laughter in his eyes before he allowed their lids to fall.

So she had gone to Tilburg with Jorina and enjoyed it immensely, for she had some money now and a pleasant companion with whom to look at the shops. She bought presents for her family, because no one had said how long she was going to stay and for all she knew she might not have the chance of shopping again. They went back after tea when the pale winter sky had darkened and the wind had gathered its strength once more. 'It's going to be a cold night,' observed Jorina as she drove her little Citroën rather too fast along the icy road. 'You're sure you're happy to come back? It is your half day, you know.'

'Yes, I don't mind a bit,' said Julia. 'After all, I've been out the whole afternoon and what would I do with myself out on a night like this?'

'Go to Oisterwijk,' laughed Jorina. 'Oh, dear, Ivo was so worried about you when he got home—you should have seen him—and Marcia vexed because he said almost nothing to her...'

Julia interrupted hastily, 'Yes, it was so silly of me. I have enjoyed my afternoon, Jorina. Thank you for taking me.'

'I enjoyed it too. We'll do it again—there are still the Christmas presents to buy. We don't have such a gay time in Holland as you do in England because we have St Nikolaas first. But we do have a party and a tree and little gifts. You must wear that lovely pink dress you showed me.'

They talked clothes for the rest of the journey and went into the house, still talking, their faces glowing with the cold and the thought of Christmas ahead, and found Marcia sitting where they had left her with a book in her hand, gazing wistfully into the fire with a sad face which didn't deceive Julia one bit. She turned to look at them as they came in, pretending surprise, and remarked in a resigned voice,

'There you are—I'm sure you must have had a delightful time. How I wish I were able to enjoy the simple pleasures of life!'

Julia murmured encouraging as she glanced casually at the book in her patient's lap—and then glanced

again, for it was a different one from the volume of
Virgil Marcia had been reading when she and Jorina
had left; this one was a prosy tome on mediaeval
religion, twice as large as Virgil and with a different
coloured binding. When Jorina presently went from
the room Julia asked,

'Did Mijnheer de Winter come to see you, Miss
Jason?' and was rewarded by Marcia's slight flush
and frown.

'How strange that you should ask, nurse. As a matter of fact he did—to bring me another book.' She
went on in self-assured way, 'It was such a cold afternoon I persuaded him to stay and have tea with
me.'

'How nice—and now, if you're not tired, supposing
we walk around the house for a little while? There's
no one about and I daresay you're tired of sitting all
the afternoon.'

She saw the flush appear again. So Marcia hadn't
been sitting still all the afternoon! Julia, promenading
up and down the hall with her patient, tried to guess
what she was up to.

She was on the point of asking in a roundabout
fashion when Ivo came in from the hospital and Marcia, never one to miss an opportunity to attract attention to herself, cried,

'Oh Ivo, look at little me—aren't I splendid? I feel
so small and fragile and I'm sure I should fall over
if it were not for Nurse Pennyfeather's arm—isn't it
fortunate that she's such a stoutly built girl?'

Ivo threw off his coat, saying good evening as he
did so, then, with the faintest hint of a smile, he
turned to study Julia.

'No,' he said mildly, 'not stoutly built—shapely if you like, curvy if I am permitted to say so, but definitely not stout.'

Julia gave an enchanting gurgle of laughter. 'What a relief! I was beginning to feel like the village blacksmith.'

His smile widened. 'I can think of nothing less like,' he said, and they laughed at each other across the hall and Marcia, her well-modulated voice a little sharp, asked, 'Have you had a busy day, Ivo? I daresay your patients have been difficult…'

He was still looking at Julia, but now he turned politely to face her. 'No, not in the least, for the greater part of the time they're under the anaesthetic.' He looked at Julia again. 'Did you have a good time in Tilburg? But surely you should have the evening free as well?'

Julia tried not to look too pleased because he had remembered to ask.

'Lovely, thank you. Yes, I should be free, I suppose, but I'm quite happy about it—there's nothing for me to do on an evening like his.'

They were sitting down to dinner when Ivo said,

'No one minds if I take Julia to the cinema in Oisterwijk, do they?' He looked round the table at his father's and sister's approving faces, Marcia's affronted stare and Julia's astonished one. 'It's her half day,' he added blandly. 'I don't see why she should be forced to remain in—you agree, Marcia?'

'Well, of course—if Nurse wishes to go out she is entitled to, I suppose, although I should have thought a quiet evening with a book…'

Ivo was staring at her and Julia noticed that he had

his father's trick of lowering his lids so that it was hard to see his eyes.

'It's an old film,' he said mildly, turning to Julia. '*The Sound of Music*, if you can bear to see it again.'

'Oh, rather! I loved it.'

'A film I've never seen,' remarked Marcia tartly. 'A sentimental fairy tale, so I've been told.'

'Very sentimental,' agreed Ivo gravely, 'just the thing to round off a half day.'

Half an hour later, warmly coated and wearing the fur bonnet, Julia danced downstairs and into the sitting room, to stop short at the door. Ivo was standing just inside the room and Marcia was addressing him in the clear tones she affected and which Julia could not but hear.

'It's very good of you, Ivo, to sacrifice your evening in this way,' her patient was saying. 'I was looking forward to a pleasant conversation, but of course Nurse must have her amusement. I can only hope you won't be bored to tears.'

Julia stood in the hall and said to Ivo's back, 'I'm ready,' in a rather small voice. He turned and raked her with a bright glance before bidding Marcia goodnight and closing the door behind him. The moment he had done so, Julia said urgently, 'I couldn't help hearing—I—I didn't think—I wouldn't dream of spoiling your evening.'

He tucked her arm firmly into his. 'The only way my evening will be spoilt is if you don't come. It's just exactly what I need after a hard day's work.' He smiled as he spoke and ushered her into the car and got in beside her. 'The cinema's small,' he went on easily, 'and the audience is sometimes noisy—will you mind?'

'No,' said Julia happily, and meant it.

They had seats at the back of the crowded hall; they were narrow and not very well-sprung, and her companion by reason of his size was very close. It seemed the most natural thing in the world for him to take her hand in his and hold it throughout the performance. Even when the lights went up half way through, he didn't let go and she was content to let it remain there.

It was bitterly cold when they came out of the cinema and Ivo said, 'Coffee, I think, don't you?' and swept her across the street to De Wapen van Oisterwijk, where in an atmosphere redolent of the evening's dinner, cigars and the faint sharp tang of Genever, they sat in the pleasant little coffee room.

'The film was marvellous,' said Julia. 'Thank you for taking me. I don't suppose it was quite your cup of tea, though?'

'My what?' Ivo stared at her over his cup, 'Oh, I see—aren't men sentimental?'

'I don't know. I've never known one well enough to ask. But wasn't it a bit lowbrow for you?'

A muscle twitched at the corner of Ivo's mouth. 'No. Don't you know James well enough to ask him?'

She shook her head. 'No. Besides, he's not the sort of person you'd ask.'

'Then you'd better not marry him.' He spoke lightly. 'If you've finished perhaps we had better go.'

She looked idly at the clock on the wall behind him and gasped,

'It's after eleven, Ivo! I should have been back ages

ago—what will Miss Jason do? How will she get to bed? I should never...'

'Panicking, Miss Pennyfeather?' His look was mocking. 'It's your half day, isn't it? I asked Jorina to help Marcia to bed—she can, you know, and I fancy that Marcia has become stronger in this last week—you must be having a good effect upon her.'

They were walking back to the car and he had tucked her arm in his again. 'I thought so too,' said Julia soberly. 'I wondered'—she hesitated—'I wondered if she were to go out in the car—you know, for a short trip or to see the shops—if she would enjoy it. Just to drive through a town when the shops are lighted up would make a change for her. I'm sure she's well enough.'

She didn't look at him as she spoke because she didn't want to see pleasure at the idea on his face. It wasn't until they were sitting in the car that he asked, 'You think that would be a good idea?'

She looked at him, a little puzzled because his voice had sounded almost reluctant. 'Well, you could ask her,' she suggested tentatively. 'It's almost Christmas; she might like to buy some presents.'

'So she might. And you, when will you buy yours?'

It seemed as though he didn't want to talk about Marcia. Julia said lightly, 'I've got some already, and I shall get the rest when I go into Tilburg again.'

He started the car. 'Very well, I'll take you both in one day next week—will that do?'

'Yes, but...'

'But what, Miss Pennyfeather?'

'Well, will you suggest it to Miss Jason and when she says yes, you could ask me as a kind of afterthought—otherwise it might look as though we'd arranged it all first and that might hurt her feelings.'

He made a small sound which could have been a laugh. 'If I were James I should come after you and marry you out of hand, my dear Miss Pennyfeather.'

'Why? And why do you call me Miss Pennyfeather?'

'You don't like it? But I always think of you as the magnificent Miss Pennyfeather. You are, you know, and you're not only quite beautiful, you're—alive.'

He stopped the car in front of the house, turned towards her, slid an arm around her shoulders and kissed her hard.

When she had her breath again she said with a kind of stunned politeness, 'Thank you for a very nice evening, Ivo.'

His face was only an inch or two from her own and he was smiling a little. 'I haven't enjoyed myself so much for a long time,' he said softly. 'No, that's not quite true. I enjoyed every minute of our stay at Drumlochie House.'

He got out and walked round the car's bonnet and opened the door for her. She went inside without saying anything more, only a quiet goodnight as she went up the stairs.

Her patient's light was still on. Julia pushed the half open door a little wider and looked into the room. Marcia was in bed with a book open in front of her. She said with gentle resignation,

'So you're back, Nurse Pennyfeather. The performance must have been a long one.' Her pale eyes searched Julia's vivid face. 'You look as though you've enjoyed yourself, but I hope you won't make a habit of this—I had the greatest difficulty in getting up the stairs.'

'I'm sorry,' said Julia, not sorry at all and at the same time appalled at her own feelings. She should be feeling guilty; spending the evening with Ivo while his Marcia lay in bed, only she didn't, because she was so very sure that Marcia didn't love Ivo, and she was almost as sure that Ivo didn't love Marcia, only perhaps he hadn't realised it yet. She said now, 'You managed very well by yourself yesterday—perhaps you were a little nervous.'

Marcia picked up her book. 'I'm never nervous,' she stated repressively. 'Now I'm sure you want to go to bed; you must be tired.'

'Not a bit,' said Julia comfortably. 'How can enjoying oneself make one tired? The film was delightful, you know, after these peculiar modern ones. I'll go and get ready for bed and then come back in case you might want something.'

But when she went back in half an hour's time, Marcia's light was out.

It was the following evening when Ivo broached the subject of Christmas. 'Shall we give our usual party?' he asked Jorina. 'Christmas Eve, I think, don't you? Marcia will be able to enjoy it.' He turned to look at her. 'You might even like to dance a few steps.'

'Naturally I shall do my best to enter into the spirit of Christmas,' Marcia was at her most gracious. 'And if you ask me, Ivo, I'm sure I'll have the strength to take a few steps of a slow foxtrot.'

Julia kept her eyes on the cloth she was embroidering; someone ought to tell her patient that the slow foxtrot wasn't often danced these days. No one did; Ivo said merely in his kind way, 'That will be delightful. And what about shopping? I'm sure you are well enough to come into Tilburg with me one day and choose your presents. It will only be a question of crossing the pavement from the car to the shop. We could manage that—better still, let us take Julia with us to make it easier for you.'

Julia chose a strand of silk with care, threaded her needle and took a few stitches, waiting for Marcia's reply.

'Oh, presents—I'd almost forgotten about them. Am I really strong enough? It would be very pleasant, provided you don't let me get tired.' She laughed her little tinkling laugh. 'How silly I am to say that, for you wouldn't do that, would you, Ivo?'

'No, certainly not, I've had too much to do with polio cases.'

And that, thought Julia judiciously, wasn't what Marcia had meant at all. She said aloud, 'Yes, of course I'll come if you think it would help at all. It might save Miss Jason unnecessary fuss if I hold the parcels and so on.'

So it was arranged, and an afternoon two days ahead was set aside for the expedition, giving Marcia, as Julia pointed out, plenty of time to decide what she wanted to buy.

Mijnheer de Winter came the next morning while everyone but Julia was out. She left him sitting with Marcia and went to fetch him some coffee, as they had just had theirs. Marcia had greeted him with unconcealed pleasure; apparently she still lived in the

days when servants—and Julia had no doubt in her
mind that she ranked as that in her patient's eyes—
were like furniture, neither seeing nor hearing. Julia
went slowly down to the kitchen, her thoughts centred
on the look Marcia had exchanged with her visitor
and the length of their handclasp. She poured the coffee, put it on a tray and bore it upstairs, wondering
as she went what Ivo thought of this odd friendship.
He didn't strike her as the kind of man who would
take kindly to playing second fiddle to anyone else,
especially when it concerned the woman he was going
to marry. She loitered on the landing, struck by the
thought that she had never actually heard him say that
he was going to marry Marcia. Nor, for that matter,
had Marcia said so, although she had been quick
enough to let Julia know that was what she expected.

Julia took in the rapidly cooling coffee, set it tidily
on the table by Mijnheer de Winter's chair and retired
to the desk in the window where she kept her charts
and reports, but she had barely reached it when Marcia said gently, 'Oh, Nurse, do go and have half an
hour to yourself. I shall be quite all right, and you
must have so much to do.'

Julia went downstairs again; contrary to her patient's supposition she had nothing to do. She began
to wander round the hall, studying the pictures. She
was outstaring the penetrating and beady black eyes
of a tyrannical old lady in a plum-coloured dress with
a bustles, when the front door opened and Ivo came
in. Her first sensation was one of delight at seeing
him, the second of apprehension in case he went
bounding upstairs before she had a chance to mention—oh, so casually—that Mijnheer de Winter had

got there first. He cast his coat down rather untidily on the nearest chair, said hullo and then, 'I had no idea that my appearance had the power to make you look like that.'

'Like what?' asked Julia, playing for time.

'As though I'd caught you in the middle of some heinous crime. Have I?'

Julia laughed hollowly. 'No, of course not. You surprised me.'

He was standing just inside the door, and although his eyes were neither black nor beady, it was obvious that the old lady with the bustle had handed on the penetrating stare.

'Whose car is that outside?' he asked.

She should have been ready for that question; instead she uttered,

'Well—that is…'

He put his hands in his pockets and leaned comfortably against the wall, all day at his disposal. 'Do tell,' he invited silkily.

'Of course I'll tell,' she said crossly. 'It's no secret—it's Mijnheer de Winter's.'

He repeated the name. 'Do I know him?' he inquired.

'How should I know?' snapped Julia, getting more and more cross. If only the wretched little man would come downstairs and answer Ivo's questions for himself!

'Visiting Marcia?' Ivo's voice was very smooth. 'In that case I'll go up and see for myself, since you're so charmingly ill-tempered and secretive.'

He went upstairs unhurriedly without giving her time to answer, which was just as well, because she had nothing to say. She didn't think he was going to like Marcia's visitor, nor was he going to like Marcia forgetting to mention his visits, especially as she harped continuously upon her loneliness—almost, it had seemed to Julia, reproaching Ivo with it. She went into the kitchen and put the coffee on again, then wandered round the house, not quite liking to go upstairs but wondering if it would help if she did. She had just made up her mind to do so when she heard steps on the staircase and Ivo's voice, speaking with the icy civility of a well-mannered man determined not to show his illhumour. The front door opened and shut and a moment later Ivo lounged through the kitchen door.

'What a detestable fellow,' he remarked. 'No wonder you didn't want me to meet him.' He shot her a sudden fierce glance. 'And it seems that I knew all about him, or so. Marcia told me just now.'

Julia said quickly, 'I daresay if you were busy you might have forgotten—it's not important, is it—and if you had other things on your mind...'

'I had nothing important on my mind until a short time ago, and I should make it plain to you that I seldom forget anything which I am told.' He grinned suddenly. 'Aren't you going to offer me some coffee?'

She had a cup with him, there in the kitchen while he told that he was unexpectedly free because the surgeon who was to have taken the list had 'flu.

'Do you have a list this afternoon?' asked Julia.

'In Breda, yes. A pity you aren't free, I'd take you with me.'

She had been unable to prevent the look of pleasure

on her face, although she said quietly enough, 'That
would have been pleasant, but I think it's a bit too
far for Miss Jason, don't you?' and instantly wished
she hadn't said it because his face hardened into a
grimness which she couldn't bear to see. Before she
could stop herself she asked impulsively, 'Can I help,
Ivo—is—is something the matter?'

He passed his coffee cup, his face once more
smoothly bland. 'You're the last one to help me, dear
girl,' he said lightly. 'Is there any more coffee?'

She felt snubbed. She supposed he had fallen out
with his Marcia, in which case, she thought crossly,
it was his own affair. She left him to his coffee and
went upstairs to her patient, who looked up as she
went in and said with a roguish smile, 'There you are,
nurse. Oh dear, how awkward that Ivo should come
home while August was here. I'm sure he's not a
jealous man—no more than any man would be in the
circumstances,' she simpered at Julia, who felt sick,
wondering how Ivo could bear the girl, 'but I must
tell you a little secret, just between us girls. I've never
mentioned Aug—Mijnheer de Winter to Ivo, there
seemed no need, so I pretended that I had written and
told him about his visits. I flatter myself that my quick
thinking saved the situation.' She smiled, her eyes
wary. 'Don't you agree?'

'No,' said Julia instantly, 'I don't. I can't think why
you should have to tell a lie about something so trivial. Jorina thinks that Ivo knows about him too, so
you must have told her the same tale—you ever said
something of the sort to me. I can't see any reason
for deceit.'

She crossed the room and picked up Marcia's walking stick and handed it to her silently. It was more than likely that her patient would dismiss her on the spot. She did no such thing, however. 'One can see, Nurse Pennyfeather,' she said archly, 'that you've never been in love.'

Julia resisted an impulse to give her patient a poke with the stick where it would hurt most. She was a little tired of being patronised by someone so foolishly out of date as Miss Jason.

'Are you engaged to Ivo?' she asked, and was astonished at herself for asking it.

Marcia looked outraged; Julia, watching her, thought that her pale prettiness masked a petty nature and that none of her feelings, good or bad, ran deep.

'My dear nurse, that's rather a personal matter, but since you have made it your business to ask, we have an understanding—before Ivo went to Edinburgh, indeed, before I was stricken down.'

Julia felt rage and sorrow working strongly under her neat uniform; she damped them down firmly. 'In that case,' she said briskly, 'it's a very good thing that you aren't stricken any longer. Another few weeks and you should be ready to go down the aisle.'

Marcia cast her a well-bred look of loathing. 'Nurse Pennyfeather, I don't care for vulgar remarks such as that.'

'Vulgar?' asked Julia, the bit well between her nice regular white teeth. 'What's vulgar about getting married? Now, if I'd proposed getting you fit enough to live in sin...'

Miss Jason, forgetting that she was still a semi-invalid walked quite briskly across the room. She hissed: 'You coarse, over-blown creature!'

'I feel sure you will apologise, Marcia,' said Ivo from the door. His voice was steely, so were his eyes. 'I am aware that you did not mean that, but if it was a joke, you'll be the first to agree with me that it was in very poor taste.'

Julia kept her back to him. 'It's quite all right,' she said matter-of-factly, 'Miss Jason was—was joking. Did you see how well she walked across the room without her stick?' She added a little breathlessly: 'It was my fault—I was joking about your wedding, and I had no right to do it.'

She swung round to face him and was shocked at the dark look on his face, although his voice was calm enough. 'In that case, you can cry quits, I imagine. Yes, Marcia, saw you walking—how clever of you to keep it a secret from us all. Another few days and you will be fit to travel.'

Marcia said quickly in a small soft voice, 'Oh, Ivo, I couldn't possibly do it again. I can't think what happened, but I feel so weak and helpless now.' Whereupon Julia, her feelings still much inflamed, put down the stick and said in a well-controlled voice,

'In that case, I'm sure the doctor will be only too glad to help you—I'll go on down and get your chair ready.'

She smiled bleakly at them both and whisked through the door without waiting for them to answer.

Lunch was a little difficult. Julia, who would have preferred to have gone to her room and had a good cry, did her best, but Marcia remained stonily polite, answering when she was spoken to but making no remarks of her own volition; in anyone else it would be sulking, but somehow she managed to convey a sad air of dolour which effectively damped everyone's efforts to keep the conversation light. Julia rose from the table with a sense of relief, and having seen her patient settled for the afternoon in the sitting room, begged to be excused. It was time for her three hours' freedom—she intended taking a long walk; the exercise would tire her out nicely and at the same time allow her to think. She flung on her clothes with little regard to her appearance and flew downstairs and out of the door straight into Ivo, waiting on the other side. He said mildly, 'I'll give you a lift. You're not due back until about five, I gather?'

Julia nodded, twitching her fur bonnet straight and tugging on her gloves. 'But I don't want a lift—I'm going for a walk.'

As though she were a refractory child, he answered, 'Oh, nonsense,' caught her by the arm and marched her to the car and bundled her in briskly, paying no attention when she reiterated, 'I'm going for a walk,' but getting in beside her and driving off in the direction of Oisterwijk. It was only when they were through its main street, on the road to Tilburg, that she ventured to ask, 'Where are we going?'

'I told you—I've a couple of cases in Breda this afternoon.'

She looked at him with something like horror. 'But that's miles away!'

'Your geography is sadly at fault, you'll have to study a map. Breda is fifteen miles from Tilburg, which we are rapidly approaching. It's half past one, the list is at two o'clock, so we have plenty of time. Why were you in such a hurry?'

'I—I wanted some fresh air.'

He was looking straight ahead, driving fast as he always did, with a nonchalance which was deceiving until you looked at the speedometer.

'I'm sorry Marcia upset you this morning. You must forgive her, she's been very ill.'

'It didn't matter, really it didn't,' she found herself protesting too much. 'She must hate being so inactive.' As she said it she remembered very clearly how well Marcia had walked across the room, and he had seen it too, although she had been clever enough to pretend it was a flash in the pan. Julia went on quickly, 'Miss Jason has quite a lot of shopping to do in Tilburg—it should be fun.'

A stupid remark, she thought, and he must have thought so too, for he didn't bother to reply, but as the outskirts of Breda closed in on them he said suddenly, 'I think we must plan a really merry Christmas, don't you? What a pity we can't keep it up until Twelfth Night, as they used to. What is that poem in English, something about "The first day of Christmas…"'

Julia obliged with a few verses, and when she got to the fifth day, stopped to remark. 'Five gold rings is a bit much, you know. Where would she wear them?'

'I shouldn't think it mattered; obviously her true love wanted to make certain that she knew he loved her.'

'Oh, well, there couldn't be much doubt about that, could there?' said Julia, once more lighthearted. 'I mean, one ring would be nice, but five—what more could any girl want?'

He didn't answer because they had stopped by the

Casualty entrance at the hospital. 'Hop out, dear girl,' he said. 'I'll take you to Zuster Bos before I go up to theatre.'

Zuster Bos was middle-aged and round; she had round blue eyes to match her rotund person and a delightful smile. She nodded vigorously to all that Ivo had to say, chuckled, shook Julia by the hand, said in quaintly accented English, 'Go away, bad boy,' and turned her attention to her guest.

Casualty was almost empty; the accidents, said Zuster Bos in difficult English helped out with a good deal of miming, were more frequent in the morning when the workers were still sleepy and perhaps a little careless—and the evening, when they were tired.

'Are you busy here?' asked Julia, prepared to enjoy herself.

'The book,' said Zuster Bos, and led her over to a desk at which a nurse sat writing. She looked up and smiled as they approached and handed over the Day Book, which Julia saw was exactly the same as the one in her own hospital, only the entries were in Dutch. But she could see the number of entries that it was a busy unit and would have enjoyed trying to decipher the various cases, but her mentor plucked her arm and led her to the office where she found herself drinking a cup of coffee and answering, in her turn, a great many questions about her own work. She said politely, 'Your English is very good Sister,' and was rewarded by a beaming smile.

'Yes? I learn in the war—I was young girl, but I nurse...' She paused, at a loss for a word.

'Men who escaped?' tried Julia, and watched the little woman's brow clear. 'Yes, they speak no

Dutch—I speak English.' She shrugged her plump shoulders and laughed cosily. It was a pity that at that moment an ambulance should shrill its way to the entrance and she had to go. But not for long. 'Not bad,' she announced as she sat down once more, 'Zuster van Rijk and Zuster Laagemaat can do all. It is,' she paused again, 'too much drug.'

'An overdose?' Julia guessed. 'Do you get a lot too? So do we.'

They talked happily together, helping each other when they came to words they didn't know. They were absorbed in the technique of resuscitation when Ivo came back. Julia watched him walking through Cas to the office. The nurses looked at him as they passed and he greeted them pleasantly without noticing their admiring glances. He looked relaxed and cheerful and very good-looking indeed. Julia turned her face away in case the admiration on her face showed too.

She was sorry to leave Zuster Bos, but as Ivo pointed out, it was already after half past two. He took her round the hospital, as he had promised, strolling from ward to ward where she was greeted more often than not in her own language and with a degree of friendliness she hadn't expected.

They walked back to the entrance. 'Is Tilburg hospital like this one?'

'Very similar. I go to Eindhoven sometimes, there's a splendid one there, and s'Hertogenbosch.'

'Where?'

He laughed and repeated the name, and standing in the hospital entrance oblivious of curious passers-by, made her repeat it too until she had it right, and only then did they get into the car again. They were outside the town when Julia saw a signpost to Roosendaal and remarked that she had thought that town to be in the opposite direction to Tilburg.

'And so it is, but you don't suppose I can travel any farther without tea, do you?' He glanced at her. 'Don't fidget, we've plenty of time. There's a place at Princenhage, just along this road.'

They stopped at the Mirabelle restaurant and went inside to a warmth very welcome after the cold outside. They had tea, each with their own little pot which amused Julia very much, and some rich and elaborate cakes, which, she declared, were a shame to eat, although she contradicted her words by eating hers to the last crumb, and when pressed to have a second, did so. She licked a morsel of cream off her pretty mouth with the tip of her tongue and sighed contentedly. 'I oughtn't to have them,' she said, although the remark was purely rhetoric, 'I shall get fat.'

He smiled lazily at her across the table. 'Never,' he said. 'You'll stay as you are for ever and ever.'

Julia pushed back her chair and put on her gloves and said lightly to cover her feelings, 'So now I'm indestructible as well as stoutly built!' and giggled so infectiously that he laughed too.

The shopping expedition the next day was, on the whole, a success. Marcia, well wrapped against the cold, was as excited as she would allow herself to be and even though it turned out that most of the shopping was for herself, it was pleasant to spend most of the afternoon in the bigger stores, even though her insistence on being treated as an invalid became a little irksome towards the end. Only once did she show any desire to do anything for herself and that was to post a handful of letters, something in which she was frustrated by Ivo, despite her protests. Julia, watching him putting them into the letter box, saw that he was looking at each of them in turn; she knew when he saw the one addressed to Mijnheer de Winter because of his quick frown. He said nothing, however, and nothing in his manner indicated that he was annoyed, although she caught Marcia's faintly worried look. Possibly Ivo had asked her not to continue her friendship with de Winter, but they weren't likely to discuss it before her. They had tea presently and Ivo was at his most amusing and if anything, kinder and more considerate of Marcia than he had been before. Julia, sitting in the back of the car on their way home, watched him in the gloom, bending his head to hear what Marcia had to say, and when Marcia laughed, which was often, Julia clenched her hands tightly in her lap, hurting them, as if by doing so she could ease the hurt in her heart.

She avoided him for the next day or two, and although they saw each other at meals and in the sitting room there was always someone else there. And on the third day, when she was free after one o'clock, she walked into Oisterwijk and did her Christmas shopping; a quite handsome coffret of eau de Cologne for Marcia, a tobacco pouch for Doctor van den Werff, handkerchiefs—fine linen ones—for Ivo and for Jorina some French soap as well as the teacloth she had embroidered. For Bep she found a scarf and for the girl who came up from the village every day to work, a box of chocolates. She went straight to her room when she got back, did up her parcels and put them away at the back of the big cupboard in her bedroom, then went down to dinner. It was during that meal that Doctor van den Werff remarked,

'It seems to me that Julia has a very bad bargain for her half day; it is in fact no half day at all. Here she is, back here with us, whether she likes it or not, because there's nothing for her to do.' He looked across the table at her, smiling. 'Do you mind, Julia?'

She smiled back, 'No, not at all. I've letters to write and those will take me all the evening. I had a nice afternoon in Oisterwijk too. One day when it's fine, I shall go for a long walk.'

Ivo looked up from the pear he was peeling for Marcia. 'Well take care if you do, there's quite a lot of fen country around here and this time of year it's rough underfoot.'

Julia thanked him politely and lapsed into silence once more while Marcia, with a sad little smile, won- dered out aloud and at some length when she would be able to go for a long walk—or, she added bravely, if she ever would again.

'I can't see why not,' said Julia kindly. 'Why not come into the garden with me tomorrow morning? We needn't go far and the worst that can happen is for you to fall over, when I shall pick you up again.'

They all laughed except Marcia, who flushed faintly and said gently,

'How kind of you to offer, nurse, but I couldn't trust myself to you—I need someone big and strong.' She glanced at Ivo as she spoke and he said placidly, 'That sounds like me, but unfortunately I'm going away for a couple of days.' He looked up briefly. 'I can't see what harm there would be in going with Julia as long as there's no ice about—you said yourself she was robust.'

Julia, who had just taken some wine, choked on it, laughing. 'I'll never live that down, shall I?' she declared cheerfully.

She went back to her room as soon as dinner was over because she felt that they expected her to, but once there she wrote no letters at all, for the only one she had to answer was an angry one from her brother, full of approaches and pointing out how selfish she had become. She sat, instead, in a chair, doing nothing until bedtime. She heard Marcia, with Ivo as escort, come upstairs and there Jorina to make sure Marcia was safely in bed. She felt a fraud, sitting there doing nothing and being paid handsomely for it. They would surely send her back to England directly after Christmas. She went on sitting idly, long after the others came to bed. Ivo was last of all; she heard him in the garden with Ben and then presently come indoors again. The house was quite silent when at last she went to bed herself.

CHAPTER SIX

THE OPPORTUNITY to go for a walk came sooner than Julia had expected, for two days later Ivo, back from wherever he had been, took Marcia into Tilburg in the morning. She had complained with her usual steely gentleness that her hair looked terrible, adding at the same time that she quite understood that no one could spare the time to take her to the hairdresser, but when Julia had immediately offered to go with her and Jorina had offered to drive them she refused on the grounds that she was selfishly taking up their time. It was inevitable that she contrived to tell Ivo in such a way that she gained his instant attention and the promise to take her himself on his way to hospital, and when Julia had asked if she was to go too, Marcia had said quite cheerfully, having gained her own ends,

'Of course not, Nurse Pennyfeather—you may have your free time this morning, that will make a nice change for you.' Whereupon Ivo had said, 'Why not have a lift in with us, Julia? There must be something you can amuse yourself with for a couple of hours.'

But Julia had declined because she considered he had listened too readily to Marcia's curdled account of her efforts to get to the hairdresser while he was away—besides, the less she saw of him the better. She had thanked him politely in a serene voice which

betrayed nothing of her true feelings and declared her
intention of taking a walk.

She tried not to think about Ivo and Marcia while
she changed into her outdoor clothes. It was cold and
a little misty outside and the sky was a mass of thick
grey clouds, but there was always the chance that the
sun would shine. She tucked a scarf into the neck of
her top coat and tied the fur bonnet securely. She had
studied a local map the previous evening and knew
just where she was going. She ran downstairs and put
her head round the kitchen door, called goodbye to
Jorina and went out of the house.

The heath stretched away beyond the woods behind
the house, and according to the map, it was criss-
crossed by bicycle paths. She intended to take one of
these as far as the village of Breukelen about three
miles away and then return along another of the paths.

The wind stung her cheeks and whipped her black
hair from under her bonnet, but it was exhilarating
and the exercise did her good, and presently, glowing
with warmth, she slowed her pace a little the better
to think. She would have to go back to England
soon—after Christmas, she thought, and if Marcia
was going home shortly, would it not be a good idea
if they were to travel together. But was Marcia going
home? She had said nothing to that effect; perhaps
she intended to remain until she married Ivo. The
thought of it made Julia catch her breath and was
swamped by the idea she had kept buried until now.
Ivo wasn't in love with Marcia; he didn't want to
marry her, although perhaps he had been attracted to
her when they first met, for she was undoubtedly a
very clever girl and in her way attractive too, but the

pity he had shown her when she was taken ill had
been mistakenly—or deliberately?—misconstrued as
love by Marcia and he had been unable to let her see
that she was wrong because she had been so ill. Perhaps he had thought that an absence of six months
would terminate the affair in a gentler fashion. But it
hadn't, or so it seemed to Ivo at least, and Julia had
the uneasy suspicion that if he thought that Marcia
still loved him he would never do anything to hurt
her because in some way Marcia had made him feel
responsible for her illness. Julia was certain that this
wasn't the case, but she had no proof. It was a pity
that Ivo held such lofty principles. She said loudly in
exasperation, 'Old-fashioned bunkum—no one behaves like that any more,' and knew even as she said
it that Ivo did.

   She began to walk faster as if to get away from her
thoughts, and when she came to a fork in the path,
took the right-hand one without really noticing. It was
some time later when she realised that she must have
taken the wrong direction, for by now she should have
reached the village. She stood still, trying to get her
bearings, and decided that the path would probably
end at some houses at least. But it didn't; she had
walked steadily for some time now and it had no end,
she stopped again and felt the first drops of freezing
rain sting her face. She hadn't noticed that the sky,
already grey, had become almost black behind her,
and she would have to find shelter as quickly as possible. There were woods to the right of her. She
looked at them carefully and decided that they must
be part of the woods she had walked through when
she had started out—if so, she had only to reach them

and then walk in their shelter in the direction she had
come from.

With the rain had come a gale of wind, whistling
through the trees so that their branches creaked and
groaned about her head, caring twigs and smaller
branches with it. She was tired by now and very cold
as well as hungry, and once or twice, in the dimness
under the trees, she fell. It was only too apparent that
she was lost, and in the blinding rain, even if she
ventured away from the woods, she had little hope of
finding her way. The sensible thing to do was to keep
on walking; she knew from the map that the area of
heath and fen land round Oisterwijk was a rough tri-
angle, bounded by roads, so sooner or later, she was
bound to strike one or other of them. Not too much
later, she hoped, for it was after two o'clock now and
getting dark, with the rain still pouring from an un-
broken pall of cloud.

She went on walking, beginning to get a little
frightened, for the night would be long and cold and
although she would have liked to rest, she dared not
in case she fell asleep. Someone would have missed
her by now—Jorina or Bep. Doctor van den Werff
would have been out on his rounds and wouldn't
know anyway, and neither would Ivo, who would
probably stay in Tilburg with Marcia until the weather
cleared. She stumbled a little and fell into a small
hollow between two fir trees. It was dry, covered in
pine needles and sheltered from the wind. She hadn't
meant to rest, but it was warmer there and surely five
minutes wouldn't hurt. Julia sat down, drew her knees
up under her chin, clasped her gloved hands round

them and rested her head upon them. She was asleep within seconds.

She was roused by a hand on her shoulders, shaking her roughly awake. A voice—Ivo's voice—was telling her, equally roughly, that she was a damned little idiot. He pulled her to her feet, which were numb to the knees so that she lurched against him, and tore off her gloves to rub her cold hands.

'You fool!' he said violently, as he rubbed. 'Haven't you got the sense to keep moving in weather like this—and what possessed you to walk all these miles?'

He stopped his rubbing for a moment, flung an arm around her shoulders to hold her steady and poured some brandy down her throat in a ruthless fashion which left her spluttering and choking, and then resumed his work.

'Ugh!' uttered Julia, gaining strength from the brandy. 'Leave me alone—shouting at me like that. You're hurting me!'

He sat her down with a thump, pulled off a boot and started on her foot. When he spoke it was forcefully and in his own language. He sounded furious, and what with too much brandy on an empty stomach and pain from the reviving circulation of her hands she felt most peculiar. She said in a voice that choked a little, 'I got lost.'

He put the boot back on again, and took off the other one.

'What possessed you—' he began harshly, and then in a rigidly controlled voice: 'Jorina told me you left the house before eleven—do you know the time now?'

Julia gave a weak but spirited snort. 'How can I? It's dark. When I looked at my watch it was just after three, but that must be half an hour or so ago.'

He gave her a look of such fierceness through the gloom that she caught her breath. 'It's after six o'clock,' he said dryly.

She shivered violently. 'It can't be—I sat down for a minute.'

'It was pure chance that I found you—you know what would have happened if I hadn't?'

'Well, I suppose I should have gone on sleeping.'

'And died of exposure.' He sounded grim.

'I—I didn't think of that,' she faltered a little. 'Have you been looking for me for a long time?'

'Rub your hands together and then clap them. Since we got home at about one o'clock.'

Julia was stricken into silence. She ventured at last, 'Just you?'

'No. Until it became really dark and the weather got too bad, we all searched—which meant leaving Marcia alone in the house. We left this stretch of the woods until last because it didn't seem possible that you could get so far.'

She said stupidly, 'But I'm not far. I'm on my way back to your house. If I had walked straight on…'

'You would have eventually come to the village of Oirschot—ten kilometres from Oisterwijk—that is, if you had wakened up.'

'You must be mistaken.'

He put on her boot and stood her on her feet again and gave her a little shake. 'For God's sake stop arguing with me,' he said loudly, then caught her close and kissed her so fiercely that she had no breath.

'Fool,' he declared. 'Fool!' and let her go so suddenly
that she almost fell. If her mind as well as her body
hadn't been so numbed, she would most certainly
have given this piece of rudeness the answer it so
richly deserved, for she felt certain that it was directed
against herself, but her teeth were chattering so much
that she found it impossible to speak. She made a
small, indignant noise and he said harshly,

'Too cold to talk, eh? That's a good thing, now I
shan't have to listen to your excuses all the way
home.' His voice was so furiously angry that Julia
felt her eyes fill with tears and was thankful for the
dark, but even as she had thought, he turned his torch
on her face. She felt his arm round her once more,
but this time it was gentle and comforting. He said in
a quite different voice, 'Drink this, dear girl—I know
you dislike it, but it will help to warm you.'

She swallowed obediently and the spirit's warmth
crept over her, making her feel more cheerful as well
as less cold, although the tears ran down her cheeks
still. But she made no attempt to wipe them away,
she had indeed forgotten them; she sniffed a little forlornly and began to walk wordlessly, urged on by his
arm in the light from the torch. It seemed a long way
to the car; she stumbled along beside him as he strode
ahead, unworried by the rain and the wind and the
blackness of the early evening, but presently they
came with unexpected suddenness out of the woods
and on to a road and she saw the Jensen's lights.

Ivo picked her up and tossed her into the seat beside his without a word, then got in beside her, and
at the same time she became aware that Ben was in
the car too, warm and doggy-smelling. He leaned his

shaggy head over the back of her seat and licked her gently, then at a quiet word from Ivo, he slid between them to settle at her feet. Julia felt his solid warmth envelop her feet and legs and said through chattering teeth, 'Dear Ben...'

'He'll warm you up,' said Ivo in a perfectly ordinary voice as he wrapped a blanket around her shoulders. 'He wanted to come with me, but he's been looking for you too all the afternoon and he's—as you so aptly say—dog-tired.'

He didn't say any more, but turned the car with a good deal of skill on the icy road and started for home. The car skidded several times on the way back, but Julia, now that the effects of the brandy were wearing off, was feeling too miserable to notice anything as trivial—her thoughts were entirely of Ivo's anger with her. It had perhaps been foolish of her to have gone so far, but she hadn't got lost deliberately, it was something which could have happened to anyone. She said out loud,

'How intolerant you are!'

Ivo laughed, sounding amused and irritated too. 'You do me less than justice—at any moment now you will be telling me that it was my fault that you got lost.' He sighed. 'Didn't you look to see where you were going when you started out?'

Julia clutched Ben round the reassuring thickness of his neck as the car went into another skid. 'Of course I did, but I was thinking. I—I must have taken a wrong turning.'

'What were you thinking of, Julia?'

She said a little too quickly, 'I don't remember.'

'Liar,' he observed blandly, and didn't speak again

until they slid to a halt before the house. The door was opened before they had stopped, revealing Bep and behind her Doctor van den Werff and Jorina. Julia, still cold and stiff despite Ben's best efforts, was glad of Ivo's arm as they went inside, although she essayed a smile as the three of them crowded round her.

'A hot bath,' said Doctor van den Werff, 'a hot drink too. How do you feel, Julia? You poor child, I feel responsible.'

Julia, who had expected a scolding or at least reproaches for being so stupid, felt a strong desire to burst into tears again. Kindness was something she hadn't reckoned with and her voice wobbled a bit as she said, 'I'm sorry I was so silly and gave you all so much trouble,' and was patted and soothed by the three of them, but all Ivo did was to say, 'You'd better do as you're told or we shall have you sneezing over us all.'

She nodded without looking at him and followed Bep upstairs with Jorina, an arm round her waist, beside her. As they went she heard Ivo ask his father, 'Where's Marcia?' which had the effect of starting her tears again, to her own great surprise and when she mumbled an apology, Jorina said kindly, 'You're tired and I expect you were frightened too—I should have been—and it must have been very cold, yes?'

'Yes,' said Julia.

She went downstairs a couple of hours later, warm once more and looking exactly as she always did in her neat uniform, save for her beautiful face which was a little pale. They were all in the sitting room and while Ivo had nothing to say his father called to

her to go and sit with him and asked her very kindly
if she felt well enough to stay up. 'We put dinner
back,' he explained, 'but you can just as easily have
it in bed if you wish.'

Julia said shyly, 'That's very kind of you, doctor,
but I feel quite well, thank you, only very foolish.'
She glanced across the room to where Marcia was
sitting by the fire. 'I'm so sorry, Miss Jason,' she
began, 'for being such a nuisance—I hope I didn't
spoil your day or cause you any inconvenience.'

Miss Jason bowed her head in graceful acknowl-
edgement of this apology and said with a sickening
graciousness, 'Well, I daresay it has taught you a lesson, nurse. You are, I imagine, an impetuous young
woman, lacking the intellectual powers of the more
intelligent person, who would have given all the as-
pects of a walk in the country at this time of year the
deliberation they deserve.'

Julia took a few moments to unwind this prosy
speech and make sense of it. She didn't care for it all;
she was willing to admit that she had been at fault,
but she wasn't going to be preached over. She opened
her mouth to say so and was forestalled in the nick
of time by Ivo, who said smoothly,

'Most unjust, Marcia, as well as making a great
fuss about nothing. We have all been lost at some
time or other, found, and brought home. There's nothing so special about going for a walk even at this time
of year, and not all of us find it necessary to weigh
the pros and cons before we do so.' He turned to
Jorina and said easily,

'Do you remember the time you went to find St
Nikolaas—how old were you? Five? You looked like

a snowman when I found you and you kicked me all the way home because I wouldn't let you go on looking for him.' They laughed together and Jorina answered, 'And what about that time you felt sure you'd failed your exams and came in frozen stiff in the middle of my birthday party after Father found you walking round in circles?' She laughed across at Julia, seemingly unaware of the indignant look still on Julia's face. 'You've no idea what a horror Ivo was— still is. Is your brother like that?'

Julia smiled despite herself. Her brother was as unlike Ivo as chalk from the proverbial cheese. She shook her head. 'I can't remember him ever doing anything to give anyone a moment's unease.'

'The fellow sounds like a dead bore,' observed Ivo carelessly.

'He is.' She saw the little smile curl the corners of his mouth and added hastily, 'He's a very worthy sort of person.'

Ivo got up. 'I'll not attempt to compete,' he stated lightly. 'Who's for a drink?'

It was when, a moment or two later, he handed her a glass of sherry that she remembered, far too vividly, the brandy he had poured down her throat in such an unceremonious fashion a few hours previously, and flushed up to her eyes under his amused look. But he didn't say anything and presently went to sit by Marcia again, and Julia, to her secret satisfaction, couldn't help but notice that his manner towards her was a little cool.

There were still several days to Christmas; Julia spent them in encouraging her patient to overcome what slight disability remained; determined to atone for the nuisance she had been and doggedly accepting Miss Jason's chastening lectures, given in her gentle, modulated voice, which she delivered at least once a day, and if there was time, twice, so that presently Julia began to feel herself a slightly inferior being, only tolerated because of her patient's high-minded principles. Her common sense told her that this was not, indeed, the fact, but she was fast losing her self-assurance, especially as she saw very little of Ivo, and when she did, he treated her with a casual politeness which made it impossible to talk to him. Not that she had any desire to talk to him, she told herself vigorously; let him marry his wretched Marcia and take the consequences—in five years' time he would be as dreary as his wife; he would probably wear goloshes and never drive at more than forty miles an hour and they would have one, or worse, no children because Marcia would feel herself to be too delicate. Julia, making her patient's bed, thumped the pillows with quite unnecessary vigour.

It was that evening at dinner that Jorina announced that she intended going to the Hague the following day. Klaas was there for a couple of days, she said, and she would combine seeing him with some shopping.

'What sort of shopping?' her father wanted to know.

'Well, there's the party in two days' time, and I might see something I liked.' She turned to Julia. 'Come with me, its time you had a day to yourself. Besides, you'll see nothing of Holland before you go back.'

Julia agreed silently; she hadn't had a day off since

she had arrived and although she was paid a handsome salary, she would have liked the opportunity of spending some of it. All the same, it had been made clear to her when she accepted the job that she was to have two half days a week; nothing had been said about a whole day. She said now,

'Thank you, Jorina, but that would mean the whole day away, you know, and you would be away too— I can't leave Miss Jason alone.'

Doctor van den Werff put down his knife and fork. 'Why ever not?' he asked. 'Jorina won't be leaving until ten o'clock or thereabouts; plenty of time to get Marcia downstairs and Bep can do anything needed once she is down. You'll be back long before bedtime.' He smiled pleasantly at Marcia. 'You won't mind? It will be splendid practice for you, for you won't be needing a nurse much longer, you know. The quicker you become independent, the better, eh?'

Thus addressed, there was nothing Marcia could do but agree, albeit sourly, and she looked even more sour when Ivo said casually,

'I've no cases at the hospital tomorrow, how about going in my car? I think that's a better idea than you driving that tin box of yours, Jorina, and we'll get there much faster. Besides, the roads aren't too good and you never could cope with a skid. There are a number of things I want to do in the Hague.'

Jorina agreed so quickly that Marcia looked up suspiciously, but Ivo's face was merely blandly inquiring and Jorina looked so innocent that any doubts she had were discarded. And Julia listening to this exchange, had no doubts at all; even if Ivo spent the whole day going about his own business there was still the drive there and back. When he gave her an enquiring look she said at once, 'I should very much like to go. I've been reading a book about the Hague and there are several places I should like to see.'

The next morning saw very little improvement in the weather. A light frosting of snow had fallen during the night and the sky was leaden. Although she wasn't a nervous girl, Julia was glad that Ivo would be driving and not Jorina. She thought about it with pleasure as she got Marcia downstairs and comfortably settled with the day's paraphernalia around her. She was still thinking about it as she dressed herself with extra care. She hadn't many clothes with her, she put on the brown wool dress, covered it with her top-coat, arranged the fur bonnet upon her dark head, snatched up her gloves and handbag and danced downstairs. She hadn't seen Ivo that morning, and the awful thought that he might have changed his mind about driving to the Hague crossed her mind as she entered the sitting room.

He hadn't. He was sitting, ready dressed to go out, on the arm of a chair, reading the paper and carrying on a desultory conversation with Marcia while he did so. He put the paper down as Julia went in and said, 'Hullo, there you are. Jorina has gone to the kitchen to see Bep.' He got to his feet then swept her out of the room, saying over his shoulder as he went, 'Goodbye, Marcia—I'll do my best to get that book for you.'

Julia, gabbling farewells as they went, was walked across hall and outside to where the car was waiting, but when he opened the door and said genially, 'Get in, dear girl,' she hung back and enquired if Jorina wouldn't prefer to sit in front, whereupon he gave her a little push with the remark, 'I've never met such a woman for arguing,' and shut the door upon her, then before she could think of a suitable answer Jorina arrived and got into the back of the car saying,

'Don't anyone talk to me until I say so—I'm making lists of food for the party. Ivo, you'll see to the drinks? I'll go into Lensvelt Nicola and get some petits fours...' There was a pause while she wrote busily. 'And there's that place in the Lange Vooruit where they sell those cheesy things, and I want some shoes and another handbag if I see one I like.'

They were already half way to Tilburg. 'Does Klaas come at the top or bottom of the list?' asked Ivo.

'Top, of course. If you drop me outside Metz—he said he's going to wait until I come. What are you going to do, Julia?'

'I'm going to the top of St Jacobskerk tower to see the view,' said Julia promptly, 'and then the Mauritshuis, and then I'm going to take a look at the Huis den Bosch. I can't go in, but all the same I'd like to see it.'

The rest of the journey passed pleasantly enough, and for Julia it was a delight, for she had Ivo beside her and just for a few hours she was determined to forget Marcia and her own imminent return to England. It was high time she made a few plans for her future, for she had nowhere to go, only to her brother's house, and he, although he would give her house room, would hardly welcome her with open arms after the way she had treated him. But it all seemed very far away from the flat, wintry landscape

they were passing through; she concentrated on studying the places of interest pointed out to her and joined
in the cheerful talk without giving a hint of her more
sombre thoughts.

The Hague, once they had reached the heart of the
city, was everything she had imagined an old Dutch
city to be, for although Tilburg had pleased her very
much and she had liked Breda, the Hague seemed,
once they were through the suburbs, like a city from
the Golden Age. They set Jorina down outside Metz,
a shop which Julia resolved to explore should she find
the time, and then went through the city to the Huis
den Bosch where Ivo stopped the car.

'Will this suit you?' he wanted to know cheerfully.
'You can't get lost—just follow the road back into
the city again.'

Julia looked behind her. 'But it's miles!'

'Oh no—two perhaps, no more.'

She eyed him a little uncertainly. 'Where—where
shall I meet you, then?'

'Now as to that, supposing we get out of the car
and you can take your fill of the Huis den Bosch as
we walk along and discuss it.'

He took her arm and marched her along briskly,
away from the main road, and Julia, having looked
her fill, said politely, 'Thank you, I've had a good
look.' She paused and went on a little apprehensively,

'If you would tell me your plans.'

He halted abruptly, and she with him. 'That's better. First you refuse to have lunch with me, and then
you try to brush me off... My plans depend upon you,
Julia. You'll waste a great deal of time on your own,
you know, and you may not get the chance to come

again. Supposing I take you back now and leave you in the Noordeinde—a shopping centre where you can't get lost. What I have to do won't take above an hour. I'll wait for you at the spot where I put you down presently. We'll have lunch and then go wherever you want. Jorina won't be ready until six o'clock.' Julia, before she could stop herself, said, 'Oh, how lovely!' and then, 'I shall be a nuisance to you—you said you had things to do.' She stared up at him, her eyes shining, her face eager, despite her words, to meet his own eyes, bright and intent and with an expression she couldn't read. An instant later she felt his arms around her.

'So I did,' he said calmly, 'and this was one of them,' and he bent his head to kiss her. And Julia, her common sense blown away by the winter wind whistling around them, kissed him back. Even as she did so, she was regretting it; she couldn't very well have prevented him from kissing her, but there was absolutely no need to return his kiss. She said as lightly as her voice would allow, 'What silly things one does at Christmas,' and even achieved a laugh with it as she slipped out of his arms, to feel immediately and illogically put out because he gave no sign of minding. She caught herself wondering how Marcia would have reacted; there was no way of telling what his own feelings were, although she fancied she could see amusement behind the calmness of his face.

He didn't answer her remark, only asked casually, 'Have you any shopping to do? Will an hour be long enough?'

'Oh, plenty,' said Julia. If he was going to be casual, she could be too. 'I don't intend to do much shopping, only look.'

He talked with a disarming friendliness as they drove to the centre of the city and left her, with strict instructions to be on that same spot in about an hour's time. Julia watched the Jensen slide away in the traffic and felt lost. But the shop windows were diverting, and she wandered along, wishing she could buy a great many of the things she saw, but beyond one or two trifles, she didn't dare because she would soon be out of work; even if she went back to her hospital, she wouldn't get any money for the rest of the month, and she didn't think her brother would think of paying her if she went there. She stared into the window of a tiny boutique, exhibiting in its window exactly the kind of party dress any girl would fall for. It had no price ticket, and presently she walked on, staring up at the old houses above the shops; it would be delightful to go into a shop like that and buy the dress without even asking the price. But it was the jewellers' shops which caught her attention. She looked in each one, and it was while she was feasting her eyes upon the contents of one of their windows that she saw Ivo coming out of an even more opulent jeweller's across the street. He was stuffing a small box into a pocket as he came through the door and judging from the satisfied look on the face of the man who had opened it for him, he had spent a lot of money…a ring for Marcia? A wedding ring? Julia turned her back upon both Ivo and her thoughts and plunged through the door before her, for if she didn't Ivo would surely see her.

She found herself in a richly furnished shop housing a great many showcases containing antique silver, diamond tiaras and suchlike expensive trifles. She gazed unhappily at a trio of diamond bracelets, displayed with studied carelessness upon dark blue velvet, and when a young man approached her and said something in Dutch she turned her pretty, worried face to his and said apologetically,

'I don't want to buy anything—there was someone I didn't want to meet...'

She looked so forlorn and so beautiful that he instantly dismissed the idea that she was a thieves' accomplice and smiled kindly at her.

'Please stay if you wish,' he said in quite beautiful English, and went to the door to study the street, and Julia came to peer over his shoulder. 'He's gone,' she breathed thankfully. 'I'll go—it was kind of you...'

He opened the door for her and she went out into the Noordeinde once more, to stare unseeingly at the shops until it was time to meet Ivo.

He was waiting for her, although she was a little early, but she could see no car. 'I haven't kept you waiting?' she asked. 'The shops are so delightful.'

He smiled and raised an eyebrow. 'And you have bought nothing? I find that a miracle. Jorina would have an armful of parcels by now.'

Julia smiled, wanting to point out that if she had the money his sister had at her disposal she would have no difficulty in rivalling her spending powers. Did he actually think that she didn't like clothes?

He must have guessed her thoughts, for he inquired, 'Didn't you see anything at all you would have liked to buy?'

She nodded. 'Any number. There was a dress—a

party dress with no price on it—an extravagant dress.'
She added hastily because he made a sudden hasty
movement and she was afraid he might insist on going back to look at it, and still worse, buy it, 'Not the
kind of dress I could ever wear.'

He smiled and took her arm. 'That's an arguable
point,' he observed. 'Now let's have a meal.'

They didn't have to walk far, round the corner into
Molenstraat to the Park Hotel and into its restaurant
over-looking the gardens of a former royal palace.
Julia, who hadn't expected anything as grand, went
away to take off her bonnet and returned, quite unconscious of the stares directed at her dark loveliness,
to find that Ivo had ordered the drinks.

'I chose this place,' he explained, 'because it is
close to most of the places you want to visit.'

He lifted a finger and the hovering waiter handed
them menu cards and stepped back to a discreet distance. Julia studied hers with deep interest. As far as
she could see, everything that anyone could possibly
want was on it.

'A starter?' prompted Ivo. 'How about Mousse
d'Avocat? If you like avocado pears.' Julia, who had
never eaten one, had no intention of telling him so,
she nodded and chose soufflé de Turbot Hollandaise,
leaving him to decide upon quenelle of pike Nantua
before going into conference with the wine waiter, but
once the important question of what they were going
to eat had been settled, he gave her his undivided
attention.

'And what do you think of our shops?' he wanted
to know.

'Super,' said Julia briefly, 'only expensive.' She was eating her avocado pear and finding it delicious.

He agreed. 'And of course it is Christmas—the shops show all their most tempting wares. Did you look at any jewellery?'

Julia kept her eyes on her plate and wished that she didn't flush so easily. 'Yes—they're marvellous. The diamonds!'

'You like diamonds?'

She was surprised into looking at him. 'Me? Of course—I imagine all women do.'

'A safe choice for a man to make, you think?' He sounded only casually interested.

Julia eyed her turbot with a sudden lack of appetite. 'Very safe,' she said, but surely he would have asked Marcia...? 'But women don't have to have diamonds, you know. I should think most of them are quite happy with—with turquoises or garnets or something similar.'

'Rubies?' he asked lightly, smiling.

So it was rubies for Marcia; Julia wondered if he knew that bit about a good woman being above rubies; probably not. She said woodenly,

'Definitely rubies,' and he went on to talk about something else. It was when they were eating dessert—mangoes in champagne—that he remarked, 'How delightful the meals were in Drumlochie House—I often think of them.'

Julia, full of false cheer from the wine and the champagne and Cointreau which had enwrapped the mangoes, smiled at him. 'Me too. But the meals weren't all that good, you know. I expect it was because we were all hungry for most of the time and cold as well.'

'Lord, yes. Those bedrooms—mine was like an ice house.'

She remembered him lying on the great bed, fast asleep, and smiled. 'You looked like a petrified knight on a tomb,' she said, and went a little pink when he said on a laugh, 'Did I? I shan't tell you what you looked like.'

She avoided his eye, concentrating on her coffee cup. The conversation was back on their old easy footing, and it wouldn't do. Marcia's long face floated in the air before her, looking reproachful, and much as Julia disliked her, she couldn't take advantage of her behind her back. She asked briskly, 'Where are we going first? And can you really spare the time?'

He assured her that he could and suggested the Ridderzaal, followed by a visit to the Mauritshuis museum, and lastly the tower of St Jacobskerk. If there was any time over from these treats he declared that he would see that no second of it was wasted. The afternoon arranged, they set off for the Ridderzaal, where the beamed roofs, stained glass windows and flags which adorned the walls of this thirteenth-century building satisfied even Julia's lively imagination. There weren't many visitors on such a cold afternoon, and the guide, about to conduct a handful of people round, asked without much interest if they wished to join his party, but Ivo, after a short parley, walked her off in the opposite direction to the one in which the guide was taking and they ambled around undisturbed and almost alone, while he explained the history of the old place at some length.

The museum was just behind the Ridderzaal, housed in a beautiful sixteenth-century house. Here they dawdled amongst the Rembrandts, Vermeers, Franz Hals and a number of other equally famous painters, with Julia displaying a knowledge of these treasures which, it amused her to see, rather surprised her escort. He said at length, 'You know a great deal.'

'Not really,' she answered honestly, 'but when I was a student nurse I hadn't a great deal of money so I spent a lot of time in museums and picture galleries.' They were standing in front of Rembrandt's self-portrait and she smiled at him over her shoulder and surprised a look on his face which set her heart beating a great deal faster than it should. She plunged at once into the first topic of conversation which entered her head, which was, not surprisingly, Rembrandt. She kept up quite a dissertation on him, rivalling her patient in both length and dullness, and only stopped when Ivo said gently,

'It's all right, dear girl—I'm not sure why you took fright, but there is no harm in us recapturing our happy times at Drumlochie House, is there?'

'No,' said Julia instantly, 'but it was easy and natural somehow, wasn't it, to be friends—I suppose it was because we were cut off from everything, in our own world. Now we're normal again and it seems unreal.' She gave him a frank look. 'You're different, too.'

They were walking slowly past priceless paintings which neither of them saw. 'And you are just the same,' said Ivo slowly. 'That's what makes it so hard.' With which cryptic remark she had to be content.

They went up the tower of St Jacobskerk after that, climbing the steps slowly and then standing to admire the view while Ivo pointed out the landmarks around them, recounting old tales and snatches of legends as he did so, so that each one came alive as he spoke. He told her about the village of Haghe, where William the Second had had his hunting lodge, which over the years, had become a town and finally the city it was before them, still keeping its name 'The Hedge'. Only the threatening dusk sent them down at last, to hurry through the streets to Formosa for tea, where they lingered, talking of unimportant things, and Julia, forgetful of everything but the delightful present, was happy.

Only later as they walked down Noordeinde to where Ivo had left his car did she remember, with sudden and painful vividness, Ivo coming out of the jeweller's shop that morning, but she dismissed it instantly and gave herself up to the delightful make-believe world of the present. The future, and Marcia, could be faced when she got back; meanwhile she stopped, obedient to Ivo's hand on her arm, to admire a windowful of toys, and vied with him in picking out which she would have chosen if she had been a child again.

They had only been in the car a minute or so when Jorina joined them, her arms full of parcels and bubbling over with happiness because she had spent the whole afternoon with Klaas.

'He's coming to the party, of course,' she explained to Julia as Ivo threaded his way through the city's heart and out of it through the suburbs. 'He'll stay the night and spend Christmas Day with us—then I shall go back with him to his family in Arnhem.' She drew a breath and went on, 'I found some shoes—brown calf with black patent leather trimming—a little expensive, but just what I wanted.'

She rattled on happily for the rest of the journey home, unnoticing of the other two's silence, but when they were nearly home she asked,

'And what did you two do?'

Julia told her, with occasional comments from Ivo as she did so, making it last as long possible because it was easier to talk than to sit and think. They were all very gay by the time Ivo drew up in front of the house; they went inside together, still laughing and talking, to part in the hall, the girls to go upstairs and Ivo, after taking off his coat, to enter the sitting room, the books he had promised Marcia under his arm.

Julia hardly spoke to him that evening, for after dinner he went to his study and didn't come out until after she had coaxed Marcia up to bed. She went to her own room herself once she had her patient safely between the sheets, for she was tired after her day's sightseeing and even more wearied from Marcia's low-voiced utterances, all of which reiterated her selfless wish to see others enjoying themselves even at the expense of her own comfort and happiness. She had taken care to utter none of these remarks in front of Ivo, though; to him she had been appealingly wistful, interested in their day in the Hague, and while expressing her delight at the success of the outing, managed to convey, without uttering a word to that effect, that both he and Julia had been both selfish and thoughtless.

Julia, brushing her hair with a violence calculated

to tear it out by the roots, remembered Ivo's slight frown as he had listened to Marcia and gave her patient credit for being clever. She got into bed, her mind a prey to a multitude of thoughts, all of them unhappy. She was almost asleep when she remembered that Ivo had kissed her; probably it had meant nothing to him and it had really no right to mean anything to her. All the same, she smiled as she closed her eyes.

CHAPTER SEVEN

THE NEXT DAY was Christmas Eve, and after weeks of bad weather the sun shone from a pale blue sky, giving the frost it wasn't strong enough to disperse an added sprinkle. Julia, going to see how her patient was before breakfast, stopped for a moment to look out of one of the landing windows and admire the wintry scene. It was still not full daylight, although the sun was making a brave blaze of colour on the flat horizon, and somewhere outside she could hear Bep calling to Lien, who came from the village each day to help in the house. Their voices, very clear in the frosty air, sounded cheerful, and that, combined with the sunshine and the aromatic smell of coffee from the kitchen, contrived to put Julia into a cheerful frame of mind; it was, after all, Christmas and a time of good fellowship. She went to Marcia's room, determined to be kind and considerate and even to try and like her patient a little.

It was a pity that Marcia wasn't of the same mind; she greeted Julia with a cross face, a muttered greeting and a rather tart request to hand her a book lying just out of reach. Julia handed it to her, forbearing to mention that she could have quite easily got it for herself, adjusted her patient's pillows to a nicety and went downstairs to see if the post had arrived. It had; she sorted Marcia's scanty mail and went along to the kitchen to get her early morning tea tray, delaying for a few minutes in order to practice her scanty Dutch on Bep before going upstairs. She had deposited the tray, handed over the letters and was on her way to the door when she was stopped.

'Nurse Pennyfeather, I must see Ivo at once—ask him to come to me immediately.' Marcia cast down the letter she had been reading and when Julia didn't move, repeated, 'Do go at once!'

Julia stayed just where she was. She said composedly, 'Ivo's having breakfast—he has to go to Eindhoven this morning. Had you forgotten?'

Miss Jason looked at her through narrowed eyes. 'I don't care if he has to go to Timbuktu,' she pronounced with surprising venom. 'He must come and see me!' She tapped the discarded letter with a nicely manicured hand. 'Did you know that Mijnheer de Winter hasn't received an invitation to the party this evening? After all his kindness to me! I shall refuse to go unless he is invited immediately. Go downstairs and say so, and be quick about it!'

Julia walked slowly back to the bed and stood looking down at the bad-tempered face staring up at her. A pity Ivo couldn't see his Marcia now—Julia suspected that this was neither the first nor the last time her patient had allowed her façade of angelic serenity to slip. She said in a reasonable voice, her own temper nicely under control,

'I don't much care for the way in which you speak to me, Miss Jason. I'm here to look after you, not to be ordered around or expected to run to and fro at your beck and call. You are no longer helpless; you might try to realise that, I think, and behave with more consideration to those around you. If you could remember that we might get on quite well.'

She smiled kindly at the astonished face turned to hers and went without haste from the room.

Ivo was in the hall, putting on his overcoat as she descended the staircase. He gave her the briefest of glances, said, 'Good morning, Julia,' in an absent-minded fashion and made for the door so that she was forced to put on a turn of speed to reach it when he did. She said without preamble, 'Marcia wants to see you urgently—she asks that you should go to her now.'

He paused with his hand on the door. 'Well, I can't—didn't you tell her that I was going to Eindhoven? Come to think of it, I told her myself yesterday evening.'

'You must,' said Julia firmly, and when he turned a baleful eye upon her: 'It's no good looking at me like that—you didn't invite Mijnheer de Winter, and Miss Jason says that if he doesn't come, she won't either. She's upset.'

She saw his frown as he pushed his briefcase and gloves into her hands and turned and ran up the stairs, two at a time. She stood at the door, trying not to hear the faint murmur of voices from her patient's room, and presently he came down again, his face bleak, took his gloves and case without a word, opened the door and went away. She heard the car tearing down the lane and roar down the road, apparently driven by a maniac.

The morning went badly after that. It seemed that Marcia hadn't got her way and as a result she sulked, although when Jorina was around she became merely sadly resigned, which was a great deal worse. However, Julia did her best to take no notice of her patient's ill-humour, but encouraged her to do her exercises in a spirited fashion and when she was asked to turn up the hem of the dress her patient intended wearing to the party, did so, although the time spent on it bit deep into her free afternoon.

The dress was a drab purple, skinnily cut, with a neckline which exposed far too much of Marcia's boniness, but when Julia suggested, with all the tact in the world, that the silk jersey hanging in the wardrobe was one of the prettiest dresses she had seen for a long time, she met with no success.

'I daresay you do like it, nurse,' quoth Miss Jason, 'but with my slender figure I'm able to wear these clinging styles. You, of course, think otherwise, and naturally so, I expect you feel just a teeny bit envious of us willowy creatures. It must be difficult for you big girls to stay in the fashion.'

Julia murmured a nothing in reply; she had a nice taste in clothes and had never considered that fashion had passed her by—indeed, from the admiring glances wolf whistles she collected when out walking, she had always felt that she was as least as eye-catching as the next girl. She thought of the pink wool hanging in her cupboard and took comfort from it.

The party was to be quite a big affair, with a family dinner party at half past seven and the rest of the guests arriving about nine for what Jorina had called a chatty evening with dancing. But Julia, when she peeped into the drawing room, decided that for once Jorina's English hadn't been quite accurate, for the room, a large one, had been cleared for dancing, its magnificent old furniture arranged round its white-painted walls, and the silky carpet rolled up and carried off to some cupboard or other by Bep. There were flowers everywhere, and when Julia put her head round the dining room door, there were flowers there too, and the table, already decked with a lace cloth and a great deal of silver and glass, had a magnificent centre-piece of holly and ivy with Father Christmas, complete with sleigh and reindeer, in the middle.

Jorina came in while Julia was admiring the flowers and said, 'Nice, eh? You like it, I hope. We have twelve for dinner and there will be about fifty people coming afterwards. A nice large party, but this time, bigger than usual, but there is room enough for everyone.'

She moved a bowl of hyacinths from one table to another and asked,

'And Marcia, she feels better now? Does she come to the party after all?' She didn't wait for Julia to answer but went on, 'And why are you not off duty, Julia?'

'I've been altering a dress for Marcia,' said Julia, and choked back a laugh as Jorina exclaimed, 'Not tighter, I hope, or cut lower in the neck—if there are no curves what is the point of letting everyone see?'

She turned round as Bep came into the room with a tray of coffee.

'Now we will sit down and drink our coffee—how fortunate that Marcia feels that she should rest. Was Ivo very angry this morning?'

Julia accepted her cup. 'Very,' she stated simply, remembering his bleak face. They sipped in a comfortable silence, broken by Jorina.

'I wish to talk,' she stated flatly. 'I have wished to talk for many days now. I talk to Vader and he laughs a little and says things have a way of putting themselves right, and I talk to Ivo and that is worse, for although he listens and is polite he is also very angry, so now I talk to you because I think that we are friends.'

Julia heard her with mixed feelings. Jorina was going to talk about Marcia and Ivo. That she didn't like Marcia, Julia was pretty sure, probably she disliked the idea of having her for a sister-in-law... She said a little unhappily, 'Well, I suppose it's all right and I'm glad you think of me as a friend, I like you too, but would Ivo mind?'

'Of course he would mind, but you will not tell and I certainly shall not.' She went on as Julia had expected she would, 'It is about Marcia.' She took Julia's cup and refilled it, then refilled her own. 'You see he doesn't love her—I don't suppose he ever did. Only when they first met she was clever...' Julia gave her a questioning look and she went on quickly, 'I will explain. A long time ago, when Ivo was twenty— twenty-one, he met a girl—she was pretty and—and *frivol*—how do you say?'

'Frivolous?' essayed Julia. 'Bird-witted?'

Jorina nodded. 'Yes—she led Ivo by the nose, she was so very pretty, you see, and gay and amusing and a little naughty, and then after a few months she married someone else with a great deal of money, and although Ivo has plenty of money too, it was not enough, so for years he had not loved any girl.

'And then last year he meets Marcia at some lecture or other and I think that someone has told her about him because she does not try to flirt or attract him, only she lets him see that she has a good brain and that she reads Greek and Latin and is a very serious person, so he thinks, "Here is a girl who is not after my money or out for a good time", and they become friendly and go to lectures and theatres and concerts—all very dull. Then she is taken ill, and while she is still in hospital Ivo has to go to Edinburgh, and although I am quite sure he has never mentioned marriage to her, she hints and suggests…it is as if she has convinced him that he was responsible for her getting polio—I do not know how.'

'Where did Marcia catch it?' asked Julia quickly.

'At a party to which Ivo took her. She did not wish to go because it was to be gay with dancing, but he persuaded her, and it was after that that she became ill.' She shrugged her shoulders. 'So when she is able to leave hospital she asks that she may come and stay with us until she is strong enough to travel, and because Ivo is not here and we do not know how he feels about her, we agree. But six months is a long time and I think—I know that Ivo does not wish to marry her, but she pretends to him that she loves him very dearly, so he is kind to her, for she is ill and perhaps he thinks that in his absence her feelings will change and everything will arrange itself. But you see how she behaves towards him, Julia; she will marry him, although she does not love him, and I shall not forgive her.'

'Can't you tell her—I mean how Ivo feels?' hazarded Julia. 'No—he wouldn't stand for that, would he? Can't he tell her?'

'Not Ivo. You see, he thinks that she loves him and she pretends—you think that she pretends too?'

'Yes, she doesn't care a row of buttons for him,' said Julia vehemently, and then had to pause to explain about the row of buttons. 'She's in love—as far as she can be—with that awful de Winter man.'

'Then why doesn't she tell Ivo that she doesn't love him?'

Julia thought about this and then said slowly, 'I'm not sure,' although she was almost certain she was. Marcia had been flattered by Ivo's attention—who wouldn't have been? Probably she had decided to marry him within a few weeks of meeting him, but was far too clever to let him see that. When she became ill she had made the most of Ivo's pity and concern for her; possibly she had written him letters calculated to keep that concern alive while he was away—and then August de Winter had come along and in her odd way, she had fallen in love with him, but because she was uncertain of him she had refused to let Ivo go, and now, although she didn't want him any more, she was going to keep up her deception until Julia had returned to England and there was no likelihood of Ivo falling in love with her...because he had fallen in love with her, she wasn't sure how much, and it seemed unlikely that she would ever know. She could of course go to Ivo and tell him about Marcia and August de Winter, and he would despise her for it. She sighed and said, 'Marcia is a very clever woman and there's nothing we can do about it. He'll have to find out for himself and let's hope it won't be too late when he does.'

Jorina surveyed her narrowly, her nice blue eyes

thoughtful. 'Is it not strange,' she said, 'that we are unable to say to each other what we would wish to say? One day, perhaps. What shall we do? I had thought of telling Ivo, but I cannot—I suppose you would not?'

Julia gave her a horrified look. 'Me? Heavens, no! Not for all the tea in China.'

She had to explain that too, she was still doing so when Doctor van den Werff came in and asked with some surprise if they didn't intend to change. 'I know it's still early, but I daresay you'll take a long time, and we shall need a drink before everyone arrives.'

He smiled at them both and went away again and Julia got up to go.

'I don't take long to change, actually, but Marcia will need help.'

Her patient dressed with more eagerness than Julia had expected, and it was while she was zipping the dreary purple up its back that Marcia said coolly, 'I telephoned Mijnheer de Winter while you were downstairs and asked him to come on my own account. Since Ivo disregarded my wishes I was forced to take matters into my own hands.'

Julia fastened the little hook at the top of the zip. 'To dinner?' she asked with admirable calm. 'There are guests, that will make the numbers wrong. And he's not one of the family.'

Miss Jason admired herself in the pier glass. 'Nor are you, nurse,' her voice was spiteful, 'and Ivo should have thought of that—he must learn to have some regard for my wishes.'

Julia tried again. 'But, Miss Jason, it's not your party—you're a guest in the house.'

Marcia turned round to face her, without, Julia noticed mechanically, any difficulty. 'And what business is that of yours? Perhaps you're afraid you'll be asked to dine in your room in order to make the numbers right.' She turned back again and smiled slowly at her reflection. 'This colour suits me—I'll rest now if you want to go.'

Julia went. If she changed very quickly she would have time to go and tell Jorina so that something could be done about dinner. She raced through her bath and was about to put on her dress when she decided to find Jorina at that very moment and not wait any longer. She flung on her dressing gown and with her feet thrust into slippers and her hair streaming blackly down her back, she ran across to Jorina's room, tapped on the door and went in. Jorina was there, also in her dressing gown, and Ivo, still in his dark grey suit, was sitting on the end of her bed.

'Oh, lord,' said Julia helplessly, and turned to go, to be stopped by Ivo's half-laughing: 'Don't run away, Julia—it's not the first time I've seen you in a dressing gown with your hair dripping round your shoulders. What's the matter? Or have you come to borrow something feminine I'm not supposed to know about?'

Julia advanced into the room. 'Look,' she said urgently, 'I wasn't going to tell you, but since you're here—and you'll know soon enough anyway—Marcia has just told me she's invited Mijnheer de Winter to dinner and I feel mean telling you because I'm sure she didn't mean me to.' She ignored Ivo's laugh and went on, 'But you had to know, because that'll make thirteen at table and that would never do—I'll have dinner in my room, it's such a good idea and no one will be any the wiser. Actually I didn't think of it, Marcia did...'

'The devil she did,' said Ivo, and then seriously, 'There's no question of you not coming to dinner,' and she realised then that he was indeed very angry. 'I'll telephone someone—we'll sit down fourteen. There's no need to tell Marcia, for there's no point in arguing about it at this late hour. Thank you for telling us, dear girl—no one need know, just we three, and Bep of course, but she's a tower of silence!' He smiled suddenly and Julia felt her heart slide away into a spiralling pulse. 'Hadn't you better finish dressing, dear Miss Pennyfeather? You look sensational as you are, but no one would eat anything if you appeared at table like that.'

He accompanied her to the door and opened it and as she went past him murmured wickedly, 'If you need any help I'd be delighted.'

She cast him a withering glance and flew down the passage and heard his laugh as she shut her door.

As she dressed it occurred to her that he hadn't been much upset by Marcia's conduct; she had been prepared to be sympathetic, but now it seemed that sympathy was wasted on him.

She put on the new pink dress, piled her hair elegantly and scented her person with 'Femme' before studying herself in the long mirror on the wall. The dress suited her with its high neck and long sleeves and the simplicity of its cut. She went along to Marcia's room to remind her that it was time to join the family downstairs and tried not to notice the inimical look in Marcia's eyes as they lighted upon her. Miss Jason, although ready, was unwilling to go down.

'Kindly go and fetch Ivo,' she said. 'I should like him to help me downstairs.'

It was on the tip of Julia's tongue to tell her that she needed no help, but there was no point in spoiling what she hoped was to be a delightful evening. She went downstairs and had reached the bottom step as Ivo came out of his study. She stammered a little as she spoke to him because he looked handsomer than ever in his dinner jacket, as well as a little remote, but there was nothing remote about his greeting. He walked across the hall towards her and took her hands, held her arms wide and studied her with cool leisure. 'Delightful,' he pronounced, and for a moment she thought that he was going to say something else, but he didn't, so she gave him Marcia's message, standing there, still holding hands, and was a little surprised when he said lightly,

'Ah, yes—this is Marcia's great night, isn't it?'

'Because she's going to dance?'

She didn't understand why he smiled. 'That among other things,' he said in a teasing voice, and led her across the hall to the sitting room where the rest of the dinner party were gathering, and handed her over to his father before he went upstairs, to return very soon with Marcia clinging to his arm. Hard on their heels came August de Winter, looking nervous, and Julia, who disliked him very much, found it in her heart to pity him because of the perfect and icy politeness, with which he was greeted by Ivo and his father; anyone with a thinner skin might have turned tail and left the party on some trumped-up excuse, but he seated himself on a sofa beside Marcia and began a low-voiced conversation with her, while Ivo, looking too bland for Julia's peace of mind, turned to greet the last and fourteenth guest. And no wonder he had looked so bland, she thought, and was thankful that she had wasted no sympathy on him, as he obviously needed none. The girl who came in was small and blonde and very pretty with laughing blue eyes and a gaiety which was infectious. She was wearing the sort of dress most girls long to wear and dared not, and she greeted Ivo with a disturbing familiarity which troubled Julia a little, and the rest of the company with charm, and then, as if drawn by a magnet, fastened like a leech upon Mijnheer de Winter, who was, willy-nilly, prised from Marcia with a neatness which could only earn Julia's wholehearted approbation. She felt almost sorry for the man struggling to withstand the laughing blue eyes of this dolly, against whom he had no chance, and at the same time retain his dignity in Marcia's eyes. He gave up the struggle very soon and was led away, leaving her on the sofa where she was immediately joined by Doctor van den Werff, who, disregarding her discomfiture, broke at once into easy conversation.

Dinner was fun, at least for Julia, who had Ivo's other brother, Pieter, on one side of her and an uncle on the other—the uncle was, as was to be expected, a doctor too. They talked lightheartedly and made her laugh a great deal as they ate their way through oyster soup, filet of beef Meurice and gateau St Honoré, washed down with a variety of wines which certainly contributed, as far as she was concerned, to a delightful meal. It was a leisurely one too; by the time they had all repaired to the drawing room, they were joined almost at once by the first of the guests, and when someone started a CD player, everyone took to the floor. Julia, partnered by yet another cousin who begged her to call him Bill, watched Marcia rise to her feet and circle the room slowly with Ivo, an action made all the more conspicuous because they were doing the foxtrot while everyone else was gyrating in a more up-to-date fashion. Her partner watched them too and observed,

'Is that the young lady who was stricken by polio? A marvellous recovery—in fact she looks as though she's been recovered for some time.'

'Are you a doctor?' asked Julia suspiciously.

He smiled at her charmingly. She thought he was rather nice, not young any more, but possessed of a friendly manner and a pair of twinkling eyes which could, she suspected, be keen as well.

'Yes, my dear young lady; married, with three children, otherwise I would be sitting out with you on the stairs. Has anyone ever told you that you're beautiful?'

'Yes,' said Julia tranquilly, 'they have, but thank you just the same. What made you say that about Miss Jason?'

She was right about the eyes; they became keen on the instant. 'Nothing, my dear, nothing—only it seems to me that she's been here a very long time. In my experience fairly mild cases—fairly severe ones too—respond well to modern treatment and—pull their weight once they are on their feet. I should have thought she would have wanted to go home. Has she no family?'

'Oh, yes—her father's a solicitor in England, some-where in the Midlands.'

He made an amused face. 'I don't like your Mid-lands. I also would not wish to return there. What do you think of Lise?'

'She's the prettiest thing I've seen for weeks,' Julia said sincerely.

They were joined then by more people and almost at once Julia was asked to dance again; this time her partner was young, and although his English wasn't good, they carried on an animated conversation, un-derstanding each other very well, laughing a good deal as they danced. She had a number of partners after that and would doubtless have danced all night if she hadn't caught sight of Marcia, sitting between two great-uncles, and looking discontented. Julia, who had no idea of the time, and didn't really care, deduced that Marcia had had enough of the party; she slipped between the dancers and joined the little group.

'I wondered if you were tired, Miss Jason,' she began, although Miss Jason didn't look tired, only cross which, Julia thought sympathetically, was nat-ural enough, for there was no sign of Ivo and none of August de Winter. 'I thought you danced beauti-fully,' she went on. 'What a triumph after all those months.'

'I fail to see what triumph there is in dancing round a room, Nurse Pennyfeather. I shall go to bed in half an hour, if you could remember I shall be glad of your help.'

'I'll remember,' said Julia, and smiled at the two old gentlemen as she slipped away. If she had only half an hour of the evening left, it would be nice to dance until the last moment of it. She was passing the open door to the hall when Ivo's arm shot out and caught her gently.

'There you are,' he said pleasantly. 'We haven't danced, dear Miss Pennyfeather.' He swung her into the crowd. 'Having a good time?'

'Super. Marcia wants to go to bed in half an hour though, and I shall go up with her. I—I saw her dancing. She was marvellous.'

She looked up at him and he returned her look with a half smile.

'I think August de Winter has enjoyed himself too,' he remarked silkily.

Julia was stricken by a sudden thought. 'Did you do it on purpose, Ivo?'

He made no pretence of not knowing what she meant. 'Of course, dear girl, surely you know by now how disagreeable I can be?' He smiled again, his blue eyes fierce, and then said in quite a different voice,

'Has anyone told you that you look beautiful this evening? You do. I like that demure pink thing—you put every other woman here in the shade, Julia.'

'Who's Lise?' asked Julia, who had been longing to know all the evening.

'Pretty, isn't she? She's theatre sister at Tilburg hospital. Jealous, dear girl?'

Julia went pink. She said much too quickly, 'Of course not, how ridiculous,' and knew that she was, wildly jealous. 'Anyway, why ask me? Is that why you invited her?' she went on, following her own train of thought. She gave him a severe look which he ignored.

'She can't hold a candle to you, Julia. James must be mad to let you out of his sight.'

'Oh, James—pooh,' said Julia impatiently. 'I shan't marry him.'

'No, I know that. Why do you keep looking at the clock?'

She reminded him about Marcia and said hesitantly, 'Would you like to dance with her once more, or—or talk to her before she goes to bed?'

For answer he drew her through the door they were passing. The hall was dimly lighted and empty as they walked over to the fire burning in the steel grate at the back of the hall.

'You're going to miss the rest of the party,' he said kindly. 'Come down again even if everyone has gone. I want to wish you a Happy Christmas before we go to bed.'

They went back together through the babel of laughter and talk and when they reached Marcia, Ivo helped her to her feet and in the little silence which had fallen, said pleasantly, 'I'm sure you're all glad to see what a marvellous recovery Marcia has made. She's going to her room now, but don't think that that signals the end of the evening.'

He smiled, his face calm, but when he would have gone to the door with her, Marcia held back, shaking her head playfully at him in a manner which Julia found quite nauseating. 'You're all so kind,' she said, 'and I am so happy. I should say—we are so happy.' She looked up at Ivo who, Julia was relieved to see, wore a polite, impersonal air of friendliness; if he loved Marcia, then he was hiding it most successfully, and now would have been a wonderful time to have announced his intention to marry—if he was going to marry. With a sudden uplift of spirits she realised that he wasn't going to do anything of the sort, but equally, he wasn't going to humiliate Marcia either. It was the cousin from Utrecht who said exactly the right thing.

'Well, of course we're all happy,' he remarked loudly. 'You're cured, Marcia, which means you're happy because you're the patient, and Ivo's happy because he's the doctor, and we're all happy because you have been able to enjoy the party. Let's drink a toast to that.'

The toast was drunk and Julia, watching Marcia, could see that she was furiously angry.

As she had expected, her patient took a long time to undress, she complained in a low, pained voice as each garment was removed and avowed that permanent damage had been done by reason of the exercise she had been persuaded, against her will, to take. 'I should never have danced,' she stated in the brave, resigned voice she affected when she wished to draw attention to herself. 'But of course, Ivo insisted.'

'There was no reason why you shouldn't,' observed Julia cheerfully, determined to be nice despite her opinion of Marcia's behaviour at the party. 'I know you've been ill a long time, but you're as good as new again, you know. You can't stay an invalid all your life.'

Miss Jason had nothing to say to this, instead she complained once again, this time about the ache in her legs.

'Only your muscles—time they were used a little more,' said Julia reassuringly, but despite her strong feelings, her hands were gentle as, without any show of impatience, she began to massage her patient's legs. By the time she had finished and Marcia had declared herself ready to sleep, they could hear the last of the cars driving away; the guests had gone, the party was over. All the same, Julia, when she found herself free, did as she had promised and went downstairs to a house strangely quiet after the cheerful hubbub of the evening. The fire in the hall was dying down; its heat had brought out the scent of the flowers in a great bowl on one of the console tables and she sniffed appreciatively as she passed it on the way to the drawing room. The drawing room was empty, but when she went into the sitting room it was to find Doctor van den Werff, his three sons, his daughter-in-law and Jorina and Klaas clustered round the fire, a tray of coffee in the middle and the whisky decanter to hand.

Jorina said comfortably, 'We've been talking about the party. Did you enjoy it too?' and when Julia said that she had, very much, they all started talking about it once more, and continued to do so until Doctor van den Werff got up to go to bed, followed, in ones and twos by everyone else, but when Julia went to follow them, Ivo said softly, 'Not you, Julia—stay a few minutes longer.' So she stayed, sitting back comfortably in the deep chair, watching the flickering fire and not talking at all. Ivo had nothing to say either, but it was peaceful there together; somehow there seemed no need for words. But when the clock struck a silvery half hour she roused herself, exclaiming,

'The time! I simply must go to bed,' and was taken aback when Ivo said quietly, 'There is really no need to talk, is there?' and smiled in such a way that she got to her feet rather more hastily than she had intended. 'It was a lovely party,' she gabbled. 'I'll say goodnight,' but Ivo had stood up with her and before she could move away had caught her hands in his.

'It's Christmas Day, Julia—the first day of Christmas.' He let her hands go and fished around in his pocket, to produce a small jeweller's box of red leather and then lift her hand to curl the fingers round it. 'I hope you'll like it, dear Miss Pennyfeather.'

She opened her hand and looked at the box. 'May I open it now?' she asked in a small voice, and taking his silence for consent, lifted the lid. There were earrings inside, resting on white velvet. They were early Victorian, she guessed, small golden crescents ornamented with filigree work in the centre of which was suspended a red stone, set in gold—they looked like rubies, but as it wasn't very likely that Ivo would buy her rubies, she supposed them to be paste, but paste or not, the earrings were very beautiful. She said so in a warm voice and asked if they were Dutch, and when he said briefly, 'Yes,' she went on, 'Thank you, Ivo, what a lovely present. I want to try them on.'

She smiled at him and went across to the baroque mirror on the wall and slipped the delicate little hooks in, swinging her pretty head from side to side to see the effect. She began. 'They're much too…' but was interrupted by his, 'No, they are not, Julia,' and something in his voice prevented her from going on, so she said instead, 'Thank you. Ivo—what a lovely way to start the first day of Christmas.' She smiled at him in the mirror and he said lightly, 'Wear them tomorrow, Julia—think of them as a small return for what you have done for Marcia, if you will.'

'Very well, Ivo. And now I think I'll go to bed. Good night.'

In her room, she took the earrings out of her ears and laid them back in their little box; they had done nothing to discourage her impossible daydreams; it was time she used a little common sense. She got into bed and late though it was, spent some considerable time poring over the time-tables she had purchased in Oisterwijk, so that she could return to England with the least possible fuss, just as soon as Doctor van den Werff suggested she should do so.

She was early for breakfast next morning, but Jorina was already at breakfast with Ivo and her father, although no one else had come down. They greeted her with a cheerful chorus of Merry Christmases and she sat down, to find a small pile of gaily wrapped packages by her plate. She jumped up again at once and said, a little confused, 'Oh, I left mine upstairs— I wasn't quite sure—I'll get them.'

She was back in a minute to give her own small presents before opening her own. Bep's was first—a small Delft blue candlestick, complete with its blue candle. The second was a French silk scarf in coffee patterned with greens and blues, from Jorina, and lastly there was a large square box, which turned out to be marrons glacés, most extravagantly packed and beribboned, from the doctor. She had scarcely finished thanking them when Jorina asked, 'What did Ivo give you?'

Julia glanced at him across the table. He had finished his breakfast and was sitting back in his chair, very relaxed, smiling a little.

'Earrings,' she said simply, 'quite beautiful. Gold crescents with red stones.' She smiled widely, remembering them. 'I shall wear them when I change.'

By the time she was free from her duties, everyone had gone to church. It would have been nice to have gone too, even in a foreign language church would have made the day more Christmassy. She had hoped that Marcia might have expressed a wish to go with the family, but she had protested gently when she had been invited to join them, and Julia had spent the greater part of the morning encouraging her to exercise herself, something she was loath to do.

They all met again at lunchtime, for although Jorina had come upstairs with a request that Marcia and Julia should go down for drinks, Marcia had refused on the grounds that her legs ached. Julia spent half an hour massaging them once more before her patient felt fit for the journey downstairs, and when they eventually reached the sitting room it was to find the men closeted in Ivo's study, enjoying themselves from the sound of things, and Jorina and her sister-in-law sitting together, drinking sherry. They greeted Marcia kindly enough, but their kindliness didn't quite make up for the reception she had expected, for she said in some surprise, 'I had expected everyone to be here...'

Jorina offered her a drink, was refused and said, 'Well, you know what men are—they're in Ivo's study, drinking whisky—they'll be out presently.'

Marcia sat down, took the various packages from Julia which she had been bidden to carry downstairs, and said, 'Well, in that case…' and handed Jorina her gift with a flowery speech which its contents hardly merited. Julia, eyeing it, decided she could have well done without it, had it been offered to her; perhaps she had been lucky in the bookmark after all, for Jorina was staring nonplussed as *The Seven Types of Ambiguity* and quite obviously searching for the right words with which to express her thanks.

The other men came in then and Marcia gave first doctor and then Ivo their gifts and then accepted theirs with a girlish flutter which caused Julia to get up and walk over to the window, from where she watched the doctor unwrap a diary which he exclaimed over politely, tactfully omitting to mention that he received several of exactly the same pattern, free each Christmas, from the various pharmaceutical firms enjoying his patronage. Ivo thanked her gravely too his face blandly polite as he exhibited a tie, a floral one very gay and aggressively nylon—and he, Julia was certain, wore nothing but pure silk, handmade, and those in dark rich colours. And for Bep, Marcia had nothing at all, which didn't worry her in the least, for after her own careless, 'Oh, her—I'd forgotten,' she undid her own presents. And very dull too, thought Julia while her patient exclaimed rapturously over a Greek-English dictionary which the doctor had thoughtfully given her and a beautifully bound volume of Montaigne's Essays from Ivo—not a very loving gift, thought Julia, and felt a guilty delight in her earrings.

Lunch, a light meal, because they were going to dine traditionally that evening, passed off smoothly enough, and Julia, watching Ivo discreetly through her long lashes, could see nothing in his pleasant friendly manner towards Marcia to suggest that he was in love with her, although she was shrewd enough to realise that he wasn't a man to show his feelings in public—at least, she amended, only if his feelings got the better of him, and those, she considered, he had nicely under control. It was a pity she could tell nothing from his face. He was looking at her now and she hadn't heard a word he said.

'Daydreaming,' he remarked. 'I'll have to say it all again. What are you going to do this afternoon?'

'Go for a walk,' she replied promptly, because it was the first thing to enter her head.

'I'll come with you if I may,' he said easily. 'I could do with some exercise.'

Without looking at her Julia knew that Marcia was annoyed, although when she spoke, that young woman's voice was as well modulated as always, although faintly long-suffering.

'Ivo,' she said, 'I had hoped that we might have had a pleasant afternoon—do you know, we've hardly talked since you have been back?'

'Indeed?' Ivo was at his silkiest, but perhaps it was because he was still annoyed about August de Winter and wanted to teach her a lesson. Julia frowned; she didn't care be used for his convenience—she wouldn't go for a walk...

'This evening, perhaps,' Ivo went on vaguely with a pleasant smile. 'Shouldn't you rest now?' He glanced across at Jorina. 'We're dining early, aren't we, Jorina—?' and when she nodded continued to Marcia, 'There are a few friends coming in this evening, you don't want to be too tired.'

They got up from the table and as they did so he said to Julia,

'Hadn't you better hurry up and change, or we shall have no time for our walk,' and because there seemed to be a little pause in the talk as he spoke, Julia said meekly that yes, she would go right away.

It was barely a quarter of an hour later when she came flying down the stairs again, warmly wrapped against the cold, the fur bonnet tied securely under her chin, her feet snug in high leather boots. She pulled on her gloves as she reached the last stair and looked around for Ivo. He was lounging in his study doorway, watching her, and as she exclaimed, 'Oh, there you are,' crossed the hall to meet her, exclaiming,

'You look so happy, dear girl. Why is that?'

She was happy, but it was impossible to tell him that it was because she was going to spend the afternoon with him. 'It's Christmas,' she stated, as though that explained everything.

They started off briskly, for although, for once, the sun was shining and the sky was almost clear of clouds, there had been a heavy frost during the night and it was cold.

They walked in silence, and Julia, trying to think of something ambiguous that would hold no pitfalls conversationwise, asked, 'Was the church full?'

He tucked a hand beneath her elbow. 'Yes, very. I wish you could have been there. I had hoped that you might be.'

'So did I, but I couldn't have left Marcia. She was tired after the party—it was wonderful to see her dancing.'

His hand tightened and she winced from the pain. 'Don't let's talk about her, not now, Julia. Let's pretend we're back at Drumlochie House.'

On the way back Julia asked, 'How many people are coming tonight, Ivo?'

'Oh, a dozen or so—mostly neighbouring doctors and friends from the hospitals—they don't stay late. I'm afraid it's a splendid chance for us to talk shop. Jorina will be glad to have you there to break us up when we get too engrossed.'

'Jorina's a dear,' said Julia with conviction. 'She'll be a wonderful wife. Klaas is a lucky man.'

Ivo stopped to stare down at her. 'And whoever gets you for a wife will be a lucky man too, Julia.'

Her heart sank a little; it seemed as though he took it for granted that she would marry; someone in England, in the future neither of them knew anything about. She told herself she was being foolish and said too brightly, 'Oh, no, he won't. I don't think I'm very good with money and I love pretty clothes and I'm not in the least clever.'

'You sound ideal,' said Ivo, and put up a hand and pushed her bonnet to the back of her head so that her black hair spilled out. He pushed that aside too, gently. 'You're wearing the earrings,' he said, and smiled a little.

'Of course. Aren't they lovely?' she wanted to know, and went pink when he said, 'Almost as lovely as you, Julia.'

He bent and kissed her gently and said, as he had said before, 'Only a seasonal greeting,' and then tucked her hair back inside the bonnet and pulled it forward. And Julia, shaken by his quiet, serious face, said, as she too had said, 'Yes—well, shouldn't we be going back?'

That night, lying in bed with the house quiet around her and only the wind in the trees outside to disturb her thoughts, Julia tried to make plans again, but it was of no use and she allowed her thoughts to drift instead to the pleasant evening they had all enjoyed. For it had been that; they had dined off roast turkey with its attendant chestnut stuffing and cranberry sauce and what Jorina described as English vegetables culled from an old copy of Mrs Beeton's cookery book. There was even a Christmas pudding, and Julia had found it rather touching that Jorina had gone to such pains to have everything just right. They had finished with crackers to pull and the champagne which Ivo had produced had loosened their tongues to a gaiety which even Marcia joined in.

Later, when the guests had arrived, it had been fun too; they had teased her in their beautiful English about the few words of Dutch she managed to say and she had laughed with them, not in the least put out, and even contrived to add to her vocabulary. Somehow Ivo had been beside her for the greater part of the evening, and when everyone had gone and she was waiting at the foot of the stairs while Marcia said her goodnights, he had come to her and asked her if she had had a happy day. She had nodded, her eyes alight with happiness, the earrings dancing, and had longed to ask him if he had been happy too—and didn't dare for fear of the answer. So she had smiled at him, saying nothing, her vivid face aglow, forgetful of her feelings, and then turned to see Marcia watching them from the drawing room door.

She hadn't been surprised when Marcia, as she was getting ready for bed, asked her who had given her the earrings; she had been able to answer naturally enough that it was Ivo. 'Something to remind me of Holland when I go back,' she said lightly, and Marcia had said nothing to that, nor had she made answer when presently Julia wished her goodnight.

In her own room she had taken the earrings off and laid them carefully away in their little box. She didn't think she would wear them for a long time, not until she could bear to think of Ivo without wanting to burst into tears—something which she immediately did.

CHAPTER EIGHT

JULIA, SLEEPING HEAVILY after a wakeful night, was roused by Jorina's knock early the next morning. She was already dressed in her outdoor things and said happily,

'Klaas and I are just off. The others have just gone—I know it's early, but I wanted to say goodbye, as I shan't be back for a day or two. There's the date to fix for the wedding and several things to decide about the flat, and Klaas is free until the twenty-eighth.'

She sat down on the end of the bed and looked closely at Julia.

'You look—have you been crying? I do believe you have. Has Ivo been beastly to you? He can be a perfect fiend if he loses his temper. The trouble is, it's hard to tell when he does, because he goes all remote.'

Julia shook her head. 'No, it's not Ivo.' Perhaps it would have been better if he had been remote and stayed that way, then she could have nurtured a dislike of him.

'Oh—it's Marcia, is it? I expect she took exception to the earrings—they're rather nice, aren't they? I like rubies.' Jorina ignored Julia's open mouth and went on smoothly, 'It's her own fault. I mean, if you're fool enough to despise such things, you deserve to get dry-as-dust books, don't you? You know, Julia,

I'm beginning to wonder if she will ever go back to
England. I asked Ivo and he looked like a thunder-
cloud and told me to keep my nose out of his business—there's a brother for you! But all that awful
coyness at the party—I mean, anyone listening to her
might have thought…it's going to make it much
harder for him.'

'Why?' asked Julia, trying to look disinterested.

'Well, as long as he thought Marcia was really in
love with him I believe he would have gone to any
length not to hurt her, but now he knows about August de Winter, he'll wait his chance to—to disengage
himself without making her look a fool—though I
wouldn't be so nice about it, I can tell you. Only I
hope she'll give him the chance.'

She jumped up, exclaiming, 'Well, have a pleasant
time. It's the second day of Christmas, after all,
though I don't think we're quite as merry about it as
you are in England with your Boxing Day.'

She smiled and nodded and was gone, and a minute
or two later Julia heard the car leaving the house. She
got up then, for Christmas or no Christmas, Marcia
needed to be coaxed through her exercises and helped
in a dozen small ways.

She was a little late for breakfast because Marcia
had awakened a little grumpy and was ready to find
fault with everything, and Julia, reminding herself that
perhaps her patient didn't feel as well as usual, was
patient and calm and good-natured with her until at
length Marcia pronounced herself satisfied.

Father and son were already at table as she entered
the dining room, between them they sat her down,
rang for fresh coffee and offered her the bread basket,

and although they both gave her similar searching glances neither of them commented upon her pale cheeks, but wished her a good morning and reminded her they would be going to Utrecht in the afternoon.

The morning passed slowly, the more so because there was no sign of Ivo when they went downstairs, only his father and a handful of friends who had called in to wish them the compliments of the season, and drink their health in the doctor's excellent sherry. They chatted politely to the two girls, their nice manners standing them in good stead when Marcia rather patronisingly complimented them on their English. One of them, who Julia knew was a professor of surgery at Breda hospital with an English degree as well as several Dutch ones, wanted to know what Marcia thought of his own language, 'For,' said he, 'of course you will have learned to speak it while you have been with us all these months, Miss Jason.' He had smiled blandly at her and when she had confessed that she knew no Dutch at all he turned to Julia and asked,

'And you, young lady—you have been with us long enough to be able to say *ja* or *neen*, have you not?'

Julia gave him the benefit of her nicest smile and said, '*Ja*, Professor,' and went on to recite her meagre, badly pronounced vocabulary, and when she had finished everyone cried 'Bravo!' and raised their glasses, declaring that she had made a very good start, to which she cheerfully agreed, joining in their laughter, and while she laughed suddenly wondered where Ivo was, for he should most certainly have been there. She looked round carefully to make sure she hadn't missed him and caught the doctor's eye; she blushed when he walked across the room to her and asked quietly, 'Looking for Ivo, are you not? He went out to see a child—he shouldn't be long.'

But he was; they waited lunch for half an hour, and when he still hadn't come home, the three of them sat down to cold turkey and salad and a rich pudding of Bep's own make. They had almost finished when he joined them with a murmured word of apology and started his own lunch while they stayed at the table, drinking their coffee and keeping him company, entertaining him with an account of their visitors that morning.

Ivo obviously had something on his mind; he would tell his father after lunch, but in the meantime there seemed no reason for them all to sit in gloom. The conversation, such as it was, was sustained until Ivo began on his coffee, when Julia said,

'Miss Jason, shall we go to the sitting room? I'm sure the doctors want to talk shop, and they wouldn't want to bore us.' Which wasn't quite true. Julia for one was dying to know what could have happened to make Ivo look so serious. She pushed back her chair and hoped Marcia would do the same, but even as she did so, Ivo said, 'No, Julia, don't go,' and turned to Marcia. 'I must ask you to do without Julia for a day or two, Marcia—I need her help for an emergency in Oisterwijk.'

Julia sat very still, watching him; he hadn't bothered to ask her if she wanted or was willing to help. She reflected that sometimes it was nice to be taken for granted in such matters and wondered what the emergency might be. As did Marcia.

'Unless it's very urgent, I don't see how you can

ask that of me,' she said. She gave him a melting look and pouted, 'I need such a lot of care, Ivo.'

Julia bit back her explosive opinion of this remark and waited to hear what Ivo would say.

'It is urgent—there's a case of polio in Biezel. It's only a small village, but a lot of the children who live there come into Oisterwijk to school. There are two other cases I'm not quite certain about. I've done lumbar punctures and sent them in to the path lab in Tilburg, but we can't get a result in under two days. I think we should do a mass inoculation—that's why I want Julia.'

Julia took this piece of news calmly; emergencies cropped up frequently in her working life and she had learnt not to get flustered. But Marcia was more than flustered. She exclaimed in a voice shrill with feeling, 'Polio—and you dare to sit down to table with us, Ivo! It's criminal, we may all become infected!'

He gave her a slow thoughtful look and said with patient courtesy,

'I'm neither criminal nor negligent, Marcia. You yourself are quite immune, and we three have at some time or other in our lives been immunized.'

'I still think it's running unnecessary risks to my health. You can't take Nurse Pennyfeather from me. I'm quite unable to look after myself, and I refuse to be looked after by someone who has become open to infection.'

Julia, watching Ivo, knew now what Jorina had meant when she had told her that Ivo became remote when he was angry. He seemed a different man, although his expression was still pleasant enough as he said patiently,

'You are perfectly able to look after yourself now, Marcia. From your letters, you know, I had the impression that you had made little or no progress, but that is not so, is it? You are well, or almost so. A day or so without Julia to fetch and carry for you will give you all the stimulus you need.'

Julia inquired, 'The child—how old is he?'

Ivo smiled at her and passed his cup for more coffee. 'It's a she—twelve years old and unfortunately goes to school in Oisterwijk. She went to a children's party there on Christmas Eve, too. Her mother told me that she didn't feel well when she went but insisted on going.'

'She's very ill?'

He nodded. 'Yes—all the classic symptoms, and paralysis has set in. I got her into hospital. I must go back and have a look at the other two.'

Marcia spoke and they both turned to look at her, a little guilty because they had quite forgotten she was there. 'What about me?' she wanted to know. 'What am I supposed to do all alone here—what about the dinner party this evening?'

'No dinner party, I'm afraid,' said Ivo in what Julia considered to be far too careless a tone. 'If we mean to do a mass immunisation, we shall need to get organised, and that will take the rest of the day. We'll have to get hold of the school health authorities and find out which children have been immunised, for a start. They'll come first, then the contacts—everyone, in fact.'

'Oisterwijk too?' asked Julia. Her mind boggled at the thought of all the odd Dutch names to be written on to the official forms someone was bound to produce.

Ivo nodded; as though he had read her thoughts he said,

'It won't be too bad. We've our own medical records and almost everyone in the area is a patient of one or other of us. If we have to do the lot I'll find someone to do the writing. You'll be of more use to us with a swab and a syringe in your hand.'

Julia looked relieved. 'What's to be done first?'

'The practical Nurse Pennyfeather!' He looked, just for a moment, almost gay. 'If, when you've made sure Marcia has all she wants in the sitting room, you would come to my study—we'll check through the cards of the children who were at the party and make sure they have all been immunized. That at least we can do.' And in answer to her look of inquiry, 'Yes, I remembered to get a list of the children who were there—that's what you wanted to know, wasn't it?'

Long before they were finished there were two more calls to children who had been taken ill. Julia went with Ivo and laid out the lumbar puncture set while he examined them, and then, masked and gowned, held them in a neat curve while he did it. He worked quickly and accurately and with complete relaxation, and he was kind to the parents as well as his little patients, who, sadly enough, were very ill. Ivo arranged for them to go to hospital, then set about inoculating everyone who had been in contact with the children during the last few days.

When they returned from the second case it was to find that Doctor van den Werff had contacted the health authorities and arranged for supplies of vaccine as well as syringes and needles to be delivered—he had notified the police too and arranged to take over the school houses in Beizel and Oisterwijk. 'I said we'd start at seven tomorrow morning,' he explained calmly.

Julia felt a little guilty about Marcia, left alone all the afternoon, and expected her to be sulky and difficult, so she was completely knocked off balance by that young lady's manner. It was a mixture of sweet sympathy and eagerness to hear about their activities, allied with subtle turning of the tables against Julia, which happily the men didn't seem to notice.

Julia stole a look at Ivo and saw the little furrow between his brows again, and when she got up to go on some errand for the doctor, he gave her a look which chilled her with its bleakness. Presently he followed her to make sure that she had packed everything they would need for the morning and his manner, although friendly, was remote, as though he were deep in thought and had no time for her. Jorina had said that he would never hurt Marcia, and Julia was beginning to think that she was right, especially as he felt responsible for her illness... They finished at length, and only as she was leaving the surgery did he look directly at her and say quietly. 'Thanks, Julia,' and then, 'You don't understand, do you?'

And she, knowing perfectly well what he meant, paused at the door to reply, 'Yes, I do, Ivo. I expect if I were you I should do the same as you intend to do,' and was surprised to see his face suddenly crease into a smile. 'No, you wouldn't, Miss Pennyfeather, you're much too nice, but thank you for your good opinion even though it's sadly inaccurate.'

It was still very dark when she got up the next morning; she had seen Bep the night before about Marcia's breakfast and any help she might need during the day, so all she had to do was to drink her coffee and eat the toast provided for her. Both men had already breakfasted, they informed her as they left her at table, with the warning that they would be at the front door in ten minutes.

It had been arranged that Ivo, with Julia to help him, should hold the clinic in the schoolhouse in Oisterwijk and that his father, with the help of a borrowed nurse from Tilburg, should take the smaller one in Beizel which, they hoped, would be finished in a day, leaving them free to join Ivo, together with a team of doctors and nurses from the hospital. The whole operation, allowing for setbacks and the absence of the doctors from time to time, should be completed in three days. They had been assured of the fullest co-operation from the Health Department and if they found themselves snowed under they could always ask for help, although, over the holidays, the staff problem was difficult.

They left the house together, Doctor van den Werff driving himself in the Mercedes, and Julia sitting beside Ivo in the Jensen.

There was already a group of people outside the school when they arrived. From somewhere or other Ivo had conjured up two clerical helpers who proceeded to sit themselves at two desks, the cards piled before them. They looked like housewives, not very young but pleasant and calm. Ivo, taking off his coat and hanging it with Julia's on a peg behind the door of the classroom they were using, introduced them as

Mevrouw Cats and Mevrouw van Bek, and hardly giving the ladies time to do more than smile at each other, said, 'Julia, I shall want you to draw up the injections and swab the arms, right?' He glanced at her. 'If I have to go away, you must carry on. Don't bother about anything else, just keep on with the jabs.' He smiled at her briefly and said, 'Right—let's get started.'

It seemed to Julia that the queue snaking slowly past Mevrouw Cats and Mevrouw van Bek never diminished. Even working fast—and Ivo, she discovered, worked very fast—they seemed to make no impression upon it whatsoever. At first it was the young mothers with babies—the babies, unaware of what was happening, remained happy enough, sucking down the three drops of vaccine, nicely flavoured, before their mothers rolled up their sleeves ready for Ivo's needle. But presently the babies petered out a little and the toddlers—those who, for some reason or other, had never been immunised—arrived. Not liking the idea at all, they fought, screaming at the tops of their powerful little lungs while they were divested of their outer garments, resisting at every button and every zip and sliding with the smooth slipperiness of cooked macaroni in and out of their mothers' grasps until caught and held firmly in Julia's lap as Ivo slid the needle in.

The older children were a little easier, although there seemed a great many of them; but they were beginning to make an impression on the piles of cards at last, or so it seemed until Ivo went away. A young woman had come running in as he was about to inoculate a small girl's arm and disregarding everyone around her, had burst into speech. Ivo finished with the little girl, pulled her blonde pigtail gently and got up. 'There's another child,' he said. 'Just keep things going until I get back, will you, dear girl?'

Julia, already piling syringes, needles, swabs and spirit bottle handily, nodded. 'I hope it's not bad,' she said briefly, and gave him a little smile as she turned to the next patient, then remembered to say over her shoulder, 'Leave the address—just in case.'

She was glad of that half an hour later when a man came pushing through the waiting queue and addressed her urgently. She waited until he had finished and then asked 'Doctor?' and when he nodded, copied the address Ivo had left and gave it to the man, glancing at the clock as she did so. It was already gone eleven o'clock and the queue had doubled in size.

It was almost half past one when Ivo finally appeared, to take off his overcoat, put on his white coat and mask again and pick up the syringe Julia was holding ready. He plunged the needle in, grinned at the small boy who was getting it and said,

'Nice work, Julia—sorry you've been on your own.' He looked round the room, his quiet eyes missing nothing. 'A good crowd still—the more the better.'

Julia swabbed the arm before her. 'You got the second message?'

'Yes—I sent the first child to hospital. This one isn't too bad, but he's gone too, of course. Now get that gown off and go across the road to the hotel. Ask for coffee and sandwiches and sit down and eat them—I'll pay later on. You can have fifteen minutes. When you come back I'll go.'

They hardly spoke again, only when it had something to do with their work, and although she was beginning to get tired, Julia would have liked the afternoon to last for ever because Ivo was there with her, but four o'clock came and a relief medical team with it, and with barely a pause in the work, they took over, and Julia found herself outside in the tree-lined main street of the little town, being urged towards the Jensen.

'I'll run you home first,' said Ivo, 'before I start my visits.'

She got in beside him. 'No—there's no need, and it would be a dreadful waste of time—I'm quite happy sitting in the car.'

He gave her a grateful look. 'Accommodating girl,' he said lightly, 'there aren't very many. You can go to sleep if you like.'

But she didn't go to sleep, she thought, and as he was speeding home after his final visit she asked tentatively, 'Doesn't Jorina usually help you with the surgery when it's a big one?'

'Yes—why?'

'Well, wouldn't I do instead? I believe I could manage. I've been thinking about it—and it would save you and your father some time if I sent the people in when you ring...'

He swung the car into the little lane and stopped unfussily exactly in front of the door. 'Clever Julia,' he said with kindly mockery. 'Why not? It'll certainly help, but what about language?'

'Well, I shan't need to say much, shall I? I'll manage, and if I get stuck I'll come to you for help.'

They got out of the car. 'You're not too tired?' he

asked, and she said at once, 'No more than you or
Doctor van den Werff are.' They went into the house
then, to be met by Bep with the welcome news that
she had tea waiting for them.

'I'll put on another uniform first,' said Julia, and
disappeared to her room. When she came down ten
minutes later, Ivo was in the sitting room with Marcia,
who, Julia immediately observed, was being gentle
and understanding and very much the brave little
woman again. She paused in her talk with Ivo just
long enough to give Julia a brief smile which held
triumph and complacency, letting her see how easy it
was to get a man's attention, even if she weren't a
black-haired beauty who knew all about germs and
cultures and how to bake bread. And Julia, always a
girl to accept a challenge, smiled back, ignoring Ivo
and applying herself to her tea, while she listened to
the intelligent questions Marcia was putting to Ivo.
The girl was really very clever, but she wasn't, it
seemed, to have it all her own way, for when Doctor
van den Werff came in a few minutes later, he took
the conversation in the politest way imaginable into
his own hands, and, almost as though he had been
listening at the door, proceeded to praise Julia in
glowing terms for her part in the day's work; something which she found embarrassing, for she had, before this, worked far harder on a hospital ward, where
it had been taken for granted and gone unthanked.
She was about to remark on this when she caught the
doctor's eye upon her; he was smiling and looked so
very like Ivo that she smiled back with a warmth of
which she was quite unaware. A moment later he had
half-closed his eyes, leaving her to wonder what he

had been thinking. But he had most effectively broken up the conversation Marcia had started with Ivo, and it cheered Julia a little to see how quickly Ivo left her side with some light excuse and went to sit by his father, discussing their plans for the next day.

Presently they got up and went away to Ivo's study, and presently, too, it was six o'clock, and to her relief she went to usher the first of the patients into the waiting room at the side of the house.

They finished just before eight o'clock and went in to a late dinner—a meal at which Marcia shone both in appearance and conversation, for Julia was by now too tired to do more than push her cap straight on her rather untidy hair and scrub her capable little hands for the hundredth time that day. Nor did she contribute much to the talk, leaving it to Marcia to continue in her role of sympathetic listener and interested questioner. She had looked up once or twice during the meal to find Ivo's eyes upon her, but beyond a half smile and an odd word, he hadn't addressed her directly except to invite her agreement or opinion upon some point touching their work.

They hadn't been in the sitting room for more than half an hour before Ivo suggested that as they would be starting at seven the next morning, she might like to go to bed, and when she had hesitated he said easily, 'Bep can take Marcia upstairs if she needs help, but I don't imagine she does. In any case, did you not say that you didn't require Julia's services any more, Marcia?' His voice was smooth, though he was smiling, and Marcia's long face became wary.

'I'm sure Nurse is anxious to get back to England,'

she said in the gentle voice Julia so disliked, 'but I suppose she will stay until your little crisis is over.'

Ivo answered her a little coldly, 'If you mean by "little crisis" the risk of a great number of people—mostly young—suffering from the same illness which you have yourself had and from which you have so successfully recovered—yes.'

Which remark, uttered in a silky voice, got Julia to her feet, because probably they intended to discuss her departure and she had very little energy to contribute to the discussion, even if they invited her to do so. She said goodnight rather abruptly and went up to bed, and lay awake until two o'clock in the morning, telling herself, each time she turned over her pillow and rearranged the bedclothes, that as far as she was concerned, the sooner she went home the better.

In consequence the next morning she presented a pale face at breakfast, and when Ivo asked her kindly if she would rather not go with him to Oisterwijk, she snapped, 'Of course I shall come—why do you ask?' and frowned so forbiddingly that he said mildly, 'well, don't slay me, Julia. I only wondered if you felt too tired.'

She poured a second cup of coffee. 'I'm not in the least tired,' she informed him haughtily, and was even crosser when he said carelessly,

'Oh, good, just bad-tempered.'

The desire to say something telling concerning those who worked and those who sat at home doing nothing, while quite unfair, was nevertheless very great. Against her better judgment she had her mouth open to utter something along these lines when Doc-

tor van den Werff forestalled her by remarking
smoothly that as she had been such a great help on
the previous evening he hoped that she would be prepared to lend a hand that evening as well. 'I shall be
finished at Beizel by midday,' he went on, 'so Nurse
and I will join you two and the team coming out from
Tilburg. We should finish some time tomorrow.'

He gave her a smile of great charm and turned to
Ivo. 'We should get the results of the culture by midday,' he observed. 'I hope we caught it in time...
thank God most of the babies had been at least partly
immunised.'

The conversation was on safe ground once more
and stayed so for the remainder of the meal and during the short drive to the schoolhouse, although Julia,
for her part, remained a little cold. He had, after all,
accused her of being bad-tempered.

The day went much the same as the previous one
had, although now that there were more doctors and
nurses they got through many more patients. But they
still kept on coming; not only from Oisterwijk itself
but from the outlying farms and smallholdings and
hamlets tucked away in the heath surrounding the little town.

Between twelve and two o'clock they went, team
by team, to eat a quick lunch, and Julia, whose temper
was quite restored, found herself looking forward to
half an hour in Ivo's company; she was of course in
his company now, and had been all the morning, but
working together was not the same as just being together; they had exchanged barely half a dozen words
and those concerned their work. It was a pity that
just as they were leaving the schoolhouse, someone

should come after them with a message that Ivo was wanted on the telephone. She crossed the street alone and went into the coffee room, where she ordered their coffee and ham rolls and sat down to wait—half an hour wasn't long and five minutes of it had gone already. Ivo came shortly after, though; there was still twenty minutes of time—away from work perhaps she could steer the conversation round to the vexed question of when she was to leave. It was like turning the knife in a wound to bring it up, but Marcia had mentioned it twice already; had in fact disclaimed her need for a nurse any longer. She was only still with them because they needed another pair of hands.

Her carefully laid plans were wasted; all Ivo talked about were the results of the CSF cultures—the first one was through and it was positive, as everyone had expected it would be. She listened to him speculating as to how many more cases they might expect, nodding agreement to his quick-thinking statistics as though she had worked them out for herself, whereas she wasn't actually listening at all.

'Wasted breath,' said Ivo suddenly, and she pinkened under his quizzical look. She said, 'Yes—no, that is, it's very interesting. Ivo, I want to ask you, when am I...' to be interrupted by his brisk, 'Time we went back, come along.'

He got to his feet and paid the bill, then accompanied her back to the schoolhouse, where they were once more plunged in work and spoke hardly a word to each other until four o'clock when their relief arrived.

Julia had hoped to talk to him again on the way home; there would be time between his visits, but today he didn't give her the opportunity to go with him but drove her straight back to the house, set her down at the door, said that he would be back in an hour or so and tore off down the lane again.

She felt better when she had bathed and put on another uniform. She did her face and hair carefully and dabbed a little Chanel Number Five here and there; it might not be quite the thing for a girl in uniform, but it gave her a badly needed uplift, and she might need that because Marcia would be the only one in the sitting room and Marcia wanted her out of the way. She went slowly downstairs and slowed to a halt half-way down, because the sitting room door had opened and Marcia and August de Winter were standing together silhouetted against the soft glow of the room's lamps. Julia watched them as they kissed, too surprised to move, and went on watching as Mijnheer de Winter crossed the hall and let himself out into the evening, while Marcia went back into the sitting room and shut the door gently. Only then did Julia continue on her way, wondering if what she had just seen had been actual fact or just her tired imagination. She stood for a few moments in the hall, listening for a car, but there was no sound; Mijnheer de Winter had either walked or parked his car somewhere along the road. She opened the sitting room door and went in. Marcia was draped on one of the sofas, languidly turning the pages of some tome or other, but she looked up as Julia went in and said, 'Oh, there you are. Well, at least you're someone—I have been lonely all day by myself.'

'And that,' said Julia vulgarly and in a towering rage, 'is a load of old trot! I've just this minute seen you and Mijnheer de Winter kissing each other good-bye. Has he been here all day? I suppose that just because Ivo said he would do his visits after the clinic, you banked on me being with him and not coming home until five or thereabouts. Well, I came home at four!' She crossed the room and stood in front of Marcia, glowing with indignation. 'You seem to think that the whole lot of us are blind and deaf to your goings-on. Well, I for one am not! It's sickening the way you bleat to Ivo about your loneliness and self-sacrifice and bravery each time you see him, while all the time you're none of these things.'

Julia drew a deep breath, looking quite magnificent. 'You are,' she said clearly and unhurriedly, 'a complete fraud. I knew it the moment I set eyes on you—Oh, you had polio, but not as badly as you would have everyone believe, and you've recovered from it weeks ago. I suppose when you came here to stay you had made up your mind to marry Ivo—you bamboozled him into feeling responsible for you getting polio in the first place, didn't you, because he persuaded you to go to a party where there was someone already infected—but I doubt if that was ever proved. I expect you put the idea into everyone's head and no one thought to disbelieve you. Well, I disbelieve you, Marcia. And then you met August de Winter, but you had to go on pretending you loved Ivo, didn't you, so that you could stay here and you could see your August as often as possible while he made up his mind.' She stared down at Marcia, her dark eyes flashing with her wrath. 'You're a harpy,' she said deliberately, 'and a complete fraud!' Then she sat down and waited to hear what Marcia would say.

For once Marcia found words difficult to come by and when she did speak her low measured voice had become almost strident.

'How dare you—' she began, and then with a vicious little smile, 'You're in love with Ivo, aren't you? I know that—that's why I said I didn't want you any more. I don't want him, not now, but I'll take good care that you don't get him. Don't think you'll get away with anything, dear, dear Julia, for you won't. What I intend to do is my own business, but you'll know soon enough...' She broke off as Bep came in with the tea tray, murmuring, '*'N beetje laat,*' as she set it down by Julia, and Julia wondered if she and Marcia would have stayed silent for ever and ever if Bep hadn't been late.

They drank their tea in silence and when they had finished Marcia went back to her book, just as though Julia wasn't there, while Julia picked up *Elsevier's Weekblad* and turned to the small ads page, because by reading the columns of bedsitters to let and help in the house wanted, she had picked up several useful words. They were still sitting, the picture of silent companionship, when Doctor van den Werff came in an hour later. He left again after a few pleasantries, pleading work in his surgery, and was followed shortly after by Ivo, who came in, sat down and drank the cup of coffee Bep insisted that he should have, talking idly as he did so, before getting up in his turn. He was halfway to the door when Marcia said with gentle firmness, 'Ivo, I want to talk to you—could you manage a few minutes some time this evening?'

He stood with his hand on the door and said with his usual courtesy, 'Why, of course, Marcia. After surgery, I should think—no, we had better say after dinner. We can be comfortable in my study.' He glanced at the great Zaandse clock on the wall. 'I must go now, though—surgery starts in ten minutes and I've some telephone calls to make first.'

He left the room and a few minutes later Julia got up and went out of the room too to admit the first patient. Neither Marcia nor Julia looked at each other as she went, nor did they speak.

The surgery went well, although it was packed out. Halfway through it Julia slipped into Doctor van den Werff's surgery and asked,

'Shall I ask Bep to delay supper?—the waiting room's still full.'

He looked up from the notes he was reading. 'Do that, Julia. How many patients are there still to see?'

'Four for Ivo, six for you.'

'I wonder if they're quick ones?' He started to shuffle through the patients' cards before him in a rather untidy fashion. Julia took them away from him, restored them to order and said,

'An old man with ear muffs and a Vandyck beard is the next—he's deaf, then a mother with a baby who's got the earache; a girl who looks as though she's going to have twins within the hour, a woman with a black eye, and a fierce old lady with a very small boy who's got a nasty cold.'

Dr van den Werff sat back in his chair and laughed. 'My dear Julia, how very observant you are—shall we tell Bep forty minutes or so?'

She nodded and went to the door and his voice, so very like his son's followed, 'Am I right in thinking that you and Marcia have—er—fallen out?'

Julia turned to face him. 'Yes, we've quarrelled. How did you know?'

'You must give Ivo the credit for that. He's perceptive. He's also very deep; perhaps you didn't know that?'

Julia said carefully, 'It doesn't really matter if I know or not, does it?' and went out, shutting the door carefully behind her.

They sat down to a late dinner presently, and to a conversation which, while easy enough on the part of the two men, sounded decidedly false when the ladies took part, for they were careful not to address each other directly unless it was unavoidable and then with a politeness which was quite awe-inspiring. But neither gentleman gave any hint of unease; they talked at random about the contents of the newspapers, the forthcoming marriage of Jorina and the possibility of skating if the frost held for a few days more. This remark prompted Julia to ask if everyone skated as a matter of course.

'Certainly we do,' said Ivo. 'We learn as soon as we can toddle and we skate every winter until our legs grow too stiff to support us. Do you skate, Julia?'

'A little—not very well. I fall down a lot.'

'How fortunate,' said Marcia sweetly, 'that there's plenty of you to take the shock.' She laughed as she said it so that everyone should know that it was a joke, and Julia, not to be outdone, laughed too.

'Falling down doesn't matter in the least,' said Ivo, just as though Marcia hadn't spoken. 'We all do it at first. A little practice and you'll be as good as everyone else.'

The conversation took on a new lease of life; they

talked about sport in its various forms for the rest of the meal. But the meal couldn't last for ever; presently Julia found herself in the sitting room with Doctor van den Werff, listening to the receding footsteps of Marcia and Ivo crossing the hall to his study.

They came back almost an hour later, Marcia looking very pleased with herself and Ivo looking bland. Only when Julia looked at him closely she saw that his eyes weren't bland at all. She sat stubbornly in her chair, looking serenely unaware of anything untoward. If she was to be hauled over the coals then and now, he could get on with it. She told herself she hadn't any intention of running away, nor was she afraid of him. All the same, when after half an hour of desultory talk, first Marcia and then Doctor van den Werff got up to go to bed, she felt decidedly nervous, but she sat on. She had bought some wool before Christmas to knit herself a sweater; she plied her needles now as though her very life depended on getting it finished within the next hour or so.

Ivo spoke and she dropped a stitch. 'You know what Marcia wanted to see me about?'

She skewered the stitch. 'Yes—at least I think I do.'

'Did you call her a fraud, Julia?'

Her needles click-clacked along half a row. 'Yes.'

'May I ask why?'

'No harm in asking,' said Julia flippantly, and fell to counting stitches.

'You also called her a harpy?'

'Thirty-six, thirty-seven...' she raised her head. 'Quite right.' After a moment she asked, 'Did I say thirty-seven?'

He said nastily, 'Put that damn knitting down—you're only using it to hide behind.'

Julia flared up at this undoubtedly true remark. 'I am not! I could have sneaked off to bed…'

'And I,' he said silkily, 'would have come and hauled you out again.' He got up and walked to the window and back again. 'Why did you do it, Julia? Why in heaven's name…' He came to a halt in front of her chair and stood looking down at her. His voice was calm now even though she was aware that he was seething with rage. 'Couldn't you have left well alone?'

She wondered what he meant by that. She began, 'Do you know—'and stopped. Impossible to tell him about August de Winter being there that afternoon; for a moment she wondered if that was what Marcia had told him too, in which case he already knew. But he didn't, for he said in a reasonable voice—the kind of voice an exasperated grown-up might have used to an annoying child—'Marcia had been alone all day; probably she had become lonely and low-spirited, and you burst in without any warning and call her a—a harpy!' A muscle at the side of his mouth twitched as he said it.

Julia gathered up her knitting. 'Is that what she told you?' she asked. 'Then why bother to ask me? I'm so obviously in the wrong, aren't I?'

She got to her feet and swept out of the room, her lovely head high. In her room she undressed rapidly and when she was ready for bed, sat down and laboriously unpicked the knitting she had done, for the pattern was sadly awry, crying silently as she did so.

She was greeted at breakfast by Doctor van den

Werff's friendly good morning and by Ivo's bland pleasantness. Both gentlemen, after taking a searching glance at her face, refrained from hoping that she had had a good night, desired her to help herself to anything she required, and went back to the discussion they had been having when she joined them.

'I shall go to Sneek,' said Doctor van den Werff. 'Your grandfather's house is there and empty most of the year. I shall enjoy living in it and I can indulge in a little gentle sailing when I feel like it. And of course you can all come for holidays whenever you wish; think how convenient it will be to send the children up to me later on.' He added a little wistfully, 'Your mother was very happy there.'

Ivo said, 'Yes,' in a quiet voice and then more briskly, 'A little young to retire, isn't it, Vader?' He smiled across the table. 'Barely sixty.'

'Oh, I daresay I'll do a little part-time work of some sort, but I shall enjoy my freedom. You'll need a partner, Ivo. Theo, if he'll consider it in a year or so.'

'Yes, of course, but there's time enough…a year, two. You're not in too great a hurry, I hope, Vader?'

'No, and there's a good deal to be done to the house in Sneek—' He went on to enumerate such alterations as he had in mind and Julia stared at her empty plate, half listening. So Ivo had made a decision to marry Marcia; yesterday evening probably when they had been so long in his study and Marcia had looked so pleased with herself—as well she might with the prospect of living in the lovely old house for the rest of her days and with Ivo for a husband. She finished her coffee and when the doctor paused she said in a quiet little voice,

'I should like to return to England as soon as it can be arranged, doctor. I—I've been offered a job in my old hospital. They don't want to wait and I'm not needed here any more; I'm only wasting your money.'

If Doctor van den Werff was surprised at her request, shot at him out of the blue in such a fashion, he said nothing about it, merely looked at her with sharp blue eyes and said, 'Ah, yes, of course, Julia. We shall finish at the school today, so supposing we have a little talk—let me see—tomorrow morning. That gives us plenty of time.'

She agreed, wondering why they should need time; he must have known that it was time for her to leave them. She went to get her coat and came downstairs in time to hear Ivo say, 'I'll deal with it in my own way…' He stopped when he saw her and she was left to speculate as to exactly what he was intending to deal with. She sat in the car beside him, cudgelling her brains, and came to no conclusion at all. They were almost in Oisterwijk when he asked, 'This job— have you been offered it, Julia?'

She was, on the whole, a truthful girl, so she said now, 'Well, not exactly—but they said when I left they would always have me back.'

'So you have arranged nothing? You have no job to go to?'

She said crossly, because he had found her out in her small deception.

'Please don't bother about me. I shall go to my brother's in any case for a short time.'

'Ah, yes,' she heard the faint mockery in his voice, 'and from what you have told me, you will enjoy that.'

They had arrived at the schoolhouse. She made a small frustrated sound and got out of the car and went inside to where the last remnant of their patients awaited them.

CHAPTER NINE

THEY WERE finished before midday. The last patient went through the door and the clearing up began at once and was quickly done now that there was a sufficiency of nurses and helpers. Ivo had a brief conversation in Dutch with his father and then said to Julia,

'You'll go home with Father, please, I shan't be coming home just yet,' and then to his father, this time in English, 'You'll do those visits for me? I'll fit in the rest when I come back.'

He lifted a hand to them both and went away and a little later Julia got into Doctor van den Werff's car and went back to the house. But when they arrived he made no effort to get out with her, remarking mildly,

'No, I'm not coming in—I've a couple of visits, I'll do them now. Don't wait lunch—I'll get some coffee and something to eat.'

He reversed the car and shot back down the lane. He drove with the same speed and skill as his son, and Julia, watching him go, felt a little pang, because she liked him very much. It was a pity that his wife had died ten years ago; Jorina had told her that her parents had been devoted to each other and that they had been—still were—a close-knit family. Julia went into the house, thinking that at least he would never be lonely with his grandchildren of the future visiting him at Sneek. He would be a delightful grandfather, just as Ivo would be a delightful father to his children, which, thought Julia sourly, would be a good thing if they were to have Marcia for a mother.

She found Marcia already in the dining room and with a brief hullo she sat down opposite her and helped herself to coffee, and because she didn't want Marcia to know how worried she was, she ate a good lunch, choking down every mouthful with a determination which did her credit, while Marcia, in a silence which could be felt, watched her. They separated after the meal, Marcia to return to the sitting room and Julia to go to her room where she wrote a letter to her brother, a letter which took some time and much thought before she was satisfied with it. It was almost four o'clock by the time she was ready and she went downstairs again; there would be tea presently in the sitting room. She went in and was at once aware that a storm was about to break over her head.

Marcia was sitting by the fire, not in her usual graceful semi-recumbent position, but upright, ready to do battle, her fingers beating a tattoo on the book she was holding. Julia watched the fingers, thankful to know that Marcia was as nervous as she was, and decided not to sit down. She felt, quite erroneously, that while she was on her feet she had a slight advantage. She wandered over to the old gilded mirror hanging beside the fireplace and composedly straightened her cap, waiting for her companion to speak. She didn't have to wait very long; Marcia flung her book from her and said in a high voice,

'I suppose you think I can't see through your little

game, Nurse Pennyfeather. Ivo would be a fine catch for a penniless half-educated girl such as you are, wouldn't he? You could lead a lady's life, no doubt. I wonder what you did in order to persuade him to bring you here in the first place—and ruby earrings indeed! I wonder what you did to get those?'

She paused, staring at Julia with spiteful eyes, and Julia, her teeth clenched to guard a fierce impulsive tongue, carefully tucked a stray end under her cap and miraculously said nothing.

'You've forced yourself upon him; do you think I haven't seen you laughing at him and talking silly nonsense to make him laugh too—getting lost in order to attract attention to yourself; pretending that you're interested in learning Dutch? Well, it's done you no good, has it? I talked to Ivo, you see—Oh, I didn't tell tales, I'm not such a fool,' she laughed, 'but I suggested this and hinted at that and let a few things drop…he thinks nothing of you now; once you're back in England he'll forget you, and you can go when you like—you're no longer my nurse.'

'As to that,' said Julia calmly, 'I don't feel I can do that. Doctor van den Werff is my employer, you know. I'll go when he tells me to. You could of course ask him to dismiss me, but you would have to give some reason for that. You tried once before without much success, didn't you?' She took out her compact and powdered her beautiful nose, and the action calmed her so that she was able to ask without heat,

'Why do you want Ivo to think you're in love with him? It would be easy enough to tell him that you wanted to marry Mijnheer de Winter, wouldn't it?'

Marcia smiled. 'You're a fool, aren't you? I shall

go on letting Ivo think that I'm in love with him until you've gone back to England, then I can drop him when I'm ready, once August...' She paused and asked with genuine astonishment, 'You don't think I'll step down for you, do you?'

Julia turned back to the mirror and started, quite unnecessarily, on her hair once more because it would keep her calm and she needed all the calm she could muster. She was about to speak when she saw that the half-open door reflected in the mirror had been opened wider and Ivo was standing there. She had no idea how long he had been there or how much he had heard. She drew a deep breath to stop the pounding of her heart and raised her voice, speaking in loud clear tones, calculated to reach his ears.

'No,' she said, 'I didn't, but I'm not quite a fool, you know. You never needed a nurse; I imagine that you were walking quite well some time before I came. I wondered about that a lot, but it wasn't until yesterday afternoon when I saw you and Mijnheer de Winter kissing each other that I knew for certain. You've been using Ivo for your own ends, haven't you, because you don't love him, do you? You have no idea what loving someone is, although you and Mijnheer de Winter enjoy a desiccated form of it, I suppose—quoting Latin tags.' She turned away from the mirror and looked at Marcia. 'How dare you,' she was speaking, if anything, louder than ever in her anxiety that Ivo shouldn't miss a word, 'use Ivo to egg on that miserable little man—Ivo's worth a hundred of him!' She saw, out of the corner of her eye, that Ivo had moved. 'I said you were a fraud and a harpy, and I'll say it again...'

She was interrupted by Ivo's voice, so cold that it
sent a shiver down her spine. 'That will do, Julia, and
you had no reason to raise your voice like that, you
know, I heard you very easily. Perhaps you would be
good enough to leave us. I think Marcia and I have—
er—a misunderstanding to clear up.'

He was standing in front of her now and when she
looked at him and met his eyes, it was to find them
hooded like his father's and the calmness of his face
told her nothing. She turned on her heel and left them
together.

It took her just under ten minutes to change out of
her uniform and into her outdoor clothes, and in that
time, too, she packed her case. It took her another
two minutes to write a very brief note to Doctor van
der Werff and count the money in her purse. She had
ample to get her back to England and once she was
there she didn't much mind what happened. She
closed her door soundlessly, then went quietly down
the stairs and out of the front door and down the lane
to the road. Her case was heavy, but she didn't notice
that; she was busy trying to remember about buses
and trains and boats to England; she would go to Oisterwijk first, because she could catch a bus to Tilburg
from there, and in Tilburg she could get on a train to
Rotterdam and go on to the Hook of Holland in time
to pick up the night boat. She had plenty of time, even
allowing for the walk to Oisterwijk, and she thought
it unlikely that anyone would notice her absence for
an hour or two and by then she would be in the train,
and Ivo and Marcia would have had their talk and
cleared up their misunderstandings and either become
reconciled—with a suitable Latin tag, she thought

wildly, or agreed to part, in either case they would be far too concerned with their own affairs to worry about her.

She shivered in the cold wind and looked doubtfully at the sky, along whose horizon great sulky clouds were piling themselves; it only needed to snow. She walked on steadily, her mind quite empty of thought now, although now and again she looked behind her at the singularly empty road, because hope dies hard and although she tried to damp down the thought, Ivo might come after her. She had thought once or twice hat he might love her a little, but now she didn't know any more. If he did he would surely follow her; she took one final look down the empty road. Apparently he wasn't going to; she must be out of her mind to even entertain the idea.

She reached the bus stop at last and joined the queue, which wasn't a queue at all but just a large group of people who, when the bus arrived, would jostle and push their way on to it in a good-natured and ruthless manner; she would have to be ruthless too; it would never do to he left behind. She put down her case and looked about her. Her companions were mostly women with shopping baskets and children, although there were one or two men, standing rock firm, well to the front. She hoped the bus would be along soon and wouldn't be too full as she looked nervously at the sky. As she did so a snowflake fell softly on to her nose.

The Jensen snarled to a halt beside her and Ivo got out, put her case on the back seat and said in a voice which gave nothing away,

'Get in, Julia.' She didn't budge, and the women

on either side of her turned to look, arranging their baskets comfortably over their arms; it was dull waiting for the bus and here was a small diversion—besides, they knew Ivo by sight. He smiled at them and raised his hat and murmured, '*Dag, Dames*,' and they chorused a '*Dag, Doctor*,' back at him, pleased to be recognised. He said something else to them too, to make them smile and nudge each other and stare with curious friendly eyes at Julia.

'Don't be pig-headed, dear girl,' he said in English, 'they're on my side.' He laughed a little and she found her voice at last, treacherously shaky.

'I couldn't care less,' she said pettishly, and then, because she couldn't help herself, 'How did you know I'd be here?'

'A process of elimination.' His voice was very decided as he went on, 'Now get in, my dear, because the car's on a bus stop and I'm in grave danger of getting a *procesverbaal*.'

She didn't know what that was, but it sounded official and she concluded that it was, for as the car slid away from the pavement a policeman on a bicycle came towards them in a purposeful way. Ivo waved to him and the man looked at him and smiled and cycled on. Ivo turned the car and sped back the way she had come, all without saying a word. It was only when, to her bewilderment, they had passed the house and he had turned the Jensen into a country road leading out into the heath that he slowed his pace and asked gently,

'Dear heart, why did you go, without a word to anyone and in such a hurry?' and when she made a small sound of protest: 'Oh, I've got your note to Father in my pocket. Tell me.'

She savoured the delight of being his dear heart and then said in a low voice, 'I couldn't have stayed. You see, it was deliberate—all the things I said to Marcia; I saw you in the mirror and I wanted you to hear, and then I—I thought how awful if you loved her after all and I'd spoilt it all for you for always, so I went away quickly because it wouldn't have taken you long to discover—Marcia would have...'

Julia stopped speaking because she felt like crying and she would have to conquer her desire to burst into tears before she could continue.

'I had no idea that you were such a virago,' remarked Ivo on a half laugh, 'but I did tell you to leave well alone, Julia, my darling. Do you think that I am blind—though I have been blind, haven't I? But I had to talk to de Winter and make sure that I was justified in breaking the imaginary understanding I was supposed to have with Marcia.'

Julia heaved a gulping sob. 'Oh, dear,' she sounded forlorn, 'I needn't have said any of those awful things, but I didn't know...' She looked out of the car window and said uncertainly, 'I got lost here...'

Ivo had halted the car. He got out and went round the bonnet, helped her out and took her arm and started walking over the bone-hard ground towards the woods.

'So did I, my dear darling, at least my heart did—to you.' He stopped and turned her round to face him, then bent his head and kissed her mouth. 'That's not quite true,' he said a long minute later, 'I lost it when you opened the door at Drumlochie House and told me in your lovely voice to hurry up and come in out of the cold. My Julia, I've not been cold since because you warm me with your sweetness and gaiety and beauty. But it was here I found you curled up asleep and I knew when I saw you that I couldn't go on without you. I've brought you here to tell you so.'

They had reached the edge of the trees by now and he stopped again, but Julia held back a little. 'Marcia,' she demanded, 'did she mind?'

Ivo shook his head. 'I don't imagine so—you see, de Winter said that he would come and fetch her within the hour and she and I—we had known that we had no feeling for each other, and you know why I couldn't break with her, not until I knew for certain about de Winter. She'll marry him and live happily ever after.'

'Reading Greek poetry to each other,' said Julia, and added in a doubtful voice, 'I'm not a clever girl,' and was gathered close and kissed by way of a very satisfactory answer.

'My darling girl, I want a wife, not a walking dictionary. A wife who is so beautiful that I can't stop looking at her or thinking about her and who buys extravagant clothes and wants diamonds for her birthday and makes bread and loves children—and loves me.'

'I like the bit about the diamonds,' said Julia. 'It's very tempting, but I can't say yes if you don't ask me.'

She stared up at him, her face glowing and her eyes bright and Ivo said, 'I should have asked you the moment I set eyes on you. Will you marry me, my darling Julia?'

Julia smiled. 'Yes, thank you, Ivo, I will. Indeed I don't know what else I would have done if you didn't want me.'

There was only one answer to a remark like that. When at length Ivo loosed her, he asked, 'Do you know which day it is, my dearest?'

Julia, deep in her own delightful thoughts, frowned. 'December the twenty-ninth,' she said at length.

'The fifth day of Christmas,' said Ivo. 'You said once that five gold rings would be more than any girl could want and I said it was a way in which her true love could prove to her that he loved her.'

He took an arm from her shoulders and plunged a hand into his pocket, then opened his hand to show her what he held.

'You see? I went to the Hague and got them after I had seen de Winter. I couldn't think of a better way of convincing you that I love you and always shall.'

He looked at her very tenderly as he pushed the fur bonnet back so that he could hook the little gold rings in her ears. 'I cheated a little with this one,' he said as he fastened the gold bracelet on one wrist, 'but not with this.' He pulled off her glove and slipped a gold ring, set with three most beautiful diamonds, on to her finger. 'And this one—you'll have to wait for this one, my dearest, until we marry.'

Julia watched the diamonds sparkle in the deepening dusk and then stretched up to kiss him. 'Thank you five times, darling Ivo, and when will that be?'

His arm tightened around her so that she could scarcely breathe.

He said, 'We'll wait until the polio scare is over, then we'll go to England and I'll get a special licence.

Unless you want a grand wedding with a cake and bridesmaids?' He kissed her gently and then with great fierceness. 'In which case we should have to wait. Please don't make me wait, Julia.'

She closed her eyes with resolution upon a tantalizing vision of herself in white satin and a tulle veil. She said clearly, 'I don't want to wait either, Ivo.' She paused to smile at him. 'We'll find a small church in the country and just get married.'

She was going to enlarge upon this idea, but was prevented from doing so because Ivo kissed her again, a long, gentle, satisfying kiss. When she had her breath again she added, 'I shall, of course, wear my five gold rings!'

Christmas Masquerade
by
Debbie Macomber

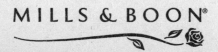
MILLS & BOON®

For Tara
A woman of grace, charm and sensitivity
Thank you

Prologue

The blast of a jazz saxophone that pierced the night was immediately followed by the jubilant sounds of a dixieland band. A shrieking whistle reverberated through the confusion. Singing, dancing, hooting and laughter surrounded Jo Marie Early as she painstakingly made her way down Tulane Avenue. Attracted by the parade, she'd arrived just in time to watch the flambeaux carriers light a golden arc of bouncing flames from one side of the street to the other. Now she was trapped in the milling mass of humanity when she had every intention of going in the opposite direction. The heavy Mardi Gras crowds hampered her progress to a slow crawl. The observation of the ''Fat Tuesday'' had commenced two weeks earlier with a series of parades and festive balls. Tonight the celebrating culminated in a frenzy of singing, lively dancing and masqueraders who roamed the brilliant streets.

New Orleans went crazy at this time of year, throwing a city-wide party that attracted a million guests. After twenty-three years, Jo Marie thought she would be accustomed to the maniacal behavior in the city she loved. But how could she criticize when she was a participant herself? Tonight, if she ever made it out of this crowd, she was attending a private party dressed as Florence Nightingale. Not her most original costume idea, but the best she could do on such short notice. Just this morning she'd been in a snowstorm in Minnesota and had arrived back this afternoon to hear the news that her roommate, Kelly Beaumont, was in the hospital for a tonsillectomy. Concerned, Joe Marie had quickly donned one of Kelly's nurse's uniforms so she could go directly to the party after visiting Kelly in the hospital.

With a sigh of abject frustration, Jo Marie realized she was being pushed in the direction opposite the hospital.

"Please, let me through," she called, struggling against the swift current of the merrymaking crowd.

"Which way?" a gravelly, male voice asked in her ear. "Do you want to go this way?" He pointed away from the crowd.

"Yes...please."

The voice turned out to be one of three young men who cleared a path for Jo Marie and helped her onto a side street.

Laughing, she turned to find all three were dressed as cavaliers of old. They bowed in gentlemanly fashion, tucking their arms at their waists and sweeping their plumed hats before them.

"The Three Musketeers at your disposal, fair lady."

"Your rescue is most welcome, kind sirs," Jo Marie shouted to be heard above the sound of the boisterous celebration.

"Your destination?"

Rather than try to be heard, Jo Marie pointed toward the hospital.

"Then allow us to escort you," the second offered gallantly.

Jo Marie wasn't sure she should trust three young men wearing red tights. But after all, it was Mardi Gras and the tale was sure to cause Kelly to smile. And that was something her roommate hadn't been doing much of lately.

The three young men formed a protective circle around Jo Marie and led the way down a less crowded side street, weaving in and out of the throng when necessary.

Glancing above to the cast iron balcony railing that marked the outer limits of the French Quarter, Jo Marie realized her heroes were heading for the heart of the partying, apparently more interested in capturing her for themselves than in delivering her to the hospital. "We're headed the wrong way," she shouted.

"This is a short cut," the tallest of the trio explained humorously. "We know of several people this way in need of nursing."

Unwilling to be trapped in their game, Jo Marie broke away from her gallant cavaliers and walked as quickly as her starched white uniform would allow. Dark tendrils of her hair escaped the carefully coiled

chignon and framed her small face. Her fingers
pushed them aside, uncaring for the moment.

Heavy footsteps behind her assured Jo Marie that
the Three Musketeers weren't giving up on her so
easily. Increasing her pace, she ran across the street
and was within a half block of the hospital parking
lot when she collided full speed into a solid object.

Stunned, it took Jo Marie a minute to recover and
recognize that whatever she'd hit was warm and lean.
Jo Marie raised startled brown eyes to meet the intense gray eyes of the most striking man she had ever
seen. His hands reached for her shoulder to steady
her.

"Are you hurt?" he asked in a deep voice that was
low and resonant, oddly sensuous.

Jo Marie shook her head. "Are you?" There was
some quality so mesmerizing about this man that she
couldn't move her eyes. Although she was self-
consciously staring, Jo Marie was powerless to break
eye contact. He wasn't tall—under six feet so that she
had only to tip her head back slightly to meet his look.
Nor dark. His hair was brown, but a shade no deeper
than her own soft chestnut curls. And he wasn't handsome. Not in the urbane sense. Although his look and
his clothes spoke of wealth and breeding, Jo Marie
knew intuitively that this man worked, played and
loved hard. His brow was creased in what looked like
a permanent frown and his mouth was a fraction too
full.

Not tall, not dark, not handsome, but the embodi-
ment of every fantasy Jo Marie had ever dreamed.

Neither of them moved for a long, drawn-out moment. Jo Marie felt as if she'd turned to stone. All

those silly, schoolgirl dreams she'd shelved in the back of her mind as products of a whimsical imagination stood before her. He was the swashbuckling pirate to her captured maiden, Rhett Butler to her Scarlett O'Hara, Heathcliff to her Catherine....

"Are you hurt?" He broke into her thoughts. Eyes as gray as a winter sea narrowed with concern.

"No." She assured him with a shake of her head and forced her attention over her shoulder. Her three gallant heroes had discovered another female attraction and had directed their attention elsewhere, no longer interested in following her.

His hands continued to hold her shoulder. "You're a nurse?" he asked softly.

"Florence Nightingale," she corrected with a soft smile.

His finger was under her chin. Lifting her eyes, she saw his softly quizzical gaze. "Have we met?"

"No." It was on the tip of her tongue to tell him that yes they had met once, a long time ago in her romantic daydreams. But he'd probably laugh. Who wouldn't? Jo Marie wasn't a star-struck teenager, but a woman who had long since abandoned the practice of reading fairy tales.

His eyes were intent as they roamed her face, memorizing every detail, seeking something he couldn't define. He seemed as caught up in this moment as she.

"You remind me of a painting I once saw," he said, then blinked, apparently surprised that he'd spoken out loud.

"No one's ever done my portrait," Jo Marie mur-

mured, frozen into immobility by the breathless bewilderment that lingered between them.

His eyes skidded past her briefly to rest on the fun-
seeking Musketeers. "You were running from
them?"

The spellbinding moment continued.

"Yes."

"Then I rescued you."

Jo Marie confirmed his statement as a large group
of merrymakers crossed the street toward them. But
she barely noticed. What captured her attention was
the way in which this dream man was studying her.

"Every hero deserves a reward," he said.

Jo Marie watched him with uncertainty. "What do
you mean?"

"This." The bright light of the streetlamp dimmed
as he lowered his head, blocking out the golden rays.
His warm mouth settled over hers, holding her pris-
oner, kissing her with a hunger as deep as the sea.

In the dark recesses of her mind, Jo Marie realized
she should pull away. A man she didn't know was
kissing her deeply, passionately. And the sensations
he aroused were far beyond anything she'd ever felt.
A dream that had become reality.

Singing voices surrounded her and before she could
recognize the source the kiss was abruptly broken.

The Three Musketeers and a long line of others
were doing a gay rendition of the rumba. Before she
could protest, before she was even aware of what was
happening, Jo Marie was grabbed from behind by the
waist and forced to join in the rambunctious song and
dance.

Her dark eyes sought the dream man only to discover that he was frantically searching the crowd for her, pushing people aside. Desperately, Jo Marie fought to break free, but couldn't. She called out, but to no avail, her voice drowned out by the song of the others. The long line of singing pranksters turned the corner, forcing Jo Marie to go with them. Her last sight of the dream man was of him pushing his way through the crowd to find her, but by then it was too late. She, too, had lost him.

Chapter One

"You've got that look in your eye again," pixie-faced Kelly Beaumont complained. "I swear every time you pick me up at the hospital something strange comes over you."

Jo Marie forced a smile, but her soft mouth trembled with the effort. "You're imagining things."

Kelly's narrowed look denied that, but she said nothing.

If Jo Marie had felt like being honest, she would have recognized the truth of what her friend was saying. Every visit to the hospital produced a deluge of memories. In the months that had passed, she was certain that the meeting with the dream man had blossomed and grown out of proportion in her memory. Every word, every action had been relived a thousand times until her mind had memorized the smallest detail, down to the musky, spicy scent of him. Jo Marie had never told anyone about that night of the Mardi

Gras. A couple of times she'd wanted to confide in Kelly, but the words wouldn't come. Late in the evenings after she'd prepared for bed, it was the dream man's face that drifted into her consciousness as she fell asleep. Jo Marie couldn't understand why this man who had invaded her life so briefly would have such an overwhelming effect. And yet those few minutes had lingered all these months. Maybe in every woman's life there was a man who was meant to fulfill her dreams. And, in that brief five-minute interlude during Mardi Gras, Jo Marie had found hers.

"...Thanksgiving's tomorrow and Christmas is just around the corner." Kelly interrupted Jo Marie's thoughts. The blaring horn of an irritated motorist caused them both to grimace. Whenever possible, they preferred taking the bus, but both wanted an early start on the holiday weekend.

"Where has the year gone?" Jo Marie commented absently. She was paying close attention to the heavy traffic as she merged with the late evening flow that led Interstate 10 through the downtown district. The freeway would deliver them to the two-bedroom apartment they shared.

"I saw Mark today," Kelly said casually.

Something about the way Kelly spoke caused Jo Marie to turn her head. "Oh." It wasn't unnatural that her brother, a resident doctor at Tulane, would run into Kelly. After all, they both worked in the same hospital. "Did World War Three break out?" Jo Marie had never known any two people who could find more things to argue about. After three years, she'd given up trying to figure out why Mark and Kelly couldn't get along. Saying that they rubbed each other the wrong way seemed too trite an explanation. Antagonistic behavior wasn't characteristic of either of them. Kelly was a dedicated nurse and Mark a struggling resident doctor. But when the two were together, the lightning arced between them like a turbulent electrical storm. At one time Jo Marie had thought Kelly and Mark might be interested in each other. But after months of constant bickering she was forced to believe that the only thing between them was her overactive imagination.

"What did Mark have to say?"

Pointedly, Kelly turned her head away and stared out the window. "Oh, the usual."

The low, forced cheerfulness in her roommate's voice didn't fool Jo Marie. Where Kelly was concerned, Mark was merciless. He didn't mean to be cruel or insulting, but he loved to tease Kelly about her family's wealth. Not that money or position was that important to Kelly. "You mean he was kidding you about playing at being a nurse again." That was Mark's favorite crack.

One delicate shoulder jerked in response. "Sometimes I think he must hate me," she whispered, pretending a keen interest in the view outside the car window.

The soft catch in Kelly's voice brought Jo Marie's attention from the freeway to her friend. "Don't mind Mark. He doesn't mean anything by it. He loves to tease. You should hear some of the things he says about my job—you'd think a travel agent did nothing but hand out brochures for the tropics."

Kelly's abrupt nod was unconvincing.

Mentally, Jo Marie decided to have a talk with her

big brother. He shouldn't tease Kelly as if she were his sister. Kelly didn't know how to react to it. As the youngest daughter of a large southern candy manufacturer, Kelly had been sheltered and pampered most of her life. Her only brother was years older and apparently the age difference didn't allow for many sibling conflicts. With four brothers, Jo Marie was no stranger to family squabbles and could stand her own against any one of them.

The apartment was a welcome sight after the twenty-minute freeway drive. Jo Marie and Kelly thought of it as their port in the storm. The two-floor apartment buidling resembled the historic mansion from *Gone With the Wind*. It maintained the flavor of the Old South without the problem of constant repairs typical of many older buildings.

The minute they were in the door, Kelly headed for her room. "If you don't mind I think I'll pack."

"Sure. Go ahead." Carelessly, Jo Marie kicked off her low-heeled shoes. Slouching on the love seat, she leaned her head back and closed her eyes. The strain of the hectic rush hour traffic and the tension of a busy day ebbed away with every relaxing breath.

The sound of running bathwater didn't surprise Jo Marie. Kelly wanted to get an early start. Her family lived in an ultramodern home along Lakeshore Drive. The house bordered Lake Pontchartrain. Jo Marie had been inside the Beaumont home only once. That had been enough for her to realize just how good the candy business was.

Jo Marie was sure that Charles Beaumont may have disapproved of his only daughter moving into an apartment with a "nobody" like her, but once he'd

learned that she was the great-great granddaughter of
Jubal Anderson Early, a Confederate Army colonel,
he'd sanctioned the move. Sometime during the Civil
War, Colonel Early had been instrumental in saving
the life of a young Beaumont. Hence, a-hundred-and-
some-odd years later, Early was a name to respect.

Humming Christmas music softly to herself, Jo
Marie wandered into the kitchen and pulled the orange juice from the refrigerator shelf.

"Want a glass?" She held up the pitcher to Kelly
who stepped from the bathroom, dressed in a short
terry-cloth robe, with a thick towel securing her
bouncy blond curls. One look at her friend and Jo
Marie set the ceramic container on the kitchen
counter.

"You've been crying." They'd lived together for
three years, and apart from one sad, sentimental
movie, Jo Marie had never seen Kelly cry.

"No, something's in my eye," she said and snif-
fled.

"Then why's your nose so red?"

"Maybe I'm catching a cold." She offered the
weak explanation and turned sharply toward her
room.

Jo Marie's smooth brow narrowed. This was
Mark's doing. She was convinced he was the cause
of Kelly's uncharacteristic display of emotion.

Something rang untrue about the whole situation
between Kelly and Mark. Kelly wasn't a soft, southern belle who fainted at the least provocation. That
was another teasing comment Mark enjoyed hurling
at her. Kelly was a lady, but no shrinking violet. Jo
Marie had witnessed Kelly in action, fighting for her

patients and several political causes. The girl didn't back down often. After Thanksgiving, Jo Marie would help Kelly fine-tune a few witty comebacks. As Mark's sister, Jo Marie was well acquainted with her brother's weak spots. The only way to fight fire was with fire she mused humorously. Together, Jo Marie and Kelly would teach Mark a lesson.

"You want me to fix something to eat before you head for your parents?" Jo Marie shouted from the kitchen. She was standing in front of the cupboard, scanning its meager contents. "How does soup and a sandwich sound?"

"Boring," Kelly returned. "I'm not really hungry."

"Eight hours of back-breaking work on the surgical ward and you're not interested in food? Are you having problems with your tonsils again?"

"I had them out, remember?"

Slowly, Jo Marie straightened. Yes, she remembered. All too well. It had been outside the hospital that she'd literally run into the dream man. Unbidden thoughts of him crowded her mind and forcefully she shook her head to free herself of his image.

Jo Marie had fixed herself dinner and was sitting in front of the television watching the evening news by the time Kelly reappeared.

"I'm leaving now."

"Okay." Jo Marie didn't take her eyes off the television. "Have a happy Thanksgiving; don't eat too much turkey and trimmings."

"Don't throw any wild parties while I'm away." That was a small joke between them. Jo Marie rarely dated these days. Not since—Mardi Gras. Kelly couldn't understand this change in her friend and affectionately teased Jo Marie about her sudden lack of an interesting social life.

"Oh, Kelly, before I forget—" Jo Marie gave her a wicked smile "—bring back some pralines, would you? After all, it's the holidays, so we can splurge."

At any other time Kelly would rant that she'd grown up with candy all her life and detested the sugary sweet concoction. Pralines were Jo Marie's weakness, but the candy would rot before Kelly would eat any of it.

"Sure, I'll be happy to," she agreed lifelessly and was gone before Jo Marie realized her friend had slipped away. Returning her attention to the news, Jo Marie was more determined than ever to have a talk with her brother.

The doorbell chimed at seven. Jo Marie was spreading a bright red polish on her toenails. She grumbled under her breath and screwed on the top of the bottle. But before she could answer the door, her brother strolled into the apartment and flopped down on the sofa that sat at right angles to the matching love seat.

"Come in and make yourself at home," Jo Marie commented dryly.

"I don't suppose you've got anything to eat around here." Dark brown eyes glanced expectantly into the kitchen. All five of the Early children shared the same dusty, dark eyes.

"This isn't a restaurant, you know."

"I know. By the way, where's money bags?"

"Who?" Confused, Jo Marie glanced up from her toes.

"Kelly."

Jo Marie didn't like the reference to Kelly's family wealth, but decided now wasn't the time to comment. Her brother worked long hours and had been out of sorts lately. "She's left for her parents' home already."

A soft snicker followed Jo Marie's announcement.

"Damn it, Mark, I wish you'd lay off Kelly. She's not used to being teased. It really bothers her."

"I'm only joking," Mark defended himself. "Kell knows that."

"I don't think she does. She was crying tonight and I'm sure it's your fault."

"Kelly crying?" He straightened and leaned forward, linking his hands. "But I was only kidding."

"That's the problem. You can't seem to let up on her. You're always putting her down one way or another."

Mark reached for a magazine, but not before Jo Marie saw that his mouth was pinched and hard. "She asks for it."

Rolling her eyes, Jo Marie continued adding the fire-engine-red color to her toes. It wouldn't do any good for her to argue with Mark. Kelly and Mark had to come to an agreement on their own. But that didn't mean Jo Marie couldn't hand Kelly ammunition now and again. Her brother had his vulnerable points, and Jo Marie would just make certain Kelly was aware of them. Then she could sit back and watch the sparks fly.

Busy with her polish, Jo Marie didn't notice for several minutes how quiet her brother had become. When she lifted her gaze to him, she saw that he had a pained, troubled look. His brow was furrowed in thought.

"I lost a child today," he announced tightly. "I couldn't understand it either. Not medically, I don't mean that. Anything can happen. She'd been brought in last week with a ruptured appendix. We knew from the beginning it was going to be touch and go." He paused and breathed in sharply. "But you know, deep down inside I believed she'd make it. She was their only daughter. The apple of her parents' eye. If all the love in that mother's heart couldn't hold back death's hand, then what good is medical science? What good am I?"

Mark had raised these questions before and Jo Marie had no answers. "I don't know," she admitted solemnly and reached out to touch his hand in reassurance. Mark didn't want to hear the pat answers. He couldn't see that now. Not when he felt like he'd failed this little girl and her parents in some obscure way. At times like these, she'd look at her brother who was a strong, committed doctor and see the doubt in his eyes. She had no answers. Sometimes she wasn't even sure she completely understood his questions.

After wiping his hand across his tired face, Mark stood. "I'm on duty tomorrow morning so I probably won't be at the folks' place until late afternoon. Tell Mom I'll try to make it on time. If I can't, the least you can do is to be sure and save a plate for me."

Knowing Mark, he was likely to go without eating until tomorrow if left to his own devices. "Let me fix you something now," Jo Marie offered. From his unnatural pallor, Jo Marie surmised that Mark couldn't even remember when he'd eaten his last decent meal, coffee and a doughnut on the run excluded.

He glanced at his watch. "I haven't got time. Thanks anyway." Before she could object, he was at the door.

Why had he come? Jo Marie wondered absently. He'd done a lot of that lately—stopping in for a few minutes without notice. And it wasn't as if her apartment were close to the hospital. Mark had to go out of his way to visit her. With a bemused shrug, she followed him to the front door and watched as he sped away in that run-down old car he was so fond of driving. As he left, Jo Marie mentally questioned if her instincts had been on target all along and Kelly and Mark did hold some deep affection for each other. Mark hadn't come tonight for any specific reason. His first question had been about Kelly. Only later had he mentioned losing the child.

"Jo Marie," her mother called from the kitchen. "Would you mind mashing the potatoes?"

The large family kitchen was bustling with activity. The long white counter top was filled with serving bowls ready to be placed on the linen-covered dining room table. Sweet potato and pecan pies were cooling on the smaller kitchen table and the aroma of spice and turkey filled the house.

"Smells mighty good in here," Franklin Early proclaimed, sniffing appreciatively as he strolled into the kitchen and placed a loving arm around his wife's waist.

"Scat," Jo Marie's mother cried with a dismissive wave of her hand. "I won't have you in here sticking your fingers in the pies and blaming it on the boys. Dinner will be ready in ten minutes.''

Mark arrived, red faced and slightly breathless. He kissed his mother on the cheek and when she wasn't looking, popped a sweet pickle into his mouth. ''I hope I'm not too late.''

''I'd say you had perfect timing,'' Jo Marie teased and handed him the electric mixer. ''Here, mash these potatoes while I finish setting the table.''

''No way, little sister.'' His mouth was twisted mockingly as he gave her back the appliance. ''I'll set the table. No one wants lumpy potatoes.''

The three younger boys, all in their teens, sat in front of the television watching a football game. The Early family enjoyed sports, especially football. Jo Marie's mother had despaired long ago that her only daughter would ever grow up properly. Instead of playing with dolls, her toys had been cowboy boots and little green army men. Touch football was as much a part of her life as ballet was for some girls.

With Mark out of the kitchen, Jo Marie's mother turned to her. ''Have you been feeling all right lately?''

''Me?'' The question caught her off guard. ''I'm feeling fine. Why shouldn't I be?''

Ruth Early lifted one shoulder in a delicate shrug. ''You've had a look in your eye lately.'' She turned and leaned her hip against the counter, her head tilted at a thoughtful angle. ''The last time I saw that look was in your Aunt Bessie's eye before she was married. Tell me, Jo Marie, are you in love?''

Jo Marie hesitated, not knowing how to explain her feelings for a man she had met so briefly. He was more illusion than reality. Her own private fantasy. Those few moments with the dream man were beyond explaining, even to her own mother.

"No," she answered finally, making busy work by placing the serving spoons in the bowls.

"Is he married? Is that it? Save yourself a lot of grief, Jo Marie, and stay away from him if he is. You understand?"

"Yes," she murmured, her eyes avoiding her mother's. For all she knew he could well be married.

Not until late that night did Jo Marie let herself into her apartment. The day had been full. After the huge family dinner, they'd played cards until Mark trapped Jo Marie into playing a game of touch football for old times' sake. Jo Marie agreed and proved that she hadn't lost her "touch."

The apartment looked large and empty. Kelly stayed with her parents over any major holidays. Kelly's family seemed to feel that Kelly still belonged at home and always would, no matter what her age. Although Kelly was twenty-four, the apartment she shared with Jo Marie was more for convenience sake than any need to separate herself from her family.

With her mother's words echoing in her ear, Jo Marie sauntered into her bedroom and dressed for bed. Friday was a work day for her as it was for both Mark and Kelly. The downtown area of New Orleans would be hectic with Christmas shoppers hoping to pick up their gifts from the multitude of sales.

As a travel agent, Jo Marie didn't have many walk-in customers to deal with, but her phone rang continuously. Several people wanted to book holiday vacations, but there was little available that she could offer. The most popular vacation spots had been booked months in advance. Several times her information was accepted with an irritated grumble as if she were to blame. By the time she stepped off the bus outside her apartment, Jo Marie wasn't in any mood for company.

No sooner had the thought formed than she caught sight of her brother. He was parked in the lot outside the apartment building. Hungry and probably looking for a hot meal, she guessed. He knew that their mother had sent a good portion of the turkey and stuffing home with Jo Marie so Mark's appearance wasn't any real surprise.

"Hi," she said and knocked on his car window. The faraway look in his eyes convinced her that after all these years Mark had finally learned to sleep with his eyes open. He was so engrossed in his thoughts that Jo Marie was forced to tap on his window a second time.

"Paging Dr. Early," she mimicked in a high-pitched hospital voice. "Paging Dr. Mark Early."

Mark turned and stared at her blankly. "Oh, hi." He sat up and climbed out of the car.

"I suppose you want something to eat." Her greeting wasn't the least bit cordial, but she was tired and irritable.

The edge of Mark's mouth curled into a sheepish grin. "If it isn't too much trouble."

"No," she offered him an apologetic smile. "It's just been a rough day and my feet hurt."

"My sister sits in an office all day, files her nails, reads books and then complains that her feet hurt."

Jo Marie was too weary to rise to the bait. "Not

even your acid tongue is going to get a rise out of me tonight."

"I know something that will," Mark returned smugly.

"Ha." From force of habit, Jo Marie kicked off her shoes and strolled into the kitchen.

"Wanna bet?"

"I'm not a betting person, especially after playing cards with you yesterday, but if you care to impress me, fire away." Crossing her arms, she leaned against the refrigerator door and waited.

"Kelly's engaged."

Jo Marie slowly shook her head in disbelief. "I didn't think you'd stoop to fabrications."

That familiar angry, hurt look stole into Mark's eyes. "It's true, I heard it from the horse's own mouth."

Lightly shaking her head from side to side to clear her thoughts, Jo Marie still came up with a blank. "But who?" Kelly wasn't going out with anyone seriously.

"Some cousin. Rich, no doubt," Mark said and straddled a kitchen chair. "She's got a diamond as big as a baseball. Must be hard for her to work with a rock that size weighing down her hand."

"A cousin?" New Orleans was full of Beaumonts, but none that Kelly had mentioned in particular. "I can't believe it," Jo Marie gasped. "She'd have said something to me."

"From what I understand, she tried to phone last night, but we were still at the folks' house. Just as well," Mark mumbled under his breath. "I'm not about to toast this engagement. First she plays at being nurse and now she wants to play at being a wife.''

Mark's bitterness didn't register past the jolt of surprise that Jo Marie felt. ''Kelly engaged,'' she repeated.

''You don't need to keep saying it,'' Mark snapped.

''Saying what?'' A jubilant Kelly walked in the front door.

''Never mind,'' Mark said and slowly stood. ''It's time for me to be going, I'll talk to you later.''

''What about dinner?''

''There's someone I'd like you both to meet,'' Kelly announced.

Ignoring her, Mark turned to Jo Marie. ''I've suddenly lost my appetite.''

''Jo Marie, I'd like to introduce you to my fiancé, Andrew Beaumont.''

Jo Marie's gaze swung from the frustrated look on her brother's face to an intense pair of gray eyes. There was only one man on earth with eyes the shade of a winter sea. The dream man.

Chapter Two

Stunned into speechlessness, Jo Marie struggled to maintain her composure. She took in a deep breath to calm her frantic heartbeat and forced a look of pleasant surprise. Andrew Beaumont apparently didn't even remember her. Jo Marie couldn't see so much as a flicker of recognition in the depth of his eyes. In the last nine months it was unlikely that he had given her more than a passing thought, if she'd been worthy of even that. And yet, she vividly remembered every detail of him, down to the crisp dark hair, the broad, muscular shoulders and faint twist of his mouth.

With an effort that was just short of superhuman, Jo Marie smiled. "Congratulations, you two. But what a surprise."

Kelly hurried across the room and hugged her tightly. "It was to us, too. Look." She held out her hand for Jo Marie to admire the flashing diamond. Mark hadn't been exaggerating. The flawless gem mounted in an antique setting was the largest Jo Marie had ever seen.

"What did I tell you," Mark whispered in her ear.

Confused, Kelly glanced from sister to brother. "Drew and I are celebrating tonight. We'd love it if you came. Both of you."

"No," Jo Marie and Mark declared in unison.

"I'm bushed," Jo Marie begged off.

"...and tired," Mark finished lamely.

For the first time, Andrew spoke. "We insist." The deep, resonant voice was exactly as Jo Marie remembered. But tonight there was something faintly arrogant in the way he spoke that dared Jo Marie and Mark to put up an argument.

Brother and sister exchanged questioning glances, neither willing to be drawn into the celebration. Each for their own reasons, Jo Marie mused.

"Well—" Mark cleared his throat, clearly ill at ease with the formidable fiancé "—perhaps another time."

"You're Jo Marie's brother?" Andrew asked with a mocking note.

"How'd you know?"

Kelly stuck her arm through Andrew's. "Family resemblance, silly. No one can look at the two of you and not know you're related."

"I can't say the same thing about you two. I thought it was against the law to marry a cousin." Mark didn't bother to disguise his contempt.

"We're distant cousins," Kelly explained brightly. Her eyes looked adoringly into Andrew's and Jo Marie felt her stomach tighten. Jealousy. This sickening feeling in the pit of her stomach was the green-eyed monster. Jo Marie had only experienced brief tastes of the emotion; now it filled her mouth until she thought she would choke on it.

"I...had a horribly busy day." Jo Marie sought frantically for an excuse to stay home.

"And I'd have to go home and change," Mark added, looking down over his pale gray cords and sport shirt.

"No, you wouldn't," Kelly contradicted with a provocative smile. "We're going to K-Paul's."

"Sure, and wait in line half the night." A muscle twitched in Mark's jaw.

K-Paul's was a renowned restaurant that was ranked sixth in the world. Famous, but not elegant. The small establishment served creole cooking at its best.

"No," Kelly supplied, and the dip in her voice revealed how much she wanted to share this night with her friends. "Andrew's a friend of Paul's."

Mark looked at Jo Marie and rolled his eyes. "I should have known," he muttered sarcastically.

"What time did you say we'd be there, darling?"

Jo Marie closed her eyes to the sharp flash of pain at the affectionate term Kelly used so freely. These jealous sensations were crazy. She had no right to feel this way. This man...Andrew Beaumont, was a blown-up figment of her imagination. The brief moments they shared should have been forgotten long ago. Kelly was her friend. Her best friend. And Kelly deserved every happiness.

With a determined jut to her chin, Jo Marie flashed her roommate a warm smile. "Mark and I would be honored to join you tonight."

"We would?" Mark didn't sound pleased. Irritation rounded his dark eyes and he flashed Jo Marie a look that openly contradicted her agreement. Jo Marie wanted to tell him that he owed Kelly this much for all the teasing he'd given her. In addition, her look pleaded with him to understand how much she needed his support tonight. Saying as much was impossible, but she hoped her eyes conveyed the message.

Jo Marie turned slightly so that she faced the tall figure standing only a few inches from her. "It's generous of you to include us," she murmured, but discovered that she was incapable of meeting Andrew's penetrating gaze.

"Give us a minute to freshen up and we'll be on our way," Kelly's effervescent enthusiasm filled the room. "Come on, Jo Marie."

The two men remained in the compact living room. Jo Marie glanced back to note that Mark looked like a jaguar trapped in an iron cage. When he wasn't pacing, he stood restlessly shifting his weight repeatedly from one foot to the other. His look was weary and there was an uncharacteristic tightness to his mouth that narrowed his eyes.

"What do you think," Kelly whispered, and gave a long sigh. "Isn't he fantastic? I think I'm the luckiest girl in the world. Of course, we'll have to wait until after the holidays to make our announcement official. But isn't Drew wonderful?"

Jo Marie forced a noncommittal nod. The raw disappointment left an aching void in her heart. Andrew should have been hers. "He's wonderful." The words came out sounding more like a tortured whisper than a compliment.

Kelly paused, lowering the brush. "Jo, are you all right? You sound like you're going to cry."

"Maybe I am." Tears burned for release, but not for the reason Kelly assumed. "It's not every day I lose my best friend."

"But you're not losing me."

Jo Marie's fingers curved around the cold bathroom sink. "But you are planning to get married?"

"Oh yes, we'll make an official announcement in January, but we haven't set a definite date for the wedding."

That surprised Jo Marie. Andrew didn't look like the kind of man who would encourage a long engagement. She would have thought that once he'd made a decision, he'd move on it. But then, she didn't know Andrew Beaumont. Not really.

A glance in the mirror confirmed that her cheeks were pale, her dark eyes haunted with a wounded, perplexed look. A quick application of blush added color to her bloodless face, but there was little she could do to disguise the troubled look in her eyes. She could only pray that no one would notice.

"Ready?" Kelly stood just outside the open door.

Jo Marie's returning smile was frail as she mentally braced herself for the coming ordeal. She paused long enough to dab perfume to the pulse points at the hollow of her neck and at her wrists.

"I, for one, am starved," Kelly announced as they returned to the living room. "And from what I remember of K-Paul's, eating is an experience we won't forget."

Jo Marie was confident that every part of this evening would be indelibly marked in her memory, but not for the reasons Kelly assumed.

Andrew's deep blue Mercedes was parked beside Mark's old clunker. The differences between the two men were as obvious as the vehicles they drove.

Clearly ill at ease, Mark stood on the sidewalk in front of his car. "Why don't Jo Marie and I follow you?"

"Nonsense," Kelly returned, "there's plenty of room in Drew's car for everyone. You know what the traffic is like. We could get separated. I wouldn't want that to happen."

Mark's twisted mouth said that he would have given a weeks' pay to suddenly disappear. Jo Marie studied her brother carefully from her position in the back seat. His displeasure at being included in this evening's celebration was confusing. There was far more than reluctance in his attitude. He might not get along with Kelly, but she would have thought that Mark would wish Kelly every happiness. But he didn't. Not by the stiff, unnatural behavior she'd witnessed from him tonight.

Mark's attitude didn't change any at the restaurant. Paul, the robust chef, came out from the kitchen and greeted the party himself.

After they'd ordered, the small party sat facing one another in stony silence. Kelly made a couple of attempts to start up the conversation, but her efforts were to no avail. The two men eyed each other, looking as if they were ready to do battle at the slightest provocation.

Several times while they ate their succulent Shrimp Remoulade, Jo Marie found her gaze drawn to Andrew. In many ways he was exactly as she remembered. In others, he was completely different. His voice was low pitched and had a faint drawl. And he wasn't a talker. His expression was sober almost to the point of being somber, which was unusual for a man celebrating his engagement. Another word that her mind tossed out was disillusioned. Andrew Beaumont looked as though he was disenchanted with life. From everything she'd learned he was wealthy and successful. He owned a land development firm. Delta Development, Inc. had been in the Beaumont family for three generations. According to Kelly, the firm had expanded extensively under Andrew's direction.

But if Jo Marie was paying attention to Andrew, he was nothing more than polite to her. He didn't acknowledge her with anything more than an occasional look. And since she hadn't directed any questions to him, he hadn't spoken either. At least not to her.

Paul's special touch for creole cooking made the meal memorable. And although her thoughts were troubled and her heart perplexed, when the waitress took Jo Marie's plate away she had done justice to the meal. Even Mark, who had sat uncommunicative and sullen through most of the dinner, had left little on his plate.

After K-Paul's, Kelly insisted they visit the French Quarter. The others were not as enthusiastic. After an hour of walking around and sampling some of the best jazz sounds New Orleans had to offer, they returned to the apartment.

"I'll make the coffee," Kelly proposed as they climbed from the luxury car.

Mark made a show of glancing at his watch. "I think I'll skip the chicory," he remarked in a flippant tone. "Tomorrow's a busy day."

"Come on, Mark—" Kelly pouted prettily "—don't be a spoil sport."

Mark's face darkened with a scowl. "If you insist."

"It isn't every day I celebrate my engagement. And, Mark, have you noticed that we haven't fought once all night? That must be some kind of a record."

A poor facsimile of a smile lifted one corner of his mouth. "It must be," he agreed wryly. He lagged behind as they climbed the stairs to the second-story apartment.

Jo Marie knew her brother well enough to know he'd have the coffee and leave as soon as it was polite to do so.

They sat in stilted silence, drinking their coffee.

"Do you two work together?" Andrew directed his question to Jo Marie.

Flustered she raised her palm to her breast. "Me?"

"Yes. Did you and Kelly meet at Tulane Hospital?"

"No, I'm a travel agent. Mark's the one in the family with the brains." She heard the breathlessness in her voice and hoped that he hadn't.

"Don't put yourself down," Kelly objected. "You're no dummy. Did you know that Jo Marie is actively involved in saving our wetlands? She volunteers her time as an office worker for the Land For The Future organization."

"That doesn't require intelligence, only time," Jo

Marie murmured self-consciously and congratulated herself for keeping her voice even.

For the first time that evening, Andrew directed his attention to her and smiled. The effect it had on Jo Marie's pulse was devastating. To disguise her reaction, she raised the delicate china cup to her lips and took a tentative sip of the steaming coffee.

"And all these years I thought the LFTF was for little old ladies."

"No." Jo Marie was able to manage only the one word.

"At one time Jo Marie wanted to be a biologist," Kelly supplied.

Andrew arched two thick brows. "What stopped you?"

"Me," Mark cut in defensively. "The schooling she required was extensive and our parents couldn't afford to pay for us both to attend university at the same time. Jo Marie decided to drop out."

"That's not altogether true." Mark was making her sound noble and self-sacrificing. "It wasn't like that. If I'd wanted to continue my schooling there were lots of ways I could have done so."

"And you didn't?" Again Andrew's attention was focused on her.

She moistened her dry lips before continuing. "No. I plan to go back to school someday. Until then I'm staying active in the causes that mean the most to me and to the future of New Orleans."

"Jo Marie's our neighborhood scientist," Kelly added proudly. "She has a science club for children every other Saturday morning. I swear she's a natural with those kids. She's always taking them on hikes and planning field trips for them.''

"You must like children." Again Andrew's gaze slid to Jo Marie.

"Yes," she answered self-consciously and lowered her eyes. She was grateful when the topic of conversation drifted to other subjects. When she chanced a look at Andrew, she discovered that his gaze centered on her lips. It took a great deal of restraint not to moisten them. And even more to force the memory of his kiss from her mind.

Once again, Mark made a show of looking at his watch and standing. ''The evening's been—'' he faltered looking for an adequate description ''—interesting. Nice meeting you, Beaumont. Best wishes to you and Florence Nightingale.''

The sip of coffee stuck in Jo Marie's throat, causing a moment of intense pain until her muscles relaxed enough to allow her to swallow. Grateful that no one had noticed, Jo Marie set her cup aside and walked with her brother to the front door. ''I'll talk to you later,'' she said in farewell.

Mark wiped a hand across his eyes. He looked more tired than Jo Marie could remember seeing him in a long time. ''I've been dying to ask you all night. Isn't Kelly's rich friend the one who filled in the swampland for that housing development you fought so hard against?''

"And lost." Jo Marie groaned inwardly. She had been a staunch supporter of the environmentalists and had helped gather signatures against the project. But to no avail. ''Then he's also the one who bought out Rose's,'' she murmured thoughtfully as a feeling of dread washed over her. Rose's Hotel was in the French Quarter and was one of the landmarks of Louisiana. In addition to being a part of New Orleans' history, the hotel was used to house transients. It was true that Rose's was badly in need of repairs, but Jo Marie hated to see the wonderful old building destroyed in the name of progress. If annihilating the breeding habitat of a hundred different species of birds hadn't troubled Andrew Beaumont, then she doubted that an old hotel in ill-repair would matter to him either.

Rubbing her temple to relieve an unexpected and throbbing headache, Jo Marie nodded. "I remember Kelly saying something about a cousin being responsible for Rose's. But I hadn't put the two together."

"He has," Mark countered disdainfully. "And come up with megabucks. Our little Kelly has reeled in quite a catch, if you like the cold, heartless sort."

Jo Marie's mind immediately rejected that thought. Andrew Beaumont may be the man responsible for several controversial land acquisitions, but he wasn't heartless. Five minutes with him at the Mardi Gras had proven otherwise.

Mark's amused chuckle carried into the living room. "You've got that battle look in your eye. What are you thinking?"

"Nothing," she returned absently. But already her mind was racing furiously. "I'll talk to you tomorrow."

"I'll give you a call," Mark promised and was gone.

When Jo Marie returned to the living room, she

found Kelly and Andrew chatting companionably. They paused and glanced at her as she rejoined them.

"You've known each other for a long time, haven't you?" Jo Marie lifted the half-full china cup, making an excuse to linger. She sat on the arm of the love seat, unable to decide if she should stay and speak her mind or repress her tongue.

"We've known each other since childhood." Kelly answered for the pair.

"And Andrew is the distant cousin you said had bought Rose's."

Kelly's sigh was uncomfortable. "I was hoping you wouldn't put two and two together."

"To be honest, I didn't. Mark figured it out."

A frustrated look tightened Kelly's once happy features.

"Will someone kindly tell me what you two are talking about?" Andrew asked.

"Rose's," they chimed in unison.

"Rose's," he repeated slowly and a frown appeared between his gray eyes.

Apparently Andrew Beaumont had so much land one small hotel didn't matter.

"The hotel."

The unexpected sharpness in his voice caused Jo Marie to square her shoulders. "It may seem like a little thing to you."

"Not for what that piece of land cost me," he countered in a hard voice.

"I don't think Drew likes to mix business with pleasure," Kelly warned, but Jo Marie disregarded the well-intended advice.

"But the men living in Rose's will have nowhere to go."

"They're bums."

A sadness filled her at the insensitive way he referred to these men. "Rose's had housed homeless men for twenty years. These men need someplace where they can get a hot meal and can sleep."

"It's a prime location for luxury condominiums," he said cynically.

"But what about the transients? What will become of them?"

"That, Miss Early, is no concern of mine."

Unbelievably Jo Marie felt tears burn behind her eyes. She blinked them back. Andrew Beaumont wasn't the dream man she'd fantasized over all these months. He was cold and cynical. The only love he had in his life was profit. A sadness settled over her with a weight she thought would be crippling.

"I feel very sorry for you, Mr. Beaumont," she said smoothly, belying her turbulent emotions. "You may be very rich, but there's no man poorer than one who has no tolerance for the weakness of others."

Kelly gasped softly and groaned. "I knew this was going to happen."

"Are you always so opinionated, Miss Early?" There was no disguising the icy tones.

"No, but there are times when things are so wrong that I can't remain silent." She turned to Kelly. "I apologize if I've ruined your evening. If you'll excuse me now, I think I'll go to bed. Good night, Mr. Beaumont. May you and Kelly have many years of happiness together." The words nearly stuck in her throat but she managed to get them out before walking from the room.

"If this offends you in any way I won't do it." Jo Marie studied her roommate carefully. The demonstration in front of Rose's had been planned weeks ago. Jo Marie's wooden picket sign felt heavy in her hand. For the first time in her life, her convictions conflicted with her feelings. She didn't want to march against Andrew. It didn't matter what he'd done, but she couldn't stand by and see those poor men turned into the streets, either. Not in the name of progress. Not when progress was at the cost of the less fortunate and the fate of a once lovely hotel.

"This picket line was arranged long before you met Drew."

"That hasn't got anything to do with this. Drew is important to you. I wouldn't want to do something that will place your relationship with him in jeopardy."

"It won't."

Kelly sounded far more confident than Jo Marie felt.

"In fact," she continued, "I doubt that Drew even knows anything about the demonstration. Those things usually do nothing to sway his decision. In fact, I'd say they do more harm than good as far as he's concerned."

Jo Marie had figured that much out herself, but she couldn't stand by doing nothing. Rose's was scheduled to be shut down the following week...a short month before Christmas. Jo Marie didn't know how anyone could be so heartless. The hotel was to be torn down a week later and new construction was scheduled to begin right after the first of the year.

Kelly paused at the front door while Jo Marie picked up her picket sign and tossed the long strap of her purse over her shoulder.

"You do understand why I can't join you?" she asked hesitatingly.

"Of course," Jo Marie said and exhaled softly. She'd never expected Kelly to participate. This fight couldn't include her friend without causing bitter feelings.

"Be careful." Her arms wrapped around her waist to chase away a chill, Kelly walked down to the parking lot with Jo Marie.

"Don't worry. This is a peaceful demonstration. The only wounds I intend to get are from carrying this sign. It's heavy."

Cocking her head sideways, Kelly read the sign for the tenth time. Save Rose's Hotel. A Piece Of New Orleans History. Kelly chuckled and slowly shook her head. "I should get a picture of you. Drew would get a real kick out of that."

The offer of a picture was a subtle reminder that Drew wouldn't so much as see the sign. He probably wasn't even aware of the protest rally.

Friends of Rose's and several others from the Land For The Future headquarters were gathered outside the hotel when Jo Marie arrived. Several people who knew Jo Marie raised their hands in welcome.

"Have the television and radio stations been notified?" the organizer asked a tall man Jo Marie didn't recognize.

"I notified them, but most weren't all that interested. I doubt that we'll be given air time."

A feeling of gloom settled over the group. An unexpected cloudburst did little to brighten their mood. Jo Marie hadn't brought her umbrella and was drenched in minutes. A chill caused her teeth to chatter and no matter how hard she tried, she couldn't stop shivering. Uncaring, the rain fell indiscriminately over the small group of protesters.

"You little fool," Mark said when he found her an hour later. "Are you crazy, walking around wet and cold like that?" His voice was a mixture of exasperation and pride.

"I'm making a statement," Jo Marie argued.

"You're right. You're telling the world what a fool you are. Don't you have any better sense than this?"

Jo Marie ignored him, placing one foot in front of the other as she circled the sidewalk in front of Rose's Hotel.

"Do you think Beaumont cares?"

Jo Marie refused to be drawn into his argument. "Instead of arguing with me, why don't you go inside and see what's holding up the coffee?"

"You're going to need more than a hot drink to prevent you from getting pneumonia. Listen to reason for once in your life."

"No!" Emphatically Jo Marie stamped her foot. "This is too important."

"And your health isn't?"

"Not now." The protest group had dwindled down to less than ten. "I'll be all right." She shifted the sign from one shoulder to the other and flexed her stiff fingers. Her back ached from the burden of her message. And with every step the rain water in her shoes squished noisily. "I'm sure we'll be finished in another hour."

"If you aren't, I'm carting you off myself," Mark shouted angrily and returned to his car. He shook his finger at her in warning as he drove past.

True to his word, Mark returned an hour later and followed her back to the apartment.

Jo Marie could hardly drive she was shivering so violently. Her long chestnut hair fell in limp tendrils over her face. Rivulets of cold water ran down her neck and she bit into her bottom lip at the pain caused by gripping the steering wheel. Carrying the sign had formed painful blisters in the palms of her hands. This was one protest rally she wouldn't soon forget.

Mark seemed to blame Andrew Beaumont for the fact that she was cold, wet and miserable. But it wasn't Andrew's fault that it had rained. Not a single forecaster had predicted it would. She'd lived in New Orleans long enough to know she should carry an umbrella with her. Mark was looking for an excuse to dislike Andrew. Any excuse. In her heart, Jo Marie couldn't. No matter what he'd done, there was something deep within her that wouldn't allow any bitterness inside. In some ways she was disillusioned and hurt that her dream man wasn't all she'd thought. But that was as deep as her resentments went.

"Little fool," Mark repeated tenderly as he helped her out of the car. "Let's get you upstairs and into a hot bath."

"As long as I don't have to listen to you lecture all night," she said, her teeth chattering as she climbed the stairs to the second-story apartment. Although she was thoroughly miserable, there was a spark of humor in her eyes as she opened the door and stepped inside the apartment.

"Jo Marie," Kelly cried in alarm. "Good grief, what happened?"

A light laugh couldn't disguise her shivering. "Haven't you looked out the window lately? It's raining cats and dogs."

"This is your fault, Beaumont," Mark accused harshly and Jo Marie sucked in a surprised breath. In her misery, she hadn't noticed Andrew, who was casually sitting on the love seat.

He rose to a standing position and glared at Mark as if her brother were a mad man. "Explain yourself," he demanded curtly.

Kelly intervened, crossing the room and placing a hand on Andrew's arm. "Jo Marie was marching in that rally I was telling you about."

"In front of Rose's Hotel," Mark added, his fists tightly clenched at his side. He looked as if he wanted to get physical. Consciously, Jo Marie moved closer to her brother's side. Fist fighting was so unlike Mark. He was a healer, not a boxer. One look told Jo Marie that in a physical exchange, Mark would lose.

Andrew's mouth twisted scornfully. "You, my dear Miss Early, are a fool."

Jo Marie dipped her head mockingly. "And you, Mr. Beaumont, are heartless."

"But rich," Mark intervened. "And money goes a long way in making a man attractive. Isn't that right, Kelly?"

Kelly went visibly pale, her blue eyes filling with

tears. "That's not true," she cried, her words jerky as she struggled for control.

"You will apologize for that remark, Early." Andrew's low voice held a threat that was undeniable.

Mark knotted and unknotted his fists. "I won't apologize for the truth. If you want to step outside, maybe you'd like to make something of it."

"Mark!" Both Jo Marie and Kelly gasped in shocked disbelief.

Jo Marie moved first. "Get out of here before you cause trouble." Roughly she opened the door and shoved him outside.

"You heard what I said," Mark growled on his way out the door.

"I've never seen Mark behave like that," Jo Marie murmured, her eyes lowered to the carpet where a small pool of water had formed. "I can only apologize." She paused and inhaled deeply. "And, Kelly, I'm sure you know he didn't mean what he said to you. He's upset because of the rally." Her voice was deep with emotion as she excused herself and headed for the bathroom.

A hot bath went a long way toward making her more comfortable. Mercifully, Andrew was gone by the time she had finished. She didn't feel up to another confrontation with him.

"Call on line three."

Automatically Jo Marie punched in the button and reached for her phone. "Jo Marie Early, may I help you?"

"You won."

"Mark?" He seldom phoned her at work.

"Did you hear me?" he asked excitedly.

"What did I win?" she asked humoring him.

"Beaumont."

Jo Marie's hand tightened around the receiver. "What do you mean?"

"It just came over the radio. Delta Development, Inc. is donating Rose's Hotel to the city," Mark announced with a short laugh. "Can you believe it?"

"Yes," Jo Marie closed her eyes to the onrush of emotion. Her dream man hadn't let her down. "I can believe it."

Chapter Three

"But you must come," Kelly insisted, sitting across from Jo Marie. "It'll be miserable without you."

"Kell, I don't know." Jo Marie looked up from the magazine she was reading and nibbled on her lower lip.

"It's just a Christmas party with a bunch of stuffy people I don't know. You know how uncomfortable I am meeting new people. I hate parties."

"Then why attend?"

"Drew says we must. I'm sure he doesn't enjoy the party scene any more than I do, but he's got to go or offend a lot of business acquaintances."

"But I wasn't included in the invitation," Jo Marie argued. She'd always liked people and usually did well at social functions.

"Of course you were included. Both you and Mark," Kelly insisted. "Drew saw to that."

Thoughtfully, Jo Marie considered her roommate's request. As much as she objected, she really would like to go, if for no more reason than to thank Andrew for his generosity regarding Rose's. Although she'd seen him briefly a couple of times since, the opportunity hadn't presented itself to express her appreciation. The party was one way she could do that. New Orleans was famous for its festive balls and holiday parties. Without Kelly's invitation, Jo Marie doubted that there would ever be the chance for her to attend such an elaborate affair.

"All right," she conceded, "but I doubt that Mark will come." Mark and Andrew hadn't spoken since the last confrontation in the girls' living room. The air had hung heavy between them then and Jo Marie doubted that Andrew's decision regarding Rose's Hotel would change her brother's attitude.

"Leave Mark to me," Kelly said confidently. "Just promise me that you'll be there."

"I'll need a dress." Mentally Jo Marie scanned the contents of her closet and came up with zero. Nothing she owned would be suitable for such an elaborate affair.

"Don't worry, you can borrow something of mine," Kelly offered with a generosity that was innate to her personality.

Jo Marie nearly choked on her laughter. "I'm three inches taller than you." And several pounds heavier, but she preferred not to mention that. Only once before had Jo Marie worn Kelly's clothes. The night she'd met Andrew.

Kelly giggled and the bubbly sound was pleasant to the ears. "I heard miniskirts were coming back into style."

"Perhaps, but I doubt that the fashion will arrive in time for Christmas. Don't worry about me, I'll go out this afternoon and pick up some material for a dress."

"But will you have enough time between now and the party to sew it?" Kelly's blue eyes rounded with doubt.

"I'll make time." Jo Marie was an excellent seamstress. She had her mother to thank for that. Ruth Early had insisted that her only daughter learn to sew. Jo Marie had balked in the beginning. Her interests were anything but domestic. But now, as she had been several times in the past, she was grateful for the skill.

She found a pattern of a three-quarter-length dress with a matching jacket. The simplicity of the design made the outfit all the more appealing. Jo Marie could dress it either up or down, depending on the occasion. The silky, midnight blue material she purchased was perfect for the holiday, and Jo Marie knew that shade to be one of her better colors.

When she returned to the apartment, Kelly was gone. A note propped on the kitchen table explained that she wouldn't be back until dinner time.

After washing, drying, and carefully pressing the material, Jo Marie laid it out on the table for cutting. Intent on her task, she had pulled her hair away from her face and had tied it at the base of her neck with a rubber band. Straight pins were pressed between her lips when the doorbell chimed. The neighborhood children often stopped in for a visit. Usually Jo Marie welcomed their company, but she was busy now and interruptions could result in an irreparable mistake. She toyed with the idea of not answering.

The impatient buzz told her that her company was irritated at being kept waiting.

"Damn, damn, damn," she grumbled beneath her breath as she made her way across the room. Extracting the straight pins from her mouth, she stuck them in the small cushion she wore around her wrist.

"Andrew!" Secretly she thanked God the pins were out of her mouth or she would have swallowed them in her surprise.

"Is Kelly here?"

"No, but come in." Her heart was racing madly as he walked into the room. Nervous fingers tugged the rubber band from her chestnut hair in a futile attempt to look more presentable. She shook her hair free, then wished she'd kept it neatly in place. For days Jo Marie would have welcomed the opportunity to thank Andrew, but she discovered as she followed him into the living room that her tongue was tied and her mouth felt gritty and dry. "I'm glad you're here...I wanted to thank you for your decision about Rose's...the hotel."

He interrupted her curtly. "My dear Miss Early, don't be misled. My decision wasn't—"

Her hand stopped him. "I know," she said softly. He didn't need to tell her his reasoning. She was already aware it wasn't because of the rally or anything that she'd done or said. "I just wanted to thank you for whatever may have been your reason."

Their eyes met and held from across the room. Countless moments passed in which neither spoke. The air was electric between them and the urge to reach out and touch Andrew was almost overwhelming. The same breathlessness that had attacked her the night of the Mardi Gras returned. Andrew had to remember, he had to. Yet he gave no indication that he did.

Jo Marie broke eye contact first, lowering her gaze to the wool carpet. "I'm not sure where Kelly is, but she said she'd be back by dinner time." Her hand shook as she handed him the note off the kitchen counter.

"Kelly mentioned the party?"

Jo Marie nodded.

"You'll come?"

She nodded her head in agreement. "If I finish sewing this dress in time." She spoke so he wouldn't think she'd suddenly lost the ability to talk. Never had she been more aware of a man. Her heart was hammering at his nearness. He was so close all she had to do was reach out and touch him. But insurmountable barriers stood between them. At last, after all these months she was alone with her dream man. So many times a similar scene had played in her mind. But Andrew didn't remember her. The realization produced an indescribable ache in her heart. What had been the most profound moment in her life had been nothing to him.

"Would you like to sit down?" she offered, remembering her manners. "There's coffee on if you'd like a cup."

He shook his head. "No, thanks." He ran his hand along the top of the blue cloth that was stretched across the kitchen table. His eyes narrowed and he looked as if his thoughts were a thousand miles away.

"Why don't you buy a dress?"

A smile trembled at the edge of her mouth. To a

man who had always had money, buying something as simple as a dress would seem the most logical solution.

"I sew most of my own things," she explained softly, rather than enlightening him with a lecture on economics.

"Did you make this?" His fingers touched the short sleeve of her cotton blouse and brushed against the sensitive skin of her upper arm.

Immediately a warmth spread where his fingers had come into contact with her flesh. Jo Marie's pale cheeks instantly flushed with a crimson flood of color. "Yes," she admitted hoarsely, hating the way her body, her voice, everything about her, was affected by this man.

"You do beautiful work."

She kept her eyes lowered and drew in a steadying breath. "Thank you."

"Next weekend I'll be having a Christmas party at my home for the employees of my company. I would be honored if both you and your brother attended."

Already her heart was racing with excitement; she'd love to visit his home. But seeing where he lived was only an excuse. She'd do anything to see more of him. "I can't speak for Mark," she answered after several moments, feeling guilty for her thoughts.

"But you'll come?"

"I'd be happy to. Thank you." Her only concern was that no one from Delta Development would recognize her as the same woman who was active in the protest against the housing development and in saving Rose's Hotel.

"Good," he said gruffly.

The curve of her mouth softened into a smile. "I'll tell Kelly that you were by. Would you like her to phone you?"

"No, I'll be seeing her later. Goodbye, Jo Marie."

She walked with him to the door, holding onto the knob longer than necessary. "Goodbye, Andrew," she murmured.

Jo Marie leaned against the door and covered her face with both hands. She shouldn't be feeling this eager excitement, this breathless bewilderment, this softness inside at the mere thought of him. Andrew Beaumont was her roommate's fiancé. She had to remember that. But somehow, Jo Marie recognized that her conscience could repeat the information all day, but it would have little effect on her restless heart.

The sewing machine was set up at the table when Kelly walked into the apartment a couple of hours later.

"I'm back," Kelly murmured happily as she hung her sweater in the closet.

"Where'd you go?"

"To see a friend."

Jo Marie thought she detected a note of hesitancy in her roommate's voice and glanced up momentarily from her task. She paused herself, then said, "Andrew was by."

A look of surprise worked its way across Kelly's pixie face. "Really? Did he say what he wanted?"

"Not really. He didn't leave a message." Jo Marie strove for nonchalance, but her fingers shook slightly and she hoped that her friend didn't notice the telltale mannerism.

"You like Drew, don't you?"

For some reason, Jo Marie's mind had always referred to him as Andrew. "Yes." She continued with the mechanics of sewing, but she could feel Kelly's eyes roam over her face as she studied her. Immediately a guilty flush reddened her cheeks. Somehow, some way, Kelly had detected how strongly Jo Marie felt about Andrew.

"I'm glad," Kelly said at last. "I'd like it if you two would fall in..." She hesitated before concluding with, "Never mind."

The two words were repeated in her mind like the dwindling sounds of an echo off canyon walls.

The following afternoon, Jo Marie arrived home from work and took a crisp apple from the bottom shelf of the refrigerator. She wanted a snack before pulling out her sewing machine again. Kelly was working late and had phoned her at the office so Jo Marie wouldn't worry. Holding the apple between her teeth, she lugged the heavy sewing machine out of the bedroom. No sooner had she set the case on top of the table than the doorbell chimed.

Releasing a frustrated sigh, she swallowed the bite of apple.

"Sign here, please." A clipboard was shoved under her nose.

"I beg your pardon," Jo Marie asked.

"I'm making a delivery, lady. Sign here."

"Oh." Maybe Kelly had ordered something without telling her. Quickly, she penned her name along the bottom line.

"Wait here," was the next abrupt instruction.

Shrugging her shoulder, Jo Marie leaned against the door jamb as the brusque man returned to the brown truck parked below and brought up two large boxes.

"Merry Christmas, Miss Early," he said with a sheepish grin as he handed her the delivery.

"Thank you." The silver box was the trademark of New Orleans' most expensive boutique. Gilded lettering wrote out the name of the proprietor, Madame Renaux Marceau, across the top. Funny, Jo Marie couldn't recall Kelly saying she'd bought something there. But with the party coming, Kelly had apparently opted for the expensive boutique.

Dutifully Jo Marie carried the boxes into Kelly's room and set them on the bed. As she did so the shipping order attached to the smaller box, caught her eye. The statement was addressed to her, not Kelly.

Inhaling a jagged breath, Jo Marie searched the order blank to find out who would be sending her anything. Her parents could never have afforded something from Madame Renaux Marceau.

The air was sucked from her lungs as Jo Marie discovered Andrew Beaumont's name. She fumbled with the lids, peeled back sheer paper and gasped at the beauty of what lay before her. The full-length blue dress was the same midnight shade as the one she was sewing. But this gown was unlike anything Jo Marie had ever seen. A picture of Christmas, a picture of elegance. She held it up and felt tears prickle the back of her eyes. The bodice was layered with intricate rows of tiny pearls that formed a V at the waist. The gown was breathtakingly beautiful. Never had Jo Marie thought to own anything so perfect or so lovely. The second box contained a matching cape with an ornate display of tiny pearls.

Very carefully, Jo Marie folded the dress and cape and placed them back into the boxes. An ache inside her heart erupted into a broken sob. She wasn't a charity case. Did Andrew assume that because she sewed her own clothes that what she was making for the party would be unpresentable?

The telephone book revealed the information she needed. Following her instincts, Jo Marie grabbed a sweater and rushed out the door. She didn't stop until she pulled up in front of the large brick building with the gold plaque in the front that announced that this was the headquarters for Delta Development, Inc.

A listing of offices in the foyer told her where Andrew's was located. Jo Marie rode the elevator to the third floor. Most of the building was deserted, only a few employees remained. Those that did gave her curious stares, but no one questioned her presence.

The office door that had Andrew's name lettered on it was closed, but that didn't dissuade Jo Marie. His receptionist was placing the cover over her typewriter when Jo Marie barged inside.

"I'd like to see Mr. Beaumont," she demanded in a breathless voice.

The gray-haired receptionist glanced at the boxes under Jo Marie's arms and shook her head. "I'm sorry, but the office is closed for the day."

Jo Marie caught the subtle difference. "I didn't ask about the office. I said I wanted to see Mr. Beaumont." Her voice rose with her frustration.

A connecting door between two rooms opened. "Is there a problem, Mrs. Stewart?"

"I was just telling..."

"Jo Marie." Andrew's voice was an odd mixture

of surprise and gruffness, yet gentle. His narrowed look centered on the boxes clasped under each arm. "Is there a problem?"

"As a matter of fact there is," she said, fighting to disguise the anger that was building within her to volcanic proportions.

Andrew stepped aside to admit her into his office.

"Will you be needing me further?" Jo Marie heard his secretary ask.

"No, thank you, Mrs. Stewart. I'll see you in the morning."

No sooner had Andrew stepped in the door than Jo Marie whirled on him. The silver boxes from the boutique sat squarely in the middle of Andrew's huge oak desk.

"I think you should understand something right now, Mr. Beaumont," she began heatedly, not bothering to hold back her annoyance. "I am not Cinderella and you most definitely are not my fairy godfather."

"Would I be amiss to guess that my gift displeases you?"

Jo Marie wanted to scream at him for being so calm. She cut her long nails into her palms in an effort to disguise her irritation. "If I am an embarrassment to you wearing a dress I've sewn myself, then I'll simply not attend your precious party."

He looked shocked.

"And furthermore, I am no one's poor relation."

An angry frown deepened three lines across his wide forehead. "What makes you suggest such stupidity?"

"I may be many things, but stupid isn't one of them."

"A lot of things?" He stood behind his desk and leaned forward, pressing his weight on his palms. "You mean like opinionated, headstrong, and impatient."

"Yes," she cried and shot her index finger into the air. "But not stupid."

The tight grip Andrew held on his temper was visible by the way his mouth was pinched until the grooves stood out tense and white. "Maybe not stupid, but incredibly inane."

Her mouth was trembling and Jo Marie knew that if she didn't get away soon, she'd cry. "Let's not argue over definitions. Stated simply, the gesture of buying me a presentable dress was not appreciated. Not in the least."

"I gathered that much, Miss Early. Now if you'll excuse me, I have a dinner engagement."

"Gladly." She pivoted and stormed across the floor ready to jerk open the office door. To her dismay, the door stuck and wouldn't open, ruining her haughty exit.

"Allow me," Andrew offered bitterly.

The damn door! It would have to ruin her proud retreat.

By the time she was in the parking lot, most of her anger had dissipated. Second thoughts crowded her mind on the drive back to the apartment. She could have at least been more gracious about it. Second thoughts quickly evolved into constant recriminations so that by the time she walked through the doorway of the apartment, Jo Marie was thoroughly miserable.

"Hi." Kelly was mixing raw hamburger for meat-loaf with her hands. "Did the dress arrive?"

Kelly knew! "Dress?"

"Yes. Andrew and I went shopping for you yes-terday afternoon and found the most incredibly lovely party dress. It was perfect for you."

Involuntarily, Jo Marie stiffened. "What made you think I needed a dress?"

Kelly's smile was filled with humor. "You were sewing one, weren't you? Drew said that you were really attending this function as a favor to me. And since this is such a busy time of year he didn't want you spending your nights slaving over a sewing ma-chine."

"Oh." A sickening feeling attacked the pit of her stomach.

"Drew can be the most thoughtful person," Kelly commented as she continued to blend the ground meat. Her attention was more on her task than on Jo Marie. "You can understand why it's so easy to love him."

A strangled sound made its way past the tightness in Jo Marie's throat.

"I'm surprised the dress hasn't arrived. Drew gave specific instructions that it was to be delivered today in case any alterations were needed."

"It did come," Jo Marie announced, more miser-able than she could ever remember being.

"It did?" Excitement elevated Kelly's voice. "Why didn't you say something? Isn't it the most beautiful dress you've ever seen? You're going to be gorgeous." Kelly's enthusiasm waned as she turned around. "Jo, what's wrong? You look like you're ready to burst into tears."

"That's...that's because I am," she managed and covering her face with her hands, she sat on the edge of the sofa and wept.

Kelly's soft laugh only made everything seem worse. "I expected gratitude," Kelly said with a sigh and handed Jo Marie a tissue. "But certainly not tears. You don't cry that often."

Noisily Jo Marie blew her nose. "I...I thought I was an embarrassment...to you two...that...you didn't want me...at the party...because I didn't have...the proper clothes...and..."

"You thought what?" Kelly interrupted, a shocked, hurt look crowding her face. "I can't believe you'd even think anything so crazy."

"That's not all. I..." She swallowed. "I took the dress to...Andrew's office and practically...threw it in his face."

"Oh, Jo Marie." Kelly lowered herself onto the sofa beside her friend. "How could you?"

"I don't know. Maybe it sounds ridiculous, but I really believed that you and Andrew would be ashamed to be seen with me in an outfit I'd made myself."

"How could you come up with something so dumb? Especially since I've always complimented you on the things you've sewn."

Miserably, Jo Marie bowed her head. "I know."

"You've really done it, but good, my friend. I can just imagine Drew's reaction to your visit." At the thought Kelly's face grew tight. "Now what are you going to do?"

"Nothing. From this moment on I'll be conveniently tucked in my room when he comes for you..."

"What about the party?" Kelly's blue eyes were rounded with childlike fright and Jo Marie could only speculate whether it was feigned or real. "It's only two days away."

"I can't go, certainly you can understand that."

"But you've got to come," Kelly returned adamantly. "Mark said he'd go if you were there and I need you both. Everything will be ruined if you back out now."

"Mark's coming?" Jo Marie had a difficult time believing her brother would agree to this party idea. She'd have thought Mark would do anything to avoid another confrontation with Andrew.

"Yes. And it wasn't easy to get him to agree."

"I can imagine," Jo Marie returned dryly.

"Jo Marie, please. Your being there means so much to me. More than you'll ever know. Do this one thing and I promise I won't ask another thing of you as long as I live."

Kelly was serious. Something about this party was terribly important to her. Jo Marie couldn't understand what. In order to attend the party she would need to apologize to Andrew. If it had been her choice she would have waited a week or two before approaching him, giving him the necessary time to cool off. As it was, she'd be forced to do it before the party while tempers continued to run hot. Damn! She should have waited until Kelly was home tonight before jumping to conclusions about the dress. Any half-wit would have known her roommate was involved.

"Well?" Kelly regarded her hopefully.

"I'll go, but first I've got to talk to Andrew and explain."

Kelly released a rush of air, obviously relieved. "Take my advice, don't explain a thing. Just tell him you're sorry."

Jo Marie brushed her dark curls from her forehead. She was in no position to argue. Kelly obviously knew Andrew far better than she. The realization produced a rush of painful regrets. "I'll go to his office first thing tomorrow morning," she said with far more conviction in her voice than what she was feeling.

"You won't regret it," Kelly breathed and squeezed Jo Marie's numb fingers. "I promise you won't."

If that was the case, Jo Marie wanted to know why she regretted it already.

To say that she slept restlessly would be an understatement. By morning, dark shadows had formed under her eyes that even cosmetics couldn't completely disguise. The silky blue dress was finished and hanging from a hook on her cloest door. Compared to the lovely creation Andrew had purchased, her simple gown looked drab. Plain. Unsophisticated. Swallowing her pride had always left a bitter aftertaste, and she didn't expect it to be any different today.

"Good luck," Kelly murmured her condolences to Jo Marie on her way out the door.

"Thanks, I'll need that and more." The knot in her stomach grew tighter every minute. Jo Marie didn't know what she was going to say or even where to begin.

Mrs. Stewart, the gray-haired guardian, was at her station when Jo Marie stepped inside Andrew's office.

"Good morning."

The secretary was too well trained to reveal any surprise.

"Would it be possible to talk to Mr. Beaumont for a few minutes?"

"Do you have an appointment?" The older woman flipped through the calendar pages.

"No," Jo Marie tightened her fists. "I'm afraid I don't."

"Mr. Beaumont will be out of the office until this afternoon."

"Oh." Discouragement nearly defeated her. "Could I make an appointment to see him then?"

The paragon of virtue studied the appointment calendar. "I'm afraid not. Mr. Beaumont has meetings scheduled all week. But if you'd like, I could give him a message."

"Yes, please," she returned and scribbled out a note that said she needed to talk to him as soon as it was convenient. Handing the note back to Mrs. Stewart, Jo Marie offered the woman a feeble smile. "Thank you."

"I'll see to it that Mr. Beaumont gets your message," the efficient woman promised.

Jo Marie didn't doubt that the woman would. What she did question was whether Andrew would respond.

By the time Jo Marie readied for bed that evening, she realized that he wouldn't. Now she'd be faced with attending the party with the tension between them so thick it would resemble an English fog.

Mark was the first one to arrive the following evening. Dressed in a pin-stripe suit and a silk tie he looked exceptionally handsome. And Jo Marie didn't mind telling him so.

"Wow." She took a step in retreat and studied him thoughtfully. "Wow," she repeated.

"I could say the same thing. You look terrific."

Self-consciously, Jo Marie smoothed out an imaginary wrinkle from the skirt of her dress. "You're sure?"

"Of course, I am. And I like your hair like that."

Automatically a hand investigated the rhinestone combs that held the bouncy curls away from her face and gave an air of sophistication to her appearance.

"When will money bags be out?" Mark's gaze drifted toward Kelly's bedroom as he took a seat.

"Any minute."

Mark stuck a finger in the collar of his shirt and ran it around his neck. "I can't believe I agreed to this fiasco."

Jo Marie couldn't believe it either. "Why did you?"

Her brother's shrug was filled with self-derision. "I don't know. It seemed to mean so much to Kelly. And to be honest, I guess I owe it to her for all the times I've teased her."

"How do you feel about Beaumont?"

Mark's eyes narrowed fractionally. "I'm trying not to feel anything."

The door opened and Kelly appeared in a red frothy creation that reminded Jo Marie of Christmas and Santa and happy elves. She had seen the dress, but on Kelly the full-length gown came to life. With a lissome grace Jo Marie envied, Kelly sauntered into the room. Mark couldn't take his eyes off her as he slowly rose to a standing position.

"Kelly." He seemed to have difficulty speaking. "You...you're lovely."

Kelly's delighted laughter was filled with pleasure. "Don't sound so shocked. You've just never seen me dressed up is all."

For a fleeting moment Jo Marie wondered if Mark had ever really seen her roommate.

The doorbell chimed and three pairs of eyes glared at the front door accusingly. Jo Marie felt her stomach tighten with nervous apprehension. For two days she'd dreaded this moment. Andrew Beaumont had arrived.

Kelly broke away from the small group and answered the door. Jo Marie watched her brother's eyes narrow as Kelly stood on her tiptoes and lightly brushed her lips across Andrew's cheek. The involuntary reaction stirred a multitude of questions in Jo Marie about Mark's attitude toward Kelly. And her own toward Andrew.

When her gaze drifted from her brother, Jo Marie discovered that Andrew had centered his attention on her.

"You look exceedingly lovely, Miss Early."

"Thank you. I'm afraid the dress I should have worn was mistakenly returned." She prayed he understood her message.

"Let's have a drink before we leave," Kelly suggested. She'd been in the kitchen earlier mixing a concoction of coconut milk, rum, pineapple and several spices.

The cool drink helped relieve some of the tightness

in Jo Marie's throat. She sat beside her brother, across from Andrew. The silence in the room was interrupted only by Kelly, who seemed oblivious to the terrible tension. She chattered all the way out to the car.

Again Mark and Jo Marie were relegated to the back seat of Andrew's plush sedan. Jo Marie knew that Mark hated this, but he submitted to the suggestion without comment. Only the stiff way he held himself revealed his discontent. The party was being given by an associate of Andrew's, a builder. The minute Jo Marie heard the name of the firm she recognized it as the one that had worked on the wetlands project.

Mark cast Jo Marie a curious glance and she shook her head indicating that she wouldn't say a word. In some ways, Jo Marie felt that she was fraternizing with the enemy.

Introductions were made and a flurry of names and faces blurred themselves in her mind. Jo Marie recognized several prominent people, and spoke to a few. Mark stayed close by her side and she knew without asking that this whole party scene made him uncomfortable.

In spite of being so adamant about needing her, Kelly was now nowhere to be seen. A half hour later, Jo Marie noticed that Kelly was sitting in a chair against the wall, looking hopelessly lost. She watched amazed as Mark delivered a glass of punch to her and claimed the chair beside her roommate. Kelly brightened immediately and soon the two were smiling and chatting.

Scanning the crowded room, Jo Marie noticed that Andrew was busy talking to a group of men. The room suddenly felt stuffy. An open glass door that led to a balcony invited her outside and into the cool evening air.

Standing with her gloved hands against the railing, Jo Marie glanced up at the starlit heavens. The night was clear and the black sky was adorned with a thousand glittering stars.

"I received a message that you wanted to speak to me." The husky male voice spoke from behind her.

Jo Marie's heart leaped to her throat and she struggled not to reveal her discomfort. "Yes," she said with a relaxing breath.

Andrew joined her at the wrought-iron railing. His nearness was so overwhelming that Jo Marie closed her eyes to the powerful attraction. Her long fingers tightened their grip.

"I owe you an apology. I sincerely regret jumping to conclusions about the dress. You were only being kind."

An eternity passed before Andrew spoke. "Were you afraid I was going to demand a reward, Florence Nightingale?"

Chapter Four

Jo Marie's heart went still as she turned to Andrew with wide, astonished eyes. "You do remember." They'd spent a single, golden moment together so many months ago. Not once since Kelly had introduced Andrew as her fiancé had he given her the slightest inkling that he remembered.

"Did you imagine I could forget?" he asked quietly.

Tightly squeezing her eyes shut, Jo Marie turned back to the railing, her fingers gripping the wrought iron with a strength she didn't know she possessed.

"I came back every day for a month," he continued in a deep, troubled voice. "I thought you were a nurse."

The color ebbed from Jo Marie's face, leaving her pale. She'd looked for him, too. In all the months since the Mardi Gras she'd never stopped looking. Every time she'd left her apartment, she had silently searched through a sea of faces. Although she'd never known his name, she had included him in her thoughts every day since their meeting. He was her dream man, the stranger who had shared those enchanted moments of magic with her.

"It was Mardi Gras," she explained in a quavering voice. "I'd borrowed Kelly's uniform for a party."

Andrew stood beside her and his wintry eyes narrowed. "I should have recognized you then," he said with faint self-derision.

"Recognized me?" Jo Marie didn't understand. In the short time before they were separated, Andrew had said she reminded him of a painting he'd once seen.

"I should have known you from your picture in the newspaper. You were the girl who so strongly protested the housing development for the wetlands."

"I...I didn't know it was your company. I had no idea." A stray tendril of soft chestnut hair fell forward as she bowed her head. "But I can't apologize for demonstrating against something which I believe is very wrong."

"To thine own self be true, Jo Marie Early." He spoke without malice and when their eyes met, she discovered to her amazement that he was smiling.

Jo Marie responded with a smile of her own. "And you were there that night because of Kelly."

"I'd just left her."

"And I was on my way in." Another few minutes and they could have passed each other in the hospital corridor without ever knowing. In some ways Jo Marie wished they had. If she hadn't met Andrew that night, then she could have shared in her friend's joy at the coming marriage. As it was now, Jo Marie was forced to fight back emotions she had no right to feel. Andrew belonged to Kelly and the diamond ring on her finger declared as much.

"And...and now you've found Kelly," she stammered, backing away. "I want to wish you both a life filled with much happiness." Afraid of what her expressive eyes would reveal, Jo Marie lowered her lashes which were dark against her pale cheek. "I should be going inside."

"Jo Marie."

He said her name so softly that for a moment she wasn't sure he'd spoken. "Yes?"

Andrew arched both brows and lightly shook his head. His finger lightly touched her smooth cheek, following the line of her delicate jaw. Briefly his gaze darkened as if this was torture in the purest sense. "Nothing. Enjoy yourself tonight." With that he turned back to the railing.

Jo Marie entered the huge reception room and mingled with those attending the lavish affair. Not once did she allow herself to look over her shoulder toward the balcony. Toward Andrew, her dream man, because he wasn't hers, would never be hers. Her mouth ached with the effort to appear happy. By the time she made it to the punch bowl her smile felt brittle and was decidedly forced. All these months she'd hoped to find the dream man because her heart couldn't forget him. And now that she had, nothing had ever been more difficult. If she didn't learn to curb the strong sensual pull she felt toward him, she could ruin his and Kelly's happiness.

Soft Christmas music filled the room as Jo Marie

found a plush velvet chair against the wall and sat down, a friendly observer to the party around her. Forcing herself to relax, her toe tapped lightly against the floor with an innate rhythm. Christmas was her favorite time of year—no, she amended, Mardi Gras was. Her smile became less forced.

"You look like you're having the time of your life," Mark announced casually as he took the seat beside her.

"It is a nice party."

"So you enjoy observing the life-style of the rich and famous." The sarcastic edge to Mark's voice was less sharp than normal.

Taking a sip of punch, Jo Marie nodded. "Who wouldn't?"

"To be honest I'm surprised at how friendly everyone's been," Mark commented sheepishly. "Obviously no one suspects that you and I are two of the less privileged."

"Mark," she admonished sharply. "That's a rotten thing to say."

Her brother had the good grace to look ashamed. "To be truthful, Kelly introduced me to several of her friends and I must admit I couldn't find anything to dislike about them."

"Surprise, surprise." Jo Marie hummed the Christmas music softly to herself. "I suppose the next thing I know, you'll be playing golf with Kelly's father."

Mark snorted derisively. "Hardly."

"What have you got against the Beaumonts anyway? Kelly's a wonderful girl."

"Kelly's the exception," Mark argued and stiffened.

"But you just finished telling me that you liked several of her friends that you were introduced to tonight."

"Yes. Well, that was on short acquaintance."

Standing, Jo Marie set her empty punch glass aside. "I think you've got a problem, brother dearest."

A dark look crowded Mark's face, and his brow was furrowed with a curious frown. "You're right, I do." With an agitated movement he stood and made his way across the room.

Jo Marie mingled, talking with a few women who were planning a charity benefit after the first of the year. When they asked her opinion on an important point, Jo Marie was both surprised and pleased. Although she spent a good portion of the next hour with these older ladies, she drifted away as they moved toward the heart of the party. If Andrew had recognized her as the girl involved in the protest against the wetlands development, others might too. And she didn't want to do anything that would cause him and Kelly embarrassment.

Kelly, with her blue eyes sparkling like sapphires, rushed up to Jo Marie. "Here you are!" she exclaimed. "Drew and I have been looking for you."

"Is it time to leave?" Jo Marie was more than ready, uncomfortably aware that she could be recognized at any moment.

"No...no, we just wanted to be certain some handsome young man didn't cart you away."

"Me?" Jo Marie's soft laugh was filled with incredulity. Few men would pay much attention to her, especially since she'd gone out of her way to remain unobtrusively in the background.

"It's more of a possibility than you realize," Andrew spoke from behind her, his voice a gentle rasp against her ear. "You're very beautiful tonight."

"Don't blush, Jo Marie," Kelly teased. "You really are lovely and if you'd given anyone half a chance, they'd have told you so."

Mark joined them and murmured something to Kelly. As he did so, Andrew turned his head toward Jo Marie and spoke so that the other two couldn't hear him. "Only Florence Nightingale could be more beautiful."

A tingling sensation raced down Jo Marie's spine and she turned so their eyes could meet, surprised that he would say something like that to her with Kelly present. Silently, she pleaded with him not to make this any more difficult for her. Those enchanted moments they had shared were long past and best forgotten for both their sakes.

Jo Marie woke to the buzz of the alarm early the next morning. She sat on the side of the bed and raised her arms high above her head and yawned. The day promised to be a busy one. She was scheduled to work in the office that Saturday morning and then catch a bus to LFTF headquarters on the other side of the French Quarter. She was hoping to talk to Jim Rowden, the director and manager of the conservationists' group. Jim had asked for additional volunteers during the Christmas season. And after thoughtful consideration, Jo Marie decided to accept the challenge. Christmas was such a busy time of year that many of the other volunteers wanted time off.

The events of the previous night filled her mind.

Lowering her arms, Jo Marie beat back the unexpected rush of sadness that threatened to overcome her. Andrew hadn't understood any of the things she'd tried to tell him last night. Several times she found him watching her, his look brooding and thoughtful as if she'd displeased him. No matter where she went during the course of the evening, when she looked up she found Andrew studying her. Once their eyes had met and held and everyone between them had seemed to disappear. The music had faded and it was as if only the two of them existed in the party-filled crowd. Jo Marie had lowered her gaze first, frightened and angry with them both.

Andrew and Mark had been sullen on the drive home. Mark had left the apartment almost immediately and Jo Marie had fled to the privacy of her room, unwilling to witness Andrew kissing Kelly good-night. She couldn't have borne it.

Now, in the light of the new day, she discovered that her feelings for Andrew were growing stronger. She wanted to banish him to a special area of her life, long past. But he wouldn't allow that. It had been in his eyes last night as he studied her. Those moments at the Mardi Gras were not to be forgotten by either of them.

At least when she was at the office, she didn't have to think about Andrew or Kelly or Mark. The phone buzzed continually. And because they were short-staffed on the weekends, Jo Marie hardly had time to think about anything but airline fares, bus routes and train schedules the entire morning.

She replaced the telephone receiver after talking with the Costa Lines about booking a spring Caribbean cruise for a retired couple. Her head was bowed as she filled out the necessary forms. Jo Marie didn't hear Paula Shriver, the only other girl in the office on Saturday, move to her desk.

"Mr. Beaumont's been waiting to talk to you," Paula announced. "Lucky you," she added under her breath as Andrew took the seat beside Jo Marie's desk.

"Hello, Jo Marie."

"Andrew." Her hand clenched the ballpoint pen she was holding. "What can I do for you?"

He crossed his legs and draped an arm over the back of the chair giving the picture of a man completely at ease. "I was hoping you could give me some suggestions for an ideal honeymoon."

"Of course. What did you have in mind?" Inwardly she wanted to shout at him not to do this to her, but she forced herself to smile and look attentive.

"What would you suggest?"

She lowered her gaze. "Kelly's mentioned Hawaii several times. I know that's the only place she'd enjoy visiting."

He dismissed her suggestion with a short shake of his head. "I've been there several times. I was hoping for something less touristy."

"Maybe a cruise then. There are several excellent lines operating in the Caribbean, the Mediterranean or perhaps the inside passage to Alaska along the Canadian west coast."

"No." Again he shook his head. "Where would *you* choose to go on a honeymoon?"

Jo Marie ignored his question, not wanting to answer him. "I have several brochures I can give you that could spark an idea. I'm confident that any one of these places would thrill Kelly.'' As she pulled out her bottom desk drawer, Jo Marie was acutely conscious of Andrew studying her. She'd tried to come across with a strict business attitude, but her defenses were crumbling.

Reluctantly, he accepted the brochures she gave him. ''You didn't answer my question. Shall I ask it again?''

Slowly, Jo Marie shook her head. ''I'm not sure I'd want to go anywhere,'' she explained simply. ''Not on my honeymoon. Not when the most beautiful city in the world is at my doorstep. I'd want to spend that time alone with my husband. We could travel later.'' Briefly their eyes met and held for a long, breathless moment. ''But I'm not Kelly, and she's the one you should consider while planning this trip.''

Paula stood and turned the sign in the glass door, indicating that the office was no longer open. Andrew's gaze followed her movements. ''You're closing.''

Jo Marie's nod was filled with relief. She was uncomfortable with Andrew. Being this close to him was a test of her friendship to Kelly. And at this moment, Kelly was losing...they both were. ''Yes. We're only open during the morning on Saturdays.''

He stood and placed the pamphlets on the corner of her desk. ''Then let's continue our discussion over lunch.''

''Oh, no, really that isn't necessary. We'll be finished in a few minutes and Paula doesn't mind waiting.''

"But I have several ideas I want to discuss with you and it could well be an hour or so."

"Perhaps you could return another day."

"Now is the more convenient time for me," he countered smoothly.

Everything within Jo Marie wanted to refuse. Surely he realized how difficult this was for her. He was well aware of her feelings and was deliberately ignoring them.

"Is it so difficult to accept anything from me, Jo Marie?" he asked softly. "Even lunch?"

"All right," she agreed ungraciously, angry with him and angrier with herself. "But only an hour. I've got things to do."

A half smile turned up one corner of his mouth. "As you wish," he said as he escorted her to his Mercedes.

Jo Marie was stiff and uncommunicative as Andrew drove through the thick traffic. He parked on a narrow street outside the French Quarter and came around to her side of the car to open the door for her.

"I have reservations at Chez Lorraine's."

"Chez Lorraine's?" Jo Marie's surprised gaze flew to him. The elegant French restaurant was one of New Orlean's most famous. The food was rumored to be exquisite, and expensive. Jo Marie had always dreamed of dining there, but never had.

"Is it as good as everyone says?" she asked, unable to disguise the excitement in her voice.

"You'll have to judge for yourself," he answered, smiling down on her.

Once inside, they were seated almost immediately and handed huge oblong menus featuring a wide variety of French cuisine. Not having sampled several of the more traditional French dishes, Jo Marie toyed with the idea of ordering the calf's sweetbread.

"What would you like?" Andrew prompted after several minutes.

"I don't know. It all sounds so good." Closing the menu she set it aside and lightly shook her head. "I think you may regret having brought me here when I'm so hungry." She'd skipped breakfast, and discovered now that she was famished.

Andrew didn't look up from his menu. "Where you're concerned, there's very little I regret." As if he'd made a casual comment about the weather, he continued. "Have you decided?"

"Yes...yes," she managed, fighting down the dizzying effect of his words. "I think I'll try the salmon, but I don't think I should try the French pronunciation."

"Don't worry, I'll order for you."

As if by intuition, the waiter reappeared when they were ready to place their order. "The lady would like *les mouilles à la crème de saumon fumé,* and I'll have the *le canard de rouen braise.*"

With a nod of approval the red-jacketed waiter departed.

Self-consciously, Jo Marie smoothed out the linen napkin on her lap. "I'm impressed," she murmured, studying the old world French provincial decor of the room. "It's everything I thought it would be."

The meal was fabulous. After a few awkward moments Jo Marie was amazed that she could talk as freely to Andrew. She discovered he was a good listener and she enjoyed telling him about her family.

"So you were the only girl."

"It had its advantages. I play a mean game of touch football."

"I hope you'll play with me someday. I've always enjoyed a rousing game of touch football."

The fork was raised halfway to her mouth and Jo Marie paused, her heart beating double time. "I...I only play with my brothers."

Andrew chuckled. "Speaking of your family, I find it difficult to tell that you and Mark are related. Oh, I can see the family resemblance, but Mark's a serious young man. Does he ever laugh?"

Not lately, Jo Marie mused, but she didn't admit as much. "He works hard, long hours. Mark's come a long way through medical school." She hated making excuses for her brother. "He doesn't mean to be rude."

Andrew accepted the apology with a wry grin. "The chip on his shoulder's as big as a California redwood. What's he got against wealth and position?"

"I don't know," she answered honestly. "He teases Kelly unmercifully about her family. I think Kelly's money makes him feel insecure. There's no reason for it; Kelly's never done anything to give him that attitude. I never have understood it."

Pushing her clean plate aside, Jo Marie couldn't recall when she'd enjoyed a meal more—except the dinner they'd shared at K-Paul's the night Kelly and Andrew had announced their engagement. Some of the contentment faded from her eyes. Numbly, she folded her hands in her lap. Being here with Andrew, sharing this meal, laughing and talking with him wasn't right. Kelly should be the one sitting across the table from him. Jo Marie had no right to enjoy his company this way. Not when he was engaged to her best friend. Pointedly, she glanced at her watch.

"What's wrong?"

"Nothing." She shook her head slightly, avoiding his eyes, knowing his look had the ability to penetrate her soul.

"Would you care for some dessert?"

Placing her hand on her stomach, she declined with a smile. "I couldn't," she declared, but her gaze fell with regret on the large table display of delicate French pastries.

The waiter reappeared and a flurry of French flew over her head. Like everything else Andrew did, his French was flawless.

Almost immediately the waiter returned with a plate covered with samples of several desserts which he set in front of Jo Marie.

"Andrew," she objected, sighing his name, "I'll get fat."

"I saw you eyeing those goodies. Indulge. You deserve it."

"But I don't. I can't possibly eat all that."

"You can afford to put on a few pounds." His voice deepened as his gaze skimmed her lithe form.

"Are you suggesting I'm skinny?"

"My, my," he said, slowly shaking his head from side to side. "You do like to argue. Here, give me the plate. I'll be the one to indulge."

"Not on your life," she countered laughingly, and dipped her fork into the thin slice of chocolate cheesecake. After sampling three of the scrumptious des-

serts, Jo Marie pushed her plate aside. "Thank you,
Andrew," she murmured as her fingers toyed with the
starched, linen napkin. "I enjoyed the meal and...and
the company, but we can't do this again." Her eyes
were riveted to the tabletop.

"Jo Marie—"

"No. Let me finish," she interrupted on a rushed
breath. "It...it would be so easy...to hurt Kelly and I
won't do that. I can't. Please, don't make this so difficult for me." With every word her voice grew
weaker and shakier. It shouldn't be this hard, her heart
cried, but it was. Every womanly instinct was reaching out to him until she wanted to cry with it.

"Indulge me, Jo Marie," he said tenderly. "It's my
birthday and there's no one else I'd rather share it
with."

No one else...his words reverberated through her
mind. They were on treacherous ground and Jo Marie
felt herself sinking fast.

"Happy birthday," she whispered.

"Thank you."

They stood and Andrew cupped her elbow, leading
her to the street.

"Would you like me to drop you off at the apartment?" Andrew asked several minutes later as they
walked toward his parked car.

"No. I'm on my way to the LFTF headquarters."
She stuck both hands deep within her sweater pockets.

"Land For The Future?"

She nodded. "They need extra volunteers during
the Christmas season."

His wide brow knitted with a deep frown. "As I

recall, that building is in a bad part of town. Is it safe for you to—"

"Perfectly safe." She took a step in retreat. "Thank you again for lunch. I hope you have a wonderful birthday," she called just before turning and hurrying along the narrow sidewalk.

Jo Marie's pace was brisk as she kept one eye on the darkening sky. Angry gray thunderclouds were rolling in and a cloud burst was imminent. Everything looked as if it was against her. With the sky the color of Andrew's eyes, it seemed as though he was watching her every move. Fleetingly she wondered if she'd ever escape him...and worse, if she'd ever want to.

The LFTF headquarters were near the docks. Andrew's apprehensions were well founded. This was a high crime area. Jo Marie planned her arrival and departure times in daylight.

"Can I help you?" The stocky man with crisp ebony hair spoke from behind the desk. There was a speculative arch to his bushy brows as he regarded her.

"Hello." She extended her hand. "I'm Jo Marie Early. You're Jim Rowden, aren't you?" Jim had recently arrived from the Boston area and was taking over the manager's position of the nonprofit organization.

Jim stepped around the large oak desk. "Yes, I remember now. You marched in the demonstration, didn't you?"

"Yes, I was there."

"One of the few who stuck it out in the rain, as I recall."

"My brother insisted that it wasn't out of any sense of purpose, but from a pure streak of stubbornness." Laughter riddled her voice. "I'm back because you mentioned needing extra volunteers this month."

"Do you type?"

"Reasonably well. I'm a travel agent."

"Don't worry I won't give you a time test."

Jo Marie laughed. "I appreciate that more than you know."

The majority of the afternoon was spent typing personal replies to letters the group had received after the demonstration in front of Rose's. In addition, the group had been spurred on by their success, and was planning other campaigns for future projects. At four-thirty, Jo Marie slipped the cover over the typewriter and placed the letters on Jim's desk for his signature.

"If you could come three times a week," Jim asked, "it would be greatly appreciated."

She left forty minutes later feeling assured that she was doing the right thing by offering her time. Lending a hand at Christmas seemed such a small thing to do. Admittedly, her motives weren't pure. If she could keep herself occupied, she wouldn't have to deal with her feelings for Andrew.

A lot of her major Christmas shopping was completed, but on her way to the bus stop, Jo Marie stopped in at a used-book store. Although she fought it all afternoon, her thoughts had been continually on Andrew. Today was his special day and she desperately wanted to give him something that would relay her feelings. Her heart was filled with gratitude. Without him, she may never have known that sometimes dreams can come true and that fairy tales aren't always for the young.

She found the book she was seeking. A large leather-bound volume of the history of New Orleans. Few cities had a more romantic background. Included in the book were hundreds of rare photographs of the city's architecture, courtyards, patios, ironwork and cemeteries. He'd love the book as much as she. Jo Marie had come by for weeks, paying a little bit each pay day. Not only was this book rare, but extremely expensive. Because the proprietor knew Jo Marie, he had made special arrangements for her to have this volume. But Jo Marie couldn't think of anything else Andrew would cherish more. She wrote out a check for the balance and realized that she would probably be short on cash by the end of the month, but that seemed a small sacrifice.

Clenching the book to her breast, Jo Marie hurried home. She had not right to be giving Andrew gifts, but this was more for her sake than his. It was her thank you for all that he'd given her.

The torrential downpour assaulted the pavement just as Jo Marie stepped off the bus. Breathlessly, while holding the paper-wrapped leather volume to her stomach, she ran to the apartment and inserted her key into the dead bolt. Once again she had barely escaped a thorough drenching.

Hanging her Irish knit cardigan in the hall closet, Jo Marie kicked off her shoes and slid her feet into fuzzy, worn slippers.

Kelly should arrive any minute and Jo Marie rehearsed what she was going to say to Kelly. She had to have some kind of explanation to be giving her friend's fiancé a birthday present. Her thoughts came back empty as she paced the floor, wringing her hands. It was important that Kelly understand, but finding a plausible reason without revealing herself was difficult. Jo Marie didn't want any ill feelings between them.

When her roommate hadn't returned from the hospital by six, Jo Marie made herself a light meal and turned on the evening news. Kelly usually phoned if she was going to be late. Not having heard from her friend caused Jo Marie to wonder. Maybe Andrew had picked her up after work and had taken her out to dinner. It was, after all, his birthday; celebrating with his fiancé would only be natural. Unbidden, a surge of resentment rose within her and caused a lump of painful hoarseness to tighten her throat. Mentally she gave herself a hard shake. *Stop it,* her mind shouted. *You have no right to feel these things. Andrew belongs to Kelly, not you.*

A mixture of pain and confusion moved across her smooth brow when the doorbell chimed. It was probably Mark, but for the first time in recent memory, Jo Marie wasn't up to a sparring match with her older brother. Tonight she wanted to be left to her own thoughts.

But it wasn't Mark.

"Andrew." Quickly she lowered her gaze, praying he couldn't read her startled expression.

"Is Kelly ready?" he asked as he stepped inside the entryway. "We're having dinner with my mother."

"She isn't home from work yet. If you'd like I could call the hospital and see what's holding her up." So they were going out tonight. Jo Marie successfully managed to rein in her feelings of jealousy, having dealt with them earlier.

"No need, I'm early. If you don't mind, I'll just wait."

"Please, sit down." Self-consciously she gestured toward the love seat. "I'm sure Kelly will be here any minute."

Impeccably dressed in a charcoal-gray suit that emphasized the width of his muscular shoulders, Andrew took a seat.

With her hands linked in front of her, Jo Marie fought for control of her hammering heart. "Would you like a cup of coffee?"

"Please."

Relieved to be out of the living room, Jo Marie hurried into the kitchen and brought down a cup and saucer. Spending part of the afternoon with Andrew was difficult enough. But being alone in the apartment with him was impossible. The tension between them was unbearable as it was. But to be separated by only a thin wall was much worse. She yearned to touch him. To hold him in her arms. To feel again, just this once, his mouth over hers. She had to know if what had happened all those months ago was real.

"Jo Marie," Andrew spoke softly from behind her.

Her pounding heart leaped to her throat. Had he read her thoughts and come to her? Her fingers dug unmercifully into the kitchen counter top. Nothing would induce her to turn around.

"What's this?" he questioned softly.

A glance over her shoulder revealed Andrew holding the book she'd purchased earlier. Her hand shook as she poured the coffee. "It's a book about the early history of New Orleans. I found it in a used-book store and..." Her voice wobbled as badly as her hand.

"There was a card on top of it that was addressed to me."

Jo Marie set the glass coffeepot down. "Yes...I knew you'd love it and I wanted you to have it as a birthday present." She stopped just before admitting that she wanted him to remember her. "I also heard on the news tonight that...that Rose's Hotel is undergoing some expensive and badly needed repairs, thanks to you." Slowly she turned, keeping her hands behind her. "I realize there isn't anything that I could ever buy for you that you couldn't purchase a hundred times over. But I thought this book might be the one thing I could give you...." She let her voice fade in midsentence.

A slow faint smile touched his mouth as he opened the card and read her inscription. "To Andrew, in appreciation for everything." Respectfully he opened the book, then laid it aside. "Everything, Jo Marie?"

"For your generosity toward the hotel, and your thoughtfulness in giving me the party dress and..."

"The Mardi Gras?" He inched his way toward her.

Jo Marie could feel the color seep up her neck and tinge her cheeks. "Yes, that too." She wouldn't deny how speical those few moments had been to her. Nor could she deny the hunger in his hard gaze as he concentrated on her lips. Amazed, Jo Marie watched as Andrew's gray eyes darkened to the shade of a stormy Arctic sea.

No pretense existed between them now, only a shared hunger that could no longer be repressed. A surge of intense longing seared through her so that when Andrew drew her into his embrace she gave a small cry and went willingly.

"Haven't you ever wondered if what we shared that night was real?" he breathed the question into her hair.

"Yes, a thousand times since, I've wondered." She gloried in the feel of his muscular body pressing against the length of hers. Freely her hands roamed his back. His index finger under her chin lifted her face and her heart soared at the look in his eyes.

"Jo Marie," he whispered achingly and his thumb leisurely caressed the full curve of her mouth.

Her soft lips trembled in anticipation. Slowly, deliberately, Andrew lowered his head as his mouth sought hers. Her eyelids drifted closed and her arms reached up and clung to him. The kiss was one of hunger and demand as his mouth feasted on hers.

The feel of him, the touch, the taste of his lips filled her senses until Jo Marie felt his muscles strain as he brought her to him, riveting her soft form to him so tightly that she could no longer breathe. Not that she cared.

Gradually the kiss mellowed and the intensity eased until he buried his face in the gentle slope of her neck. "It was real," he whispered huskily. "Oh, my sweet Florence Nightingale, it was even better than I remembered."

"I was afraid it would be." Tears burned her eyes and she gave a sad little laugh. Life was filled with ironies and finding Andrew now was the most painful.

Tenderly he reached up and wiped the moisture from her face. "I shouldn't have let this happen."

"It wasn't your fault." Jo Marie felt she had to accept part of the blame. She'd wanted him to kiss her so badly. "I...I won't let it happen again." If one of them had to be strong, then it would be her. After years of friendship with Kelly she owed her roommate her loyalty.

Reluctantly they broke apart, but his hands rested on either side of her neck as though he couldn't bear to let her go completely. "Thank you for the book," he said in a raw voice. "I'll treasure it always."

The sound of the front door opening caused Jo Marie's eyes to widen with a rush of guilt. Kelly would take one look at her and realize what had happened. Hot color blazed in her cheeks.

"Jo Marie!" Kelly's eager voice vibrated through the apartment.

Andrew stepped out of the kitchen, granting Jo Marie precious seconds to compose herself.

"Oh, heavens, you're here already, Drew. I'm sorry I'm so late. But I've got so much to tell you."

With her hand covering her mouth to smother the sound of her tears, Jo Marie leaned against the kitchen counter, suddenly needing its support.

Chapter Five

"Are you all right?" Andrew stepped back into the kitchen and brushed his hand over his temples. He resembled a man driven to the end of his endurance, standing with one foot in heaven and the other in hell. His fingers were clenched at his side as if he couldn't decide if he should haul her back into his arms or leave her alone. But the tortured look in his eyes told Jo Marie how difficult it was not to hold and reassure her.

"I'm fine." Her voice was eggshell fragile. "Just leave. Please. I don't want Kelly to see me." Not like this, with tears streaming down her pale cheeks and her eyes full of confusion. Once glance at Jo Marie and the astute Kelly would know exactly what had happened.

"I'll get her out of here as soon as she changes clothes," Andrew whispered urgently, his stormy gray eyes pleading with hers. "I didn't mean for this to happen."

"I know." With an agitated brush of her hand she dismissed him. "Please, just go."

"I'll talk to you tomorrow."

"No." Dark emotion flickered across her face. She didn't want to see him. Everything about today had been wrong. She should have avoided Andrew, feeling as she did. But in some ways, Jo Marie realized that the kiss had been inevitable. Those brief magical moments at the Mardi Gras demanded an exploration of the sensation they'd shared. Both had hoped to dismiss that February night as whimsy—a result of the craziness of the season. Instead, they had discovered how real it had been. From now on, Jo Marie vowed, she would shun Andrew. Her only defense was to avoid him completely.

"I'm sorry to keep you waiting." Kelly's happy voice drifted in from the other room. "Do I look okay?"

"You're lovely as always."

Jo Marie hoped that Kelly wouldn't catch the detached note in Andrew's gruff voice.

"You'll never guess who I spent the last hour talking to."

"Perhaps you could tell me on the way to mother's?" Andrew responded dryly.

"Drew." Some of the enthusiasm drained from Kelly's happy voice. "Are you feeling ill? You're quite pale."

"I'm fine."

"Maybe we should cancel this dinner. Really, I wouldn't mind."

"There's no reason to disappoint my mother."

"Drew?" Kelly seemed hesitant.

"Are you ready?" His firm voice brooked no disagreement.

"But I wanted to talk to Jo Marie."

"You can call her after dinner," Andrew responded shortly, his voice fading as they moved toward the entryway.

The door clicked a minute later and Jo Marie's fingers loosened their death grip against the counter. Weakly, she wiped a hand over her face and eyes. Andrew and Kelly were engaged to be married. Tonight was his birthday and he was taking Kelly to dine with his family. And Jo Marie had been stealing a kiss from him in the kitchen. Self-reproach grew in her breast with every breath until she wanted to scream and lash out with it.

Maybe she could have justified her actions if Kelly hadn't been so excited and happy. Her roommate had come into the apartment bursting with enthusiasm for life, eager to see and talk to Andrew.

The evening seemed interminable and Jo Marie had a terrible time falling asleep, tossing and turning long past the time Kelly returned. Finally at the darkest part of the night, she flipped on the beside lamp and threw aside the blankets. Pouring herself a glass of milk, Jo Marie leaned against the kitchen counter and drank it with small sips, her thoughts deep and dark. She couldn't ask Kelly to forgive her for what had happened without hurting her roommate and perhaps ruining their friendship. The only person there was to confront and condemn was herself.

Once she returned to bed, Jo Marie lay on her back,

her head clasped in her hands. Moon shadows fluttered against the bare walls like the flickering scenes of a silent movie.

Unhappy beyond words, Jo Marie avoided her roommate, kept busy and occupied her time with other friends. But she was never at peace and always conscious that her thoughts never strayed from Kelly and Andrew. The episode with Andrew wouldn't happen again. She had to be strong.

Jo Marie didn't see her roommate until the following Monday morning. They met in the kitchen where Jo Marie was pouring herself a small glass of grapefruit juice.

"Morning." Jo Marie's stiff smile was only slightly forced.

"Howdy, stranger. I've missed you the past couple of days."

Jo Marie's hand tightened around the juice glass as she silently prayed Kelly wouldn't ask her about Saturday night. Her roommate must have known Jo Marie was in the apartment, otherwise Andrew wouldn't have been inside.

"I've missed you," Kelly continued. "It seems we hardly have time to talk anymore. And now that you're going to be doing volunteer work for the foundation, we'll have even less time together. You're spreading yourself too thin."

"There's always something going on this time of year." A chill seemed to settle around the area of Jo Marie's heart and she avoided her friend's look.

"I know, that's why I'm looking forward to this weekend and the party for Drew's company. By the way, he suggested that both of us stay the night on Saturday.''

"Spend the night?'' Jo Marie repeated like a recording and inhaled a shaky breath. That was the last thing she wanted.

"It makes sense, don't you think? We can lay awake until dawn the way we used to and talk all night.'' A distant look came over Kelly as she buttered the hot toast and poured herself a cup of coffee. "Drew's going to have enough to worry about without dragging us back and forth. From what I understand, he goes all out for his company's Christmas party.''

Hoping to hide her discomfort, Jo Marie rinsed out her glass and deposited it in the dishwasher, but a gnawing sensation attacked the pit of her stomach. Although she'd promised Kelly she would attend the lavish affair, she had to find a way of excusing herself without arousing suspicion. "I've been thinking about Andrew's party and honestly feel I shouldn't go—''

"Don't say it. You're going!'' Kelly interrupted hastily. "There's no way I'd go without you. You're my best friend, Jo Marie Early, and as such I want you with me. Besides, you know how I hate these things.''

"But as Drew's wife you'll be expected to attend a lot of these functions. I won't always be around.''

A secret smile stole over her friend's pert face. "I know, that's why it's so important that you're there now.''

"You didn't seem to need me Friday night.''

Round blue eyes flashed Jo Marie a look of disbelief. "Are you crazy? I would have been embarrassingly uncomfortable without you."

It seemed to Jo Marie that Mark had spent nearly as much time with Kelly as she had. In fact, her brother had spent most of the evening with Kelly at his side. It was Mark whom Kelly really wanted, not her. But convincing her roommate of that was a different matter. Jo Marie doubted that Kelly had even admitted as much to herself.

"I'll think about going," Jo Marie promised. "But I can't honestly see that my being there or not would do any good."

"You've got to come," Kelly muttered, looking around unhappily. "I'd be miserable meeting and talking to all those people on my own." Silently, Kelly's bottomless blue eyes pleaded with Jo Marie. "I promise never to ask anything from you again. Say you'll come. Oh, please, Jo Marie, do this one last thing for me."

An awkward silence stretched between them and a feeling of dread settled over Jo Marie. Kelly seemed so genuinely distraught that it wasn't in Jo Marie's heart to refuse her. As Kelly had pointedly reminded her, she was Kelly's best friend. "All right, all right," she agreed reluctantly. "But I don't like it."

"You won't be sorry, I promise." A mischievous gleam lightened Kelly's features.

Jo Marie mumbled disdainfully under her breath as she moved out of the kitchen. Pausing at the closet, she took her trusted cardigan from the hanger. "Say, Kell, don't forget this is the week I'm flying to Mazatlán." Jo Marie was scheduled to take a familiarization tour of the Mexican resort town. She'd be fly-

ing with ten other travel agents from the city and
staying at the Riviera Del Sol's expense. The luxury
hotel was sponsoring the group in hopes of having
the agents book their facilities for their clients. Jo
Marie usually took the "fam" tours only once or
twice a year. This one had been planned months before and she mused that it couldn't have come at a
better time. Escaping from Andrew and Kelly was just
the thing she needed. By the time she returned, she
prayed, her life could be back to normal.

"This is the week?" Kelly stuck her head around
the kitchen doorway. "Already?"

"You can still drive me to the airport, can't you?"

"Sure," Kelly answered absently. "But if I can't,
Drew will."

Jo Marie's heart throbbed painfully. "No," she returned forcefully.

"He doesn't mind."

But I do, Jo Marie's heart cried as she fumbled with
the buttons of her sweater. If Kelly wasn't home when
it came time to leave for the airport, she would either
call Mark or take a cab.

"I'm sure Drew wouldn't mind," Kelly repeated.

"I'll be late tonight," she answered, ignoring her
friend's offer. She couldn't understand why Kelly
would want her to spend time with Andrew. But so
many things didn't make sense lately. Without a
backward glance, Jo Marie went out the front door.

Joining several others at the bus stop outside the
apartment building en route to the office, Jo Marie
fought down feelings of guilt. She'd honestly thought
she could get out of attending the party with Kelly.
But there was little to be done, short of offending her

friend. These constant recriminations regarding Kelly and Andrew were disrupting her neatly ordered life, and Jo Marie hated it.

Two of the other girls were in the office by the time Jo Marie arrived.

"There's a message for you," Paula announced. "I think it was the same guy who stopped in Saturday morning. You know, I'm beginning to think you've been holding out on me. Where'd you ever meet a hunk like that?"

"He's engaged," she quipped, seeking a light tone.

"He is?" Paula rolled her office chair over to Jo Marie's desk and handed her the pink slip. "You could have fooled me. He looked on the prowl, if you want my opinion. In fact, he was eyeing you like a starving man looking at a cream puff."

"Paula!" Jo Marie tried to toss off her co-worker's observation with a forced laugh. "He's engaged to my roommate."

Paula lifted one shoulder in a half shrug and scooted the chair back to her desk. "If you say so." But both her tone and her look were disbelieving.

Jo Marie read the message, which listed Andrew's office number and asked that she call him at her earliest convenience. Crumbling up the pink slip, she tossed it in the green metal wastebasket beside her desk. She might be attending this party, but it was under duress. And as far as Andrew was concerned, she had every intention of avoiding him.

Rather than rush back to the apartment after work, Jo Marie had dinner in a small café near her office. From there she walked to the Land For The Future headquarters.

She was embarrassingly early when she arrived outside of the office door. The foundation's headquarters were on the second floor of an older brick building in a bad part of town. Jo Marie decided to arrive earlier than she'd planned rather than kill time by walking around outside. From the time she'd left the travel agency, she'd wandered around with little else to do. Her greatest fear was that Andrew would be waiting for her at the apartment. She hadn't returned his call and he'd want to know why.

Jim Rowden, the office manager and spokesman, was busy on the telephone when Jo Marie arrived. Quietly she slipped into the chair at the desk opposite him and glanced over the letters and other notices that needed to be typed. As she pulled the cover from the top of the typewriter, Jo Marie noticed a shadowy movement from the other side of the milky white glass inset of the office door.

She stood to investigate and found a dark-haired man with a worn felt hat that fit loosely on top of his head. His clothes were ragged and the faint odor of cheap wine permeated the air. He was curling up in the doorway of an office nearest theirs.

His eyes met hers briefly and he tugged his thin sweater around his shoulders. "Are you going to throw me out of here?" The words were issued in subtle challenge.

Jo Marie teetered with indecision. If she did tell him to leave he'd either spend the night shivering in the cold or find another open building. On the other hand if she were to give him money, she was confident it wouldn't be a bed he'd spend it on.

"Well?" he challenged again.

"I won't say anything," she answered finally. "Just go down to the end of the hall so no one else will find you."

He gave her a look of mild surprise, stood and gathered his coat before turning and ambling down the long hall in an uneven gait. Jo Marie waited until he was curled up in another doorway. It was difficult to see that he was there without looking for him. A soft smile of satisfaction stole across her face as she closed the door and returned to her desk.

Jim replaced the receiver and smiled a welcome at Jo Marie. "How'd you like to attend a lecture with me tonight?"

"I'd like it fine," she agreed eagerly.

Jim's lecture was to a group of concerned city businessmen. He relayed the facts about the dangers of thoughtless and haphazard land development. He presented his case in a simple, straightforward fashion without emotionalism or sensationalism. In addition, he confidently answered their questions, defining the difference between building for the future and preserving a link with the past. Jo Marie was impressed and from the looks on the faces of his audience, the businessmen had been equally affected.

"I'll walk you to the bus stop," Jim told her hours later after they'd returned from the meeting. "I don't like the idea of you waiting at the bus stop alone. I'll go with you."

Jo Marie hadn't been that thrilled with the prospect herself. "Thanks, I'd appreciate that."

Jim's hand cupped her elbow as they leisurely strolled down the narrow street, chatting as they went. Jim's voice was drawling and smooth and Jo Marie mused that she could listen to him all night. The lamplight illuminated little in the descending fog and would have created an eerie feeling if Jim hadn't been at her side. But walking with him, she barely noticed the weather and instead found herself laughing at his subtle humor.

"How'd you ever get into this business?" she queried. Jim Rowden was an intelligent, warm human being who would be a success in any field he chose to pursue. He could be making twice and three times the money in the business world that he collected from the foundation.

At first introduction, Jim wasn't the kind of man who would bowl women over with his striking good looks or his suave manners. But he was a rare, dedicated man of conscience. Jo Marie had never known anyone like him and admired him greatly.

"I'm fairly new with the foundation," he admitted, "and it certainly wasn't what I'd been expecting to do with my life, especially since I struggled through college for a degree in biology. Afterward I went to work for the state, but this job gives me the opportunity to work first hand with saving some of the— well, you heard my speech."

"Yes, I did, and it was wonderful."

"You're good for my ego, Jo Marie. I hope you'll stick around."

Jo Marie's eyes glanced up the street, wondering how long they'd have to wait for a bus. She didn't want their discussion to end. As she did, a flash of midnight blue captured her attention and her heart dropped to her knees as the Mercedes pulled to a stop alongside the curb in front of them.

Andrew practically leaped from the driver's side. "Just what do you think you're doing?" The harsh anger in his voice shocked her.

"I beg your pardon?" Jim answered on Jo Marie's bchalf, taking a step forward.

Andrew ignored Jim, his eyes cold and piercing as he glanced over her. "I've spent the good part of an hour looking for you."

"Why?" Jo Marie demanded, tilting her chin in an act of defiance. "What business is it of yours where I am or who I'm with?"

"I'm making it my business."

"Is there a problem here, Jo Marie?" Jim questioned as he stepped forward.

"None whatsoever," she responded dryly and crossed her arms in front of her.

"Kelly's worried sick," Andrew hissed. "Now I suggest you get in the car and let me take you home before...." He let the rest of what he was saying die. He paused for several tense moments and exhaled a sharp breath. "I apologize, I had no right to come at you like that." He closed the car door and moved around the front of the Mercedes. "I'm Andrew Beaumont," he introduced himself and extended his hand to Jim.

"From Delta Development?" Jim's eyes widened appreciatively. "Jim Rowden. I've been wanting to meet you so that I could thank you personally for what you did for Rose's Hotel."

"I'm pleased I could help."

When Andrew decided to put on the charm it was like falling into a jar of pure honey, Jo Marie thought. She didn't know of a man, woman or child who couldn't be swayed by his beguiling showmanship. Having been under his spell in the past made it all the more recognizable now. But somehow, she realized, this was different. Andrew hadn't been acting the night of the Mardi Gras, she was convinced of that.

"Jo Marie was late coming home and luckily I remembered her saying something about volunteering for the foundation. Kelly asked that I come and get her. We were understandably worried about her taking the bus alone at this time of night."

"I'll admit I was a bit concerned myself," Jim returned, taking a step closer to Jo Marie. "That's why I'm here."

As Andrew opened the passenger's side of the car, Jo Marie turned her head to meet his gaze, her eyes fiery as she slid into the plush velvet seat.

"I'll see you Friday," she said to Jim.

"Enjoy Mexico," he responded and waved before turning and walking back toward the office building. A fine mist filled the evening air and Jim pulled up his collar as he hurried along the sidewalk.

Andrew didn't say a word as he turned the key in the ignition, checked the rearview mirror and pulled back onto the street.

"You didn't return my call." He stopped at a red light and the full force of his magnetic gray eyes was turned on her.

"No," she answered in a whisper, struggling not to reveal how easily he could affect her.

"Can't you see how important it is that we talk?"

"No." She wanted to shout the word. When their eyes met, Jo Marie was startled to find that only a few inches separated them. Andrew's look was centered on her mouth and with a determined effort she averted her gaze and stared out the side window. "I don't want to talk to you." Her fingers fumbled with the clasp of her purse in nervous agitation. "There's nothing more we can say." She hated the husky emotion-filled way her voice sounded.

"Jo Marie." He said her name so softly that she wasn't entirely sure he'd spoken.

She turned back to him, knowing she should pull away from the hypnotic darkness of his eyes, but doing so was impossible.

"You'll come to my party?"

She wanted to explain her decision to attend—she hadn't wanted to go—but one glance at Andrew said that he understood. Words were unnecessary.

"It's going to be difficult for us both for a while."

He seemed to imply things would grow easier with time. Jo Marie sincerely doubted that they ever would.

"You'll come?" he prompted softly.

Slowly she nodded. Jo Marie hadn't realized how tense she was until she exhaled and felt some of the coiled tightness leave her body. "Yes, I'll...be at the party." Her breathy stammer spoke volumes.

"And wear the dress I gave you?"

She ended up nodding again, her tongue unable to form words.

"I've dreamed of you walking into my arms wearing that dress," he added on a husky tremor, then shook his head as if he regretted having spoken.

Being alone with him in the close confines of the car was torture. Her once restless fingers lay limp in her lap. Jo Marie didn't know how she was going to avoid Andrew when Kelly seemed to be constantly throwing them together. But she must for her own peace of mind...she must.

All too quickly the brief respite of her trip to Mazatlán was over. Saturday arrived and Kelly and Jo Marie were brought to Andrew's home, which was a faithful reproduction of an antebellum mansion.

The dress he'd purchased was hanging in the closet of the bedroom she was to share with Kelly. Her friend threw herself across the canopy bed and exhaled on a happy sigh.

"Isn't this place something?"

Jo Marie didn't answer for a moment, her gaze falling on the dress that hung alone in the closet. "It's magnificent." There was little else that would describe this palace. The house was a three-story structure with huge white pillars and dark shutters. It faced the Mississippi River and had a huge garden in the back. Jo Marie learned that it was his mother who took an avid interest in the wide variety of flowers that grew in abundance there.

The rooms were large, their walls adorned with paintings and works of art. If Jo Marie was ever to doubt Andrew's wealth and position, his home would prove to be a constant reminder.

"Drew built it himself," Kelly explained with a proud lilt to her voice. "I don't mean he pounded in every nail, but he was here every day while it was being constructed. It took months."

"I can imagine." And no expense had been spared from the look of things.

"I suppose we should think about getting ready," Kelly continued. "I don't mind telling you that I've had a queasy stomach all day dreading this thing."

Kelly had! Jo Marie nearly laughed aloud. This party had haunted her all week. Even Mazatlán hadn't been far enough away to dispel the feeling of dread.

Jo Marie could hear the music drifting in from the reception hall by the time she had put on the finishing touches of her makeup. Kelly had already joined Andrew. A quick survey in the full-length mirror assured her that the beautiful gown was the most elegant thing she would ever own. The reflection that came back to her of a tall, regal woman was barely recognizable as herself. The dark crown of curls was styled on top of her head with a few stray tendrils curling about her ears. A lone strand of pearls graced her neck.

Self-consciously she moved from the room, closing the door. From the top of the winding stairway, she looked down on a milling crowd of arriving guests. Holding in her breath, she placed her gloved hand on the polished bannister, exhaled, and made her descent. Keeping her eyes on her feet for fear of tripping, Jo Marie was surprised when she glanced down to find Andrew waiting for her at the bottom of the staircase.

As he gave her his hand, their eyes met and held in a tender exchange. "You're beautiful."

The deep husky tone in his voice took her breath away and Jo Marie could do nothing more than smile in return.

Taking her hand, Andrew tucked it securely in the crook of his elbow and led her into the room where the other guests were mingling. Everyone was meeting for drinks in the huge living room and once the

party was complete they would be moving up to the
ballroom on the third floor. The evening was to cul-
minate in a midnight buffet.

With Andrew holding her close by his side, Jo Marie had little option but to follow where he led. Moving from one end of the room to the other, he introduced her to so many people that her head swam
trying to remember their names. Fortunately, Kelly
and Andrew's engagement hadn't been officially announced and Jo Marie wasn't forced to make repeated
explanations. Nonetheless, she was uncomfortable
with the way he was linking the two of them together.

"Where's Kelly?" Jo Marie asked under her
breath. "She should be the one with you. Not me."

"Kelly's with Mark on the other side of the room."

Jo Marie faltered in midstep and Andrew's hold
tightened as he dropped his arm and slipped it around
her slim waist. "With Mark?" She couldn't imagine
her brother attending this party. Not feeling the way
he did about Andrew.

Not until they were upstairs and the music was
playing did Jo Marie have an opportunity to talk to
her brother. He was sitting against the wall in a high-
backed mahogany chair with a velvet cushion. Kelly
was at his side. Jo Marie couldn't recall a time she'd
seen her brother dress so formally or look more handsome. He'd had his hair trimmed and was clean
shaven. She'd never dreamed she'd see Mark in a
tuxedo.

"Hello, Mark."

Her brother looked up, guilt etched on his face. "Jo
Marie." Briefly he exchanged looks with Kelly and
stood, offering Jo Marie his seat.

"Thanks," she said as she sat and slipped the high-heeled sandals from her toes. "My feet could use a few moments' rest."

"You certainly haven't lacked for partners," Kelly observed happily. "You're a hit, Jo Marie. Even Mark was saying he couldn't believe you were his sister."

"I've never seen you look more attractive," Mark added. "But then I bet you didn't buy that dress out of petty cash either."

If there was a note of censure in her brother's voice, Jo Marie didn't hear it. "No." Absently her hand smoothed the silk skirt. "It was a gift from Andrew...and Kelly." Hastily she added her roommate's name. "I must admit though, I'm surprised to see you here."

"Andrew extended the invitation personally," Mark replied, holding his back ramrod stiff as he stared straight ahead.

Not understanding, Jo Marie glanced at her roommate. "Mark came for me," Kelly explained, her voice soft and vulnerable. "Because I...because I wanted him here."

"We're both here for you, Kelly," Jo Marie reminded her and punctuated her comment by arching her brows.

"I know, and I love you both for it."

"Would you care to dance?" Mark held out his hand to Kelly, taking her into his arms when they reached the boundary of the dance floor as if he never wanted to let her go.

Confused, Jo Marie watched their progress. Kelly was engaged to be married to Andrew, yet she was gazing into Mark's eyes as if he were her knight in shining armor who had come to slay dragons on her behalf. When she'd come upon them, they'd acted as if she had intruded on their very private party.

Jo Marie saw Andrew approach her, his brows lowered as if something had displeased him. His strides were quick and decisive as he wove his way through the throng of guests.

"I've been looking for you. In fact, I was beginning to wonder if I'd ever get a chance to dance with you." The pitch of his voice suggested that she'd been deliberately avoiding him. And she had.

Jo Marie couldn't bring herself to meet his gaze, afraid of what he could read in her eyes. All night she'd been pretending it was Andrew who was holding her and yet she'd known she wouldn't be satisfied until he did.

"I believe this dance is mine," he said, presenting her with his hand.

Peering up at him, a smile came and she paused to slip the strap of her high heel over her ankle before standing.

Once on the dance floor, his arms tightened around her waist, bringing her so close that there wasn't a hair's space between them. He held her securely as if challenging her to move. Jo Marie discovered that she couldn't. This inexplicable feeling was beyond argument. With her hands resting on his muscular shoulders, she leaned her head against his broad chest and sighed her contentment.

She spoke first. "It's a wonderful party."

"You're more comfortable now, aren't you?" His fingers moved up and down her back in a leisurely exercise, drugging her with his firm caress against her bare skin.

"What do you mean?" She wasn't sure she understood his question and slowly lifted her gaze.

"Last week, you stayed on the outskirts of the crowd afraid of joining in or being yourself."

"Last week I was terrified that someone would recognize me as the one who had once demonstrated against you. I didn't want to do anything that would embarrass you," she explained dryly. Her cheek was pressed against his starched shirt and she thrilled to the uneven thump of his heart.

"And this week?"

"Tonight anyone who looked at us would know that we've long since resolved our differences."

She sensed more than felt Andrew's soft touch. The moment was quickly becoming too intimate. Using her hands for leverage, Jo Marie straightened, creating a space between them. "Does it bother you to have my brother dance with Kelly?"

Andrew looked back at her blankly. "No. Should it?"

"She's your fiancée." To the best of Jo Marie's knowledge, Andrew hadn't said more than a few words to Kelly all evening.

A cloud of emotion darkened his face. "She's wearing my ring."

"And...and you care for her."

Andrew's hold tightened painfully around her waist. "Yes, I care for Kelly. We've always been close." His eyes darkened to the color of burnt silver. "Perhaps too close."

The applause was polite when the dance number finished.

Jo Marie couldn't escape fast enough. She made an excuse and headed for the powder room. Andrew wasn't pleased and it showed in the grim set of his mouth, but he didn't try to stop her. Things weren't right. Mark shouldn't be sitting like an avenging angel at Kelly's side and Andrew should at least show some sign of jealousy.

When she returned to the ballroom, Andrew was busy and Jo Marie decided to sort through her thoughts in the fresh night air. A curtained glass door that led to the balcony was open, and unnoticed she slipped silently into the dark. A flash of white captured her attention and Jo Marie realized she wasn't alone. Inadvertently, she had invaded the private world of two young lovers. With their arms wrapped around each other they were locked in a passionate embrace. Smiling softly to herself, she turned to escape as silently as she'd come. But something stopped her. A sickening knot tightened her stomach.

The couple so passionately embracing were Kelly and Mark.

Chapter Six

Jo Marie woke just as dawn broke over a cloudless horizon. Standing at the bedroom window, she pressed her palms against the sill and surveyed the beauty of the landscape before her. Turning, she glanced at Kelly's sleeping figure. Her hands fell limply to her side as her face darkened with uncertainty. Last night while they'd prepared for bed, Jo Marie had been determined to confront her friend with the kiss she'd unintentionally witnessed. But when they'd turned out the lights, Kelly had chatted happily about the success of the party and what a good time she'd had. And Jo Marie had lost her nerve. What Mark and Kelly did wasn't any of her business, she mused. In addition, she had no right to judge her brother and her friend when she and Andrew had done the same thing.

The memory of Andrew's kiss produce a breathlessness, and surrendering to the feeling, Jo Marie closed her eyes. The infinitely sweet touch of his mouth seemed to have branded her. Her fingers shook as she raised them to the gentle curve of her lips. Jo Marie doubted that she would ever feel the same overpowering rush of sensation at another man's touch. Andrew was special, her dream man. Whole lifetimes could pass and she'd never find anyone she'd love more. The powerful ache in her heart drove her to the closet where a change of clothes were hanging.

Dawn's light was creeping up the stairs, awaking a sleeping world, when Jo Marie softly clicked the bedroom door closed. Her overnight bag was clenched tightly in her hand. She hated to sneak out, but the thought of facing everyone over the breakfast table was more than she could bear. Andrew and Kelly needed to be alone. Time together was something they hadn't had much of lately. This morning would be the perfect opportunity for them to sit down and discuss their coming marriage. Jo Marie would only be an intruder.

Moving so softly that no one was likely to hear her, Jo Marie crept down the stairs to the wide entry hall. She was tiptoeing toward the front door when a voice behind her interrupted her quiet departure.

"What do you think you're doing?"

Releasing a tiny, startled cry, Jo Marie dropped the suitcase and held her hand to her breast.

"Andrew, you've frightened me to death."

"Just what are you up to?"

"I'm...I'm leaving."

"That's fairly easy to ascertain. What I want to

know is why." His angry gaze locked with hers, refusing to allow her to turn away.

"I thought you and Kelly should spend some time together and...and I wanted to be gone this morning before everyone woke." Regret crept into her voice. Maybe sneaking out like this wasn't such a fabulous idea, after all.

He stared at her in the dim light as if he could examine her soul with his penetrating gaze. When he spoke again, his tone was lighter. "And just how did you expect to get to town. Walk?"

"Exactly."

"But it's miles."

"All the more reason to get an early start," she reasoned.

Andrew studied her as though he couldn't believe what he was hearing. "Is running away so important that you would sneak out of here like a cat burglar and not tell anyone where you're headed?"

How quickly her plan had backfired. By trying to leave unobtrusively she'd only managed to offend Andrew when she had every reason to thank him. "I didn't mean to be rude, although I can see now that I have been. I suppose this makes me look like an ungrateful house guest."

His answer was to narrow his eyes fractionally.

"I want you to know I left a note that explained where I was going to both you and Kelly. It's on the nightstand."

"And what did you say?"

"That I enjoyed the party immensely and that I've never felt more beautiful in any dress."

A brief troubled look stole over Andrew's face.

"Once," he murmured absently. "Only onece have you been more lovely." There was an unexpectedly gentle quality to his voice.

Her eyelashes fluttered closed. Andrew was reminding her of that February night. He too hadn't been able to forget the Mardi Gras. After all this time, after everything that had transpired since, neither of them could forget. The spell was as potent today as it had been those many months ago.

"Is that coffee I smell?" The question sought an invitation to linger with Andrew. Her original intent had been to escape so that Kelly could have the opportunity to spend this time alone with him. Instead, Jo Marie was seeking it herself. To sit in the early light of dawn and savor a few solitary minutes alone with Andrew was too tempting to ignore.

"Come and I'll get you a cup." Andrew led her toward the back of the house and his den. The room held a faint scent of leather and tobacco that mingled with the aroma of musk and spice.

Three walls were lined with leather-bound books that reached from the floor to the ceiling. Two wing chairs were angled in front of a large fireplace.

"Go ahead and sit down. I'll be back in a moment with the coffee."

A contented smile brightened Jo Marie's eyes as she sat and noticed the leather volume she'd given him lying open on the ottoman. Apparently he'd been reading it when he heard the noise at the front of the house and had left to investigate.

Andrew returned and carefully handed her the steaming earthenware mug. His eyes followed her gaze which rested on the open book. "I've been read-

ing it. This is a wonderful book. Where did you ever
find something like this?''

"I've known about it for a long time, but there
were only a few volumes available. I located this one
about three months ago in a used-book store.''

"It's very special to me because of the woman who
bought it for me.''

"No.'' Jo Marie's eyes widened as she lightly
tossed her head from side to side. "Don't let that be
the reason. Appreciate the book for all the interesting
details it gives of New Orleans' colorful past. Or admire the pictures of the city architects' skill. But don't
treasure it because of me.''

Andrew looked for a moment as if he wanted to
argue, but she spoke again.

"When you read this book ten, maybe twenty,
years from now, I'll only be someone who briefly
passed through your life. I imagine you'll have trouble remembering what I looked like.''

"You'll never be anyone who flits in and out of
my life.''

He said it with such intensity that Jo Marie's fingers tightened around the thick handle of the mug.
"All right,'' she agreed with a shaky laugh. "I'll admit I barged into your peaceful existence long before
Kelly introduced us but—''

"But,'' Andrew interrupted on a short laugh, "it
seems we were destined to meet. Do you honestly
believe that either of us will ever forget that night?''
A faint smile touched his eyes as he regarded her
steadily.

Jo Marie knew that she never would. Andrew was
her dream man. It had been far more than mere fate

that had brought them together, something almost spiritual.

"No," she answered softly. "I'll never forget."

Regret moved across his features, creasing his wide brow and pinching his mouth. "Nor will I forget," he murmured in a husky voice that sounded very much like a vow.

The air between them was electric. For months she'd thought of Andrew as the dream man. But coming to know him these past weeks had proven that he wasn't an apparition, but real. Human, vulnerable, proud, intelligent, generous—and everything that she had ever hoped to find in a man. She lowered her gaze and studied the dark depths of the steaming coffee. Andrew might be everything she had ever wanted in a man, but Kelly wore his ring and her roommate's stake on him was far more tangible than her own romantic dreams.

Taking an exaggerated drink of her coffee, Jo Marie carefully set aside the rose-colored mug and stood. "I really should be leaving."

"Please stay," Andrew requested. "Just sit with me a few minutes longer. It's been in this room that I've sat and thought about you so often. I'd always hoped that someday you would join me here."

Jo Marie dipped her head, her heart singing with the beauty of his words. She'd fantasized about him too. Since their meeting, her mind had conjured up his image so often that it wouldn't hurt to steal a few more moments of innocent happiness. Kelly would have him for a lifetime. Jo Marie had only today.

"I'll stay," she agreed and her voice throbbed with the excited beat of her heart.

"And when the times comes, I'll drive you back to the city."

She nodded her acceptance and finished her coffee. "It's so peaceful in here. It feels like all I need to do is lean my head back, close my eyes and I'll be asleep."

"Go ahead," he urged in a whispered tone.

A smile touched her radiant features. She didn't want to fall asleep and miss these precious moments alone with him. "No." She shook her head. "Tell me about yourself. I want to know everything."

His returning smile was wry. "I'd hate to bore you."

"Bore me!" Her small laugh was incredulous. "There's no chance of that."

"All right, but lay back and close your eyes and let me start by telling you that I had a good childhood with parents who deeply loved each other."

As he requested, Jo Marie rested her head against the cushion and closed her eyes. "My parents are wonderful too."

"But being raised in an ideal family has its drawbacks," Andrew continued in a low, soothing voice. "When it came time for me to think about a wife and starting a family there was always a fear in the back of my mind that I would never find the happiness my parents shared. My father wasn't an easy man to love. And I won't be either."

In her mind, Jo Marie took exception to that, but she said nothing. The room was warm, and slipping off her shoes, she tucked her nylon-covered feet under her. Andrew continued speaking, his voice droning on as she tilted her head back.

"When I reached thirty without finding a wife, I became skeptical about the women I was meeting. There were some who never saw past the dollar signs and others who were interested only in themselves. I wanted a woman who could be soft and yielding, but one who wasn't afraid to fight for what she believes, even if it meant standing up against tough opposition. I wanted someone who would share my joys and divide my worries. A woman as beautiful on the inside as any outward beauty she may possess."

"Kelly's like that." The words nearly stuck in Jo Marie's throat. Kelly was everything Andrew was describing and more. As painful as it was to admit, Jo Marie understood why Andrew had asked her roommate to marry him. In addition to her fine personal qualities, Kelly had money of her own and Andrew need never think that she was marrying him for any financial gains.

"Yes, Kelly's like that." There was a doleful timbre to his voice that caused Jo Marie to open her eyes.

Fleetingly she wondered if Andrew had seen Mark and Kelly kissing on the terrace last night. If he had created the picture of a perfect woman in his mind, then finding Kelly in Mark's arms could destroy him. No matter how uncomfortable it became, Jo Marie realized she was going to have to confront Mark about his behavior. Having thoughtfully analyzed the situation, Jo Marie believed it would be far better for her to talk to her brother. She could speak more freely with him. It may be the hardest thing she'd ever do, but after listening to Andrew, Jo Marie realized that she must talk to Mark. The happiness of too many people was at stake.

Deciding to change the subject, Jo Marie shifted her position in the supple leather chair and looked to Andrew. "Kelly told me that you built the house yourself."

Grim amusement was carved in his features. "Yes, the work began on it this spring."

"Then you've only been living in it a few months?"

"Yes. The construction on the house kept me from going insane." He held her look, revealing nothing of his thoughts.

"Going insane?" Jo Marie didn't understand.

"You see, for a short time last February, only a matter of moments really, I felt my search for the right woman was over. And in those few, scant moments I thought I had met that special someone I could love for all time."

Jo Marie's heart was pounding so fast and loud that she wondered why it didn't burst right out of her chest. The thickening in her throat made swallowing painful. Each breath became labored as she turned her face away, unable to meet Andrew's gaze.

"But after those few minutes, I lost her," Andrew continued. "Ironically, I'd searched a lifetime for that special woman, and within a matter of minutes, she was gone. God knows I tried to find her again. For a month I went back to the spot where I'd last seen her and waited. When it seemed that all was lost I discovered I couldn't get the memory of her out of my mind. I even hired a detective to find her for me. For months he checked every hospital in the city, searching for her. But you see, at the time I thought she was a nurse."

Jo Marie felt moisture gathering in the corner of her eyes. Never had she believed that Andrew had looked for her to the extent that he hired someone.

"For a time I was convinced I was going insane. This woman, whose name I didn't even know, filled my every waking moment and haunted my sleep. Building the house was something I've always wanted to do. It helped fill the time until I could find her again. Every room was constructed with her in mind."

Andrew was explaining that he'd built the house for her. Jo Marie had thought she'd be uncomfortable in such a magnificent home. But she'd immediately felt the welcome in the walls. Little had she dreamed the reason why.

"Sometimes," Jo Marie began awkwardly, "people build things up in their minds and when they're confronted with reality they're inevitably disappointed." Andrew was making her out to be wearing angel's wings. So much time had passed that he no longer saw her as flesh and bone, but a wonderful fantasy his mind had created.

"Not this time," he countered smoothly.

"I wondered where I'd find the two of you." A sleepy-eyed Kelly stood poised in the doorway of the den. There wasn't any censure in her voice, only her usual morning brightness. "Isn't it a marvelous morning? The sun's up and there's a bright new day just waiting for us."

Self-consciously, Jo Marie unwound her feet from beneath her and reached for her shoes. "What time is it?"

"A quarter to eight." Andrew supplied the information.

Jo Marie was amazed to realize that she'd spent the better part of two hours talking to him. But it would be time she'd treasure all her life.

"If you have no objections," Kelly murmured and paused to take a wide yawn, "I thought I'd go to the hospital this morning. There's a special...patient I'd like to stop in and visit."

A patient or Mark, Jo Marie wanted to ask. Her brother had mentioned last night that he was going to be on duty in the morning. Jo Marie turned to Andrew, waiting for a reaction from him. Surely he would say or do something to stop her. Kelly was his fiancée and both of them seemed to be regarding their commitment to each other lightly.

"No problem." Andrew spoke at last. "In fact I thought I'd go into the city myself this morning. It is a beautiful day and there's no better way to spend a portion of it than in the most beautiful city in the world. You don't mind if I tag along with you, do you, Jo Marie?"

Half of her wanted to cry out in exaltation. If there was anything she wished to give of herself to Andrew it was her love of New Orleans. But at the same time she wanted to shake both Andrew and Kelly for the careless attitude they had toward their relationship.

"I'd like you to come." Jo Marie spoke finally, answering Andrew.

It didn't take Kelly more than a few moments to pack her things and be ready to leave. In her rush, she'd obviously missed the two sealed envelopes Jo Marie had left propped against the lamp on Kelly's nightstand. Or if she had discovered them, Kelly chose not to mention it. Not that it mattered, Jo Marie decided as Andrew started the car. But Kelly's actions revealed what a rush she was in to see Mark. If it was Mark that she was indeed seeing. Confused emotions flooded Jo Marie's face, pinching lines around her nose and mouth. She could feel Andrew's caressing gaze as they drove toward the hospital.

"Is something troubling you?" Andrew questioned after they'd dropped Kelly off in front of Tulane Hospital. Amid protests from Jo Marie, Kelly had assured them that she would find her own way home. Standing on the sidewalk, she'd given Jo Marie a happy wave, before turning and walking toward the double glass doors that led to the lobby of the hospital.

"I think Kelly's going to see Mark," Jo Marie ventured in a short, rueful voice.

"I think she is too."

Jo Marie sat up sharply. "And that doesn't bother you?"

"Should it?" Andrew gave her a bemused look.

"Yes," she said and nodded emphatically. She would never have believed that Andrew could be so blind. "Yes, it should make you furious."

He turned and smiled briefly. "But it doesn't. Now tell me where you'd like to eat breakfast. Brennan's?"

Jo Marie felt trapped in a labyrinth in which no route made sense and from which she could see no escape. She was thoroughly confused by the actions of the three people she loved.

"I don't understand any of this," she cried in frustration. "You should be livid that Kelly and Mark are together."

A furrow of absent concentration darkened Andrew's brow as he drove. Briefly he glanced in her direction. "The time will come when you do understand," he explained cryptically.

Rubbing the side of her neck in agitation, Jo Marie studied Andrew as he drove. His answer made no sense, but little about anyone's behavior this last month had made sense. She hadn't pictured herself as being obtuse, but obviously she was.

Breakfast at Brennan's was a treat known throughout the south. The restaurant was built in the classic Vieux Carre style complete with courtyard. Because they didn't have a reservation, they were put on a waiting list and told it would be another hour before there would be a table available. Andrew eyed Jo Marie, who nodded eagerly. For all she'd heard, the breakfast was worth the wait.

Taking her hand in his, they strolled down the quiet streets that comprised the French Quarter. Most of the stores were closed, the streets deserted.

"I was reading just this morning that the French established New Orleans in 1718. The Spanish took over the 3,000 French inhabitants in 1762, although there were so few Spaniards that barely anyone noticed until 1768. The French Quarter is like a city within a city."

Jo Marie smiled contentedly and looped her hand through his arm. "You mean to tell me that it takes a birthday present for you to know about your own fair city?"

Andrew chuckled and drew her closer by circling

his arm around her shoulders. "Are you always snobbish or is this act for my benefit?"

They strolled for what seemed far longer than a mere hour, visiting Jackson Square and feeding the pigeons. Strolling back, with Andrew at her side, Jo Marie felt she would never be closer to heaven. Never would she want for anything more than today, this minute, with this man. Jo Marie felt tears mist her dusty eyes. A tremulous smile touched her mouth. Andrew was here with her. Within a short time he would be married to Kelly and she must accept that, but for now, he was hers.

The meal was everything they'd been promised. Ham, soft breads fresh from the bakery, eggs and a fabulous chicory coffee. A couple of times Jo Marie found herself glancing at Andrew. His expression revealed little and she wondered if he regretted having decided to spend this time with her. She prayed that wasn't the case.

When they stood to leave, Andrew reached for her hand and smiled down on her with shining gray eyes.

Jo Marie's heart throbbed with love. The radiant light of her happiness shone through when Andrew's arm slipped naturally around her shoulder as if branding her with his seal of protection.

"I enjoy being with you," he said and she couldn't doubt the sincerity in his voice. "You're the kind of woman who would be as much at ease at a formal ball as you would fishing from the riverside with rolled-up jeans."

"I'm not Huck Finn," she teased.

"No," he smiled, joining in her game. "Just my

Florence Nightingale, the woman who has haunted me for the last nine months.''

Self-consciously, Jo Marie eased the strap of her leather purse over her shoulder. ''It's always been my belief that dreams have a way of fading, especially when faced with the bright light of the sun and reality.''

''Normally, I'd agree with you,'' Andrew responded thoughtfully, ''but not this time. There are moments so rare in one's life that recognizing what they are can sometimes be doubted. Of you, of that night, of us, I have no doubts.''

''None?'' Jo Marie barely recognized her own voice.

''None,'' he confirmed.

If that were so, then why did Kelly continue to wear his ring? How could he look at her with so much emotion and then ask another woman to share his life?

The ride to Jo Marie's apartment was accomplished in a companionable silence. Andrew pulled into the parking space and turned off the ignition. Jo Marie's gaze centered on the dashboard. Silently she'd hoped that he wouldn't come inside with her. The atmosphere when they were alone was volatile. And with everything that Andrew had told her this morning, Jo Marie doubted that she'd have the strength to stay out of his arms if he reached for her.

''I can see myself inside.'' Gallantly, she made an effort to avoid temptation.

''Nonsense,'' Andrew returned, and opening the car door, he removed her overnight case from the back seat.

Jo Marie opened her side and climbed out, not waiting for him to come around. A feeling of doom settled around her heart.

Her hand was steady as she inserted the key into the apartment lock, but that was the only thing that was. Her knees felt like rubber as the door swung open and she stepped inside the room, standing in the entryway. The drapes were pulled, blocking out the sunlight, making the apartment's surroundings all the more intimate.

"I have so much to thank you for," she began and nervously tugged a strand of dark hair behind her ear. "A simple thank you seems like so little." She hoped Andrew understood that she didn't want him to come any farther into the apartment.

The door clicked closed and her heart sank. "Where would you like me to put your suitcase?"

Determined not to make this situation any worse for them, Jo Marie didn't move. "Just leave it here."

A smoldering light of amused anger burned in his eyes as he set the suitcase down. "There's no help for this," he whispered as his hand slid slowly, almost unwillingly along the back of her waist. "Be angry with me later."

Any protests died the moment his mouth met hers in a demanding kiss. An immediate answering hunger seared through her veins, melting all resistance until she was molded against the solid wall of his chest. His caressing fingers explored the curve of her neck and shoulders and his mouth followed, blazing a trail that led back to her waiting lips.

Jo Marie rotated her head, giving him access to any part of her face that his hungry mouth desired. She

offered no protest when his hands sought the fullness
of her breast, then sighed with the way her body responded to the gentleness of his fingers. He kissed
her expertly, his mobile mouth moving insistently
over hers, teasing her with light, biting nips that made
her yearn for more and more. Then he'd change his
tactics and kiss her with a hungry demand. Lost in a
mindless haze, she clung to him as the tears filled her
eyes and ran unheeded down her cheeks. Everything
she feared was happening. And worse, she was powerless to stop him. Her throat felt dry and scratchy
and she uttered a soft sob in a effort to abate the flow
of emotion.

Andrew went still. He cupped her face in his hands
and examined her tear-streaked cheeks. His troubled
expression swam in and out of her vision.

"Jo Marie," he whispered, his voice tortured.
"Don't cry, darling, please don't cry." With an infinite tenderness he kissed away each tear and when
he reached her trembling mouth, the taste of salt was
on his lips. A series of long, drugging kisses only
confused her more. It didn't seem possible she could
want him so much and yet that it should be so wrong.

"Please." With every ounce of strength she possessed Jo Marie broke from his embrace. "I promised
myself this wouldn't happen again," she whispered
feeling miserable. Standing with her back to him, her
hands cradled her waist to ward off a sudden chill.

Gently he pressed his hand to her shoulder and Jo
Marie couldn't bring herself to brush it away. Even
his touch had the power to disarm her.

"Jo Marie." His husky tone betrayed the depths of
his turmoil. "Listen to me."

"No, what good would it do?" she asked on a quavering sob. "You're engaged to be married to my best friend. I can't help the way I feel about you. What I feel, what you feel, is wrong as long as Kelly's wearing your ring." With a determined effort she turned to face him, tears blurring her sad eyes. "It would be better if we didn't see each other again...at least until you're sure of what you want..or who you want."

Andrew jerked his hand through his hair. "You're right. I've got to get this mess straightened out."

"Promise me, Andrew, please promise me that you won't make an effort to see me until you know in your own mind what you want. I can't take much more of this." She wiped the moisture from her cheekbones with the tips of her fingers. "When I get up in the morning I want to look at myself in the mirror. I don't want to hate myself."

Andrew's mouth tightened with grim displeasure. He looked as if he wanted to argue. Tense moments passed before he slowly shook his head. "You deserve to be treated so much better than this. Someday, my love, you'll understand. Just trust me for now."

"I'm only asking one thing of you," she said unable to meet his gaze. "Don't touch me or make an effort to see me as long as Kelly's wearing your ring. It's not fair to any one of us." Her lashes fell to veil the hurt in her eyes. Andrew couldn't help but know that she was in love with him. She would have staked her life that her feelings were returned full measure. Fresh tears misted her eyes.

"I don't want to leave you like this."

"I'll be all right," she murmured miserably.

"There's nothing that I can do. Everything rests with you, Andrew. Everything."

Dejected, he nodded and added a promise. "I'll take care of it today."

Again Jo Marie wiped the wetness from her face and forced a smile, but the effort was almost more than she could bear.

The door clicked, indicating that Andrew had gone and Jo Marie released a long sigh of pent-up emotion. Her reflection in the bathroom mirror showed that her lips were parted and trembling from the hungry possession of his mouth. Her eyes had darkened from the strength of her physical response.

Andrew had asked that she trust him and she would, with all her heart. He loved her, she was sure of it. He wouldn't have hired a detective to find her or built a huge home with her in mind if he didn't feel something strong toward her. Nor could he have held her and kissed her the way he had today without loving and needing her.

While she unpacked the small overnight bag a sense of peace came over her. Andrew would explain everything to Kelly, and she needn't worry. Kelly's interests seemed to be centered more on Mark lately, and maybe...just maybe, she wouldn't be hurt or upset and would accept that neither Andrew nor Jo Marie had planned for this to happen.

Time hung heavily on her hands and Jo Marie toyed with the idea of visiting her parents. But her mother knew her so well that she'd take one look at Jo Marie and want to know what was bothering her daughter. And today Jo Marie wasn't up to explanations.

A flip of the radio dial and Christmas music drifted into the room, surrounding her with its message of peace and love. Humming the words softly to herself, Jo Marie felt infinitely better. Everything was going to be fine, she felt confident.

A thick Sunday paper held her attention for the better part of an hour, but at the slightest noise, Jo Marie's attention wandered from the printed page and she glanced up expecting Kelly. One look at her friend would be enough to tell Jo Marie everything she needed to know.

Setting the paper aside, Jo Marie felt her nerves tingle with expectancy. She felt weighted with a terrible guilt. Kelly obviously loved Andrew enough to agree to be his wife, but she showed all the signs of falling in love with Mark. Kelly wasn't the kind of girl who would purposely hurt or lead a man on. She was too sensitive for that. And to add to the complications were Andrew and Jo Marie who had discovered each other again just when they had given up all hope. Jo Marie loved Andrew, but she wouldn't find her own happiness at her friend's expense. But Andrew was going to ask for his ring back, Jo Marie was sure of it. He'd said he'd clear things up today.

The door opened and inhaling a calming breath, Jo Marie stood.

Kelly came into the apartment, her face lowered as her gaze avoided her friend's.

"Hi," Jo Marie ventured hesitantly.

Kelly's face was red and blotchy; tears glistened in her eyes.

"Is something wrong?" Her voice faltered slightly.

"Drew and I had a fight, that's all." Kelly raised

her hand to push back her hair and as she did so the
engagement ring Andrew had given her sparkled in
the sunlight.

Jo Marie felt the knot tighten in her stomach. Andrew had made his decision.

Chapter Seven

Somehow Jo Marie made it through the following days. She didn't see Andrew and made excuses to avoid Kelly. Her efforts consisted of trying to get through each day. Once she left the office, she often went to the LFTF headquarters, spending long hours helping Jim. Their friendship had grown. Jim helped her laugh when it would have been so easy to cry. A couple of times they had coffee together and talked. But Jim did most of the talking. This pain was so all-consuming that Jo Marie felt like a newly fallen leaf tossed at will by a fickle wind.

Jim asked her to accompany him on another speaking engagement which Jo Marie did willingly. The talk was on a stretch of wetlands Jim wanted preserved and it had been well received. Silently, Jo Marie mocked herself for not being attracted to someone as wonderful as Jim Rowden. He was everything a woman could want. In addition, she was convinced that he was interested in her. But it was Andrew who continued to fill her thoughts, Andrew who haunted her dreams, Andrew whose soft whisper she heard in the wind.

Lost in the meandering trail of her musing, Jo Marie didn't hear Jim's words as they sauntered into the empty office. Her blank look prompted him to repeat himself. "I thought it went rather well tonight, didn't you?" he asked, grinning boyishly. He brushed the hair from his forehead and pulled out the chair opposite hers.

"Yes," Jo Marie agreed with an absent shake of her head. "It did go well. You're a wonderful speaker." She could feel Jim's gaze watching her and in an effort to avoid any questions, she stood and reached for her purse. "I'd better think about getting home."

"Want some company while you walk to the bus stop?"

"I brought the car tonight." She almost wished she was taking the bus. Jim was a friendly face in a world that had taken on ragged, pain-filled edges.

Kelly had been somber and sullen all week. Half the time she looked as if she were ready to burst into tears at the slightest provocation. Until this last week, Jo Marie had always viewed her roommate as an emotionally strong woman, but recently Jo Marie wondered if she really knew Kelly. Although her friend didn't enjoy large parties, she'd never known Kelly to be intimidated by them. Lately, Kelly had been playing the role of a damsel in distress to the hilt.

Mark had stopped by the apartment only once and

he'd resembled a volcano about to explode. He'd left after fifteen minutes of pacing the living-room carpet when Kelly didn't show.

And Andrew—yes, Andrew—by heaven's grace she'd been able to avoid a confrontation with him. She'd seen him only once in the last five days and the look in his eyes had seared her heart. He desperately wanted to talk to her. The tormented message was clear in his eyes, but she'd gently shaken her head, indicating that she intended to hold him to his word.

"Something's bothering you, Jo Marie. Do you want to talk about it?" Dimples edged into Jim's round face. Funny how she'd never noticed them before tonight.

Sadness touched the depths of her eyes and she gently shook her head. "Thanks, but no. Not tonight."

"Venturing a guess, I'd say it had something to do with Mr. Delta Development."

"Oh?" Clenching her purse under her arm, Jo Marie feigned ignorance. "What makes you say that?"

Jim shook his head. "A number of things." He rose and tucked both hands in his pants pockets. "Let me walk you to your car. The least I can do is see that you get safely outside."

"The weather's been exceptionally cold lately, hasn't it?"

Jim's smile was inviting as he turned the lock in the office door. "Avoiding my questions, aren't you?"

"Yes." Jo Marie couldn't see any reason to lie.

"When you're ready to talk, I'll be happy to listen.'' Tucking the keys in his pocket, Jim reached for Jo Marie's hand, placing it at his elbow and patting it gently.

"Thanks, I'll remember that."

"Tell me something more about you," Jo Marie queried in a blatant effort to change the subject. Briefly Jim looked at her, his expression thoughtful.

They ventured onto the sidewalk. The full moon was out, its silver rays clearing a path in the night as they strolled toward her car.

"I'm afraid I'd bore you. Most everything you already know. I've only been with the foundation a month."

"LFTF needs people like you, dedicated, passionate, caring."

"I wasn't the one who gave permission for a transient to sleep in a doorway."

Jo Marie softly sucked in her breath. "How'd you know?"

"He came back the second night looking for a handout. The guy knew a soft touch when he saw one."

"What happened?"

Jim shrugged his shoulder and Jo Marie stopped walking in mid-stride. "You gave him some money!" she declared righteously. "And you call me a soft touch."

"As a matter of fact, I didn't. We both knew what he'd spend it on."

"So what did you do?"

"Took him to dinner."

A gentle smile stole across her features at the picture that must have made. Jim dressed impeccably in his business suit and the alcoholic in tattered, ragged clothes.

"It's sad to think about." Slowly, Jo Marie shook her head.

"I got in touch with a friend of mine from a mission. He came for him afterward so that he'll have a place to sleep at least. To witness, close at hand like that, a man wasting his life is far worse to me than..." he paused and held her gaze for a long moment, looking deep into her brown eyes. Then he smiled faintly and shook his head. "Sorry, I didn't mean to get so serious."

"You weren't," Jo Marie replied, taking the car keys from her purse. "I'll be back Monday and maybe we could have a cup of coffee."

The deep blue eyes brightened perceptively. "I'd like that and listen, maybe we could have dinner one night soon."

Jo Marie nodded, revealing that she'd enjoy that as well. Jim was her friend and she doubted that her feelings would ever go beyond that, but the way she felt lately, she needed someone to lift her from the doldrums of self-pity.

The drive home was accomplished in a matter of minutes. Standing otuside her apartment building, Jo Marie heaved a steadying breath. She dreaded walking into her own home—what a sad commentary on her life! Tonight, she promised herself, she'd make an effort to clear the air between herself and Kelly. Not knowing what Andrew had said to her roommate about his feelings for her, if anything, or the details of the argument, had put Jo Marie in a precarious position. The air between Jo Marie and her best friend was like the stillness before an electrical storm. The problem was that Jo Marie didn't know what to say to Kelly or how to go about making things right.

She made a quick survey of the cars in the parking lot to assure herself that Andrew wasn't inside. Relieved, she tucked her hands inside the pockets of her cardigan and hoped to give a nonchalant appearance when she walked through the front door.

Kelly glanced up from the book she was reading when Jo Marie walked inside. The red, puffy eyes were a testimony of tears, but Kelly didn't explain and Jo Marie didn't pry.

"I hope there's something left over from dinner," she began on a forced note of cheerfulness. "I'm starved."

"I didn't fix anything," Kelly explained in an ominously quiet voice. "In fact I think I'm coming down with something. I've got a terrible stomachache."

Jo Marie had to bite her lip to keep from shouting that she knew what was wrong with the both of them. Their lives were beginning to resemble a three-ring circus. Where once Jo Marie and Kelly had been best friends, now they rarely spoke.

"What I think I'll do is take a long, leisurely bath and go to bed."

Jo Marie nodded, thinking Kelly's sudden urge for a hot soak was just an excuse to leave the room and avoid the problems that faced them.

While Kelly ran her bathwater, Jo Marie searched through the fridge looking for something appetizing. Normally this was the time of the year that she had to watch her weight. This Christmas she'd probably end up losing a few pounds.

The radio was playing a series of spirited Christmas carols and Jo Marie started humming along. She took out bread and cheese slices from the fridge. The cupboard offered a can of tomato soup.

By the time Kelly came out of the bathroom, Jo Marie had set two places at the table and was pouring hot soup into deep bowls.

"Dinner is served," she called.

Kelly surveyed the table and gave her friend a weak, trembling smile. "I appreciate the effort, but I'm really not up to eating."

Exhaling a dejected sigh, Jo Marie turned to her friend. "How long are we going to continue pretending like this? We need to talk, Kell."

"Not tonight, please, not tonight."

The doorbell rang and a stricken look came over Kelly's pale features. "I don't want to see anyone," she announced and hurried into the bedroom, leaving Jo Marie to deal with whoever was calling.

Resentment burned in her dark eyes as Jo Marie crossed the room. If it was Andrew, she would simply explain that Kelly was ill and not invite him inside.

"Merry Christmas." A tired-looking Mark greeted Jo Marie sarcastically from the other side of the door.

"Hi." Jo Marie watched him carefully. Her brother looked terrible. Tiny lines etched about his eyes revealed lack of sleep. He looked as though he was suffering from both mental and physical exhaustion.

"Is Kelly around?" He walked into the living room, sat on the sofa and leaned forward, roughly rubbing his hands across his face as if that would keep him awake.

"No, she's gone to bed. I don't think she's feeling well."

Briefly, Mark stared at the closed bedroom door and as he did, his shoulder hunched in a gesture of defeat.

"How about something to eat? You look like you haven't had a decent meal in days."

"I haven't." He moved lackadaisically to the kitchen and pulled out a chair.

Lifting the steaming bowls of soup from the counter, Jo Marie brought them to the table and sat opposite her brother.

As Mark took the soup spoon, his tired eyes held a distant, unhappy look. Kelly's eyes had revealed the same light of despair. "We had an argument," he murmured.

"You and Kell?"

"I said some terrible things to her." He braced his elbow against the table and pinched the bridge of his nose. "I don't know what made me do it. The whole time I was shouting at her I felt as if it was some stranger doing this. I know it sounds crazy but it was almost as if I were standing outside myself watching, and hating myself for what I was doing."

"Was the fight over something important?"

Defensively, Mark straightened. "Yeah, but that's between Kelly and me." He attacked the toasted cheese sandwich with a vengeance.

"You're in love with Kelly, aren't you?" Jo Marie had yet to touch her meal, more concerned about what was happening between her brother and her best friend than about her soup and sandwich.

Mark hesitated thoughtfully and a faint grimness

closed off his expression. "In love with Kelly? I am?"

"You obviously care for her."

"I care for my cat, too," he returned coldly and his expression hardened. "She's got what she wants—money. Just look at who she's marrying. It isn't enough that she's wealthy in her own right. No, she sets her sights on J. Paul Getty."

Jo Marie's chin trembled in a supreme effort not to reveal her reaction to his words. "You know Kelly better than that." Averting her gaze, Jo Marie struggled to hold back the emotion that tightly constricted her throat.

"Does either one of us really know Kelly?" Mark's voice was taut as a hunter's bow. Cyncism drove deep grooved lines around his nose and mouth. "Did she tell you that she and Drew have set their wedding date?" Mark's voice dipped with contempt.

A pain seared all the way through Jo Marie's soul. "No, she didn't say." With her gaze lowered, she struggled to keep her hands from shaking.

"Apparently they're going to make it official after the first of the year. They're planning on a spring wedding."

"How...nice." Jo Marie nearly choked on the words.

"Well, all I can say is that those two deserve each other." He tossed the melted cheese sandwich back on the plate and stood. "I guess I'm not very hungry, after all."

Jo Marie rose with him and glanced at the table. Neither one of them had done more than shred their sandwiches and stir their soup. "Neither am I," she said, and swallowed at the tightness gripping her throat.

Standing in the living room, Mark stared for a second time at the closed bedroom door.

"I'll tell Kelly you were by." For a second it seemed that Mark hadn't heard.

"No," he murmured after a long moment. "Maybe it's best to leave things as they are. Good night, sis, thanks for dinner." Resembling a man carrying the weight of the world on his shoulders, Mark left.

Leaning against the front door, Jo Marie released a bitter, pain-filled sigh and turned the dead bolt. Tears burned for release. So Andrew and Kelly were going to make a public announcement of their engagement after Christmas. It shouldn't shock her. Kelly had told her from the beginning that they were. The wedding plans were already in the making. Wiping the salty dampness from her cheek, Jo Marie bit into the tender skin inside her cheek to hold back a sob.

"There's a call for you on line one," Paula called to Jo Marie from her desk.

"Thanks." With an efficiency born of years of experience, Jo Marie punched in the telephone tab and lifted the receiver to her ear. "This is Jo Marie Early, may I help you?"

"Jo Marie, this is Jim. I hope you don't mind me calling you at work."

"No problem."

"Good. Listen, you, ah, mentioned something the other night about us having coffee together and I said something about having dinner."

If she hadn't known any better, Jo Marie would have guessed that Jim was uneasy. He was a gentle man with enough sensitivity to campaign for the future. His hesitancy surprised her now. "I remember."

"How would you feel about this Wednesday?" he continued. "We could make a night of it."

Jo Marie didn't need to think it over. "I'd like that very much." After Mark's revelation, she'd realized the best thing to do was to put the past and Andrew behind her and build a new life for herself.

"Good." Jim sounded pleased. "We can go Wednesday night...or would you prefer Friday?"

"Wednesday's fine." Jo Marie doubted that she could ever feel again the deep, passionate attraction she'd experienced with Andrew, but Jim's appeal wasn't built on fantasy.

"I'll see you then. Goodbye, Jo Marie."

"Goodbye Jim, and thanks."

The mental uplifting of their short conversation was enough to see Jo Marie through a hectic afternoon. An airline lost her customer's reservations and the tickets didn't arrive in time. In addition the phone rang repeatedly.

By the time she walked into the apartment, her feet hurt and there was a nagging ache in the small of her back.

"I thought I heard you." Kelly sauntered into the kitchen and stood in the doorway dressed in a robe and slippers.

"How are you feeling?"

She lifted one shoulder in a weak shrug. "Better."

"You stayed home?" Kelly had still been in bed

when Jo Marie left for work. Apparently her friend had phoned in sick.

"Yeah." She moved into the living room and sat on the sofa.

"Mark was by last night." Jo Marie mentioned the fact casually, waiting for a response from her roommate. Kelly didn't give her one. "He said that the two of you had a big fight," she continued.

"That's all we do anymore—argue."

"I don't know what he said to you, but he felt bad about it afterward."

A sad glimmer touched Kelly's eyes and her mouth formed a brittle line that Jo Marie supposed was meant to be a smile. "I know he didn't mean it. He's exhausted. I swear he's trying to work himself to death."

Now that her friend mentioned it, Jo Marie realized that she hadn't seen much of her brother lately. It used to be that he had an excuse to show up two or three times a week. Except for last night, he had been to the apartment only twice since Thanksgiving.

"I don't think he's eaten a decent meal in days," Kelly continued. "He's such a good doctor, Jo Marie, because he cares so much about his patients. Even the ones he knows he's going to lose. I'm a nurse, I've seen the way the other doctors close themselves off from any emotional involvement. But Mark's there, always giving." Her voice shook uncontrollably and she paused to bite into her lip until she regained her composure. "I wanted to talk to him the other night, and do you know where I found him? In pediatrics holding a little boy who's suffering with terminal cancer. He was rocking this child, holding him in his arms and telling him the pain wouldn't last too much longer. From the hallway, I heard Mark talk about heaven and how there wouldn't be any pain for him there. Mark's a wonderful man and wonderful doctor."

And he loves you so much it's tearing him apart, Jo Marie added silently.

"Yesterday he was frustrated and angry and he took it out on me. I'm not going to lie and say it didn't hurt. For a time I was devastated, but I'm over that now."

"But you didn't go to work today." They both knew why she'd chosen to stay home.

"No, I felt Mark and I needed a day away from each other."

"That's probably a good idea." There was so much she wanted to say to Kelly, but everything sounded so inadequate. At least they were talking, which was a major improvement over the previous five days.

The teakettle whistled sharply and Jo Marie returned to the kitchen bringing them both back a steaming cup of hot coffee.

"Thanks." Kelly's eyes brightened.

"Would you like me to talk to Mark?" Jo Marie's offer was sincere, but she wasn't exactly sure what she'd say. And in some ways it could make matters worse.

"No. We'll sort this out on our own."

The doorbell chimed and the two exchanged glances. "I'm not expecting anyone," Kelly murmured and glanced down self-consciously at her attire. "In fact I'd rather not be seen, so if you don't mind I'll vanish inside my room."

The last person Jo Marie expected to find on the other side of the door was Andrew. The welcome died in her eyes as their gazes met and clashed. Jo Marie quickly lowered hers. Her throat went dry and a rush of emotion brought a flood of color to her suddenly pale cheeks. A tense air of silence surrounded them. Andrew raised his hand as though he wanted to reach out and touch her. Instead he clenched his fist and lowered it to his side, apparently having changed his mind.

"Is Kelly ready?" he asked after a breathless moment. Jo Marie didn't move, her body blocking the front door, refusing him admittance.

She stared up at him blankly. "Ready?" she repeated.

"Yes, we're attending the opera tonight. Bizet's *Carmen*," he added as if in an afterthought.

"Oh, dear." Jo Marie's eyes widened. Kelly had obviously forgotten their date. The tickets for the elaborate opera had been sold out for weeks. Her roommate would have to go. "Come in, I'll check with Kelly."

"Andrew's here," Jo Marie announced and leaned against the wooden door inside the bedroom, her hands folded behind her.

"Drew?"

"Andrew to me, Drew to you," she responded cattily. "You have a date to see *Carmen*."

Kelly's hand flew to her forehead. "Oh, my goodness, I completely forgot."

"What are you going to do?"

"Explain, what else is there to do?" she snapped. Jo Marie followed her friend into the living room.

Andrew's gray eyes widened at the sight of Kelly dressed in her robe and slippers.

"You're ill?"

"Actually, I'm feeling better. Drew, I apologize, I completely forgot about tonight."

As Andrew glanced at his gold wristwatch, a frown marred his handsome face.

"Kelly can shower and dress in a matter of a few minutes," Jo Marie said sharply, guessing what Kelly was about to suggest.

"I couldn't possibly be ready in forty-five minutes," she denied. "There's only one thing to do. Jo Marie, you'll have to go in my place."

Andrew's level gaze crossed the width of the room to capture Jo Marie's. Little emotion was revealed in the impassive male features, but his gray eyes glinted with challenge.

"I can't." Her voice was level with hard determination.

"Why not?" Two sets of eyes studied her.

"I'm...." Her mind searched wildly for an excuse. "I'm baking cookies for the Science Club. We're meeting Saturday and this will be our last time before Christmas."

"I thought you worked Saturdays," Andrew cut in sharply.

"Every other Saturday." Calmly she met this gaze. Over the past couple of weeks, Kelly had purposely brought Jo Marie and Andrew together, but Jo Marie wouldn't fall prey to that game any longer. She'd made an agreement with him and refused to back down. As long as he was engaged to another woman she wouldn't...couldn't be with him. "I won't go," she explained in a steady voice which belied the inner turmoil that churned her stomach.

"There's plenty of time before the opening curtain if you'd care to change your mind."

Kelly tossed Jo Marie an odd look. "It looks like I'll have to go," she said with an exaggerated sigh. "I'll be as fast as I can." Kelly rushed back inside the bedroom leaving Jo Marie and Andrew separated by only a few feet.

"How have you been?" he asked, his eyes devouring her.

"Fine," she responded on a stiff note. The lie was only a little one. The width of the room stood between them, but it might as well have been whole light-years.

Bowing her head, she stared at the pattern in the carpet. When she suggested Kelly hurry and dress, she hadn't counted on being left alone with Andrew. "If you'll excuse me, I'll get started on those cookies."

To her dismay Andrew followed her into the kitchen.

"What are my chances of getting a cup of coffee?" He sounded pleased with himself, his smile was smug.

Wordlessly Jo Marie stood on her tiptoes and brought down a mug from the cupboard. She poured in the dark granules, stirred in hot water and walked past him to carry the mug into the living room. All the while her mind was screaming with him to leave her alone.

Andrew picked up the mug and followed her back

into the kitchen. "I've wanted to talk to you for days."

"You agreed."

"Jo Marie, believe me, talking to Kelly isn't as easy as it seems. There are some things I'm not at liberty to explain that would resolve this whole mess."

"I'll just bet there are." The bitter taste of anger filled her mouth.

"Can't you trust me?" The words were barely audible and for an instant Jo Marie wasn't certain he'd spoken.

Everything within her yearned to reach out to him and be assured that the glorious times they'd shared had been as real for him as they'd been for her. Desperately she wanted to turn and tell him that she would trust him with her life, but not her heart. She couldn't, not when Kelly was wearing his engagement ring.

"Jo Marie." A faint pleading quality entered his voice. "I know how all this looks. At least give me a chance to explain. Have dinner with me tomorrow. I swear I won't so much as touch you. I'll leave everything up to you. Place. Time. You name it."

"No." Frantically she shook her head, her voice throbbing with the desire to do as he asked. "I can't."

"Jo Marie." He took a step toward her, then another, until he was so close his husky voice breathed against her dark hair.

Forcing herself into action, Jo Marie whirled around and backed out of the kitchen. "Don't talk to me like that. I realized last week that whatever you feel for Kelly is stronger than any love you have for me. I've tried to accept that as best I can.''

Andrew's knuckles were clenched so tightly that they went white. He looked like an innocent man facing a firing squad, his eyes resigned, the line of his jaw tense, anger and disbelief etched in every rugged mark of his face.

''Just be patient, that's all I'm asking. In due time you'll understand everything.''

''Will you stop?'' she demanded angrily. ''You're talking in puzzles and I've always hated those. All I know is that there are four people who—''

''I guess this will have to do,'' Kelly interrupted as she walked into the room. She had showered, dressed and dried her hair in record time.

Jo Marie swallowed the taste of jealousy as she watched the dark, troubled look dissolve from Andrew's eyes. ''You look great,'' was all she could manage.

''We won't be too late,'' Kelly said on her way out.

''Don't worry,'' Jo Marie murmured and breathed in a sharp breath. ''I won't be up; I'm exhausted.''

Who was she trying to kid? Not until the key turned in the front door lock five hours later did Jo Marie so much as yawn. As much as she hated herself for being so weak, the entire time Kelly had been with Andrew, Jo Marie had been utterly miserable.

The dinner date with Jim the next evening was the only bright spot in a day that stretched out like an empty void. She dressed carefully and applied her makeup with extra care, hoping to camouflage the effects of a sleepless night.

"Don't fix dinner for me, I've got a date," was all she said to Kelly on her way out the door to the office.

As she knew it would, being with Jim was like stumbling upon an oasis in the middle of a sand-tossed desert. He made her laugh, teasing her affectionately. His humor was subtle and light and just the antidote for a broken heart. She'd known from the moment they'd met that she was going to like Jim Rowden. With him she could relax and be herself. And not once did she have to look over her shoulder.

"Are you going to tell me what's been troubling you?" he probed gently over their dessert.

"What? And cry all over my lime-chiffon pie?"

Jim's returning smile was one of understanding and encouragement. Again she noted the twin dimples that formed in his cheeks. "Whenever you're ready, I'm available to listen."

"Thanks." She shook her head, fighting back an unexpected swell of emotion. "Now what's this surprise you've been taunting me with most of the evening?" she questioned, averting the subject from herself.

"It's about the wetlands we've been crusading for during the last month. Well, I talked to a state senator today and he's going to introduce a bill that would make the land into a state park." Lacing his hands together, Jim leaned toward the linen-covered table. "From everything he's heard, George claims from there it should be a piece of cake."

"Jim, that's wonderful." This was his first success and he beamed with pride over the accomplishment.

"Of course, nothing's definite yet, and I'm not even sure I should have told you, but you've heard

me give two speeches on the wetlands and I wanted
you to know.''

''I'm honored that you did.''

He acknowledged her statement with a short nod.
''I should know better than to get my hopes up like
this, but George—my friend—sounded so confident.''

''Then you should be too. We both should.''

Jim reached for her hand and squeezed it gently.
''It would be very easy to share things with you, Jo
Marie. You're quite a woman.''

Flattery had always made her uncomfortable, but
Jim sounded so sincere. It cost her a great deal of
effort to simply smile and murmur her thanks.

Jim's arm rested across her shoulder as they walked
back toward the office. He held open her car door for
her and paused before lightly brushing his mouth over
hers. The kiss was both gentle and reassuring. But it
wasn't Andrew's kiss and Jim hadn't the power to
evoke the same passionate response Andrew seemed
to draw so easily from her.

On the ride home, Jo Marie silently berated herself
for continuing to compare the two men. It was unfair
to them both to even think in that mode.

The apartment was unlocked when Jo Marie let
herself inside. She was hanging up her sweater-coat
when she noticed Andrew. He was standing in the
middle of the living room carpet, regarding her with
stone cold eyes.

One glance and Jo Marie realized that she'd never
seen a man look so angry.

''It's about time you got home.'' His eyes were
flashing gray fire.

"What right is it of yours to demand what time I get in?"

"I have every right." His voice was like a whip lashing out at her. "I suppose you think you're playing a game. Every time I go out with Kelly, you'll pay me back by dating Jim?"

Stunned into speechlessness, Jo Marie felt her voice die in her throat.

"And if you insist on letting him kiss you the least you can do is look for someplace more private than the street." The white line about his mouth became more pronounced as his eyes filled with bitter contempt. "You surprise me, Jo Marie, I thought you had more class than that."

Chapter Eight

"How dare you...how dare you say such things to me!" Jo Marie's quavering voice became breathless with rage. Her eyes were dark and stormy as she turned around and jerked the front door open.

"What do you expect me to believe?" Andrew rammed his hand through his hair, ruffling the dark hair that grew at his temple.

"I expected a lot of things from you, but not that you'd follow me or spy on me. And then...then to have the audacity to confront and insult me." The fury in her faded to be replaced with a deep, emotional pain that pierced her heart.

Andrew's face was bloodless as he walked past her and out the door. As soon as he was through the portal, she slammed it closed with a sweeping arc of her hand.

Jo Marie was so furious that the room wasn't large enough to contain her anger. Her shoulders rose and

sagged with her every breath. At one time Andrew
had been her dream man. Quickly she was learning
to separate the fantasy from the reality.

Pacing the carpet helped relieve some of the terrible tension building within her. Andrew's behavior
was nothing short of odious. She should hate him for
saying those kinds of things to her. Tears burned for
release, but deep, concentrated breaths held them at
bay. Andrew Beaumont wasn't worth the emotion.
Staring sightlessly at the ceiling, her damp lashes
pressed against her cheek.

The sound of the doorbell caused her to whirl
around. Andrew. She'd stake a week's salary on the
fact. In an act of defiance, she folded her arms across
her waist and stared determinedly at the closed door.
He could rot in the rain before she'd open that door.

Again the chimes rang in short, staccato raps.
"Come on, Jo Marie, answer the damn door."

"No," she shouted from the other side.

"Fine, we'll carry on a conversation by shouting
at each other. That should amuse your neighbors."

"Go away." Jo Marie was too upset to talk things
out. Andrew had hurt her with his actions and words.

"Jo Marie." The appealing quality in his voice
couldn't be ignored. "Please, open the door. All I
want is to apologize."

Hating herself for being so weak, Jo Marie turned
the lock and threw open the solid wood door. "You
have one minute."

"I think I went a little crazy when I saw Jim kiss
you," he said pacing the area in front of the door.
"Jo Marie, promise me that you won't see him again.

I don't think I can stand the thought of any man touching you.''

"This is supposed to be an apology?'' she asked sarcastically. "Get this, Mr. Beaumont,'' she said, fighting to keep from shouting at him as her finger punctuated the air. "You have no right to dictate anything to me.''

His tight features darkened. "I can make your life miserable.''

"And you think you haven't already?'' she cried. "Just leave me alone. I don't need your threats. I don't want to see you again. Ever.'' To her horror, her voice cracked. Shaking her head, unable to talk any longer, she shut the door and clicked the lock.

Almost immediately the doorbell chimed, followed by continued knocking. Neither of them were in any mood to discuss things rationally. And perhaps it was better all the way around to simply leave things as they were. It hurt, more than Jo Marie wanted to admit, but she'd recover. She'd go on with her life and put Andrew, the dream man and all of it behind her.

Without glancing over her shoulder, she ignored the sound and moved into her bedroom.

The restaurant was crowded, the luncheon crowd filling it to capacity. With Christmas only a few days away the rush of last-minute shoppers filled the downtown area and flowed into the restaurants at lunch time.

Seeing Mark come through the doors, Jo Marie raised her hand and waved in an effort to attract her brother's attention. He looked less fatigued than the last time she'd seen him. A brief smile momentarily brightened his eyes, but faded quickly.

"I must admit this is a surprise," Jo Marie said as her brother slid into the upholstered booth opposite her. "I can't remember the last time we met for lunch."

"I can't remember either." Mark picked up the menu, decided and closed it after only a minute.

"That was quick."

"I haven't got a lot of time."

Same old Mark, always in a rush, hurrying from one place to another. "You called me, remember?" she taunted softly.

"Yeah, I remember." His gaze was focused on the paper napkin which he proceeded to fold into an intricate pattern. "This is going to sound a little crazy so promise me you won't laugh."

The edge of her mouth was already twitching. "I promise."

"I want you to attend the hospital Christmas party with me Saturday night."

"Me?"

"I don't have time to go out looking for a date and I don't think I can get out of it without offending half the staff."

In the past three weeks, Jo Marie had endured enough parties to last her a lifetime. "I guess I could go."

"Don't sound so enthusiastic."

"I'm beginning to feel the same way about parties as you do."

"I doubt that," he said forcefully and shredded the napkin in half.

The waitress came for their order and delivered steaming mugs of coffee almost immediately afterward.

Jo Marie lifted her own napkin, toying with the pressed paper edge. "Will Kelly and...Drew be there?"

"I doubt it. Why should they? There won't be any ballroom dancing or a midnight buffet. It's a pot luck. Can you picture old 'money bags' sitting on a folding chair and balancing a paper plate on her lap? No. Kelly goes more for the two-hundred-dollar-a-place-setting affairs."

Jo Marie opened her mouth to argue, but decided it would do little good. Discussing Andrew—Drew, her mind corrected—or Kelly with Mark would be pointless.

"I suppose Kelly's told you?"

"Told me what?" Jo Marie glanced up curious and half-afraid. The last time Mark had relayed any information about Drew and Kelly it had been that they were going to publicly announce their engagement.

"She's given her two-week notice."

"No," Jo Marie gasped. "She wouldn't do that. Kelly loves nursing; she's a natural." Even more surprising was the fact that Kelly hadn't said a word to Jo Marie about leaving Tulane Hospital.

"I imagine with the wedding plans and all that she's decided to take any early retirement. Who can blame her, right?"

But it sounded very much like Mark was doing exactly that. His mouth was tight and his dark eyes were filled with something akin to pain. What a mess this Christmas was turning out to be.

"Let's not talk about Kelly or Drew or anyone for the moment, okay. It's Christmas next week." She forced a bit of yuletide cheer into her voice.

"Right," Mark returned with a short sigh. "It's almost Christmas." But for all the enthusiasm in his voice he could have been discussing German measles.

Their soup and sandwiches arrived and they ate in strained silence. "Well, are you coming or not?" Mark asked, pushing his empty plate aside.

"I guess." No need to force any enthusiasm into her voice. They both felt the same way about the party.

"Thanks, sis."

"Just consider it your Christmas present."

Mark reached for the white slip the waitress had placed on their table, examining it. "And consider this lunch yours," he announced and scooted from his seat. "See you Saturday night."

"Mark said you've given the hospital your two-week notice?" Jo Marie confronted her roommate first thing that evening.

"Yes," Kelly replied lifelessly.

"I suppose the wedding will fill your time from now on."

"The wedding?" Kelly gave her an absent look. "No," she shook her head and an aura of dejected defeat hung over her, dulling her responses. "I've got my application in at a couple of other hospitals."

"So you're going to continue working after you're married."

For a moment it didn't look as if Kelly had heard her. "Kell?" Jo Marie prompted.

"I'd hoped to."

Berating herself for caring how Kelly and Andrew lived their lives, Jo Marie picked up the evening paper and pretended an interest in the front page. But if Kelly had asked her so much as what the headline read she couldn't have answered.

Saturday night Jo Marie dressed in the blue dress that she'd sewn after Thanksgiving. It fit her well and revealed a subtle grace in her movements. Although she took extra time with her hair and cosmetics, her heart wasn't up to attending the party.

Jo Marie had casually draped a lace shawl over her shoulder when the front door opened and Kelly entered with Andrew at her side.

"You're going out," Kelly announced, stopping abruptly inside the living room. "You...you didn't say anything."

Jo Marie could feel Andrew's gaze scorching her in a slow, heated perusal, but she didn't look his way. "Yes, I'm going out; don't wait up for me."

"Drew and I have plans too."

Reaching for her evening bag, Jo Marie's mouth curved slightly upward in a poor imitation of a smile. "Have a good time."

Kelly said something more, but Jo Marie was already out the door, grateful to have escaped without another confrontation with Andrew.

Mark had given her the address of the party and asked that she meet him there. He didn't give any particular reason he couldn't pick her up. He didn't need an excuse. It was obvious he wanted to avoid Kelly.

She located the house without a problem and was

greeted by loud music and a smoke-filled room. Making her way between the dancing couples, Jo Marie delivered the salad she had prepared on her brother's behalf to the kitchen. After exchanging pleasantries with the guests in the kitchen, Jo Marie went back to the main room to search for Mark.

For all the noisy commotion the party was an orderly one and Jo Marie spotted her brother almost immediately. He was sitting on the opposite side of the room talking to a group of other young men, who she assumed were fellow doctors. Making her way across the carpet, she was waylaid once by a nurse friend of Kelly's that she'd met a couple of times. They chatted for a few minutes about the weather.

"I suppose you've heard that Kelly's given her notice," Julie Frazier said with a hint of impatience. "It's a shame, if you ask me."

"I agree," Jo Marie murmured.

"Sometimes I'd like to knock those two over the head." Julie motioned toward Mark with the slight tilt of her head. "Your brother's one stubborn male."

"You don't need to tell me. I'm his sister."

"You know," Julie said and glanced down at the cold drink she was holding in her hand. "After Kelly had her tonsils out I could have sworn those two were headed for the altar. No one was more surprised than me when Kell turns up engaged to this mystery character."

"What do you mean about Kelly and Mark?" Kelly's tonsils had come out months ago during the Mardi Gras. No matter how much time passed, it wasn't likely that Jo Marie would forget that.

"Kelly was miserable—adult tonsillectomies are

seldom painless—anyway, Kelly didn't want anyone around, not even her family. Mark was the only one who could get close to her. He spent hours with her, coaxing her to eat, spoon-feeding her. He even read her to sleep and then curled up in the chair beside her bed so he'd be there when she woke.''

Jo Marie stared back in open disbelief. "Mark did that?" All these months Mark had been in love with Kelly and he hadn't said a word. Her gaze sought him now and she groaned inwardly at her own stupidity. For months she'd been so caught up in the fantasy of those few precious moments with Andrew that she'd been blind to what was right in front of her own eyes.

"Well, speaking of our friend, look who's just arrived."

Jo Marie's gaze turned toward the front door just as Kelly and Andrew came inside. From across the length of the room, her eyes clashed with Andrew's. She watched as the hard line of his mouth relaxed and he smiled. The effect on her was devastating; her heart somersaulted and color rushed up her neck, invading her face. These were all the emotions she had struggled against from the beginning. She hated herself for being so vulnerable when it came to this one man. She didn't want to feel any of these emotions toward him.

"Excuse me—" Julie interrupted Jo Marie's musings "—there's someone I wanted to see."

"Sure." Mentally, Jo Marie shook herself and joined Mark, knowing she would be safe at his side.

"Did you see who just arrived?" Jo Marie whispered in her brother's ear.

Mark's dusty dark eyes studied Kelly's arrival and

Jo Marie witnessed an unconscious softening in his gaze. Kelly did look lovely tonight, and begrudgingly Jo Marie admitted that Andrew and Kelly were the most striking couple in the room. They belonged together—both were people of wealth and position. Two of a kind.

"I'm surprised that she came," Mark admitted slowly and turned his back to the pair. "But she's got as much right to be here as anyone."

"Of course she does."

One of Mark's friends appointed himself as disc jockey and put on another series of records for slow dancing. Jo Marie and Mark stood against the wall and watched as several couples began dancing on the makeshift dance floor. When Andrew turned Kelly into his arms, Jo Marie diverted her gaze to another section of the room, unable to look at them without being affected.

"You don't want to dance, do you?" Mark mumbled indifferently.

"With you?"

"No, I'd get one of my friends to do the honors. It's bad enough having to invite my sister to a party. I'm not about to dance with you, too."

Jo Marie couldn't prevent a short laugh. "You really know how to sweet talk a woman don't you, brother dearest?"

"I try," he murmured and his eyes narrowed on Kelly whose arms were draped around Andrew's neck as she whispered in his ear. "But obviously not hard enough," he finished.

Standing on the outskirts of the dancing couples made Jo Marie uncomfortable. "I think I'll see what

I can do to help in the kitchen,'' she said as an excuse to leave.

Julie Frazier was there, placing cold cuts on a round platter with the precision of a mathematician.

''Can I help?'' Jo Marie offered, looking around for something that needed to be done.

Julie turned and smiled her appreciation. ''Sure. Would you put the serving spoons in the salads and set them out on the dining room table?''

''Glad to.'' She located the spoons in the silverware drawer and carried out a large glass bowl of potato salad. The Formica table was covered with a vinyl cloth decorated with green holly and red berries.

''And now ladies and gentleman—'' the disc jockey demanded the attention of the room ''—this next number is a ladies' choice.''

With her back to the table, Jo Marie watched as Kelly whispered something to Andrew. To her surprise, he nodded and stepped aside as Kelly made her way to the other side of the room. Her destination was clear—Kelly was heading directly to Mark. Jo Marie's pulse fluttered wildly. If Mark said or did anything cruel to her friend, Jo Marie would never forgive him.

Her heart was in her eyes as Kelly tentatively tapped Mark on the shoulder. Engrossed in a conversation, Mark apparently wasn't aware he was being touched. Kelly tried again and Mark turned, surprise rounding his eyes when he saw her roommate.

Jo Marie was far enough to the side so that she couldn't be seen by Mark and Kelly, but close enough to hear their conversation.

"May I have this dance?" Kelly questioned, her voice firm and low.

"I thought it was the man's prerogative to ask." The edge of Mark's mouth curled up sarcastically. "And if you've noticed, I haven't asked."

"This number is ladies' choice."

Mark tensed visibly as he glared across the room, eyeing Andrew. "And what about Rockefeller over there?"

Slowly, Kelly shook her head, her inviting gaze resting on Mark. "I'm asking you. Don't turn me down, Mark, not tonight. I'll be leaving the hospital in a little while and then you'll never be bothered with me again."

Jo Marie doubted that her brother could have refused Kelly anything in that moment. Wordlessly he approached the dance floor and took Kelly in his arms. A slow ballad was playing and the soft, melodic sounds of Billy Joel filled the room. Kelly fit her body to Mark's. Her arms slid around his neck as she pressed her temple against his jaw. Mark reacted to the contact by closing his eyes and inhaling as his eyes drifted closed. His hold, which had been loose, tightened as he knotted his hands at the small of Kelly's back, arching her body closer.

For the first time that night, her brother looked completely at ease. Kelly belonged with Mark. Jo Marie had been wrong to think that Andrew and Kelly were meant for each other. They weren't, and their engagement didn't make sense.

Her eyes sought out the subject of her thoughts. Andrew was leaning against the wall only a few feet from her. His eyes locked with hers, refusing to release her. He wanted her to come to him. She couldn't. His gaze seemed to drink her in as it had the night of the Mardi Gras. She could almost feel him reaching out to her, imploring her to come, urging her to cross the room so he could take her in his arms.

With unconscious thought Jo Marie took one step forward and stopped. No. Being with Andrew would only cause her more pain. With a determined effort she lightly shook her head, effectively breaking the spell. Her heart was beating so hard that breathing was difficult. Her steps were marked with decision as she returned to the kitchen.

A sliding glass door led to a lighted patio. A need to escape for a few moments overtook her and silently she slipped past the others and escaped into the darkness of the night.

A chill ran up her arms and she rubbed her hands over her forearms in an effort to warm her blood. The stars were out in a dazzling display and Jo Marie tilted her face toward the heavens, gazing at the lovely sight.

Jo Marie stiffened as she felt more than heard someone join her. She didn't need to turn around to realize that it was Andrew.

He came and stood beside her, but he made no effort to speak, instead focusing his attention on the dark sky.

Whole eternities seemed to pass before Andrew spoke. "I came to ask your forgiveness."

All the pain of his accusation burned in her breast. "You hurt me," she said on a breathless note after a long pause.

"I know, my love, I know." Slowly he removed his suit jacket and with extraordinary concern, draped it over her shoulders, taking care not to touch her.

"I'd give anything to have those thoughtless words back. Seeing Jim take you in his arms was like waving a red flag in front of an angry bull. I lashed out at you, when it was circumstances that were at fault."

Something about the way he spoke, the emotion that coated his words, the regret that filled his voice made her feel that her heart was ready to burst right out of her breast. She didn't want to look at him, but somehow it was impossible to keep her eyes away. With an infinite tenderness, he brushed a stray curl from her cheek.

"Can you forgive me?"

"Oh, Andrew." She felt herself weakening.

"I'd go on my knees if it would help."

The tears felt locked in her throat. "No, that isn't necessary."

He relaxed as if a great burden had been lifted from his shoulders. "Thank you."

Neither moved, wanting to prolong this tender moment. When Andrew spoke it was like the whisper of a gentle breeze and she had to strain to hear him.

"When I first came out here you looked like a blue sapphire silhouetted in the moonlight. And I was thinking that if it were in my power, I'd weave golden moonbeams into your hair."

"Have you always been so poetic?"

His mouth curved upward in a slow, sensuous smile. "No." His eyes were filled with an undisguised hunger as he studied her. Ever so slowly, he raised his hand and placed it at the side of her neck.

The tender touch of his fingers against her soft skin caused a tingling sensation to race down her spine. The feeling was akin to pain. Jo Marie loved this man as she would never love again and he was promised to another woman.

"Jo Marie," he whispered and his warm breath fanned her mouth. "There's mistletoe here. Let me kiss you."

There wasn't, of course, but Jo Marie was unable to pull away. She nodded her acquiescence. "One last time." She hadn't meant to verbalize her thoughts.

He brought her into his arms and she moistened her lips anticipating the hungry exploration of his mouth over hers. But she was to be disappointed. Andrew's lips lightly moved over hers like the gentle brush of the spring sun on a hungry earth. Gradually the kiss deepened as he worked his way from one corner of her mouth to another—again like the earth long starved from summer's absence.

"I always knew it would be like this for us, Florence Nightingale," he whispered against her hair. "Even when I couldn't find you, I felt a part of myself would never be the same."

"I did too. I nearly gave up dating."

"I thought I'd go crazy. You were so close all these months and yet I couldn't find you."

"But you did." Pressing her hands against the strong cushion of his chest she created a space between them. "And now it's too late."

Andrew's eyes darkened as he seemed to struggle within himself. "Jo Marie." A thick frown marred his face.

"Shh." She pressed her fingertips against his lips.

"Don't try to explain. I understand and I've accepted it. For a long time it hurt so much that I didn't think I'd be able to bear it. But I can and I will."

His hand circled her wrist and he closed his eyes before kissing the tips of her fingers. "There's so much I want to explain and can't."

"I know." With his arm holding her close, Jo Marie felt a deep sense of peace surround her. "I'd never be the kind of wife you need. Your position demands a woman with culture and class. I'm proud to be an Early and proud of my family, but I'm not right for you."

The grip on her wrist tightened. "Is that what you think?" The frustrated anger in his voice was barely suppressed. "Do you honestly believe that?"

"Yes," she answered him boldly. "I'm at peace within myself. I have no regrets. You've touched my heart and a part of me will never be the same. How can I regret having loved you? It's not within me."

He dropped her hand and turned from her, his look a mixture of angry torment. "You honestly think I should marry Kelly."

It would devastate Mark, but her brother would need to find his own peace. "Or someone like her." She removed his suit jacket from her shoulders and handed it back to him, taking care to avoid touching him. "Thank you," she whispered with a small catch to her soft voice. Unable to resist any longer, she raised her hand and traced his jaw. Very lightly, she brushed her mouth over his. "Goodbye, Andrew."

He reached out his hand in an effort to stop her, but she slipped past him. It took her only a moment to collect her shawl. Within a matter of minutes, she was out the front door and on her way back to the apartment. Mark would never miss her.

Jo Marie spent Sunday with her family, returning late that evening when she was assured Kelly was asleep. Lying in bed, studying the darkness around her, Jo Marie realized that she'd said her final good-bye to Andrew. Continuing to see him would only make it difficult for them both. Avoiding him had never succeeded, not when she yearned for every opportunity to be with him. The best solution would be to leave completely. Kelly would be moving out soon and Jo Marie couldn't afford to pay the rent on her own. The excuse would be a convenient one although Kelly was sure to recognize it for what it was.

After work Monday afternoon, before she headed for the LFTF office, Jo Marie stopped off at the hospital, hoping to talk to Mark. With luck, she might be able to convince her brother to let her move in with him. But only until she could find another apartment and another roommate.

Julie Frazier, the nurse who worked with both Kelly and Mark, was at the nurses' station on the surgical floor when Jo Marie arrived.

"Hi," she greeted cheerfully. "I don't suppose you know where Mark is?"

Julie glanced up from a chart she was reading. "He's in the doctors' lounge having a cup of coffee."

"Great. I'll talk to you later." With her shoes making clicking sounds against the polished floor, Jo Marie mused that her timing couldn't have been more perfect. Now all she needed was to find her brother in a good mood.

The doctors' lounge was at the end of the hall and was divided into two sections. The front part contained a sofa and a couple of chairs. A small kitchen area was behind that. The sound of Mark's and Kelly's voices stopped Jo Marie just inside the lounge.

"You can leave," Mark was saying in a tight, pained voice. "Believe me I have no intention of crying on your shoulder."

"I didn't come here for that," Kelly argued softly.

Jo Marie hesitated, unsure of what she should do. She didn't want to interrupt their conversation which seemed intense, nor did she wish to intentionally stay and listen in either.

"That case with the Randolph girl is still bothering you, isn't it?" Kelly demanded.

"No, I did everything I could. You know that."

"But it wasn't enough, was it?"

Jo Marie had to bite her tongue not to interrupt Kelly. It wasn't like her roommate to be unnecessarily cruel. Jo Marie vividly recalled her brother's doubts after the young child's death. It had been just before Thanksgiving and Mark had agonized that he had lost her.

"No," Mark shouted, "it wasn't enough."

"And now you're going to lose the Rickard boy." Kelly's voice softened perceptively.

Fleetingly Jo Marie wondered if this child was the one Kelly had mentioned who was dying of cancer.

"I've known that from the first." Mark's tone contained the steel edge of anger.

"Yes, but it hasn't gotten any easier, has it?"

"Listen, Kelly, I know what you're trying to do, but it isn't going to work."

"Mark," Kelly murmured his name on a sigh, "sometimes you are so blind."

"Maybe it's because I feel so inadequate. Maybe it's because I'm haunted with the fact that there might have been something more I could have done."

"But there isn't, don't you see?" Kelly's voice had softened as if her pain was Mark's. "Now won't you tell me what's really bothering you?"

"Maybe it's because I don't like the odds with Tommy. His endless struggle against pain. The deck was stacked against him from the beginning and now he hasn't got a bettor's edge. In the end, death will win."

"And you'll have lost, and every loss is a personal one."

Jo Marie didn't feel that she could eavesdrop any longer. Silently she slipped from the room.

The conversation between Mark and Kelly played back in her mind as she drove toward the office and Jim. Mark would have serious problems as a doctor unless he came to terms with these feelings. Kelly had recognized that and had set personal relationships aside to help Mark settle these doubts within himself. He'd been angry with her and would probably continue to be until he fully understood what she was doing.

Luckily Jo Marie found a parking space within sight of the office. With Christmas just a few days away the area had become more crowded and finding parking was almost impossible.

Her thoughts were heavy as she climbed from the

passenger's side and locked her door. Just as she turned to look both ways before crossing the street she caught a glimpse of the dark blue Mercedes. A cold chill raced up her spine. Andrew was inside talking to Jim.

Chapter Nine

"Is everything all right?" Wearily Jo Marie eyed Jim, looking for a telltale mannerism that would reveal the reason for Andrew's visit. She'd avoided bumping into him by waiting in a small antique shop across the street from the foundation. After he'd gone, she sauntered around for several additional minutes to be certain he was out of the neighborhood. Once assured it was safe, she crossed the street to the foundation's office.

"Should anything be wrong?" Jim lifted two thick brows in question.

"You tell me. I saw Andrew Beaumont's car parked outside."

"Ah, yes." Jim paused and smiled fleetingly. "And that concerns you?"

"No." She shook her head determinedly. "All right, yes!" She wasn't going to be able to fool Jim, who was an excellent judge of human nature.

A smile worked its way across his round face. "He came to meet the rest of the staff at my invitation. The LFTF Foundation is deeply indebted to your friend."

"My friend?"

Jim chuckled. "Neither one of you has been successful at hiding your feelings. Yes, my dear, sweet, Jo Marie, *your* friend."

Any argument died on her tongue.

"Would you care for a cup of coffee?" Jim asked, walking across the room and filling a Styrofoam cup for her.

Jo Marie smiled her appreciation as he handed it to her and sat on the edge of her desk, crossing his arms. "Beaumont and I had quite a discussion."

"And?" Jo Marie didn't bother to disguise her curiosity.

The phone rang before Jim could answer her. Jim reached for it and spent the next ten minutes in conversation. Jo Marie did her best to keep occupied, but her thoughts were doing a crazy tailspin. Andrew was here on business. She wouldn't believe it.

"Well?" Jo Marie questioned the minute Jim replaced the receiver.

His expression was empty for a moment. "Are we back to Beaumont again?"

"I don't mean to pry," Jo Marie said with a rueful smile, "but I'd really like to know why he was here."

Jim was just as straightforward. "Are you in love with him?"

Miserably, Jo Marie nodded. "A lot of good it's done either of us. Did he mention me?"

A wry grin twisted Jim's mouth. "Not directly, but he wanted to know my intentions."

"He didn't!" Jo Marie was aghast at such audacity.

Chuckling, Jim shook his head. "No, he came to ask me about the foundation and pick up some of our literature. He's a good man, Jo Marie."

She studied the top of the desk and typewriter keys. "I know."

"He didn't mention you directly, but I think he would have liked to. I had the feeling he was frustrated and concerned about you working here so many nights, especially in this neighborhood."

"He needn't worry, you escort me to my car or wait at the bus stop until the bus arrives."

Jim made busy work with his hands. "I had the impression that Beaumont is deeply in love with you. If anything happened to you while under my protection, he wouldn't take it lightly."

Even hours later when Jo Marie stepped into the apartment the echo of Jim's words hadn't faded. Andrew was concerned for her safety and was deeply in love with her. But it was all so useless that she refused to be comforted.

Kelly was sitting up, a blanket wrapped around her legs and torso as she paid close attention to a television Christmas special.

"Hi, how'd it go tonight?" Kelly greeted, briefly glancing from the screen.

Her roommate looked pale and slightly drawn, but Jo Marie attributed that to the conversation she'd overheard between her brother and her roommate. She wanted to ask how everything was at the hospital, but doubted that she could adequately disguise her interest.

"Tonight...oh, everything went as it usually does...fine."

"Good." Kelly's answer was absentminded, her look pinched.

"Are you feeling all right, Kell?"

Softly, she shook her head. "I've got another stomachache."

"Fever?"

"None to speak of. I think I might be coming down with the flu."

Tilting her head to one side, Jo Marie mused that Kelly had been unnaturally pale lately. But again she had attributed that to painfully tense times they'd all been through in the past few weeks.

"You know, one advantage of having a brother in the medical profession is that he's willing to make house calls."

Kelly glanced her way, then turned back to the television. "No, it's nothing to call Mark about."

But Kelly didn't sound as convincing as Jo Marie would have liked. With a shrug, she went into the kitchen and poured herself a glass of milk.

"Want one?" She raised her glass to Kelly for inspection.

"No thanks," Kelly murmured and unsuccessfully tried to disguise a wince. "In fact, I think I'll head for bed. I'll be fine in the morning, so don't worry about me."

But Jo Marie couldn't help doing just that. Little things about Kelly hadn't made sense in a long time—like staying home because of an argument with

Mark. Kelly wasn't a shy, fledgling nurse. She'd stood her ground with Mark more than once. Even her behavior at the Christmas parties had been peculiar. Nor was Kelly a shrinking violet, yet she'd behaved like one. Obviously it was all an act. But her reasons remained unclear.

In the morning, Kelly announced that she was going to take a day of sick leave. Jo Marie studied her friend with worried eyes. Twice during the morning she phoned to see how Kelly was doing.

"Fine," Kelly answered impatiently the second time. "Listen, I'd probably be able to get some decent rest if I didn't have to get up and answer the phone every fifteen minutes."

In spite of her friend's testiness, Jo Marie chuckled. "I'll try to restrain myself for the rest of the day."

"That would be greatly appreciated."

"Do you want me to bring you something back for dinner?"

"No," she answered emphatically. "Food sounds awful."

Mark breezed into the office around noon, surprising Jo Marie. Sitting on the corner of her desk, he dangled one foot as she finished a telephone conversation.

"Business must be slow if you've got time to be dropping in here," she said, replacing the receiver.

"I come to take you to lunch and you're complaining?"

"You've come to ask about Kelly?" She wouldn't hedge. The time for playing games had long passed.

"Oh?" Briefly he arched a brow in question. "Is that so?"

"She's got the flu. There, I just saved you the price of lunch." Jo Marie couldn't disguise her irritation.

"You didn't save me the price of anything," Mark returned lazily. "I was going to let you treat."

Unable to remain angry with her brother for long, Jo Marie joined him in a nearby café a few minutes later, but neither of them mentioned Kelly again. By unspoken agreement, Kelly, Andrew, and Kelly's unexpected resignation were never mentioned.

Jo Marie's minestrone soup and turkey sandwich arrived and she unwrapped the silverware from the paper napkin. "How would you feel about a roommate for a while?" Jo Marie broached the subject tentatively.

"Male or female?" Dusky dark eyes so like her own twinkled with mischief.

"This may surprise you—female."

Mark laid his sandwich aside. "I'll admit my interest has been piqued."

"You may not be as keen once you find out that it's me."

"You?"

"Well I'm going to have to find someplace else to move sooner or later and—"

"And you're interested in the sooner," he interrupted.

"Yes." She wouldn't mention her reasons, but Mark was astute enough to figure it out for himself.

Peeling open his sandwich, Mark removed a thin slice of tomato and set it on the beige plate. "As long as you do the laundry, clean, and do all the cooking I won't object."

A smile hovered at the edges of her mouth. "Your generosity overwhelms me, brother dearest."

"Let me know when you're ready and I'll help you cart your things over."

"Thanks, Mark."

Briefly he looked up from his meal and grinned. "What are big brothers for?"

Andrew's car was in the apartment parking lot when Jo Marie stepped off the bus that evening after work. The darkening sky convinced her that waiting outside for him to leave would likely result in a drenching. Putting aside her fears, she squared her shoulders and tucked her hands deep within her pockets. When Kelly was home she usually didn't keep the door locked so Jo Marie was surprised to discover that it was. While digging through her purse, she was even more surprised to hear loud voices from the other side of the door.

"This has to stop," Andrew was arguing. "And soon."

"I know," Kelly cried softly. "And I agree. I don't want to ruin anyone's life."

"Three days."

"All right—just until Friday."

Jo Marie made unnecessary noise as she came through the door. "I'm home," she announced as she stepped into the living room. Kelly was dressed in her robe and slippers, slouched on the sofa. Andrew had apparently been pacing the carpet. She could feel his gaze seek her out. But she managed to avoid it, diverting her attention instead to the picture on the wall behind him. "If you'll excuse me I think I'll take a hot shower."

"Friday," Andrew repeated in a low, impatient tone.

"Thank you, Drew," Kelly murmured and sighed softly.

Kelly was in the same position on the sofa when Jo Marie returned, having showered and changed clothes. "How are you feeling?"

"Not good."

For Kelly to admit to as much meant that she'd had a miserable day. "Is there anything I can do?"

Limply, Kelly laid her head back against the back of the couch and closed her eyes. "No, I'm fine. But this is the worst case of stomach flu I can ever remember?"

"You're sure it's the flu?"

Slowly Kelly opened her eyes. "I'm the nurse here."

"Yes, your majesty." With a dramatic twist to her chin, Jo Marie bowed in mock servitude. "Now would you like me to fix you something for dinner?"

"No."

"How about something cool to drink?"

Kelly nodded, but her look wasn't enthusiastic. "Fine."

As the evening progressed, Jo Marie studied her friend carefully. It could be just a bad case of the stomach flu, but Jo Marie couldn't help but be concerned. Kelly had always been so healthy and full of life. When a long series of cramps doubled Kelly over in pain, Jo Marie reached for the phone.

"Mark, can you come over?" She tried to keep the urgency from her voice.

"What's up?"

"It's Kelly. She's sick." Jo Marie attempted to keep her voice low enough so her roommate wouldn't hear. "She keeps insisting it's the flu, but I don't know. She's in a lot of pain for a simple intestinal virus."

Mark didn't hesitate. "I'll be right there."

Ten minutes later he was at the door. He didn't bother to knock, letting himself in. "Where's the patient?"

"Jo Marie." Kelly's round eyes tossed her a look of burning resentment. "You called Mark?"

"Guilty as charged, but I wouldn't have if I didn't think it was necessary."

Tears blurred the blue gaze. "I wish you hadn't," she murmured dejectedly. "It's just the flu."

"Let me be the judge of that." Mark spoke in a crisp professional tone, kneeling at her side. He opened the small black bag and took out the stethoscope.

Not knowing what else to do, Jo Marie hovered at his side for instructions. "Should I boil water or something?"

"Call Drew," Kelly insisted. "He at least won't overreact to a simple case of the flu."

Mark's mouth went taut, but he didn't rise to the intended gibe.

Reluctantly Jo Marie did as she was asked. Andrew answered on the third ring. "Beaumont here."

"Andrew, this is—"

"Jo Marie," he finished for her, his voice carrying a soft rush of pleasure.

"Hi," she began awkwardly and bit into the corner of her bottom lip. "Mark's here. Kelly's not feeling well and I think she may have something serious. She wanted to know if you could come over.''

''I'll be there in ten minutes.'' He didn't take a breath's hesitation.

As it was, he arrived in eight and probably set several speed records in the process. Jo Marie answered his hard knock. ''What's wrong with Kelly? She seemed fine this afternoon.'' He directed his question to Mark.

''I'd like to take Kelly over to the hospital for a couple of tests.''

Jo Marie noted the way her brother's jaw had tightened as if being in the same room with Andrew was a test of his endurance. Dislike exuded from every pore.

''No,'' Kelly protested emphatically. ''It's just the stomach flu.''

''With the amount of tenderness in the cecum?'' Mark argued, shaking his head slowly from side to side in a mocking gesture.

''Mark's the doctor,'' Andrew inserted and Jo Marie could have kissed him for being the voice of reason in a room where little evidence of it existed.

''You think it's my appendix?'' Kelly said with shocked disbelief.

''It isn't going to hurt to run a couple of tests,'' Mark countered, again avoiding answering a direct question.

''Why should you care?'' Kelly's soft voice wavered uncontrollably. ''After yesterday I would have thought...''

''After yesterday,'' Mark cut in sharply, ''I realized that you were right and that I owe you an apology.''

His eyes looked directly into Kelly's and the softness
Jo Marie had witnessed in his gaze at the hospital
Christmas party returned. He reached for Kelly's
hand, folding it in his own. "Will you accept my
apology? What you said yesterday made a lot of
sense, but at the time I was angry at the world and
took it out on you. Forgive me?"

With a trembling smile, Kelly nodded. "Yes, of
course I do."

The look they shared was both poignant and tender,
causing Jo Marie to feel like an intruder. Briefly, she
wondered what Andrew was thinking.

"If it does turn out that I need surgery would you
be the one to do it for me?"

Immediately Mark lowered his gaze. "No."

His stark response was cutting and Kelly flinched.
"There's no one else I'd trust as much as you."

"I said I wouldn't." Mark pulled the stethoscope
from his neck and placed it inside his bag.

"Instead of fighting about it now, why don't we
see what happens?" Jo Marie attempted to reason.
"There's no need to argue."

"There's every reason," Andrw intervened. "Tell
us, Mark, why wouldn't you be Kelly's surgeon if
she needed one?"

Jo Marie stared at Andrew, her dark eyes filled with
irritation. Backing Mark into a corner wouldn't help
the situation. She wanted to step forward and defend
her brother, but Andrew stopped her with an abrupt
motion of his hand, apparently having read her intent.

"Who I chose as my patients is my business."
Mark's tone was dipped in acid.

"Isn't Kelly one of your patients?" Andrew questioned calmly. "You did hurry over here when you heard she was sick."

Coming to a standing position, Mark ignored the question and the man. "Maybe you'd like to change clothes." He directed his comment to Kelly.

Shaking her head she said, "No, I'm not going anywhere."

"Those tests are important." Mark's control on his anger was a fragile thread. "You're going to the hospital."

Again, Kelly shook her head. "No, I'm not."

"You're being unreasonable." Standing with his feet braced apart, Mark looked as if he was willing to take her to the hospital by force if necessary.

"Why not make an agreement," Andrew suggested with cool-headed resolve. "Kelly will agree to the tests, if you agree to be her doctor."

Tiredly, Mark rubbed a hand over his jaw and chin. "I can't do that."

"Why not?" Kelly implored.

"Yes, Mark, why not?" Andrew taunted.

Her brother's mouth thinned grimly as he turned aside and clenched his fists. "Because it isn't good practice to work on the people you're involved with emotionally."

The corners of Kelly's mouth lifted in a sad smile. "We're not emotionally involved. You've gone out of your way to prove that to me. If you have any emotion for me it would be hate."

Mark's face went white and it looked for an instant as if Kelly had physically struck him. "Hate you?" he repeated incredulously. "Maybe," he replied in brutal honesty. "You're able to bring out every other emotion in me. I've taken out a lot of anger on you recently. Most of which you didn't deserve and I apologize for that.'' He paused and ran a hand through his hair, mussing it. ''No, Kelly,'' he corrected, ''I can't hate you. It would be impossible when I love you so much,'' he announced with an impassive expression and pivoted sharply.

A tense silence engulfed the room until Kelly let out a small cry. ''You love me? All these months you've put me through this torment and you love me?'' She threw back the blanket and stood, placing her hands defiantly on her hips.

''A lot of good it did me.'' Mark's angry gaze crossed the width of the room to hold hers. ''You're engaged to Daddy Warbucks over there so what good would it do to let you know?''

Jo Marie couldn't believe what she was hearing and gave a nervous glance to Andrew. Casually standing to the side of the room, he didn't look the least disturbed by what was happening. If anything, his features were relaxed as if he were greatly relieved.

''And if you cared for me then why didn't you say something before now?'' Kelly challenged.

Calmly he met her fiery gaze. ''Because he's got money, you've got money. Tell me what can I offer you that could even come close to the things he can give you.''

''And you relate love and happiness with things?'' Her low words were scathing. ''Let me tell you exactly what you can offer me, Mark Jubal Early. You have it in your power to give me the things that matter most in my life: your love, your friendship, your respect. And...and...if you turn around and walk out that door, by heaven I'll never forgive you."

"I have no intention of leaving," Mark snapped in return. "But I can't very well ask you to marry me when you're wearing another man's ring."

"Fine." Without hesitating Kelly slipped Andrew's diamond from her ring finger and handed it back to him. Lightly she brushed her mouth over his cheeks. "Thanks, Drew."

His hands cupped her shoulders as he kissed her back. "Much happiness, Kelly," he whispered.

Brother and sister observed the scene with open-mouthed astonishment.

Turning, Kelly moved to Mark's side. "Now," she breathed in happily, "if that was a proposal, I accept."

Mark was apprently too stunned to answer.

"Don't tell me you've already changed your mind?" Kelly muttered.

"No, I haven't changed my mind. What about the hospital tests?" he managed finally, his voice slightly raw as his eyes devoured her.

"Give me a minute to change." Kelly left the room and the three were left standing, Jo Marie and Mark staring blankly at each other. Everything was happening so fast that it was like a dream with dark shades of unreality.

Kelly reappeared and Mark tucked her arm in his. "We should be back in an hour," Mark murmured, but he only had eyes for the pert-faced woman on his arm. Kelly's gaze was filled with a happy radiance that brought tears of shared happiness to Jo Marie's eyes.

"Take your time and call if you need us," Andrew said as the happy couple walked toward the door.

Jo Marie doubted that either Kelly or Mark heard him. When she turned her attention to Andrew she discovered that he was already walking toward her. With eager strides he eliminated the distance separating them.

"As I recall, our agreement was that I wouldn't try to see you or contact you again while Kelly wore my engagement ring."

Her dark eyes smiled happily into his. "That's right."

"Then let's be rid of this thing once and for all." He led her into the kitchen where he carelessly tossed the diamond ring into the garbage.

Jo Marie gasped. Andrew was literally throwing away thousands of dollars. The diamond was the largest she had ever seen.

"The ring is as phony as the engagement."

Still unable to comprehend what he was saying, she shook her head to clear her thoughts. "What?"

"The engagement isn't any more real than that so-called diamond."

"Why?" Reason had escaped her completely.

His hands brought Jo Marie into the loving circle of his arms. "By Thanksgiving I'd given up every hope of ever finding you again. I'd convinced myself that those golden moments were just a figment of my imagination and that some quirk of fate had brought us together, only to pull us apart."

It seemed the most natural thing in the world to have his arms around her. Her eyes had filled with moisture so that his features swam in and out of her vision. "I'd given up hope of finding you, too," she admitted in an achingly soft voice. "But I couldn't stop thinking about you."

Tenderly he kissed her, briefly tasting the sweetness of her lips. As if it was difficult to stop, he drew in an uneven breath and rubbed his jaw over the top of her head, mussing her hair. "I saw Kelly at her parents' house over the Thanksgiving holiday and she was miserable. We've always been close for second cousins and we had a long talk. She told me that she'd been in love with Mark for months. The worst part was that she was convinced that he shared her feelings, but his pride was holding him back. Apparently your brother has some strange ideas about wealth and position."

"He's learning," Jo Marie murmured, still caught in the rapture of being in Andrew's arms. "Give him time." She said this knowing that Kelly was willing to devote the rest of her life to Mark.

"I told Kelly she should give him a little competition and if someone showed an interested in her, then Mark would step forward. But apparently she'd already tried that."

"My brother can be as stubborn as ten men."

"I'm afraid I walked into this phony engagement with my eyes wide open. I said that if Mark was worth his salt, he wouldn't stand by and let her marry another man. If he loved her, really loved her, he'd step in."

"But he nearly didn't."

"No," Andrew admitted. "I was wrong. Mark loved Kelly enough to sacrifice his own desires to give her what he thought she needed. I realized that the night of my Christmas party. By that time I was getting desperate. I'd found you and every minute of this engagement was agony. In desperation, I tried to talk to Mark. But that didn't work. He assumed I was warning him off Kelly and told me to make her happy or I'd pay the consequences.''

The irony of the situation was almost comical. ''You were already suffering the consequences. Why didn't you say something? Why didn't you explain?''

''Oh, love, if you'd been anyone but Mark's sister I would have.'' Again his mouth sought hers as if he couldn't get enough of her kisses. ''Here I was trapped in the worst set of circumstances I've ever imagined. The woman who had haunted me for months was within my grasp and I was caught in a steel web.''

''I love you, Andrew. I've loved you from the moment you held me all those months ago. I knew then that you were meant to be someone special in my life.''

''This has taught me the most valuable lesson of my life.'' He arched her close. So close it was impossible to breath normally. ''I'll never let you out of my arms again. I'm yours for life, Jo Marie, whether you want me or not. I've had to trust again every instinct that you would wait for me. Dear Lord, I had visions of you falling in love with Jim Rowden, and the worst part was I couldn't blame you if you did. I can only imagine what kind of man you thought me.''

Lovingly, Jo Marie spread kisses over his face. ''It's going to take me a lifetime to tell you.''

''Oh, love.'' His grip tightened against the back of her waist, arching her closer until it was almost painful to breathe. Not that Jo Marie cared. Andrew was holding her and had promised never to let her go again.

"I knew something was wrong with you and Kelly from the beginning," she murmured between soft, exploring kisses. Jo Marie couldn't have helped but notice.

"I've learned so much from this," Andrew confessed. "I think I was going slowly mad. I want more than to share my life with you, Jo Marie. I want to see our children in your arms. I want to grow old with you at my side."

"Oh, Andrew." Her arms locked around his neck and the tears of happiness streamed down her face.

"I love you, Florence Nightingale."

"And you, Andrew Beaumont, will always be my dream man."

"Forever?" His look was skeptical.

She lifted her mouth to his. "For all eternity," she whispered in promise.

"An ulcer?" Jo Marie shook her head slowly.

"Well, with all the stress I was under in the past few weeks, it's little wonder," Kelly defended herself.

The four sat in the living room sipping hot cocoa. Kelly was obediently drinking plain heated milk and hating it. But her eyes were warm and happy as they rested on Mark who was beside her with an arm draped over her shoulders.

"I've felt terrible about all this, Jo Marie," Kelly continued. "Guilt is a horrible companion. I didn't know exactly what was going on with you and Andrew. But he let it be known that he was in love with you and wanted this masquerade over quickly.''

''You felt guilty?'' Mark snorted. ''How do you think I felt kissing another man's fiancée?''

''About the same way Jo Marie and I felt,'' Andrew returned with a chuckle.

''You know, Beaumont. Now that you're marrying my sister, I don't think you're such a bad character after all.''

''That's encouraging.''

''I certainly hope you get along since you're both going to be standing at the altar at the same time.''

Three pairs of blank eyes stared at Kelly. ''Double wedding, silly. It makes sense, doesn't it? The four of us have been through a lot together. It's only fitting we start our new lives at the same time.''

''But soon,'' Mark said emphatically. ''Sometime in January.''

Everything was moving so fast, Jo Marie barely had time to assimilate the fact that Andrew loved her and she was going to share his life.

''Why not?'' she agreed with a small laugh. ''We've yet to do anything else conventionally.''

Her eyes met Andrew's. They'd come a long way, all four of them, but they'd stuck it out through the doubts and the hurts. Now their whole lives stretched before them filled with promise.

*　*　*　*　*

Unexpected Engagement
by
Jessica Steele

MILLS & BOON®

Don't miss Jessica Steele's next book

VACANCY: WIFE OF CONVENIENCE

**On sale April 2005,
in Tender Romance™!**

CHAPTER ONE

LYSAN paced her room. It was early yet, but she did not wish to go downstairs. Nor could she stay in her bed. After a very troubled night she was still no further forward. What was wrong with her?

Was she just plain frigid? She had never thought so. But then, up until last night she had never *thought* about the possibility that she might be frigid at all! Nor would she have, she was fairly certain, if...

She could hear sounds of the rest of the household stirring but still had no mind to leave her room. Instead she went and sat in her bedroom chair and went over again the worries that had plagued her during the night, as if hoping that this time she might find some answers.

She was Lysan Hadley—fact. Aged twenty-two—fact. Virgin of the parish of Luscombe in Berkshire—fact. And had been engaged to Noel Whitmore for almost three months. That too was a fact. Though the way in which she must have agreed to marry him still seemed to be a trace confusing.

She had known Noel all her life. His father and her father had been partners in a prosperous wine-importing business. In fact they all worked in the firm of Hadley and Whitmore, her father now heading the company, her brother Todd heading retailing, Noel warehousing, while she did her bit on the administration side.

Lysan had known for years, as had Noel, that the two families would be delighted if she and Noel were to marry. But she had never thought of Noel in that way.

And then three months ago tragedy had struck when Noel's parents had died, his father piloting the light aircraft that had crashed, killing him and his wife instantly.

They had all been close to Susan and Vernon Whitmore and were as shocked as Noel by his parents' deaths. Noel had no other relatives and had all but lived at their home as they each grappled with their shock and grief.

He had returned to his own home on the day before the funeral, and after the small, private funeral Lysan, noticing he had been missing for quite a while, had gone looking for him.

She had found him seated at his father's desk in his study, and had been hard put not to weep with him when she'd observed the tears on his face. But before she'd had time to wonder if she should tiptoe away and leave him to the privacy of his grief he had looked up. 'Oh, Liz,' he had cried in torment, and she could no more leave him than fly.

Swiftly she had hurried to him, her arms going out to his seated figure to hold him in what comfort she might give, her soft heart bleeding for him. He had turned in his chair and had held onto her, his arms around her waist, and for quite some minutes she had held him, until she'd heard him give a shaky sigh. 'All right?' she asked as a precursor to letting go of him.

'I've no one now,' he mumbled brokenly.

'Oh, love, you have,' she denied. 'You're part of our family!'

He looked up. 'Am I?'

She gently dried his eyes. 'You always have been,' she smiled, hating to witness his distress.

'We'll be married soon?'

She stared at him wordlessly, his question a bolt out

of the blue. Marriage had never been under discussion, but—he was so distressed—what could she say? Somehow, feeling emotionally torn by what he was going through, she could not at once tell him no, he had got his wires crossed somewhere.

Then she realised he must have read her consent to his 'We'll be married soon?' in her non-answer, for a moment later her father appeared in the doorway and, 'Lysan had just agreed to marry me,' Noel announced. And if on top of his heartbreak Noel was not to be made to look foolish there was no way then that she could say otherwise.

With her parents and brother delighted at her engagement, and with her feelings for Noel never more tender in those early days of him losing both his parents, Lysan began to think she was worrying needlessly. Noel was a super person, and any female would be thrilled to be engaged to him.

Days had turned into weeks, and... Her thoughts drifted off and she had to snatch her thoughts back when she found she was again remembering the tall Chilean who, a month ago, had paid them a visit. Dante Viveros had his own wine business just south of Santiago and...

Abruptly Lysan cut her thoughts off. Grief, she should be worrying about her and Noel, not some South American whom she barely knew, and would never see again.

Hurriedly she put the intrusive memory of the fair-haired, blue-eyed Latin from her, and gave all her powers of concentration to the most important of matters—what was wrong with her?

Noel, dear Noel. She loved him; of course she did. Yet, although she had been kissed before, and many times, by Noel, when last night the intensity of his kisses had changed to passionate, and demanding, instead of being thrilled by his passion, as any engaged woman should have been, she had felt nothing but—embarrassment!

A quick glance at her watch showed that, having been up and dressed for ages, she had sat so long she was in danger of being late down to breakfast.

Lysan left her room and went down the stairs no further forward in her quest to know what was the matter with her. She entered the breakfast room unhappily recalling how astonished Noel had looked last night when she had pushed him away and in no uncertain fashion had told him to 'Cut that out!'.

Oh, grief! 'Good morning, Dad,' she greeted her father. 'Morning, Todd.'

Her father had his head buried in his mail which he was sorting through. 'Morning, poppet,' he answered absently, Marjorie, his wife, preferring her bed to such an early morning start to the day.

Lysan received a brotherly grunt from Todd who was scanning the headlines in his paper, and she took her place at the table with her mind back on the problem that had plagued her since parting from Noel last night. She felt not a whit further forward as their housekeeper, Mrs Mason, brought fresh toast to the table, and Lysan greeted her and at that moment felt an urgent need to get away for a few days in order to get her head together.

She'd had barely any holiday this year but with Christmas only about five weeks away, the Christmas rush taken care of on her side of the business, she could take some time off. Noel was due some time off too, she realised—and when she really needed some time by herself she had an idea that if she said she was going away for a few days he would want to come too.

She had to dismiss the notion to go away, and had no chance to give her problem any more thought when Todd suddenly put down his paper and asked, 'Are you driving in with Noel, or coming with us?'

Oh, heck! Noel, who lived at the other end of the village, had taken to stopping by on his way through to give her a lift into London. But she did not feel ready to see him again so soon.

'I'll drive myself, thanks, Todd,' she answered. 'I've an appointment at the hairdresser's late this afternoon. I may be late.'

'Suit yourself,' he replied equably. 'Ready, Dad?'

Lysan smiled as the two men bade her goodbye, but as soon as they had left the room so her smile too departed. Oh, Lord, now, if she didn't want to be a liar, she had to find time to visit the hairdresser.

A minute later and she was realising that if she did not get a move on she would still be there when Noel arrived. In the next instant she was on her feet and heading in the same direction as her father and brother.

'Oh, if Noel stops by would you tell him I've already left?' she asked on meeting Mrs Mason, their treasure of many years, in the hall.

'I'll tell him,' Mrs Mason agreed, and Lysan sent her a smile of thanks and went swiftly to get her car out of its garage while conscience pricked that she should perhaps have picked up the phone to tell Noel not to call. But that would have involved explanations and, since she did not have an explanation, would have meant lying to him too. Lysan salved her conscience when she recalled that if Noel was to pick her up in the morning they always mentioned something of the sort the evening before. Her thoughts were glum again as she recalled

that very little had been said between them last evening
after she had forthrightly told him to 'Cut that out!'.

Lysan was glad that since her job was no sinecure she
was fully occupied that day. She managed, however, to
fit in a visit to the hairdresser's, where, to keep her 'lie
sheet' clean, she had about half an inch trimmed off her
shoulder-length ash-blonde hair.

She had thought that Noel might try to phone her, but
that he had not indicated that he was having a bit of a
sulk. She knew he was seeing some people that night in
connection with his side of the business, and felt uncomfortable within herself that she felt a tinge of relief that
she would not see him herself that evening.

She drove home feeling very much out of sorts and
still wondering what on earth the matter with her was
that when the man whose engagement ring she wore
should suddenly become more ardent than she had ever
known him—something inside her should cause her to
freeze over.

Alleviation from the worry that was starting to get her
down came that evening at dinner when, having just
passed her mother the potatoes, she overheard her father
and brother discussing a letter that had arrived that day
from Chile.

'Chile!' she butted in to exclaim, and, entirely forgetful that they did quite a bit of business with Chile
and that the letter could have come from anyone,
'You've had a letter from Dante Viveros!'

'I'd forgotten you'd met him,' her father replied,
happy to include her in the conversation, and confirming
that the letter had been from none other. 'He's written
thanking us for entertaining him while he was in
London. You remember we all stayed in town one night
when he was here and invited him to dinner?'

She remembered—vividly. The tall, mid-thirties Chilean was all male and charming with it. She had thought at first that he quite liked her, for he had seemed pleased to meet her. But when her father had expressed regret that her fiancé couldn't be with them because he was fully employed at home attending to matters in connection with his deceased parents' estate Dante Viveros had seemed to go distant on her.

'You are formally engaged to be married, *señorita*?' he had enquired.

'Down to the ring,' Todd had replied for her, raising her left hand to show the ruby ring on her third finger. And with the casualness of brothers—'Will you sit here, Dante?'—he'd begun to look after their guest.

And, while she'd been conscious of Dante Viveros's glance on her from time to time, apart from observing the courtesies of a guest, he'd had little more to say to her. And yet she had been so aware of him. Had thought of him so often since then. Had, she owned, ejected him from her thoughts on many an occasion when she had been out with Noel.

Suddenly then she became aware that her parents and Todd were looking at her and that she had not answered her father's question. 'Of course I remember,' she smiled. 'Noel couldn't be with us because he had to find some paperwork the solicitors wanted the next day. Er— it was kind of Señor Viveros to write.'

'He would think it only good manners,' her father stated. 'He's a most honourable man,' he added, and went on, 'In his letter he very kindly suggested that if I, or any member of my family, were thinking of visiting Chile it would give him pleasure to return my hospitality.'

Why her heart should suddenly give a little flutter,

Lysan had no idea. 'Now there's something for you to think about, Todd,' she addressed her brother, who, it seemed to her, was always trotting off to visit some vineyard or other.

'Would that I could fit it in,' Todd answered seriously, having spent time in France, Italy, Portugal and Spain that year. 'Perhaps next year.'

He left it there and Lysan went up to bed early that night. She was, she admitted, feeling more out of sorts than she could ever remember. And it wasn't just Noel who was causing her to feel concerned. For when, later, she lay in bed, she all at once realised that she had been thinking along the lines that if Todd went to South America perhaps she could go with him!

Aghast at the way her thoughts had gone when given free rein, Lysan tried to settle to sleep. But she awoke many times in the night and each time found she was wishing that the blue-eyed Chilean had never written. She felt very much confused, and when she left her bed she discovered she was not only confused but restless too. It was late November, but the next year Todd had spoken of seemed light years away. She wanted to be up and doing something *now*.

She showered and dressed and, determined to think sensibly, batted away any such ridiculous notion as to try and get Todd to agree to go to Chile now.

Determinedly she put Chile out of her head—and Dante Viveros—and set about solving the problem of her in relation to Noel and to try and banish the suddenly desperate need she felt to go away, to be by herself. Then suddenly she found she was wondering why, when in these days of female emancipation she was free to go anywhere, she should think she had to wait for Todd to be free before she could go to Chile. She could just as easily go on her own!

Oh, for heaven's sake! she fumed impatiently, and went downstairs to breakfast angry at the disorder in her head that had only come about this past month. Of course she wasn't going to Chile for goodness' sake— why in the name of reason should she?

She waited for Noel that morning. 'Forgiven me?' he asked.

She didn't want to talk about it. 'Of course,' she smiled, knowing what he was referring to. She spent the rest of the journey into London with her mind only half on what he was chatting about while with the other half she fretted that surely, since they were to be married, she should be able to discuss pretty well anything with him. Yet, just by him referring to the passion that had flared in him, she had again been embarrassed.

'I'll see you tonight?' Noel queried as he walked with her to her office door.

'Come round for dinner. I'll tell Mrs Mason,' she invited, and went into her own office feeling more worried than ever. It shouldn't be like this, should it? Was it embarrassment she felt or merely shyness at this new turn in their relationship? But how could she feel shy? She had known Noel all her life!

As matters turned out, Noel did not join them for dinner that night. Some major crisis had arisen to do with warehousing in Scotland and he had flown up there to personally attend to it.

And suddenly, in the lull from her father and Todd discussing that selfsame crisis, Lysan, while slicing into a piece of potato, heard her own voice state, quite calmly, 'I've decided to take a holiday in South America.'

At once all eyes turned to her. 'What did you say, Lysan?' her father enquired, not quite believing his hearing, Lysan a very much loved daughter.

She didn't quite believe her own hearing herself, and could only think then that the pressure she had felt herself under for the last couple of days must have forced her subconscious to speak out for her. But, the words having been said, her family informed, the idea seemed all at once set like concrete. She was no further forward in trying to sort out in her head if she was just plain frigid or what the dickens was wrong. She wished she could discuss it with her mother. But her mother loved Noel like a son and might be upset with her if she thought she had upset him so soon after his parents' deaths.

'It must have been you and Todd talking about South America yesterday,' Lysan left her own thoughts to try to give some explanation to her father; for once feeling unsure about most nearly everything, the only thing she did feel sure about was that she had to get away.

'You've got that look about you that says nothing is going to make you change your mind,' her mother observed.

'Heaven help us,' Todd put in.

'Shut up,' Lysan retorted.

'Now then, you two,' Marjorie Hadley interceded, fully aware that her two offspring would go through fire and water for the other. 'Have you told Noel?'

'I've only just decided.'

'What part of South America?' her father wanted to know.

'Hmm—I haven't quite decided...'

'You'd better make it Chile. I'd be happier if I knew someone where you're going. And...'

'Father—I'm twenty-two!'

'And not my little girl any longer, by the sound of it,' he teased. 'A year ago I was "Daddy", yesterday "Dad". But today, suddenly, I'm "Father"!'

'Oh, you!' she laughed—but could hardly believe when she went to bed that night that she had actually made the decision she had and that, albeit after a good half an hour of serious discussion, her parents and brother had raised few arguments.

Well, that's it, she thought, and collapsed into her bedroom chair starting to feel slightly stunned; she'd done it now. She'd have to go. She'd have to tell Noel too, but it was thoughts of Dante Viveros that began to fill her head.

Later, wide awake and excited over what she was about to undertake, she lay awake and could not help but wonder if she might have just the tiniest attraction to Dante Viveros. Could she be engaged to one man yet feel a little bit drawn to another? Dante was so virile-looking, so sophisticated, so male, so just about everything, while Noel, dear Noel, was just—Noel.

Lysan sighed in some bewilderment. Was it possible to be frigid and yet feel her heart beat just that tiniest bit faster in a kind of panic at the thought of meeting Dante Viveros again?

Not that she would go out of her way to see him; she quieted that dart of panic. She would take a good look around Chile first and then, if she had time, she might pick up the phone and perhaps make a courtesy call to him.

Lysan took time out the following morning to have the various vaccinations her father insisted she have for her trip and to make her flight reservation, and from then until a Saturday evening at the beginning of December, when her plane destined for Santiago de Chile took off from Heathrow Airport, she did not seem to have a moment to spare.

Only when she was airborne did Lysan have time to wonder if it was all real. So much had taken place. She was taking a month off and not returning to work until the second of January, but her actual holiday in Chile was for two and a half weeks; she would be home for Christmas but, to save herself a last-minute rush, she had done her Christmas-present shopping, plus Noel's Christmas birthday present. At her office, even though things were easier, she had worked late so that, save for a few items which of their nature had to wait awhile, there was little left in her 'pending' tray.

There had seemed little chance to be alone with Noel, and he hadn't liked it when she had broken the news to him of her intended holiday. 'But I can't come with you!' he'd protested. 'I can't get away for more than a few days just now!'

'I know but, well, I haven't had a holiday in an age, and I wouldn't mind at all getting away from our damp, cold winter and finding some warm sun.'

'Can't you wait awhile? Perhaps we could go in the new year. If it wasn't for your mother insisting that we observe the social conventions and wait until my parents have been dead for a year before we marry, we could get married and...'

'Oh, Noel.' Her heart had gone out to him again to be reminded that he was still suffering the loss of his parents. 'I'll soon be back,' she'd promised.

The night before she'd left, her father had taken her to one side and given her a note of Dante Viveros's home address and his telephone number. 'If you experience any sort of difficulty, get in touch with him; I'm sure he'll help you,' he'd advised.

'What sort of difficulty would I...?' she'd begun to tease, then had seen that her parent who had always been there to guard her would feel much better about her going if she did as he asked.

'For you, anything,' she'd grinned, and had kissed his cheek and, for his sake, stowed the piece of paper he had given her in a seldom-used, small, zipped compartment of her bag.

Her parents, with Noel and Todd and Todd's latest girlfriend, had seen her off at the airport. And she had said goodbye to them without showing that she felt more than a little nervous about what she was doing, but nevertheless convinced that it was something she just had to do. Somehow, without the need to be alone to have time to sort out what was wrong with her in relation to her inability to return Noel's passion, Chile seemed to be calling her.

Apart from a stop at São Paulo, the flight was long and uneventful. Others seemed able to sleep; she could not. Her plane landed in Santiago just before noon Chilean time on Sunday, and a kind of joy seemed to immediately take a hold of her. She had arranged hotel accommodation from England, and collected her luggage off the carousel with her thoughts on a taxi to her hotel, then a glorious shower, and bed for a few hours, in that order.

She pushed her luggage trolley into the arrivals area, glad her bank had been able to get her some Chilean currency, when her heart suddenly leapt and her intention to go out into the Chilean sunshine was lost completely. For there—could she believe it?—standing right there in front of her, was none other than—Dante Viveros!

Her mouth fell open and, when there must have been a dozen or so bright remarks she could have said, she gasped, 'You're—meeting someone?'

'None other but you, *señorita*,' he replied in faultless English. And, while she was still gasping not only at seeing him so unexpectedly, but at his reply, he stretched out a hand to formally shake her by the hand, and without so much as a by-your-leave took charge of her luggage.

Lysan could only think that it was because she was so shattered to see him there so unexpectedly—when so far as she was aware he did not even live in Santiago— that without a word she allowed him to usher her outside. They had walked to where he had his car parked before she had recovered any of her scattered wits.

'How did you know which flight—what plane to— that I'd—that I was on my way to Santiago?' she at last managed to complete a semi-sensible sentence, and when he stopped to put down her cases she made the mistake of looking up.

Amused blue eyes stared down at her. 'I have no gift of magic, *señorita*,' he drawled, and, while she was not very sure how she felt to be the butt of this sophisticated man's amusement, added, 'Your father sent a fax.'

Thanks, Dad! That was all she needed—that this worldly-wise man should know her father thought she was not safe out on her own. Clearly, since it was Sunday, Dante Viveros must have a fax machine in his study the same way her father had. 'That—was thoughtful of him,' she offered as lightly as she could.

'Your father has great caring for you,' the Chilean commented.

'Yes, but—he really shouldn't have bothered you. I'm sure you have much better things to do on a Sunday than hang around airports.'

He made no reply but stood back so she should get into the passenger seat of his car. He waited only until she had moved her long, slender legs over the door-sill, then he closed the door and, hefting her cases up effortlessly, he went to stow her luggage in the boot.

Lysan was still coping with seeing him so suddenly. Coping with the fact that her father had faxed him that she was on her way. It had been in her mind to contact Dante Viveros at the end of her stay, if at all, and not at the beginning. Suddenly, though, then, and following on from her wondering what Dante Viveros might normally be engaged upon on a Sunday, and with something of a jolt, another thought hit her.

· At that moment Dante joined her in the car, and she could no more hold the question down than fly. 'Your wife, she...?' Her voice tapered off when he turned to look at her.

'I have no wife,' he informed her casually, his eyes taking in the fine contours of her face, her cloud of ash-blonde hair, her wide green eyes.

'Oh,' Lysan mumbled, wondering why on earth she should feel so pleased to hear him say that. She had somehow gained the notion that he was still a bachelor, but, at around thirty-five, good-looking into the bargain, not to mention that he wasn't without a peso or two, she calculated he must have done some pretty nifty footwork to be still footloose and running. Not that it bothered her in the slightest, of course.

Dante turned from her and started up the car. 'Your fiancé could not join you on this holiday, señorita?' he questioned as they left the airport behind.

'He's busy just now. He—' she broke off; somehow she didn't want to talk about Noel just then. Soon, she knew, she must get down to some solid thinking about Noel, and her frigidity in response to his passion. But not yet. 'My—er—hotel's the...'

'Your father mentioned it in his fax,' Dante replied, and gave his attention to the road, and Lysan settled back and looked about her.

They had been driving some while, though, when it suddenly occurred to her that the airport must be miles and miles away from the city because when she had thought they would soon be driving into a built-up area the area they were driving in seemed to be growing more and more rural. Odd, that, because on the plane it had seemed that no sooner had they flown in over the Andes than they were landing in Santiago.

She turned to her companion, intending to say as much. 'Dante,' she attracted his attention, and as he glanced at her and she recalled how she had been '*señorita*' to him from the moment he had met her at the airport she went a touch pink. 'It's all right if I call you Dante?' she enquired. Perhaps they were more formal here than they were at home.

She discovered she had nothing to get hot under the collar about when, taking his attention briefly off the road up ahead, he gave her a kindly sort of look that made her heart beat a touch faster. And, 'I insist upon it,' he said, and there was such a superb upward curve to his mouth as he said it that she forgot for quite some seconds why it was she had wanted to attract his attention in the first place.

Then she remembered. 'When do we start meeting the city?' she asked pleasantly.

'City?' he queried.

She was a degree mystified. Given that he had a trace of an accent, he spoke English as if he knew her language as well as she did. 'Santiago,' she gave him the benefit of the doubt. 'We don't seem to have hit any built-up areas yet. I just wondered how far Santiago is from the airport.'

This time he did not glance her way but, with a slight shrug of his shoulders, and keeping his eyes on the road, he answered, 'It's about a half-hour's drive.'

'Then we should soon be there,' she murmured, and might have relaxed back into her seat again.

Only, to her astonishment, she clearly heard him state, 'We would be, if we were driving in that direction.'

Lysan started at him in amazement. Did he mean he had an errand to do first before he dropped her off at her hotel? Somehow she did not think so. But, aware that she could sometimes be a little hasty, she remembered her manners and controlled the sudden rush of heat to her tongue, to state as calmly as she was able, 'I'm grateful for you meeting me at the airport, *señor*, but I could have gone to my hotel by taxi if...'

Her voice tailed off when this time he did turn his head and she was certain she discerned a hint of amusement in his expression that, having enquired if she might use his first name, she was now calling him *señor*. But Lysan was very far from amused when in everyday even tones he quietly let fall, 'I cannot allow you to stay in a hotel; I am taking you to my home.'

'You... I...' she spluttered, staring at him in utter shock. 'You cannot *allow*...!' she managed to string a few more words together.

'It is true, I cannot,' he replied urbanely.

'It is also true,' she fired, her tongue burning out of control, 'that *I* will not allow myself to stay anywhere but in a hotel. Turn this car around at once and...' Her voice tailed off when he gave her an arrogant and arctic look that would instantly have frozen boiling water. She guessed then that nobody ever gave Señor Dante Viveros orders.

'I have cancelled your hotel reserva—'

'You did wh—?' She couldn't believe it!

'While you are in Chile,' he cut her off, 'you will stay where I say you will,' he informed her in no uncertain fashion.

'Oh, will I?' she raged aggressively. And on that instant he braked, bringing the speed of the car down as he steered to the side of the road.

Halting the car, he turned to her, all in the same movement, and, the blue of his eyes darkened by his sudden anger, he grated, 'Yes, you will.' She opened her mouth but he would not allow her to say another word until he had finished. 'You are a single woman, thousands of miles away from home, with neither your father, your brother, nor your fiancé here to protect you. You may be fully emancipated and familiar with men—' Familiar with men! How *dared* he? '—but while you're here you will be under my protection.'

'Oh, no, I w—'

'Your father was right to send a fax to me. You are much too beautiful to be left running around Santiago on your own.' He thought she was beautiful! For all his tone had been matter-of-fact, some of her heat died.

'I...' she tried to protest just the same.

'I cannot leave you alone in some hotel, Lysan; you must see that.' She saw nothing of the sort, but as quickly as he had angered, so his voice had softened to be half-teasing. 'Could I leave you to drive half the men in my country crazy?' he enquired. 'That ring you wear would be no protection with some men.'

'I...' she tried again, realising that without doubt she could count him in the other half who most definitely would not be driven crazy by her. 'You exaggerate,' she replied stiffly.

'I assure you I do not. But, even so, from the respect I have for your father and brother, I must still insist that you stay in my home. My brother and his wife will be there to chaperon you should you think it necessary.'

'I shouldn't think it will be necessary at all,' she retorted coldly, not thanking him for his implication that he didn't fancy her and that, no matter how beautiful she might be, a chaperon wouldn't be necessary on his account. Mulishly she stared at him—and tried desperately hard to deny a prick of curiosity to see his home, to meet his brother and sister-in-law who obviously lived at his home.

'Well?' he demanded, clearly starting to grow impatient with her, clearly waiting for her confirmation that she would go with him to his home, but just as clearly not intending to take her anywhere *but* to his home.

Lysan stared belligerently at him. Who did he think he was? She needed time by herself to get herself sorted out, to discover why it was, when she loved Noel, his ardent embraces left her cold.

Dante Viveros stared grimly back. It was stalemate. He seemed prepared to sit there for the rest of the day. This was ridiculous. She opened her mouth—and to her amazement found she had an unexpected sense of humour when pushed into a corner with no way out.

'Thank you very much for your kind offer of hospitality,' she trotted out as any well brought up young woman might. 'I accept.' She then discovered that Dante

Viveros had a sense of humour that matched hers because as he stared at her, stared at the impish light in
her wide green eyes, suddenly his mouth started to curve
up at the corners—and he put back his head and laughed.

His teeth were superb, his face was alive, the sound
of his laughter deep and warm—the whole effect was
quite devastating, she thought.

THE landscape seemed totally rural when Dante steered his car off the main highway and towards the lush valley where he had his estate. By that time Lysan had put from her any absurd notion that she had found Dante Viveros, his face alive with laughter, in any way devastating.

By that time the emancipated part of her that wanted to be heard was objecting most strongly to the way in which she had been shanghaied. The annoyance she felt, however, was weakened by the knowledge that her father, out of his love for her—with or without the excellence of his mutual business dealings with the Chilean—trusted the man. That was why he had faxed him that she was on her way.

It was time, she well knew, to bring her manners to the fore. She was a guest, for the want of a better word. She had better start acting like one.

Having decided to be most polite but nothing more than that, Lysan's emotions underwent another change when they began to drive down into the valley. For suddenly she began to feel enchantment wash over her. Everywhere were lush grasses and green trees, with pale yellow lupins growing wild by the roadside.

The entrance to the house was gated, but someone was there to open the high and wide gates for them, and Dante, with a few words to the man, steered his car up a wide and long, tree-lined drive. It was quite magical. With strong sunlight dappling through tall trees Lysan was suddenly aware that she felt quite joyous. She tried to tell herself that no wonder she felt that way—yesterday she had left a country where everyone was muffled and coated against a cold and wet December. Who wouldn't feel joyful to be here in this warm sunshine? Somehow, though, she had the oddest notion the cause of her joy was more than that.

The notion was fleeting, and before she had time to analyse it Dante had come round to open the passenger door. She stepped out onto the gravel drive beside him. 'Welcome to my home,' he stated, and Lysan looked up into his solemn blue eyes, and quickly away again.

'Thank you,' she murmured, and as they stood for a moment in front of the superb two-storeyed building so she wanted to stay annoyed with him but found that she could not.

At least, she thought she could not, but as he escorted her into the equally splendid and large hall of the house and looked down as they halted at the bottom of the wide staircase and remarked, 'You are tired, Lysan,' she felt quite cross. She had been travelling for more than sixteen hours! She was not surprised that she looked tired—she also felt a little grubby into the bargain.

She did not thank him that he refrained from suggesting she might benefit from twenty-four hours' sleep and a soak in the tub. 'I'm quite all right, *señor*,' she replied, her voice more tart perhaps than she had intended.

'Proud as well as beautiful,' he commented, and she hated the amusement lurking in his eyes. But, before she could forget her manners and tell him what he could do with his hospitality, a dark-clad, matronly woman of about forty came hurrying along the hall. 'Ah, here is my housekeeper.'

From somewhere Lysan found a smile as he introduced Emilia to her. Then, firing a volley of Spanish at the woman, of which Lysan understood not one word, Dante turned back to her.

'I'll have your cases brought up to you. Emilia will show you to your room. In the meantime...' his mouth curved—she was sure in mischief—as he looked into her sparking green eyes '...might I suggest you rest and perhaps catch up on some of the sleep you missed on your flight?'

Suddenly and from nowhere, her sense of humour stirred. But she would not let him see. 'Thank you,' she replied quietly.

'I shall see you at dinner,' he stated smoothly, waited only to give Emilia one more instruction, then, turning, bade her, *'Adiós,'* and left her in the capable hands of his housekeeper.

Emilia's English was no better than Lysan's Spanish, but a few smiles and gestures later she showed Lysan into a lovely high-ceilinged room. It was a large room and as Lysan looked about at the furnishings, and last word in luxurious carpeting, she saw that it was more a bed-sitting room than just a bedroom.

The housekeeper went over to another door in the room to reveal the adjoining bathroom, and it seemed that barely had Lysan turned round than a manservant was bringing in her luggage. 'Thank you,' she smiled, and bravely attempted, *'Gracias!'*

The man smiled back. *'Gracias, señorita,'* he beamed, for all the world as though she had just presented him a fortune, then, with one last look at her ash-blonde hair, he respectfully went on his way. Following on his heels, however, a pleasant woman of her own age appeared in the doorway and was introduced as Auda, and had apparently arrived to unpack for her.

'No, no,' Lysan declined with a smile. 'I can do it.'

Auda looked doubtful, but Emilia returned Lysan's smile and as the two went away Lysan turned about and made for the bathroom.

She found that she had everything she would need already there for her, from the fluffiest of towels and most divine soap, right down to towelling slippers and a bathrobe. With no need to hunt up her toilet bag, Lysan ran a bath, and a few minutes later knew perfect bliss.

For an age she just lay there, indulging in the fragrant water. She thought of home and thought of Noel. But each time she tried to get down to any kind of in-depth thinking about her 'problem' her thoughts seemed to wander—and she found she was thinking of none other but Dante Viveros.

Feeling restless and confused, Lysan left her bath, towelled herself dry and donned a fluffy robe. She was, she guessed, more tired than she had thought, and she went into the bedroom, a pleased smile coming to her face. For while she had been lost to her thoughts in her bath someone had been in and left a tray of refreshments.

After eating a sandwich or two and drinking a cup of tea, Lysan unpacked, and decided that the bed looked too inviting to be ignored. She chose to lie on top of what she discovered was the most comfortable of double beds.

Over the next few hours she alternately dozed and slept. But she was awake and dressed in a shirt and light-weight trousers when a knock sounded on her door. Why her heart should leap that perhaps it might be Dante coming to tell her what time they usually dined she could not fathom.

In the next second, however, she was realising that if Dante did have such a message for her he would more likely send the maid to deliver it—probably with a note since Auda could not speak English.

Fully expecting by then to see Auda standing on the other side of the door, Lysan went swiftly over to it, and found it was not the maid who stood there but a dark-haired, late-twenties woman who smiled warmly, and, speaking slowly in English, she introduced herself. 'I am Gabina, wife of Celso, the brother of Dante.'

'Oh, hello!' Lysan's own smile tumbled out at the charming way Dante's sister-in-law introduced herself, and, extending her right hand, she said, 'Lysan Hadley,' and added, 'Come in.'

'You have everything you require?' Gabina enquired.

'Absolutely!' Lysan replied, and when Gabina looked faintly mystified at the word Lysan added, 'Yes, oh, yes.' There was even an electric hairdryer attached to the wall in the bathroom.

Gabina smiled. 'I am sorry I was not here when you come. I did not know of visit until this morning.'

Lysan wondered if Gabina Viveros was put out that out of the blue, and without her invitation, some un-known English woman had descended upon them. Her smile, though, denied that she was in any way upset, but just the same Lysan began to explain, 'I was going to go to a hotel but Dante...' when she realised she was speaking too quickly for Gabina. 'Would you like to sit down?' she invited, indicating one of the three chairs in the room.

'Thank you,' Gabina accepted, and enquired, 'Would you like some tea?'

'Not unless you would,' Lysan answered, and since Gabina required nothing either they made themselves comfortable in the well-padded chairs, and the next hour flashed by as Gabina got more and more to grips with her rusty English, and Lysan, with the help of her Spanish/English dictionary, learned a few Spanish words. Then suddenly Gabina became aware of the time and exclaimed, 'I must go and see my husband!' Getting up, she asked, 'Do you know the *sala*?'

Quickly Lysan leafed through her dictionary to find that *sala* was Spanish for large room. 'I'm afraid not,' she replied, and received another of Gabina's lovely smiles.

'I will come seven forty-five for you,' she promised, and left, and Lysan thought she had seldom met anyone so friendly and pleasant.

By the sound of it the family assembled in the drawing room before dinner. Now what should she wear? Gabina had been quietly but expensively clad. Mustn't let the side down, Lysan mused, and went over and slid back the doors of the huge wardrobe.

Tomorrow, Emilia and Auda permitting, she would hunt up an iron, but for now she was extremely glad she had thought to pack a smart and uncrushable lightweight two-piece of dark putty colour.

At seven-thirty, and feeling strangely nervous, Lysan looked at her reflection in the full-length mirror. She had left her ash-blonde hair loose, framing her face. Her delicate creamy skin required little more make-up than a touch of powder, a touch of pink lipstick, her eyes a touch of mascara. The picture that stared back at her should have given her confidence—so why was she feeling nervous?

She had never been shy about meeting people before, and anyhow she had already met Dante. Not that she was in any way nervous about seeing him again anyhow. He, she recalled, her thoughts spinning off again, had referred to her as beautiful. Did he truly think she was

beautiful? Did…? Her thoughts halted when just then a
light tap sounded on her door and Lysan rapidly got
herself together.

'You are ready?' Gabina smilingly enquired when
Lysan opened the door. Some of her nervousness started
to ebb away. Gabina was dressed in similar fashion to
herself.

Together they went along the wide landing and down
the wide and handsome staircase. There seemed to Lysan
to be a good many doors leading off the main hallway.
But it was towards one that looked a little larger than
the rest that Gabina took her. And once there she opened
it and stood back for Lysan to precede her into the room.

There were two men standing in conversation in the
centre of the room, and as Lysan recognised the taller
of the two as Dante Viveros, her host, so she started to
feel suddenly shy. Rot, she denied, and as Dante turned
and his eyes went over her so she went confidently forward.

'Good evening, Lysan, Gabina,' Dante greeted them
smoothly, coming a pace nearer. 'You haven't met my
brother Celso,' he remarked, and, turning, he performed
the introduction.

Celso Viveros, as well as being a few inches shorter
than his brother, was also a year or two younger, Lysan
judged. But she took an instant liking to him. 'Welcome
to Chile, Lysan,' he beamed warmly as they shook
hands. 'I hope your stay with us will be a very happy
one.'

'Thank you,' she murmured, and, his English very
good, she commented on the only subject she so far
knew that they had in common. 'You're in the wine
business too, I believe,' she smiled.

'I live, think and breathe it,' he replied, and added,

'Dante has told me that you work in the administration of your family's wine-import business.'

Lysan took a sideways glance at Dante. She had thought him to be looking at his brother, but he was looking at her—was that admiration she glimpsed in those blue depths? She quickly looked away again, aware that her imagination must be running riot. He had said she was beautiful, but that didn't mean he would look at her in any way admiringly.

'I...' she attempted to reply to Celso, but discovered that she was so confused suddenly that she had forgotten what it was they had been talking about.

Nor did she thank Dante Viveros that he should smoothly and with charm enter the conversation, and remind her, by saying to his brother, 'The administration side of Hadley and Whitmore will have to do without Lysan for a while. We are privileged to have her with us for the next two and a half weeks.'

He'd got that wrong but Dante chose that moment to ask what she would like to drink and moved away to fix her a martini and Gabina a sherry and the moment was lost in which to tell him so. For, even though she did have her flight back booked for two weeks next Wednesday—and regardless of Dante's 'I must...insist that you stay in my home'—there was no way she was going to stay under his roof until then.

Realising that her father must have told Dante in his fax the duration of her holiday, Lysan started to feel decidedly niggled with the male population in general.

'Your martini.' Dante was standing in front of her.

'Thank you,' she murmured coolly, and saw one of his eyebrows twitch a shade upwards at her tone.

'You did not want ice in it?' he enquired, his expression now deadpan for all she knew he was hinting that from her cool tone ice was not required.

'It's—just right.' Politeness forced the words from her—but she wanted to smile. Thankfully, at that point, Gabina came and chatted to her.

Lysan sat opposite Dante when later they took their places in the dining room, where good manners to him, as his guest, meant she should put any irritation she felt to be so press-ganged, bossed about, and, in truth, generally disturbed by him, to the back of her. While they were in company at any rate. Host or no host, though, she wasn't going to put up with any more of his arrogant edicts should he again come over all bossy and tell her 'While you're here you will be under my protection'. Now she came to think of it, she had given in far too easily! Her journey had been wearying and she had been suffering from a lack of sleep, of course, but...

'The soup is to your liking, Lysan?'

She looked up, and across the table, straight into a pair of intelligent blue eyes. The soup was home-made pea and ham. 'It's delicious,' she replied truthfully, and, regardless of her mutinous thoughts, she smiled. She immediately wanted that smile back and saw that his glance had fallen to her upward curve of her mouth.

Again she was glad to hear Gabina engage her in conversation. 'Do you cook at all, Lysan?' she asked.

'I'm afraid not,' she answered.

'Afraid?' the question came from Dante.

'One day I shall have a home of my own and shall need to cook,' Lysan looked at him to reply. 'Unless I learn to cook fairly quickly then I'm afraid my poor husband...'

She did not get to finish the sentence because all at

once a stern look crossed Dante's features and he grated, 'You are to be married soon?'

Honestly! she fumed. There she was doing her utmost to be a polite guest. It cut both ways. *And* they were in company!

She almost retorted a snappy 'If you've no objection' but from what she knew of him so far had an idea she would find his unbridled laughter at the notion he might object more humiliating than she was ready for.

She decided to take his question at face value. 'Noel's parents died just over three months ago. My mother doesn't think we should marry for a year,' she replied primly.

'And what do you think?' he demanded to know.

Feeling more than a little startled, Lysan stared at him. Quite plainly, while he obviously always wanted to be boss, he at the same time thought a woman should have a mind of her own.

'In this case, I think Mother knows best,' she answered tautly, and, uncaring if he thought her a wimp, she turned to Gabina and, finding a smile, she asked, 'Do you cook, Gabina?'

'My wife loves to be in the kitchen,' Celso answered for her. 'But for upsetting the housekeeper, Gabina would spend most of her day in the kitchen, I would swear.' Lysan could not see the sweet Gabina upsetting Emilia or anyone else. But it seemed that Celso had spoken too quickly for Gabina to fully comprehend, so while he translated into Spanish what he had said so Lysan calmed down again.

Though she did not know if it was wariness of Dante or wariness of her own tongue that shortly after dinner caused her to ask if anyone would mind if she retired. It was ten o'clock by then but in Chile apparently everyone kept late hours. She went to bed with very mixed emotions.

Lysan felt better after a good night's sleep and realised her mixed-up emotions of yesterday had stemmed from nothing more than the fact that she was tired from travelling, irked that she had given in to being bossed about, while at the same time she was attempting to adjust to her new surroundings.

Suddenly she was feeling full of life and eager to explore. In a hurry to start her day she swiftly showered, shampooed her hair and found the efficiency of the bathroom hairdryer was second to none. While leaving her hair loose at the back, she brushed the sides to the back and secured them, leaving her fine bone-structure exposed. Her idea, however, was to get some of the gorgeous sun on her face rather than to show the world the beauty of her cheekbones.

Dressed in white trousers and a white T-shirt, Lysan left her room and tripped lightly down the stairs. Before she got as far as the bottom, however, the stout front door into the hall opened and her heart gave a little flip as Dante Viveros came in.

He halted, and she halted, and as she stared at the tall, virile-looking Chilean so his glance slid over her long-legged, slender shape and came to rest on her face and pulled-back hair.

But, she recalled, nothing was going to upset her today. There was a glorious sun shining out there, and she was on holiday. Her lips formed an impish smile. *'Buenos días, señor!'* she greeted him in her best non-existent South American accent—and was truly quite fascinated when his superb mouth parted in what could only be called a fabulous grin.

'*Buenos días*, Lysan,' he replied, and, coming over to the bottom of the stairs, said, 'You obviously slept well.'

Even while it passed through her mind to wonder, Was there a barb behind his comment? Was he saying that yesterday she had been a pain? Lysan silently reiterated that nothing was going to upset her today.

She carried on down the stairs, and felt unexpectedly breathless when she stood close to him at the bottom of the stairs. She found she was having to search quite desperately for something to say to fill the moment. Though he, of course, did not seem to be one whit put out to have her standing so close.

'I—er—was looking for Gabina,' she invented, moving a step away.

'Gabina is having breakfast, I suspect.' Lysan felt a frisson of electricity shoot up her arm when, touching a hand to her elbow, he said, 'I will show you the way.'

Lysan fell in step with him the short way to the breakfast room, and again felt a nervous need to say something. 'Um—what time is breakfast—er—usually? I never thought to ask.'

'Breakfast is any time you require it,' he replied easily.

'Are you going to have yours now?'

'I had mine some hours ago.'

She stared at him in some amazement. It was only eight o'clock now. 'Do you never sleep?' she could not resist the question. Lord alone knew what time he went to bed last night yet this morning he must have been up before dawn cracked.

'I require little sleep,' Dante answered.

'That's just as well,' she tossed back, and felt light-headed all of a sudden. He stopped and opened a door along the hall and she went before him into a large but none the less comfortable breakfast room where Gabina was.

'*Buenos días*, Dante. Good morning, Lysan,' she smiled at once.

'*Buenos días*, Gabina,' Lysan answered. 'Thank you,' she turned to say to Dante who had pulled out a chair for her at the breakfast table.

'Will you have coffee with us?' Gabina asked him, out of courtesy to their guest speaking carefully in English.

'*Sí, gracias*,' he smiled to his sister-in-law, and as the housekeeper hurried into the room he enquired what Lysan would like for her breakfast.

In no time at all, or so it seemed to Lysan, she had toast, butter and marmalade in front of her while she sipped at a glass of freshly squeezed orange juice. 'Is there somewhere in particular you would like to visit today?' Gabina asked, pouring her a cup of coffee.

These were busy people. Lysan did not want to take up any of their time which they might want to use more industriously elsewhere. 'The view from my bedroom window is so lovely, I thought I might take a walk,' she smiled.

Though owned to being pleased when Gabina requested, 'May I walk with you?'

'I should like that,' she accepted, but was not quite sure how she felt when Dante put down his cup and stood up.

'If you'll excuse me,' he requested, and was halfway to the door when he stopped and turned to look at Lysan. 'I have to see the manager of one of our cellars this afternoon. You might enjoy the drive, Lysan?'

She opened her mouth to say no. 'Thank you. I think I might,' some newly awakened stranger to her replied.

It must be something in the air, she mused, when a half-hour or so later she and Gabina set off on their walk. It seemed much further down the tree-lined avenue to the wrought-iron gates than it had when she and Dante had driven up to the house yesterday. But Gabina was a super companion, which made the walking in such delightful surroundings even that bit more pleasant.

Once through the gates they strolled further into the lush valley and with every step Lysan grew more and more enchanted with it. 'Is it always like this?' she enquired in wonder.

And Gabina laughed. 'Perhaps I should not tell you of the rain.'

Lysan laughed too, realising that a valley floor of such green lushness could not happen without a plentiful supply of rain. It was the beginning of summer in Chile, she calculated, so perhaps the rainy season was over. Though in actual fact, and 'weird' though Todd called her, she had always liked the rain.

By the time they returned to the house, she knew that Gabina was the only child of a professor and his doctor wife, that Gabina had studied haute cuisine in France, and was hoping to write a cookery book, and also that she and Celso had been married a year. In turn she had told Gabina of her parents and brother and her job, and also of her fiancé. Oddly, though, and disturbingly, Lysan felt something akin to unease at having Noel's engagement ring on her finger.

'Emilia will have prepared something for lunch,' Gabina stated as they entered the house.

Wondering if Dante and Celso would be there for the midday meal, Lysan went up to her room to change, just in case Dante would want to be off straight away afterwards.

Before she knew it she found, when she had showered not many hours before, that she had showered again, and she was in the act of taking one of her smart silk dresses from her wardrobe when she caught herself up short. Good heavens, what was she thinking of? Dante was working, and had been dressed in casual trousers and sports shirt that morning. He was working this afternoon too, and since she was only going along for the ride— and in all likelihood would not even be getting out of the car—that twitchy eyebrow of his was bound to rise a centimetre or two if he saw her dressed as if to open a garden fête.

When Lysan went down the stairs again, she had dressed her hair in the same fashion as earlier that day, and had exchanged her white trousers and T-shirt for cotton trousers of the palest green and a palest green thin cotton short-sleeved shirt. She found Gabina in the dining room on her own.

'Doesn't D-Celso come home to lunch?' she enquired, and realised she had been speaking a trifle too fast when Gabina looked momentarily puzzled.

'Home?' she queried, then smiled, and answered, 'Oh, yes, sometimes. But when he is very busy he sometimes forgets about his stomach.'

From that, Lysan gathered that Celso, and Dante too, without a doubt, were not clock-watchers and that once absorbed in their work they forget time. For a fleeting moment she felt quite anxious that Dante might forget he had invited her to go with him that afternoon. Hurriedly she put any such nonsense from her. Grief— as if it mattered!

And just to show that it did not she asked, 'Are you coming too this afternoon, Gabina? Dante and I are driving to...'

'Ah, yes. I mean no,' Gabina laughed. 'Not unless you wish me to...'

'No, no, that's all right,' Lysan smiled, and suddenly started to feel anxious that, for all Gabina had not shown it, there must have been a dozen or so other matters she might have preferred to be getting on with that morning rather than walking around the estate.

She went up to her room after lunch to wash her hands, comb her hair and apply fresh lipstick. And by then anxieties were picking at her thick and fast. For by then she had started to wonder just how much she was putting Dante out! Until yesterday when he had received her father's fax, he'd had no thought of having to entertain an English woman. Not that she had asked him to house her under his roof—far from it. But...

She went down the stairs to the *sala* in a thoughtful frame of mind. 'You are ready, Lysan?'

She spun round. She had been standing looking out of the window, and had not heard him come in. 'Dante, I...'

'Something is wrong?' he asked, coming further into the room and not stopping until he was right in front of her. 'Your beautiful green eyes—so serious,' he teased gently, and most peculiarly she felt a spurt of emotion in her heart region.

'You—you were up early this morning. It wasn't so that you could get your work done because you thought you had to keep me entertained, was it?'

'Are you always so direct?' he wanted to know.

'Most times, I think,' she replied, but would not be teased out of her worry. The idea that, late to bed, he had risen early on her account appalled her. 'Have I inconvenienced y—?'

'Not in the slightest,' he cut her off to assure her.

But she was not convinced. 'I can't stay here!' she announced bluntly—and saw that he did not think very much of her announcement, his teasing manner gone in an instant.

'You cannot stay anywhere else!' he retorted sharply, his blunt tone reducing hers to nothing.

Oh, can't I? she bridled—then remembered that, in the light of the mutual and harmonious business dealings between him and her father, to go for his jugular was perhaps hardly tactful. 'It's an imposition, my being here,' she toned down what she had been going to say— so much for being direct! 'You didn't invite me—yet now you're stuck with me, and...'

'What a funny child you are.' Humour was suddenly in his voice, but she liked that no better than she liked his sharp tone.

'I am *not*,' she said haughtily, 'a child!'

'Forgive me,' he at once apologised, and, his eyes sliding down over her slender but curvy and all-womanly body before returning to her green ones, said, 'I can well see that you are physically all woman, but—'

'Don't say it!' she cut in threateningly. She was not sure she would not take a swing at him, business relationship with her father or no, if Dante Viveros dared to utter that while physically she was all woman she otherwise behaved like a child.

'Would I dare?' His eyes were suddenly dancing with amusement.

But she was not amused. Indeed she felt very much out of sorts. 'You won't take it personally, I'm sure, if I change my mind and don't come with you this afternoon,' she stated stiffly.

His amusement vanished. 'And you are not childish?'

The pig! From wanting to hit him, she went to a barely held down desire to kick him. To break his ankle.

She took a deep and steadying breath and, knowing deep down she had been looking forward to the drive all morning, suddenly, as Dante looked down at her, she found, most extraordinarily, that she was smiling. 'You're sure you want me to come?'

His eyes roved her face, and while he did not deign to answer her question he remarked, 'Your hair suits you equally drawn back from your face like that.'

Again her heart acted peculiarly. She gave a tiny, choky sort of cough. 'In that case, I'll come,' she grinned.

She was not grinning half an hour later as she sat beside him in his car wondering at the emotions Dante Viveros aroused in her. While it was true she had, when required, thumped both her brother and Noel in her growing years, never had she come anywhere close to hitting a man. She had wanted to kick his ankle too, she recalled with shame. What on earth had come over her since coming to Chile?

'You're very quiet,' Dante broke into her thoughts to observe. 'You're not still worrying?'

There was charm in his tones, a warmth. 'No,' she replied as she felt she had to. What with Dante insisting that she be his guest, it would indeed be childish to continue to fret that she might be imposing on his hospitality. 'Though...'

'Though?' he took up at once when she hesitated.

'Though I did ask Gabina to join us this afternoon.'

Dante turned his head in surprise. 'You felt the need of a chaperon?'

Oh, grief, she wished she had said nothing. She had not for a moment thought that Dante might make a pass at her. And clearly, from his—uncomplimentary—surprise, the thought to do so was a million miles from his mind. 'Of course not!' she retorted, half in embarrassment that he should read her comment that way, half in annoyance that when he himself had spoken of her being fully emancipated he should ask the question at all. 'It just occurred to me that—' she broke off wishing with all she had that she had never uttered that 'though'. But while it might seem that Dante was concentrating solely on his driving the enquiring look he gave her when once more he turned to look at her told her he was still waiting for her to answer. Suddenly hating him and his tenacity, she stated snappily, 'I shouldn't want to be a burden on Gabina's time either.' And heard him laugh! Actually heard him laugh. 'What's so funny?' she asked aggressively.

'And they say Latin women are volatile!'

She wanted to laugh, but wouldn't. What *was* it about this man that in the space of ten seconds could send her emotions from one extreme to another? 'I'm sorry,' she apologised quietly, as in all conscience she felt that she must.

'I shall forgive you,' he replied magnanimously, but looking at him Lysan was sure she saw the corners of his mouth quirk upwards. Though he was totally serious when he said, 'Do not ever think you are a burden on anyone's time. I promise you that my sister-in-law will thoroughly enjoy this time of you being here with us.'

'You think so?'

'I know it. Gabina will treat your holiday as her holiday also,' he assured her.

It was a super day; the countryside they were travelling through was fantastic. Lysan chose to believe him. She relaxed, started to unwind, and began to think that perhaps after a hard year with little time off she might be in need of this holiday.

It took them almost two hours to reach the area Dante was making for, and caused Lysan to realise that Dante's wine-producing concern must cover quite a vast area. She had thought vaguely that she might be left sitting in the car while Dante went off to complete his business. But he came round to the passenger side of the car and opened the door.

'Shall we go and find you a cup of tea?' he asked, and without waiting for her reply he escorted her over to a main office building where the manager came out to meet him.

A few pleasant minutes followed where Dante introduced Rufo Espinoza to her, and then ushered her to a comfortably furnished room where she imagined visiting VIPs were entertained.

'I shall be no more than half an hour,' he declared.

'No hurry,' she responded, and as he and his manager departed she went to take a glance out of the window.

A few minutes later a smart young woman bearing a tray of tea and pastries knocked and came in—and let go with a smiling volley of Spanish as she placed the tray down on the table.

'*Muchas gracias,*' Lysan responded, which she felt was fairly safe.

And it proved so when the young woman beamed, '*De nada,*' which Lysan thought meant 'You're welcome', and went on her way.

True to his word, Dante was back in just under half an hour, and sunlight was still there to greet them when they went outside. She moved to go over to where Dante had left his car but his hand on her arm stayed her.

Her skin tingled at the feel of his touch but he obvi-

ously felt no such surge of electricity since he casually
let go his hold and enquired, 'Would you like to take a
look at the cellar?'

'I'd love to,' she answered enthusiastically, and
walked with him some way until they reached another
building, and went in.

It was much cooler inside the cellar but Lysan barely
noticed; her attention was more absorbed in the scores
of wine-filled oak casks. 'Watch where you are walking—the floor is wet,' Dante cautioned.

She looked down as she moved on, and saw that the
floor was indeed very wet. 'Why?' she asked, when just
then a time-controlled sprinkler system went into operation and all at once spray began to rain down about her
head. 'Don't answer,' she laughed, and looked up to see
that Dante was staring at her as if taken aback to see her
take being rained down on so unexpectedly in her stride.

'You don't mind?'

'I'll soon dry.' Then she noticed that his shirt was
getting wet too. 'As will you,' she grinned—but as he
continued to stare at her so she suddenly felt most peculiarly shy. She looked away from him and, as the
sprinkler system turned itself off again, so she walked
on to an area where the vats were much, much bigger,
some no longer wooden but stainless steel. She guessed
the sprinkler system was there to keep the temperature
of the cellar down, but felt too choked to so much as
voice such a simple question.

There had been wall lights all along the many lanes
of barrels they had walked amongst, but, unexpectedly,
Lysan found they had walked to an area where there was
barely any light at all.

'Let me guess,' she found her voice as she ventured

further into the darkness. 'This is where your very old wines are matured?'

'This is where they finally rest after having been racked many times,' Dante agreed, his tone even and— close by.

Unexpectedly Lysan felt all choky again and turned hurriedly, barely knowing if she was going to take flight or what she was doing. Then it was that she discovered that Dante was much closer to her than she had thought for, turning swiftly, she cannoned straight into him.

'W—' he muttered, but added no more because she was slightly off balance.

His arms came out and round her and as he steadied her so Lysan's heart raced and she grew more confused than ever because Dante's hold on her had tightened and she could feel the manliness of his warm, broad-shouldered, firm body against her.

And oh, what a lot her imagination had to answer for. Because a moment later Dante, not in the slightest affected to have her body so close up against his, was putting her away from him and coolly declaring, 'It is too dark in here—you might trip and injure yourself.' And, putting more distance between them, he added, 'We will go, *señorita*.'

The drive back was a silent one—and this time her host made not the smallest remark to the effect that she was quiet. She had nothing to say either, Lysan owned, for while she was in shock about the emotions that had stirred in her when she had been—so briefly—in his arms Dante, every instinct was telling her, had gone cold on her.

Any other time it would have been natural for her to ask straight out what was the matter. Was it that he thought she'd been coming on to him back at that cellar? But she felt constrained to speak again.

The fact was, of course, that if his hold on her had tightened in any way it had been because he was doing his best to prevent her from falling.

Having analysed that, Lysan went on to be certain that Dante, in turn, could not imagine she had pressed against him on purpose. Nor, because he couldn't read into her mind, no matter how experienced he was, could he know of her racing heart and confusion when held by him. So where did he get off calling her '*señorita*' again?

By the time Dante was steering his car up the long drive to his home, Lysan was in high mutiny. To hell with him; she'd done nothing wrong. When he pulled up at the house she was out of the car before he could come round to the passenger's side.

Never let it be said that she forgot her manners. 'Thank you for a very entertaining afternoon,' she thanked him politely, if stiffly. His answer was a curt nod. If he had anything to add, Lysan was not waiting around to hear it.

Fuming, she turned her back on him—which she owned was rather lost on him because he turned about and went striding off somewhere—and she marched indoors.

Pig of a man, she riled up in her room and determined then that she would starve before she ate another crumb at his table. Half an hour later, however, and her mutiny faded and she had the strangest notion that she wanted to see him again. Nonsense, she immediately banished that outlandish idea to the bin.

A half-hour after that, however, and she went and took a shower. Good manners, she told herself, decreed that while she was a guest in his house she observed certain courtesies. Quite clearly he was regretting having taken her in his arms—though she couldn't see what else he could have done to steady both her and himself if they weren't to land in a heap on the floor. However, if he thought in any way that she might have misread his action and was therefore being aloof to show how wrong she had it—then she would show him very clearly that she had not been an iota disturbed by him *or* his actions.

Chance, she thought, when she entered the drawing room to find only Gabina and Celso there, would be a fine thing. 'Am I too early?' she asked by way of enquiring where Dante might be.

'Not at all,' Celso replied. 'Is it a martini?'

'Yes, please.'

'Did you enjoy the drive this afternoon?' Gabina asked while her husband went to pour Lysan a drink.

'Very much. We…' her voice tailed off when just then a sound by the door caused her to turn round. Turn round, and feel an emotion she had never felt before as she recognised that Dante had joined them, but was not alone. Coming into the room with him, indeed, hanging onto his arm, was one of the most striking women she had ever seen.

'Ondina, let me introduce our guest from England, Miss Lysan Hadley. Lysan, my—friend, Senõrita Ondina Alvarez.'

Lysan did not miss that slight pause between that 'my' and 'friend'. They're lovers, she thought, and wanted to hit him and hit her. Good God, what's wrong with me? she wondered, aghast, and from somewhere found a smile while she shook hands with the dark-haired, dark-eyed beauty.

'*Encantada de conocerle?*' Lysan offered her phrasebook 'How do you do?' and tried to like Ondina when she beamed a smile back at her.

'I am charmed to meet you,' Ondina replied—and spent the rest of the evening giving all her attention over to Dante.

Which, Lysan fumed, was fine by her because it meant that she did not have to put herself out—for good manners' sake—to talk to him. Instead she found plenty of things to discuss with Gabina and Celso until dinner came to an end. And as soon as she politely could afterwards she excused herself and went up to bed.

She was in bed when she heard a car start up outside. Dante was taking Ondina home. Hours later she was still awake. Dante was not back yet. Where did Ondina live, for heaven's sake? It must be miles and miles away. That was—that was—perhaps Dante wasn't coming home tonight?

Oh, hell. Lysan closed her eyes and pulled the bedclothes over her head. She had never felt more mixed up—and she hadn't even begun to sort out her other problem yet!

CHAPTER THREE

WHEN Lysan went down to breakfast the following morning she was positive that she did not care a button if Dante Viveros had not come home all night.

He was not in the breakfast room either though Gabina was and greeted her warmly. 'I have been thinking that today, if you wish it, we will go shopping,' she smiled.

'I'd love to,' Lysan answered—and there followed a week where she realised that Dante had been speaking no more than the truth when he had said that his sister-in-law would treat her holiday as a holiday for herself too.

Gabina—even given that Christmas was just around the corner—gave 'shop until you drop' a new meaning. She was tireless, Lysan found when each day Gabina would drive along Santiago's Avenida O'Higgins. Once they had parked the car they spent a dizzying round of coffee, shopping, an extended lunch, more shopping, afternoon tea, and a contented drive back home.

In this way, as the days went by, Lysan started to become good friends with Gabina. If she grew to know Gabina better, however, then as a result she seemed to see less and less of Dante.

Which was fine by her, Lysan decided. Although when she got out of bed on Sunday morning and realised that she had been in Chile a whole week now—save for a few hours—she was startled to realise that she was still in Dante's home as his guest!

She recalled how he had arrogantly told her that while she was in Chile she would stay where he said she would stay—but she gave no mind to that. Though she could barely believe that she had stayed in his home far longer than the few days she had thought she might. Well, she would soon put that right.

As matters turned out, however, her decision to tell Dante at breakfast that she was leaving that day became a non-starter when she joined Gabina for breakfast.

'*Buenos días*, Gabina,' she smiled, slipping into her seat as Gabina smilingly replied. She reached for the coffee-pot but Gabina was there before her pouring her a cup.

'Auda will be here soon with your toast,' she commented.

'I thought Dante might...' unplanned words started to leave Lysan. 'I mean, I—er—rather expected, since it's Sunday, that he and Celso might have breakfast at a more civilised time than in the week,' she smiled—and at once realised she had been speaking too fast.

But Gabina seemed to grasp the gist of what she was saying anyhow, for she said, 'They work. Normally they do not. But today they do. So today I thought you and I...'

'Not shopping!' Lysan exclaimed as she took on board that, out of courtesy, she was going to have to leave it until dinner this evening to thank Dante for his hospitality. It would mean delaying her departure until tomorrow but... Gabina breaking into laughter brought her away from her thoughts.

'No, not shopping. Today I thought we might, if you would like,' she inserted, 'take a drive into Santiago and visit Cerro San Cristóbel—we could walk up the hill or take the funicular.'

'Sounds good,' Lysan agreed.

It was only later, as they left the estate behind and Gabina drove towards Santiago, that Lysan belatedly realised she could just as easily have written Dante a note of thanks, packed her belongings and asked Gabina to drop her off at a hotel. She could even have checked in, slipped her cases up to her room and have still spent a good part of the day with Gabina. However, too late now.

It was another wonderful sunny day and as they approached Santiago and Lysan looked to the horizon where the mighty snow-capped Andes formed a magnificent backcloth so she decided that she was not going to fret or worry about anything. Neither Dante nor Noel nor—oh, grief, Noel! She hadn't begun to get herself sorted out about him yet!

There was a giant white statue near the summit of the hill—it was impressive. As was the view. Lysan was able to see for miles but, as she looked out over Santiago, so she experienced a dreadful feeling of restlessness.

She and Gabina opted to take the cable car down the hill but she found her thoughts were more concerned with what Dante was doing than with the view or the fact that life seemed a touch precarious when encapsulated high in the air in a small compartment for four. Was Dante still occupied working or was his work finished for the day—and was he now occupied with Ondina Alvarez?

With confusion Lysan suddenly realised that instead of sorting out her problem she seemed to be thinking more about Dante than she was about Noel!

She firmly pushed Dante out of her head, and on the drive home was able to satisfactorily see that the only reason she had given him any thought anyway was that she must, the next time she saw him, mention that she intended to leave in the morning.

When she walked down the wide staircase prior to dinner that evening, Lysan had taken pains with her appearance. She wore an elegant sleeveless dress of pale lemon silk and had dressed her ash-blonde hair in a classic knot. She had a double row of pearls at her throat and a discreet design of pearls dangled from her ears. Her other piece of jewellery was her engagement ring.

She scoffed that she had taken such care with her appearance because she needed to boost her confidence. But even while she was aware that she looked good she could not deny that she felt oddly nervous as she approached the *sala* door.

Half expecting to see Ondina Alvarez there, Lysan took a deep breath before she went in. Ondina Alvarez was not there. Neither was Gabina nor Celso—but Dante was. And all at once, as his unsmiling gaze travelled from top to toe over her, she felt a desperate need to say something.

'Er—I appear to be the first one down—except yourself that is.'

'Martini?' he answered coolly, her usual drink—and she wanted to hit him that he could be so cool.

'Sherry,' she replied, just to be perverse, but, inbred manners giving her a nudge, she added, 'Please.' What was it about this man? She didn't particularly care for sherry!

He went over to the drinks table and all Lysan could think was that she hoped Gabina and Celso would soon be here, while at the same time she knew that this was an ideal moment in which to thank him for his hospi-

tality and tell him that she would be leaving in the morning.

'Gabina and Celso are dining with friends this evening,' Dante informed her as he came and handed her
her sherry.

'Oh!' she was surprised. 'Gabina didn't mention it!
Not that she had to of—'

'Celso arranged it while Gabina was out. They haven't
seen these particular friends for some while. Did you
enjoy your day?'

'Er—yes,' she answered his tacked-on question. 'You
were working today, I believe?'

'I've discovered in business that if there has to be a
small matter that requires emergency action it always
happens on a Sunday,' he replied, a wry—and quite
charming—smile coming to his face.

Crazily, her heart fluttered. 'Your emergency is over,
I hope?' she murmured while her heartbeats settled and
she gave short shrift to any such notion that his wry look
affected her in any way whatsoever.

'As I said, it was a small one,' he answered, and a
few moments later Emilia appeared and said something
to him in their own tongue. Lysan guessed that the soup
or whatever first course they were having had been taken
to the dining room. She finished her drink and Dante
took her glass from her, his right hand brushing her left
one. 'Shall we eat?' he clipped, not a smile, wry or otherwise, about him.

Without a word Lysan preceded him from the *sala*,
her latent ankle-kicking tendencies on the loose again.
What *was* it about him?

Feeling suddenly as if she never wanted to speak to
him again, and by the look of it he felt about as affable,
Lysan tucked into her sweet red pepper starter with

every appearance of a good appetite. The truth was, though, that any appetite she'd had seemed to have unexpectedly deserted her.

Somehow or other, however, by the time the last course was over and they were drinking coffee, and probably because he, like her, felt that certain politenesses had to be observed, Lysan found that they had discussed all manner of inconsequential subjects.

Which was good. Any moment now she was going to find the right moment, Lysan determined to advise him of her departure in the morning. After that, she would go and pack. He, no doubt, since it appeared he kept late hours, would find something of interest to do. Her thoughts slid to Ondina Alvarez... 'Gabina was telling me of your Nobel Prize-winning writer,' she said in a rush, for no known reason suddenly wanting to blot thoughts of Dante with Ondina from her mind.

'Neftalí Reyes.'

'That doesn't sound like the...'

'Does his pen-name, Pablo Neruda, sound—?'

'That's the one,' she interrupted, calming down, while at the same time wondering why she should imagine thoughts of Dante with Ondina should bother her. 'Gabina was also telling me of your national dance.'

'*La Cueca*. We must make sure you see it performed before you return to England,' he remarked, and there, beautifully, was the opening she sought.

'Actually, Dante—' she used his name so he should know she was being friendly '—I'm leaving tomorrow.'

'No!'

She looked at him, startled. 'What do you mean, "No"?' she objected.

'You've only just got here!' he snarled, his darkened gaze shooting to the ring on her left hand. 'You are missing your lover so much that you cannot wait to get back to him!' he thundered.

She had no idea in which context Dante used the word 'lover' but whether he meant it in lover-bed context or lover-fiancé context that wasn't the issue. Who did this mercurial Chilean think he was?

'It isn't that. I've been...'

'Then what?' he demanded. 'You have come here for almost three weeks—yet after only a week you are determined to return to England with all speed!'

'Who said anything about returning to England?' she fired.

'You—' he broke off, and seemed to cool down a small degree. Though his eyes were still smouldering angrily when he demanded, 'Did you not?'

'No, I didn't,' she answered forthrightly. Grief, you'd have thought she'd stolen his most treasured vintage wine.

'You said you were leaving here!'

'I meant *here* here, not Chile,' she retorted, and rushed on quickly. 'I hadn't intended to stay with you at all when I arrived.' Her tone, again thanks to manners instilled in her, became more conciliatory as she added, 'And, while I thank you so much for allowing me to stay in your beautiful home and its beautiful surroundings, I only meant to stay for a few days.'

'So where are you thinking of going?' he grunted, ignoring her thanks along with her comments on his beautiful home.

'Well—I thought I'd go to the hotel I'd originally intended to stay in—in Santiago—for a start and...' Oh, heavens, she had offended him! She knew it from the way he glowered at her. 'Don't be like this, Dante,' she urged. 'I didn't mean to offend you. It's just that I want to see more of Chile, take a look around. A hotel in the centre of the capital seems a good base to—'

'If you want to see more of Chile, then I will show you,' he cut in unequivocally.

'Oh, really!' she protested, exasperated.

'Really!' he took her literally. 'Tomorrow I shall begin by taking you to Viña del Mar. We will—'

'Just a minute!' she cut in sharply, as her firm intention to leave tomorrow seemed on the edge of getting away from her. Dante stared at her—arrogance not in it. 'I can't allow you to...' her voice faded.

'You can't *allow*, *señorita*?'

'Look here!' she erupted, not liking at all that she was suddenly the bad guy—and she'd done *nothing* wrong! 'I can't possibly take you away from your work.'

'Did I not say that the reason I worked today was because I wanted some time off tomorrow?'

'You've just made that up!' she accused hotly—and all at once didn't know where on earth she was because from angry and arrogant his Latin temperament took another change and, totally unexpectedly, he laughed.

Even more unexpectedly, Lysan felt her own lips start to twitch. And, fight against it though she might, she just couldn't help it; she burst out laughing too.

This was crazy. The man was a devil. 'What time?' she asked.

He stared at her laughing mouth, his own smile fading. 'Shall we say nine-thirty?' he suggested quietly.

'Mm,' she murmured, and got to her feet. Dante rose too—their eyes met and suddenly her heart started to pound. His glance was burning into hers. She wanted to swallow, hard, but would not. 'I'll—see you in the morning,' she said as evenly as she could manage—and swiftly left the dining room.

She was up in her room before it dawned on her that when she had been certain she would that night be packing her cases she had, by agreeing to go with Dante to this place called Viña del Mar tomorrow, stated that she would not leave.

Feeling very much perplexed by this insubordinate other self, this other self that was at odds with the person she had thought herself to be, Lysan sank down into a chair for a while to try to get herself together. Yet, even while she was telling herself that this was ridiculous, she found her thoughts were wandering, and that among her other problems that occupied her was—what was she going to wear tomorrow?

Lysan left her bed on Monday morning knowing that she should have been more forceful when telling Dante that she was leaving. Though how could she have been? He had been all arrogance and anger, and then he had made her laugh—and any forcefulness she had found had crumbled.

She was still unsure about what to wear for her visit to Viña del Mar. But del Mar meant seaside, didn't it? Diamonds and a tiara would definitely not be needed.

When she went down to breakfast Lysan had opted to wear a smart lightweight short-sleeved jacket of the palest flame, with matching tailored trousers. Forgetful of her slender but curvaceous figure, she felt that a little femininity would not come amiss so left her hair loose to fall about her shoulders.

'You look—I think the word is terrific!' Gabina exclaimed the moment Lysan entered the breakfast room.

'I wasn't sure what to wear. I'm going—Dante is taking me to...'

'He said. You are dressed perfectly,' Gabina assured her.

Lysan had finished her breakfast, had been up to her room to do a last-minute titivation, and was seated in the *sala* with Gabina, when, at a few minutes before nine-thirty, Dante entered the house and came looking for her.

'Buenos días,' he greeted them both, but his glance went to Lysan, and stayed. She was sure she caught a hint of liking what he saw in his look, and all at once found a rush of her former confidence—without fully appreciating when, since she had known him, she had become a trace nervous, unsure, and perhaps a little confused! 'Are you ready, Lysan?' he enquired smoothly. And as Lysan left her chair he enquired courteously, 'You're sure you will not join us, Gabina?'

As Gabina replied that she had made other arrangements, it became clear to Lysan that he must have already asked his sister-in-law to go with them. She said goodbye to Gabina and went out to his car with him wondering if Dante wanted Gabina with them because he thought he was in for a tedious day—so that Gabina could talk to her and so save him the trouble.

Stop it! Impatient with herself, Lysan started to get angry. What in creation was happening to her? Never before had she felt so lacking in confidence.

'Are you sure you wish to take me to Viña del Mar, *señor*?' she challenged before she had time to think. Prior to her engagement there had always been some male monopolising the phone to talk to her—with not the smallest sign of finding her tedious!

Dante had been about to start up the car, but he took his hand off the ignition key and turned and stared at her, clearly astonished by both her challenging tone and her words.

For perhaps two seconds he said not a thing but just

sat and studied her mutinous expression. Then, very quietly, his tone sardonic, he enquired, 'Was it something I said?' and suddenly Lysan was on the verge of laughing again. How did he do that to her?

'I'm sorry,' she apologised at once, as she saw she must. 'I think this super sunshine in December has gone to my head.'

His gaze roved over her cascade of ash-blonde hair, and over her creamy skin and dainty features. 'A very lovely head,' he murmured, and while she began to tingle all over he asked, 'Do you intend to behave yourself today?' and she just had to grin. He stared at her a moment longer, muttered something in his own language which she had no chance at guessing at, and set the car in motion.

Viña del Mar was quite some way from where Dante had his estate. The sun was shining and to make up for her challenging attitude earlier Lysan gave herself up to enjoying the drive and to being as near a perfect companion as she could.

Although she did not have to try very hard, and, in truth in a very brief while forgot to try at all, her good humour coming naturally when Dante showed himself to be a charming person to spend a day with.

He seemed in no hurry to arrive at their destination and ignored the speed capabilities of his vehicle to just saunter along so she should admire the scenery. They drove between mountains and, by dint of tunnels blasted through, inside mountains, to come out to more brilliant sunshine. Lysan was enchanted to see acacia trees, avocado trees and flowers of every hue.

And once they reached their destination she just had to sigh in pure pleasure at the most picturesque sight of purple bougainvillaea tumbling down over the walls of one particular house. Indeed, it seemed a superb spot to have a house.

'It's gorgeous,' she breathed.

'You like it?'

'Like it' was an understatement. 'I think I'm falling a little in love with Chile,' she smiled.

'Would you like to walk around for a while?' he asked, braking to a halt.

'You think of everything,' she grinned, and was out of the car, stretching her long legs as they strolled around, Dante letting her gaze her fill at a most magnificent blue flowering plumbago, and telling her names of other flowers she had never before seen.

From there they walked on, and she discovered that Dante was able to answer yet more of her questions, when her attention was caught as they walked by a shop window full of necklets and earrings made of a lovely deep blue stone.

'Isn't that lapis lazuli?' she asked, unsure that she'd ever seen it before.

'It is,' he agreed.

'It's beautiful. Such a gorgeous deep colour.'

'And Chile is one of the few places where it is found.'

'It's mined here?'

'It is,' he answered, and enquired, 'Hungry?'

'I think I am,' she replied. 'Though I shouldn't be. I've done nothing to earn an appetite.'

He smiled, said nothing, but took her hand to assist her across a busy road, and seemed to have forgotten he still had hold of it until they walked up to a smart hotel and he let go her hand so he should open the door for her.

With the sea so close, fish seemed to be a natural choice. Dante seemed to think so too for he chose the same, and Lysan began to think that never had she been so at one with anyone else. That thought disturbed her.

'What worries you?'

Lysan blinked, and only then realised that Dante must have been watching her. 'Nothing,' she answered, finding a smile.

'You looked—troubled?' Dante persisted.

'I'm not, honestly,' she assured him, and added, when he didn't look convinced, 'How could I be when I'm here living it up, while back home my family are working away like beavers?'

'Ah!' She stared at him, wondering what the dickens that 'Ah' meant. He was not smiling, she noticed, and seemed to have withdrawn some of his warmth when he revealed his deduction from what she had said. 'You are missing your fiancé?'

In actual fact, she wasn't, but it seemed disloyal to Noel to say so. 'What do you think?' she answered, and concentrated on her fish.

Dante made no answer. And, as the meal progressed, Lysan became more and more aware that he had nothing else to say either. In silence they finished their meal and as he settled their bill Lysan went over their most recent conversation, wondering if she had said something to upset him.

She did not think she had but as they went outside again, and lest he think that by missing her fiancé she was making the best of it and, in Noel's absence, just enduring his company, she told him openly, 'I am enjoying myself with you, you know.'

For answer Dante stood stock-still. She stopped walking too and, as she looked up, so he looked down at her. Then suddenly his look changed, and became very gentle. 'Even though I'm like a bore with a sore head?' he asked very softly.

Her spine melted. 'Bear,' she replied chokily, something happening to her as she stared up into his darkened blue eyes. '*Bear* with a sore head.'

'Oh, Lysan Hadley, what a fascinating creature you are,' he breathed, and while she was by that time totally mesmerised he bent his head and touched his lips to her cheek in a kiss of apology. God help me if he ever seriously offends me and regrets it, she couldn't help thinking as her knees went to water. 'Bore is what I said, and bore is what I meant,' he said on raising his head. Then someone bumped into them, and Lysan realised she was standing on the pavement in a Chilean street, blocking someone's path without even being aware of it.

More in harmony, they began to walk on, by unspoken mutual consent enjoying an after-lunch stroll that brought them to the beach where the Pacific rolled in. At one spot Dante pointed to a rock where a family of pelicans were also enjoying the day.

Later, when they had walked along for quite some while, they came to another outcrop of rocks. 'That's a baby seal! Isn't it?' she cried, her face eager and alight as she turned to Dante. 'Oh, isn't it gorgeous?'

Suddenly then her breath caught—for instead of staring out to the distant rock she saw that Dante was looking not out to the rock but at her—something there in his expression which she could not define.

'I'm embarrassing you,' she mumbled, and turned her back to him, feeling gauche and embarrassed herself. He was a sophisticated man, for heaven's sake, and, while she had never seen a seal sitting on a rock unperturbed by the crashing sea, Dante must have seen them by the dozen.

Miserably she wished that some power would arrive and whisk her back to England—but then, to make her heart leap, she felt Dante come behind her, felt his hands on her shoulders—and her throat dried.

He gave her shoulders a small squeeze. 'Not embarrassed, little Lysan,' he bent to say softly in her right ear, 'but delighted at your innocent pleasure.'

She wanted to say something, anything, but no words would come. Yet it truly thrilled her that a man of the world such as he could still find pleasure in others' pleasure. It made him special somehow.

But she was too confused to know what to make of that. Then, whether she moved back or Dante moved forward that little bit, she did not know. But suddenly he was close up to her. She leaned back, and for a few glorious moments she rested her head on the hard wall of his chest. His muscles rippled as he moved again and, even though it was like thistledown, she was sure she felt the breath of his kiss as his lips touched the top of her head.

She was out of control, she knew it; her whole body was tingling—electric. She did the only thing she could—she moved away. That or turn round and bury her head in his chest. Dante let her go, and she stood for about a minute looking out to sea while she strove to regain control. She saw the seal's mother suddenly appear.

'Is there a colony out there?' she asked, amazed that her voice should sound so calm when everything inside her was crashing about, much like the sea and spume against the rocks.

'I wouldn't be at all surprised,' he returned amiably. 'Shall we go and find you a cup of tea?'

'I can live without having my tea-level topped up, you know,' she smiled.

'I don't believe it,' he teased, and as they exchanged amused glances so her world went back to near normal.

They returned to the car and Dante drove them the five or so miles along the coast to the charming port of Valparaíso, where they had tea, and afterwards strolled along the harbour to take a look at the ships at anchor there.

To her further pleasure, Dante did not drive straight back to his estate for dinner, but drove the seventy miles to Santiago. She had been in the same clothes all day, but so had Dante, and if he thought it was all right to call in at a smart hotel for dinner dressed as they were—though he did have a jacket in the car—who was she to argue? Besides, she was thoroughly enjoying herself and to extend the day when he could just as easily have taken her back to his home had to mean that he was not finding her at all tedious as she had earlier in the day thought he might.

'So tell me about Lysan Hadley,' Dante requested over the meal, having answered her questions all day wanting to ask some of his own.

'There's nothing to tell,' she responded with a smile.

'You expect me to believe that?'

God, the man had charm! That hint of a smile at the corners of his mouth... Desperately then did she wish she had climbed mountains, swum seas, composed an opera or won a gold medal at the Olympics. There was just nothing to tell him.

'I work, go home, and—er—that's about it.'

'No fun?'

She wished he had not said that. His fun—Ondina Alvarez—sprang to mind. Lysan smiled. It was good camouflage for the sick feeling inside that had just made itself felt. 'Well, yes, fun, plenty of it. Before Noel and I became engaged, there were—' she broke off; all hint of a smile had left Dante's mouth.

'There were?' he insisted.

'Well, before then, I was always out and about with friends.'

'Men-friends?' he questioned abruptly.

'Of course!' she exclaimed emphatically. She might be a virgin, might have gone around in a crowd, and avoided meaningful relationships—possibly because she had never particularly fancied being 'meaningful' with any of her crowd, as nice as they were—but there was no need to give Dante the impression that she had lived the life of a nun.

'You've had many men-friends?' he wanted to know.

'Well, naturally.' Grief, she'd been at college with a whole glut of them—friends all, with few exceptions.

'Humph,' he grunted—and to her seemed to be particularly sour.

'Now what did I say?' she challenged.

'You have slept with many partners?' he barked.

Her green eyes widened. The nerve of him! 'Well, I'm not as old as you so I suppose I've got some catching up to do in that department,' she exploded. And then, to her amazement, when she had never been known to back down from a fight, she discovered she had run out of steam. 'For your information,' she tilted her head to tell him coolly, 'I've not made a habit of sleeping around.'

Whether he believed her or not she did not just then care as he stared at her mutinous and proud expression. Then his glance went to her empty coffee-cup, and without another word he summoned the waiter and settled their bill.

Lysan was on her feet the moment he made a move to stand. In icy silence they walked from the restaurant and she hated, hated, hated him. He had spoiled her lovely day.

In the same icy silence they drove back to his home. Lysan thought he would just stop at the front door to let her out and then drive off to garage his car.

She knew she should thank him for taking time from his work to give the whole of that day to her, but the words to thank him just would not come. She got out of the car and, without a word, left him. Then found that her surmise that he would be garaging his car was wrong when he left the car too, and as she started to climb the steps to his home he began to climb the steps beside her.

Dante opened the door for her but still she had no words for him. All she hoped was that neither Gabina nor Celso was around. If she saw either of them she was in honour bound to exchange a few pleasantries with them, and she just did not feel up to telling anyone where they had been or how much she had enjoyed it.

Good fortune smiled on her in that she saw neither Gabina nor Celso, nor anyone else. She headed for the staircase, aware the whole of the time that Dante was going in the same direction. He's probably going up to shower and change so he can give his lady-love a call, she thought unhappily, but found she was too down to mind overmuch about that.

They reached the landing and since Dante's room lay the same way as hers it did not surprise her that he should turn in the same direction. What did surprise her, though, as she reached her door and turned from him and opened it, was that he did not go straight on to his own apartments, but, just as she was about to enter her room, he halted and called sharply, 'Lysan!'

She stopped, turned, and looked at him, and wanted to cry. He looked so serious, so grave, and after having been such a wonderful companion he was now a stranger. 'Yes?' she asked chokily, and saw his glance fix on her misty eyes, and heard him deliver something heartfelt in his own language. Then his hands were coming to hold her upper arms.

'I have made you sad, unhappy?' he questioned solemnly. She shook her head. He did not believe her. 'I had no right.'

'No right?' she enquired huskily.

'No right to question you about the men in your life. No right at all. It was unforgivable of me,' he went on, but asked nevertheless, 'But will you forgive me?'

'Oh, Dante,' she cried, and as peace washed away her unhappiness it seemed the most natural thing in the world to take that small step forward and to raise her lips to his cheek.

His grip on her arms tightened, and then his arms came around her—and it was pure bliss to rest her head on his chest—friends once again. She lifted her head to answer a compulsion to ask his forgiveness in turn— without being fully sure what she wanted his forgiveness about. She looked into his face, saw warmth in the darkened depths of his blue eyes, and all at once forgot what she had been about to say. For, unhurriedly, Dante lowered his head to hers until, lightly, gently, his mouth lay over hers.

'Dante!' she breathed his name, and as his hold on her tightened so her arms went around him. She held onto him when his kiss became seeking, and just did not know where she was when his mobile mouth teased her lips apart.

All she knew for sure was that she had never been kissed like this before—and that she wanted more. She returned his kiss, strained to get nearer to him, and was thrilled to hear his groan of emotion and was with him wholeheartedly when he moved her inside her bedroom door and shut out the outside world.

'*Querida,*' he murmured, and she was thrilled yet again. She thought *querida* meant dear, or darling, but wasn't sure about that or anything else then save that his tone was tender, his lovemaking gentle and unhurried— and that she never wanted it to stop.

'My dear,' she murmured shyly, and felt a fire of wanting lick into life within her when he pushed her jacket away from her neck and began to trace beautiful, mind-blowing kisses over her throat.

Nor did she have any protest to make when, wanting to kiss more of her bare skin, Dante's fingers came to the front of her and he began to unbutton her jacket.

She had to clutch onto him, though, when his wonderful warm mouth traced down to the valley between her breasts. When next his mouth returned to hers, his gentleness was laced with a growing passion and Lysan found herself in a world she had never been in before. Dante's sensitive fingers caressed her breasts, and she gripped onto him hard. She wanted him.

She wanted him and, save from winning a battle with shyness when she felt his fingers beneath her jacket move to her back, felt him unfastening her bra, but she had no objection to make. Nor when, unhurriedly, he removed first her jacket, and then her bra, and held her close up to him, kissing her, caressing her back. His sensitive fingers caressed to the front of her.

She swallowed hard as tenderly he cupped each naked breast in turn. 'Lysan, Lysan,' he breathed, and tasted the sweetness of her breasts, causing the tips he had made harden to harden further, throbbing their need as his moist mouth teased and caressed her.

'I...' she choked, and wanted to tell him how much she ached for him. But newness, shyness, held her back. Dante raised his head to kiss her again. She placed a hand to the side of his face. 'I've never...' she attempted to speak as his mouth left hers, but again her voice faded into nothing.

Then Dante was saying it for her. '*Mi querida*, I want you,' he cried softly, and, taking hold of her left hand from the side of his face, almost reverently, he brought her hand to his mouth, and buried a kiss in its palm.

Then, even while she stood half in the circle of his arm, glad it was dark for all she exalted in this freedom with him, glad he had not snicked on the light, she suddenly became aware that something had happened; something quite terrible had happened. For all at once, while still holding her small hand in his grasp, Dante had stiffened, and he took an abrupt step back.

'What...?' she began, her mind racing. Had her naïvety shown? Had she put him off by not co-operating fully? For all she had followed her instincts, was she supposed to do something else?

But it was not that, she discovered. For as Dante held onto her hand, as if still reluctant to let her go, so she felt him fingering the ring on her finger. Oh, God! Reality hit her at the same moment that Dante threw her hand from him as if it burned him.

'My apologies, *señorita*,' he grated formally, if on a ragged kind of breath. 'I forgot that you are engaged to be married.'

Lysan was still in shock when she heard the door close after him. She still hadn't surfaced from it ten minutes later. Oh, heavens, Dante was not the only one who had forgotten that she was engaged—so had she, completely!

CHAPTER FOUR

NEVER had Lysan spent a worse night. Over and over again she relived the day she had spent with Dante. A day that had culminated in her discovering more of this new person who had shown itself in her ever since she had set foot in Chile. How eager she had been when she had been in Dante's arms. Her face flamed as she recalled the person his ardour had flushed out.

With the coming of daylight she got out of bed and went to stare, unseeing, out of her window, and wished she had been able to find an ounce of the embarrassment that had swamped her and made her reject Noel when Noel had attempted to make love to her.

Oh, grief, but for Noel's ring on her finger and its reminder to Dante that she belonged to another man Lord knew what would have happened.

Restlessly she moved from the window and went to take a shower. But her tormented thoughts followed her. How could she have forgotten Noel so easily? Why, when she had been so embarrassed in Noel's arms, hadn't she felt embarrassed to be in Dante's arms? Oh, if only she had been! How on earth was she ever going to face Dante again?

Lysan towelled herself dry and got dressed, aware that she had not felt the least bit embarrassed to be kissed and caressed by Dante. A touch shy here and there maybe, but that was only natural, surely. It wasn't every day—or ever—that she stood semi-naked in the arms of a vibrant, all-male male!

Thank God it had been dark. The thought of seeing him again after he had caressed and kissed her curvy nakedness was enough. Thank goodness she'd had a cloak of darkness to cover her.

Perhaps she should leave right now. Would that be considered running away? She could not decide. Strangely, though, for all to leave had seemed like a good idea yesterday, Lysan found she felt more reluctant to follow that course of action today.

The time arrived when she should go down to breakfast—but she wasn't ready to see Dante again just yet. Somehow or other she was going to have to act cool and as if she had barely any memory of that which had kept her sleepless last night—and she just wasn't ready, not yet.

Lysan waited another five minutes and then realised she was being discourteous to Dante's staff by making them hold up her breakfast requirements. She left her room hoping with all she had that the man who had invaded too much of her thinking was not around.

He was not in the breakfast room when she went in, but Gabina was. Relief flooded in. '*Buenos días*, Gabina,' Lysan greeted her brightly.

'Good morning, Lysan,' Gabina smiled, and, as Lysan had known she would, she asked as she took her place at the table, 'You enjoyed your day yesterday?'

'It was super,' Lysan replied enthusiastically—come to think of it, she couldn't remember if she had thanked Dante for it. Oh, God! 'Did you have a good day with your friend?' she found out of a thin nowhere to quickly get off the subject.

'Very good,' Gabina replied. 'But we talked and talked so much, I did not complete all of my purchases.

With Christmas so close, I am starting to panic that I have bought nothing for Celso yet.'

Christmas was indeed close; everywhere was starting to look festive. 'You're going into Santiago again today?' Lysan guessed.

Gabina nodded. 'You will come with me?' she asked.

'Won't you be seeing your friend?'

'Febe has a business to run. Yesterday she took a holiday.'

Dante was given to returning to the house at any time of the day. To go to Santiago would mean she would not be around, and would cut out the risk of bumping into him. Lysan owned she still was not ready to see him again.

'I'd love to come with you,' she accepted.

'That is good,' Gabina beamed, and, glancing at her watch, she added, 'We will go in a half-hour if you wish. First I must telephone my mother.'

Lysan wished she hadn't said that. She wasn't homesick, she loved it here, but suddenly with everything that was disturbing, upsetting and totally confused within her she would not have minded at all to hear the down-to-earth sanity of her own mother's voice.

She had not realised she had made a sound, but realised that she must have done for she all at once became aware that Gabina was looking at her. 'You wish to telephone your mother also?' she enquired. And without waiting for her to answer she said, 'You must do so, Lysan. It will make your mother happy to hear that, so far away, you are in good health. There is a telephone in the *sala*.'

'I...' Lysan began to deny that she wanted to make a call to England, and then changed her mind. 'May I?' she asked.

'But of course! I will come with you to help you find the telephone numbers you will need.'

Gabina went with her to the *sala*, and, having eased her way in making the call, waited only for Lysan to say, 'Hello, Mum, it's me, Lysan,' before she left her to continue her call in private.

'Are you all right?' was her mother's first question.

'I'm fine, and having a lovely time.'

'Oh, that's good. You might like to know that it's snowing here.'

Lysan laughed. 'It's gorgeous sunshine here.'

'Life's never fair. How's your hotel?'

'Ah! Well, as a matter of fact... Did you know that Dad had sent a fax to Dante Viveros?'

'And if I did?'

A few minutes later Lysan finished telling her parent how Dante Viveros had met her at the airport, and had point-blank refused to allow her to go to a hotel but had insisted she stay in his home where his brother and sister-in-law lived.

'Well, wasn't that kind of him?' her mother gasped. But swiftly recovered, to add, 'Oh, your father will be pleased! He received a reply from his fax to the effect that Mr Viveros would meet your plane, but he would never have imagined—' she broke off, then continued, 'Your father has the greatest respect for the man and knows he will treat you most honourably.' Now didn't seem the time to say 'Mother, he was on the way to taking my virginity last night—and I was doing nothing to stop him'! Though, come to think of it, were he *not* an honourable man, he would last night have paid scant heed to that reminder of her engagement ring that she belonged to someone else. 'Don't get too comfortable there,' her mother went on. 'Remember we want you home for Christmas.'

'You think I'm missing out on all that turkey and Christmas pud?' Lysan laughed, then added, 'I shall have to go, Mum. I'll see you soon.'

'Any messages for anybody?' her mother asked, and Lysan knew she meant Noel.

Only just then the drawing-room door opened, and Dante was there. 'Er, love and kisses all round,' she managed, her face flaming, her insides churning wildly.

'Bye, sweetheart,' her mother said warmly.

'Bye.' Carefully, concentrating hard on what she was doing, as if the phone were made of egg shells, Lysan looked nowhere but at the instrument in her hand as she put the receiver back on its rest. 'Good morning,' she said coolly on looking up. And when Dante came further into the room but did not answer she added, 'I've just been speaking with my mother.'

'A woman's best friend, I believe,' he commented shortly.

'Look here, *you*!' she flared, offended, her green eyes sparking angrily. She did not need any guesses to know why he was being so acid with her, and was suddenly too angry to hide behind a natural modesty as she let rip, 'I'll take half the blame, but the other half lies at *your* door!'

A stream of furious Spanish shot from him and she could not doubt from the enraged look of him that she had just received the Chilean equivalent of 'Who the hell do you think you're talking to?'.

But it seemed she was way off beam in her surmise that he objected to being spoken to like that, because, his tone challenging, he then barked caustically, 'I expect you will now cut short your holiday and run home.'

And that made her madder than ever. All too clearly he was positive she had been complaining to her mother about him—and felt *his* honour had been called into question. 'For your information, *señor*, I have not the smallest intention of running *anywhere*,' she erupted. 'Nor would I dream of reporting to my family any of what took place between you and I last night!' Was she, quiet—for the most part—Lysan Hadley, really having this type of conversation with a man?

'You would prefer they, not forgetting your fiancé— as you were so eager to last night—knew nothing of the way you encouraged me to bed you!' he hurled back.

In a flash she was on her feet, a red mist forming in front of her eyes as—horrified to hear what he said, she discounted that he looked in any way horrified that he had said it—she let go with her right hand and struck him a monstrous blow.

She was then more mortified than horrified. It was as if every bit of her energy and anger had been drained from her in that blow, and she was totally without fury when she came to, to realise that Dante had caught hold of her in a vice-like grip and seemed about to shake her until her teeth rattled.

Another volley of Spanish hit the air and she guessed she deserved it, whatever it was he reviled her with. Then suddenly the words stopped, and as she stared apprehensively into blue eyes that were almost black in the emotion of his fury so Dante seemed to gain a little control, and, throwing her from him with such force that she all but lost her balance, 'Keep away from me this day, *señorita*!' he snarled.

That's no way to treat a door, she fumed, anger returning as he slammed from the *sala* with such force that she would not have been surprised to see the supporting wall fall down. So if she was so angry, why did she feel like bursting into tears?

'I am so sorry to keep you waiting,' Gabina apologised when a half-hour later she joined Lysan in the *sala*.

'Don't worry about it,' Lysan smiled. In actual fact she had needed all of that half an hour to try to calm down after that brush—violent brush—with Dante.

'It is my mother,' Gabina explained. 'We just talk and talk—and forgot the time. Your call to your mother was all right?'

'Yes, thanks. It was good to talk to her for a while.'

Lysan tried to get enthusiastic over Gabina's shopping, but with her thoughts tripping to Dante the whole while, for all her efforts not to think about the wretched man, she found her enthusiasm was in short supply. Oh, how she wished she had not allowed him to goad her into hitting him. Ye gods, never had she been so emotionally moved to *want* to hit a man, much less put all her weight behind the blow—slight though her weight might be.

It was all his fault, she decided in desperation. She hadn't asked him to kiss her—she hadn't backed away, though, when he had, prompted an unwanted but all-honest voice of her conscience.

Oh, to hell with it, she fumed, and concentrated her energies on what she could get Gabina for Christmas. She had been so friendly to her and must have left some of her own pursuits to keep her company, Lysan felt, so that a Christmas gift could be part of a grateful thanks as well.

Dante was her host, so perhaps she should buy him a gift too. Oh, rats. What about Celso? She couldn't leave a present for Gabina and Dante without giving to Celso, in the same way she could not buy gifts for Gabina and Celso without giving to Dante.

Realising that she was getting bogged down by thoughts of wanting to do the 'right' thing, Lysan left the puzzle of what to do for the best and decided that she would truly like to get Gabina something. To that end, on the pretext of going to the ladies' room, Lysan left the café where they were resting and drinking coffee, and raced to purchase a delicate porcelain crinolined lady which Gabina had fallen in love with and almost bought as a Christmas gift for her mother, before realising it was in her own taste and not her mother's.

Lysan was again in high anxiety as she dressed to go down to dinner that night. 'Keep away from me this day, *señorita*,' Dante had threatened. Did he mean this evening too? Of course he didn't, said her head. Besides... Oddly, but she had to admit it was true, from not wanting to see him that morning, she had the most urgent feeling of wanting to see him. As if...

She dismissed any such notion. He had been more than a match for her forthrightness this morning, and that had stung so that, too incensed for words, she had physically lashed out at him. For that blow, she owed him an apology.

When, at her usual time, Lysan went down to the *sala* prior to dinner that evening, she was wearing a deceptively simple dress of black silk jersey. She had piled her ash-blonde hair in a sophisticated style at the top of her head—the contours of her face shown off to perfection. She knew she looked good and needed to know it.

She was still wondering what had happened to her and her confidence that she needed to know she was looking her best when she opened the *sala* door. The first person she saw was Dante, the second—Ondina Alvarez. With barely any halt in her step, though with perhaps the smallest upward tilt to her chin, Lysan went forward.

'*Buenas tardes*, Ondina,' she smiled; she'd do this right if it killed her. 'How nice to see you again.'

'*Buenas tardes*, Lysan,' Ondina replied civilly, but spared Lysan a return of her lie by smiling at Dante and charming him with a string of Spanish.

'What would you like to drink?' Celso asked, and while he went to pour her martini Lysan—aloof to Dante—went to chat to Gabina while at the same time she was outraged. How dared he invite that woman here? Without a doubt he had last Monday bedded Ondina Alvarez—and last night he had almost bedded *her*! Yet, not twenty-four hours later, he had the nerve to bring that woman into the same room as her! To *hell* with any apology—she'd love to have a go at the other side of his face!

She glanced his way and saw he was looking at her. Solemn-faced, unsmiling, she stared at him. He was unsmiling too as for two seconds they hostilely held eye contact. Then he turned back to Ondina and smiled broadly at something the dark-eyed, good-looking woman had said.

Hating him like poison, Lysan turned to Gabina and smilingly asked if she had been able to find a gift suitable for her mother yet.

Conversation at dinner was lively, but Lysan found that her hate for Dante had sorely affected her appetite. But somehow or other she got through the meal. She had thought the whole evening would end without Dante addressing one single, solitary word to her. Nor did he directly. But, to prove he had not entirely forgotten her existence, when they somehow lit on the subject of favourite places, everyone, who had been speaking in

English for her benefit, suddenly erupted into Spanish. That was until Dante cut into the conversation. 'Our guest might wish to join in,' he suggested smoothly.

'Oh, I'm sorry!' Gabina apologised at once for herself, Celso and Ondina. 'I was so anxious to impress that Puerto Varas is much prettier than my husband's choice that I forgot.'

'Don't worry,' Lysan smiled, and, laughing lightly, added, 'If there's any fault it's mine, for not taking the trouble to learn your language when you have troubled to learn mine.'

Gabina smiled, happy once more. 'Do you have a favourite place?' she asked, and Lysan could not readily answer her. In view of the antipathy she felt towards Dante, wild horses would not get her to admit that she thought where she was, this very place where he had his home, was somewhere rather special.

She looked across the table to him, her gaze going to the left side of his face where she had hit him. It was galling that there was not so much as a mark on him—her hand felt bruised enough by the contact for her to have fractured his jaw—yet not a mark! She slid her green gaze to his eyes—and saw he had been watching her—and guessed from the glint that came to his eyes that he had a fair idea of what was going through her mind. Hope your teeth rot, she thought sweetly—and wouldn't have been at all surprised if he'd read that too as he glanced from her to make a remark to his brother—and she caught the flash of his superb white and never healthier teeth.

She was glad when dinner ended and a general move was made in the direction of the *sala*. But it had been a strain keeping up the pretence that everything in her life was wonderful. And she had had enough.

'Would you excuse me?' she asked generally, and saw Dante give her a sharp look—but it was Gabina who answered.

'You are well, Lysan?'

'Oh, grief, yes,' she replied blithely. 'It's just that I've a letter to write...'

'You write to your *novio* every day?' Ondina asked.

Lysan guessed *novio* was her fiancé. Stuff Dante Viveros and his 'Who shall I bed this Monday?' policy... 'Every day,' she lied—and could not resist a flick of a glance to him. His face was inscrutable, she saw. Though—was that a flicker of something in his eyes, an angry flicker that said, I hope you told him of the abandoned way you were with me when you wrote to him last night? She favoured him with her uppity profile, but went up to her room facing the fact that she had never felt so down.

She refused to listen for sounds of him and Ondina leaving, and for sounds of him not coming back, and went and stood under the shower for an age, wishing that the sound of running water would block out all thought as well as sounds of a departing car.

She used the blow-dryer to dry her newly washed hair and got into a fresh nightdress and climbed into bed to snick off her light and to know with a certainty that her stay in Dante's lovely home was over.

That knowledge kept her awake for half the night. She was going to leave, she knew that. After the way she had clung to him, after the way he had not flinched from openly telling her she had encouraged him to bed her— and, to crown it all, after the way she had let fly with that right-hander, pride alone if nothing else demanded that she packed and went. The only wonder to her was that she had waited almost a whole day to realise that!

He had objected strongly on Sunday when she had told him she was leaving, but she doubted he would put up any protest tomorrow when she told him she was off.

Busily she planned how she would go about it. There had been frost between them tonight; albeit that they had both taken pains that no one else should know it, she had been aware of that frost. But, hopefully, they would part amicably tomorrow. Not that she thought the coldness between them would worry Dante one iota. But because her father would still have dealings with his firm, and because Dante would still have dealings with her father's firm, she felt it only right that she should behave with as much friendliness as she could muster.

Eventually Lysan managed to get off to sleep, but it seemed that barely had she closed her eyes than a pounding should start in her head. She opened her eyes. The pounding was still there. Then suddenly, just as it began to dawn on her that it wasn't a pounding in her head but that someone was knocking on her door, so that door opened and Dante was coming over to her bed.

'There is a phone call for you,' he said without preamble, looking down at her from his tall height.

Usually Lysan came awake rapidly. She blamed the fact that she must have only managed a couple of hours' sleep that night for the fact that she was so dull-witted that morning.

'A phone call?' she questioned, more conscious of the fact that she hadn't a scrap of make-up on and that her hair was all over the place—and that Dante, larger than life, was standing over her.

'You've heard of the telephone?'

Sarcastic swine! In an instant she had pushed back the covers and angrily jumped out of bed. Unfortunately it was all too quick. She knew she was going to topple over the minute she stood up, found she was too close to him for comfort, and took a too rapid step backward— knocking her leg on the bed in the process.

'Oh!' she cried, but before she could fall strong arms and hands had shot out to grab her.

To be in Dante's arms was heaven. Her anger disappeared as nothing. Momentarily she leaned against him, felt safe in the harbour of his arms. He was shirt- and trouser-clad and all at once the warmth of his body was burning into her.

Desperately she strove to remain sane. When had she ever thought herself frigid? This man only had to hold her and... From somewhere she found the strength to pull out of his hold. It coincided with Dante moving back a step.

Then he spotted her robe at the bottom of her bed. 'Here, put this on,' he said gruffly, his eyes moving from her face to where the peaks of her breasts had hardened and were showing through the soft silk of her nightdress.

She saw a muscle move in his temple, but as Lysan came more fully awake and realised the clinging material of her nightdress left little to the imagination she grabbed at the robe he held out. 'Where?' she asked. 'Which phone?' Distractedly she pushed a swathe of tousled hair from her face.

'Come with me,' he grunted, and, taking his eyes from the action of her hand, he abruptly turned about and headed for the door.

Lysan chased after him, shrugging into the robe and doing it up as she went. Down the stairs they went and into a room she had not been in before. It was Dante's study. He pointed to the phone. As she had thought it had a fax facility.

She went past him and picked up the phone. 'Hello.'

'You took your time,' grumbled Noel pleasantly.

'Noel!' she cried. 'Is anything wrong?'

'Wrong? Why should there be? I just got to the office, remembered your mother saying last night that you were staying in Dante Viveros's home, and, having got his number from your father, thought I'd like to give my best girl a ring.'

'And forgot that if it's getting on for ten in England it must be getting on for six in the morning here.'

'Oh, damn! Do you mind?'

'Not a bit,' Lysan softened. 'It's good to hear you.' She heard an impatient kind of sound behind her, and spun round to see that Dante was still in the study with her. She wished he had half of Gabina's manners in the 'I'll leave you to your telephone call' department. Then realised that since he was up and dressed he must have been putting in a few hours at his desk—probably to make up for having Monday off—and was waiting impatiently for her to finish her conversation so he could have his study back.

'How's it going, this holiday? Are you enjoying it? Are you...?' he paused, and then asked seriously, 'Are you missing me at all?'

Oh, Noel, she thought sadly, and knew at that exact moment that, love him though she did, that love was that of a sister to a brother. She knew then, painfully, that she was going to have to hurt him! Knew because...

'Of course, but I'm also having a super time,' she replied, tears springing to her eyes as she realised that she must break her engagement to Noel, and cause him unhappiness.

'Not so good that you won't want to come back, I hope?' he asked, and sounded just that little bit worried.

What could she do? No way could she tell him over

the phone that she could not marry him—she owed him better than that. 'I'm—looking forward to coming home,' she lied.

'Good. I'd better go now and start some work. But don't forget it's my birthday on Christmas Day, and that I want two presents,' he joked, and Lysan felt worse than ever at what she was going to have to do.

'You won't let me forget, I'm sure,' she said gently, and said goodbye wanting nothing more than to hide away in some dark corner and howl her eyes out.

She turned round and had no idea that there was the shine of tears in her eyes until Dante, standing nowhere but right in front of her, blocking her way, stared grimly at her, and snarled, 'You miss him so much that you weep!'

She choked on a breath. Even while he looked at her as if he could easily throttle her, she knew... It had been there long enough. Staring her in the face had she but seen. But now she knew. Had known while she was speaking with Noel that she—was in love with Dante Viveros. And, while coping with the shock of that, something else she knew too was that she was going to guard at all costs that he never found out how she felt about him.

'Of course I miss Noel,' she retorted, no mistake about it. 'I'm engaged to him!'

'It took a phone call from him to make you remember!' Dante snarled, and Lysan wondered how she could love him yet at the same time hate him. But she was under no illusion about what he was so obliquely referring to, and it had never been her way to duck an issue.

'I remember more than that!' she flew, her green eyes sparking, anger aiding her in her time of utmost need. 'I also remember that it was you who took me into your arms, not the other way about!'

'And you objected!' Sarcasm wasn't in it.

'You pig! You utter pig!' she yelled, and, feeling in danger of belting him another one, she pushed past him and raced along the hall and up the stairs.

Tears of sadness had given way to tears of fury by the time she had reached her room. That was it! She was leaving. Nothing was going to stop her.

A short while later, however, and her anger began to abate. So much, though, for her wanting to part amicably from Dante! And so much too for her thought that nothing would stop her leaving. She was still going; nothing had changed that. But now she loved him—and it seemed to her now that, far from stopping her from going, Dante would come and help her pack!

CHAPTER FIVE

HER head was a ferment of worried thoughts as Lysan waited for her normal time to go down to breakfast to arrive. After her angry flight from Dante she had showered and dressed and had started to pack her belongings. But as busy as she kept herself she could not stop the thoughts that rioted in her head.

She loved that arrogant swine, was in love with him, and there was not a thing she could do about it! How it had come about when she had seemed to spend half her time hating him was a mystery. But it was there, and no amount of wishing, or trying to dissect the how and why of it, would make it go away.

With the love she had for Dante uppermost, she supposed she should be grateful to him. Prior to meeting him she had been extremely worried that there was something wrong with her that Noel's more passionate kisses embarrassed her. Since knowing Dante, since he had held her in his arms, she had learned that there was not a thing wrong with her. She was not frigid. She was a normal woman with a normal woman's responses to a man she was in love with.

And there, in relation to Noel, lay her problem. She had grown up with Noel. As Todd was her brother, so Noel, always seeming to be at her home or she and Todd at his, had become another brother. And, as a brother, she loved him and always would. But she could never marry him.

Only now—now that she knew what really being in

love felt like—was she able to put her sisterly love for Noel into perspective. Indeed, she even began to wonder if perhaps Noel was so very much in love with her that way after all. Had it been that at the time they had become engaged, with his world falling apart, he had just needed someone to cling onto?

He was stronger now, though, starting to adjust to his parents not being there. Would he be so very upset? One thing was for certain—she could not marry him.

Another thing that was for certain was that she did not look forward to going home. Oh, grief, she would have to tell not only Noel but her family too! Her parents and Todd had been so pleased...

Lysan's feeling of wretchedness was not helped by the knowledge that her parents and brother would be disappointed that she was not going to marry Noel.

At last it was time to go down to breakfast and as Lysan left her room so her nerves started to jangle. There was a fair chance that Dante would not be about. There was also a fair chance that he would be. She knew she was going to hide her true feelings from him and guessed, because she was her father's daughter, that he would treat her with every courtesy when she told him she was leaving.

In actual fact, though, she did not get to find out how courteously Dante would speed her on her way. Because after entering the breakfast room and greeting Gabina she discovered that Dante, along with Celso, had gone to spend the day at one of the vineyards many miles distant and would not be back until nightfall.

A treacherous weakness invaded Lysan. It would be impolite to leave without seeing Dante again, that treachery reasoned as Gabina went on, 'So we have the whole day. Would you like to walk, or shop, or ride?'

'Actually, Gabina,' Lysan answered on a moment of courage, 'I'm leaving today.' There, it was out; there was no going back. No weakly changing her mind—she mustn't; she couldn't. She hardened her heart at the thought that Dante would most likely breathe a sigh of relief to find her gone on his return home.

'You're leaving!' Gabina exclaimed. 'But—does Dante know?'

'He—er—I saw him first thing this morning,' Lysan prevaricated, not wanting Gabina to put up any objections, not now, not now the matter was decided. 'There was a telephone call from England.'

'You are called home?'

'Er—no,' Lysan answered. She liked Gabina so well, and hated having lied to her by implying that Dante had known first thing that morning that she was leaving.

'But where are you going? Santiago?' Gabina looked puzzled.

Since it seemed that she and Gabina drove into Santiago most days, Lysan realised that she might be a touch offended that she should leave to go and stay in some hotel there.

'I thought I might—um...' From a great worried nowhere, Lysan suddenly remembered some of the conversation at dinner the previous evening. 'You've whetted my appetite to see your favourite place, Puerto Varas,' she pulled out of thin air.

'You're going to Puerto Varas?'

'Is it very far?'

'From here—near seven hundred miles, I think.'

Lysan didn't know that she wanted to be that far away from Dante, but then realised just how crazy she was being. Soon she would be *thousands* of miles away from him, not hundreds!

'Is there a train?'

'There is, but you could fly to Puerto Montt, which is near to Puerto Varas. Oh!' she broke off. 'My cousin Urso lives in Puerto Montt. He will meet you...'

'No, no. I don't want that!' Lysan quickly exclaimed, feeling awful. 'Your cousin must be very busy...'

Her arguments were useless, she discovered, forced to give up when Gabina, whose English had come on a great deal in the time she had been there, seemed not to comprehend her assertions that she would be all right on her own and did not require anyone to meet her.

An hour ago she had not so much as considered a journey to Puerto Varas, Lysan reflected as, arrangements made by Gabina for her to catch the overnight train to Puerto Montt, she returned upstairs to finalise her packing.

To take a plane down would have been quicker but she was in no hurry. The problem of her love for Dante would go with her no matter how speedily she put some distance between them.

She felt honour-bound to write him a note, but found that far far more difficult than she would have imagined. Knowing a little of the man, she felt he would scorn any trite phrasing, though she had no intention of writing any of what she truly felt about leaving for fear he might read some of how she felt about him.

In the end, 'Dear Dante, Thank you for the kindness of your hospitality whilst I was with you. I shall remember your home with pleasure, Lysan' was what, after many starts, had to suffice.

There was a knock on her door; it was a female knock and nothing at all like the sound that had wakened her from her slumbers that morning. Lysan opened the door to Gabina and invited her in.

'A present for you,' Gabina smiled, holding out a gift-wrapped parcel.

'Oh, Gabina, you...'

'It pleases me to give this to you for Christmas. We do not open our presents until Christmas Eve, so I ask you to open this at midnight then, and to think of us in Chile, and we will think of you.'

'Oh, what a lovely thing to say,' Lysan murmured, and, turning, took from the bed her own gift-wrapped parcel for Gabina. 'Will you open this one at midnight too?' And when Gabina fairly beamed in delight she said regretfully, 'I haven't anything for Celso yet.'

'It is not necessary. He has nothing for you either,' Gabina laughed, and Lysan felt she was parting from a good friend.

Neither did Lysan have a gift for Dante but she did have a letter for him. 'Would you give that to Dante for me, please?' she asked, and when Gabina looked a shade enquiringly at her Lysan explained, 'It is a note of thank-you.'

Despite her protests, Gabina insisted on driving her to the railway station in Santiago, and Lysan, also despite Gabina's protests, insisted on settling with her for the sleeping compartment which Gabina had booked. Then Gabina went and spoke with the carriage conductor, and came back to report, 'Just in case you are confused to know where you are, he will come and tell you when you reach Puerto Montt. You will arrive there tomorrow afternoon, and my cousin will meet you.'

'You rang him!' Lysan exclaimed, startled; apart from mentioning her cousin at breakfast, Gabina had said not another word about him.

'But of course! He has to work so will meet your train, take you to a hotel in Puerto Montt I have booked for you, and the day after he will come and take you to Puerto Varas and show you around. So,' Gabina went on, 'you must wait until someone comes to you and tells you his name is Urso Ibanez, and...'

'I...' Protests by the dozen were by then queuing up on Lysan's tongue. But, realising that Gabina had done all she had only for her benefit, she swallowed down what she would have said, and settled for asking, 'How will your cousin Urso know me?'

At which Gabina burst out laughing. 'I have told him how you look. I do not think there will be many with hair your beautiful colour getting off the train at Puerto Montt. It is time to go now. I hope you will write to me from England,' Gabina requested.

'I will,' Lysan promised, and, feeling suddenly as close to Gabina as a sister she had never had, she impulsively gave her a quick hug.

She felt strangely bereft once the train had pulled out of the station. She had just, voluntarily, cut herself off from the man she loved. It was a desolate feeling, even if in seven days' time she would have severed all contact when she flew back to England.

Dante and her father would still communicate, of course. And, she realised, she might hear of Dante from time to time if she kept up a correspondence with Gabina.

An hour later she realised that dinner was being served and she walked down to the train's dining car and had taken a stab at ordering from the Chilean menu, when it dawned on her that any letters coming from Gabina could contain not only references to Dante but also his lady-love, Ondina Alvarez.

How would she take it if Gabina wrote that Ondina and Dante were to be married? Lysan's appetite promptly disappeared. Dammit, she fumed, was she to be tormented like this for the rest of her life? She picked up her fork and aimed it at her prawn and salad starter as if she meant business.

When she returned to her compartment her bed had been made up, but for all the sleep she got it might just as well have not been. At dawn she washed and dressed and sat looking out of the window, and grew more and more in love with Chile as she watched as the landscape gave way to lush green plains abundant with trees, on past a whole field of ox-eye daisies, making the field a patchwork of white. Then thoughts of Dante started to intrude again. She pushed him away, and concentrated to where the scene, though still rural, had changed again, to where a potato crop grew and chickens pecked, to corrugated-roofed houses, gardens, with roses growing—and all too soon Dante was back in her head again.

Lysan stretched her legs by going along to the dining car for breakfast and, seeing someone eating scrambled eggs out of a pan, opted for the same, and then returned to her compartment.

She was not hungry at lunchtime so stayed where she was and concentrated her thoughts on how she would get through to Urso Ibanez when she met him that she did not need him to show her around Puerto Varas tomorrow. She was grateful to both him and Gabina—of course she was—but, she owned, even without Gabina's cousin putting himself out on her behalf, she just was not very good company just then.

In fact she had never felt more unhappy in her life when the carriage conductor came and indicated that they would shortly be arriving in Puerto Montt.

'*Gracias,*' she smiled, and earned herself a quick firing of rapid Spanish, none of which she understood. '*No hablo español,'* she told him, which was meant to convey that she didn't speak Spanish, but he did not understand a word of her Spanish either.

But in any event he took charge of her luggage as the train stopped, and she said goodbye to her compartment and, because she owed it to the man who was meeting her not to wear a dismal face, she pinned a pleasant look on her face. She was just about to step down from the train, though, when, clearly knowing which compartment she had been booked into, she found herself staring down into the face of a man whom she had last seen nearly seven hundred miles back. A man who should not be here, but was!

'*You!*' she gasped, her heart racing, her brain racing, while at the same time she fought with all she had to hide the wonder, the delight to see him again.

'The same,' Dante drawled drily. 'Have you taken root there or are you going to let the people behind you out?'

Put like that, she had to move. But even as his hand came out to her arm to assist her, even as she stood on the platform beside him, Lysan still could not believe it.

'What are you doing here?' she gasped.

'I could ask you the same question!'

She started to recover. Oh, dear; by the sound of it, Dante was not as pleased as she'd thought he might be that she had departed while his back was turned. 'I did write to you,' she offered.

'Thank you for letting me know you dislike my home so much!' he clipped.

'I never said anything of the sort!'

'You didn't have to; it was all there in your "remember your home with pleasure" note.'

'You'd have read it wrong no matter what I'd written, by the sound of it!'

'You're saying I got it wrong and that you didn't lie when you convinced Gabina that I knew you were leaving?' he challenged forthrightly.

He'd got her there! 'Well—er—' She took a deep breath and, loving him so totally and completely, she came out fighting. 'Well, I'm not standing here on a railway platform having an argument with you all day,' she answered shortly. 'I'm being met!'

So saying, she stared up at him with defiant sparking green eyes. In turn he stared down at her. Then, his expression giving no heed to her angry stubbornness, he caught a firm hold of her arm, and before she could utter another word he informed her curtly, 'You have been. By me!' and steered her along the platform and out to a car where by some miracle—and, fuming, she knew he wouldn't have had it any other way—her luggage had arrived and was being looked after. 'Get in!' Dante instructed her shortly, opening up the passenger door while he went to deal with her luggage and its attendant.

For the sake of dignity she had allowed him to guide her to his vehicle but, even while she appreciated she must have offended his honour, and even if she did love him so much that her heart was threatening to burst into song just to see him again, there were limits! She had had enough of his bossy orders. He could take some of hers for a change.

'You can just take my cases right out of there again!' she commanded when, her luggage stowed in the boot, he walked back to see why she had not complied with his 'Get in!'. Her answer was an icy stare. She was not going to back down. 'Gabina has arranged for her cousin to meet me,' she informed him frostily.

Oh, my word—frosty! His displeased look was positively arctic! 'I,' he clipped, 'unarranged it!'

'You did what!'

'I rang Urso Ibanez and told him not to bother!'

'You did—*what*? How d—?'

'Get in!'

Like hell she would! Then she noticed that they seemed to have an audience. And, while it did not seem to bother Dante in the slightest that several people had stopped to watch them slugging it out, she began to feel more than a little self-conscious.

'You really are the most bossy, most—'

'And you really are the most insolent, most infuriating woman I've ever met!' he sliced in before she could finish. Then, while she was winding herself up, audience or no audience, to go for his jugular, he completely disarmed her by adding shortly, 'Oh, look at you—even angry beyond enduring you're beautiful.' She stared at him, guessed from his impatient movement that he was annoyed to have complimented her when he had not meant to. But he had complimented her, and she loved him and it did her heart good to hear him again say he thought her beautiful. So that when, his patience at an end, apparently, he demanded, 'Are you going to get in voluntarily or...?' she found herself moving.

'Well, if you put it like that,' she murmured, and got into the car—she thought she saw his lips twitch as he closed the door on her, but it was such a brief moment, she could not be sure.

By the time he had joined her in the car Lysan had discounted entirely that her comment had amused him, and was on the way to telling herself that she had better buck her ideas up if she didn't want him trampling all over her, when he ordered, not a sign of being amused about him, 'Do your seat belt up!'

And neither was she amused. Did he *have* to be so bossy? She gritted her teeth and did up her seat belt. 'Gabina has booked me into a hotel in Puerto Montt,' she thought she'd better tell him as he started up the car.

'I know,' he replied—and to her astonishment added, 'I unbooked it.'

Really, he was the giddy limit! 'My God, you take a lot on yourself!' she erupted before she could think further.

'Whatever that means, I'm sure you're right,' he replied, and there *was* a smile in his voice, she was sure of it. And charm too—and it was all too much.

For the moment Lysan felt too overwhelmed by what had taken place in such a short space of time, and was too devastated by him, to be able to think at all clearly.

Then she suddenly became alert. If Dante wasn't taking her to her hotel... 'Where are you taking me?' she demanded, and, realising only then that he must have flown down to Puerto Montt to get there before her, she questioned hotly, 'Not to the airport?'

'And deprive you of your such urgent desire to see Puerto Varas that you cared not what rules you offended in your desire to get there?'

'I didn't think—after our—um—set-to this morning— that you'd mind all that much if I didn't wait around to tell you in person I was leaving,' she answered sniffily.

He did not speak again and neither did she. She had asked him where he was taking her and, since she felt certain from his reply that he was not taking her to any airport, she'd be hanged if she would ask him again.

They motored on; it was sunny outside. She thought of the snow back home, and quickly switched her mind away. She had enough problems here without getting into thoughts of the problems that awaited her in England.

She was aware that they must have left Puerto Montt some miles away, but they had gone about ten to twelve miles, and Lysan's determination not to ask again where he was taking her had started to weaken, when they arrived in a town and Dante pulled up outside a hotel.

'Where are we?' she asked.

'Puerto Varas—where else?'

Oh, Dante; he had, despite her crossness, brought her to stay in the spot Gabina must have told him she wanted to see. Thankfully, he had left the car, and in between his coming round to the passenger's side she had got herself more of one piece.

Someone came to take care of their luggage and as it disappeared up to their rooms so she stood beside Dante as he completed the reservation particulars at the desk.

It was a small and friendly hotel, and their rooms were on the first floor. 'We'll take the stairs,' Dante decided, and escorted her to the staircase. She thought he would leave her at the door, but realised she should have known better when, clearly deciding to inspect her accommodation, he went in with her and looked about.

It was a lovely room, light and airy, but as Lysan looked to the picture window she gasped with pleasure. 'It's stunning!' she gasped. 'Absolutely stunning.' And could do no more than hurry to the window to stare out at the view of the most fabulous clear blue lake that stretched for miles. 'Oh, Dante!' she cried. 'Did you ever seen anything so fabulous?'

He did not answer. She turned and flicked a glance at him and saw he seemed arrested by her face. She turned back to the window. Was she gauche, naïve? Oh, grief, she wished she were more sophisticated.

'It is fabulous, as you say,' Dante said softly, coming over and standing close by.

Lysan found she had difficulty in concentrating on the view just then. She was deeply aware of closeness, close as he had to be if he wanted to look out of the window too. 'Er—what's the lake called?' she asked, searching for some semblance of normality, when nothing seemed normal any more.

'Lago Llanquihue,' he answered.

'What are those mountains—on the distant shore?' she asked. 'Is that cloud or snow on them?'

'A little of both,' he replied, and furthered her education by adding, 'They're volcanoes.'

'No!' she gasped. And, gazing in awe and delight, she asked, 'Extinct?'

'I hope so,' he murmured drily, and she just had to turn and look at him to see if he was smiling. He was, the most wonderful teasing, amused, wonderful look on him. Suddenly, though as she stared up at him, so as his eyes searched her face all humour went from him. 'You look tired,' he remarked.

Any sign of good humour went from her too. 'You know how to flatter a girl!' she snapped tartly. 'You try sleeping on a train!

'I have, and I did.'

'*You* would!'

He laughed. 'You're still beautiful,' he remarked. Oh, how she loved him. 'I'll see you at dinner—why not have a rest before then?' he suggested.

'Oh, I think I shall manage without falling asleep over my soup,' she replied coolly, and wished straight away that she hadn't been so cool when, favouring her with a 'suit yourself' look, Dante left her to get on with it.

She went straight to the bathroom mirror once he had gone. Where did he get off telling her she looked tired? She couldn't see any difference. Though she had to own that even if she couldn't see signs of tiredness then little sleep last night and only a couple of hours' sleep the night before made a try out on that bed most definitely appealing.

First of all, though, she gave herself up to the luxury of a non-moving, non-rocking shower. There had been one on the train but that sort of acrobat she was not. Under the shower joy started to get to her that she had not yet, as she had thought, said goodbye to Dante. How marvellous that he was here, that—if her cool tone hadn't made him decide he wanted more congenial company to sup with—she would have dinner with him that evening!

After her shower, Lysan donned some underwear and a robe and shook out the dress she would wear that night and hung it in the steamy bathroom for any creases to drop out. And only then did she go and test the bed for comfort.

Oh, bliss! She had no intention of going to sleep, but stared at the lake, at the mountains, and at the waters of Lago Llanquihue, and thought of Dante, dear, wonderful Dante. He shouldn't have flown down to check that she was all right. No way did he owe that kind responsibility to her father, but—her eyelids started to droop, and a loving smile feathered her mouth—she was so glad that he had.

Something disturbed her; she opened her eyes to find Dante staring down at her. 'I did knock, and you didn't lock the door after I left,' he told her sternly.

She wouldn't get cross. He was here, miracle of miracles, he was here, and she loved him—and she wouldn't get cross. 'This is getting to be a habit,' she murmured sleepily, recalling with no effort whatsoever how yesterday he had knocked on her door and had aroused her from her slumbers.

He shrugged. 'You managed to get some rest, I see,' he commented drily.

She had no defence; he'd come in and caught her at it. 'I always obey orders,' she offered demurely, knowing she should leap off the bed and get moving but not wanting to end so quickly these few moments with him.

'Like hell you do,' he replied amiably, and to her delight came and sat down on the side of her bed. She moved her legs over to make room for him. 'I can get Room Service to send you something up if you don't feel like going down.'

And deprive her of his company? No way! 'Is it dinnertime already?'

'Hungry?'

'Starving,' she grinned. In direct contrast to the way she had felt on the train, she could eat a meal of the proverbial horse variety. 'I'll get up,' she added, and began to sit up. Her movement brought her head close to his head. Their eyes met, and held. 'It won't take me long to get ready,' she said, her voice all husky suddenly.

Gently, unhurriedly, Dante's hands came up and he cupped her face in his hands, and while her heart thundered he said, 'Not a scrap of make-up and your hair all fluffed about you—are you sure you're not sixteen?'

'That's what clean living does for a girl,' she quipped; she wanted to be a sophisticated twenty-two, not an innocent sixteen!

Dante took his hands from her face and stood up. 'Can you be ready in half an hour?' he asked.

'Watch me move,' she grinned, and because to have him in her room was suddenly much too much, and she did not want him calling for her again, she added, 'I'll see you in the bar in under that time.'

Her hair was all over the place and the minute he went she set to work on it. Oh, heavens, twenty-five minutes to go and her hair was still out of control. A bit like her, really, she couldn't help but think as she dashed around so as not to keep Dante waiting.

He was seated in the bar lounge of the hotel when, her hair smoothly secured in a knot at the back of her head, though with stray tendrils flying which she could do nothing about, she joined him.

'Martini?' he enquired, rising to his feet when he saw her heading his way.

Tonight she wouldn't be difficult, though from what she could conveniently remember she was only ever difficult in retaliation. 'A martini would be lovely,' she smiled, and as he gave her order to an attentive waiter she took the padded chair next to Dante's chair.

The lounge area of the hotel looked out over Lake Llanquihue, and Lysan knew she had never been happier than now as she sat sipping her drink and chatting, surprisingly easily, she discovered, to the cultured man by her side.

At one stage he stretched out a hand and, with sensitive fingers, tucked a stray few strands of hair behind her ear; she went breathless, and stared at him, her skin alive from his touch.

'Do you mind?' he thought to enquire.

She shook her head, for the moment having no words. She looked out to the lake—and said the first thing to come into her head. 'Are there fish in there?' she asked, and could have groaned out loud. Of course there were fish in the lake—it was vast and must be miles across and wide. 'Forget I asked that,' she added quickly, not wanting him of all people to think her brainless. 'How big is the lake; have you any idea?'

No wonder she loved him; he was charming, and didn't seem to think her an idiot at all. 'Quite big,' he replied teasingly. 'I believe it's one of the largest lakes in South America.' And while she stared at him, spell-bound, he asked, 'Would you like another martini, or would you prefer to eat now?'

Lysan dropped her eyes from his, she had to; she quite urgently needed to get herself together. Just to be with him was making her backbone wilt.

'Did I mention I was starving?' she raised her head to murmur demurely.

Amusement lit his eyes. He looked away. She saw he had glanced to the dining-room door. 'We had better go now,' he started getting to his feet.

Lysan followed suit, but for all she had declared her-self starving she had barely any idea of what food passed between her lips. Though she did have an idea what wine it was, because, as the first course ended and they were midway through the second, she became so aware of him that she just had to break into conversation, to say some-thing, anything, to ease this breathless feeling in her that came from just looking at him.

'Is this one of yours?' she asked of the excellent Cabernet Sauvignon they were drinking with their meal.

Dante shook his head. 'Occasionally, I try others. This is Don Melchor, a wine from the Puente Alto vineyard. What do you think of it?'

It was, in fact, one of the most palatable wines she

had tasted. 'Do I get sent to my room without pudding if I say it's superb?' she asked, grinning impishly.

He looked at her mouth, then her hair, and finally he looked deep into her green eyes. 'Who could deny you anything?' he questioned quietly.

Can I have you, to keep, to love and look after? she wanted to reply, and was hurt because she *was* to be denied his love—and he would always be able to look after himself without needing the help of her.

But she would rather die than he should know of her hurt, of her love for him, and she again had to search for something, some subject, which might help while she got back on a more even keel.

'I'm sorry you've come all this way,' she blurted out, and wanted to bite her tongue—it was coming out all wrong.

To her relief, however, Dante chose to be more amused than annoyed. 'Should I leave straight away?' he questioned, his tone serious but the uplift at one corner of his mouth, his wonderful mouth, giving him away.

'I didn't mean it like that!' she said at once, and realised immediately that she would have to go carefully here—she was within an ace to telling him just how much she did not mean it.

Just at that moment, however, a waiter came to remove the used dishes, and another one came to request what else they would like. They both ordered a caramel and Lysan looked about at other diners while caramel and coffee were brought to the table.

'This is delicious,' she looked across at Dante to comment as she dipped her spoon into her dessert.

'So how *did* you mean it?'

'I'd thought you'd forgotten.'

'Forgive me, Lysan, I forget little of the *señorita* from England.'

He really *was* too charming for his own good—or hers either for that matter, she couldn't help thinking. But, since it seemed he was not ready to let the subject go, she began, 'What I meant was that—er—I owe you an apology that, because of me, you've had to leave your work.' He stared at her, his expression telling her absolutely nothing. She wished he would say something, anything—then started to worry that she had offended his honour more deeply than she knew by leaving his home the way she had. 'The valley where you have your home is lovely,' she went on quickly, 'and I really grew fond of your home, but—'

'Then why leave?' he cut in before she could finish.

Oh, help. There was only one way out of this. 'I shouldn't want to get too attached to it,' she smiled.

'You could live there?' he questioned, and seemed so serious that her heartbeats thundered and she felt breathless again.

But there could be nothing more behind his question than an everyday, pass-the-mealtime-conversation sort of enquiry, which meant she had to answer in kind. 'Don't tempt me,' she replied lightly. 'You might never be rid of me!' His blue eyes seemed to have darkened, and as she looked at him so Lysan started to panic. There was something in that searching look in those dark blue depths which warned her. Had she given away that not only had she fallen in love with the valley, and his home, but the owner as well? 'I'll be all right here on my own!' she did not waste a moment to tell him, smiled, and found demolishing the rest of her dessert of paramount interest.

'You're trying to tell me something?' Dante addressed her bent head.

She looked up, surveyed his cool expression, and just knew, without a doubt, that she was going to offend him again unless she was very, very careful. Devil take it, was there ever such a man? She felt she was walking on eggs where he was concerned sometimes. She took a steadying breath. 'What I'm saying, Dante, is that while I can't get over how…' she searched and found the word '…kind of you it was…' she faltered; his brow had come down; he didn't like the word 'kind', she could tell '…to fly down,' she pressed gamely on, 'to check that I was— um—all right I'm quite able to look after myself.' He did not like that either. 'What I'm trying to say is that now that I'm no longer under your roof you needn't— if you do—feel responsible for me, because…' Whew, it was warm in here!

'You want me to leave?'

She sighed. He was back to being arctic again. 'It isn't like that.' No way did she want him to leave; oh, why, oh, why had she got started on this? 'It's just that I'm conscious that you're taking time off from your work on my account and…' Dammit, she was very near squirming like a worm on a pin here! She did not like the simile, and exploded in anger, 'Are you leaving tomorrow or not?'

Frustratedly she glared at him. She had started out being nice, being placatory, and while knowing she was going to suffer nothing but heartache when he had gone she would, at that moment, have quite happily bashed his head in.

Loftily he stared at her down his arrogant nose. 'I might leave tomorrow,' he deigned to tell her, and paused, scrutinised her mutinous face—and then deliberately added, 'and then again I might not.'

Lysan stared back; she felt the corners of her mouth start to twitch. She didn't want to laugh; she didn't. But—and she could not decide if he had meant to be amusing—all of a sudden laughter was bubbling up inside her. And, a moment later, would not be denied. Her lips curved upwards, parted. 'Swine!' she murmured.

She saw his eyes on her mouth and as his stern look started to vanish she began to panic again. To her ears that 'Swine!' she'd uttered had sounded much too loving.

His glance went to her plate, to her now empty coffee-cup. 'Have you had sufficient?' he enquired politely.

'Ample,' she replied, still worrying.

'Would you care to stroll around the square after your meal?' he asked courteously.

Would she not! But she felt weak, vulnerable, and the better option seemed to be to get somewhere where she could be alone; letter-writing again came in handy. 'I've a letter I need to write!' she stated without giving herself time to think.

And that was when all sign of Dante being in any way affable promptly disappeared. 'Your fiancé is a very lucky man,' he replied stiffly, and with an impatient kind of movement got to his feet.

Lysan took the hint and rose from the table. 'He thinks so too!' she snapped. *'Buenas noches, señor,'* she added shortly, and left him.

She went up to her room feeling very much out of sorts. Dante had not answered her pithy 'goodnight' and tomorrow—when his 'I might not' had hinted that he might stay a day in Puerto Varas—it was now certain that he would be taking a plane back to Santiago!

CHAPTER SIX

LYSAN got up the following morning wanting to go to Dante's room to say goodbye to him before he left. Then she felt suddenly certain that he had already left Puerto Varas and, because of that last thought—the thought that she had already said goodbye to him—she was unable to find the view from her window as enchanting as it had been yesterday.

Dressed in a white, short-sleeved cotton two-piece, she went down to breakfast in a disconsolate frame of mind. It wasn't going to get any better; she knew that. She crossed the foyer and went along a wide corridor and then as she entered the dining room the sun suddenly came out!

As if drawn by some invisible magnet her glance went to a table near the window. Dante had not left! He was still here! Her heart lifted and joy entered her being. Nor was he being all arrogant and 'get on with it' in relation to her snappy parting from him last night. But he was looking her way and having spotted her, to show he bore her no ill will, he courteously rose to his feet, indicating that he expected her to join him.

With a spring in her step she breezed across the room to him. 'Hello,' she smiled warmly by way of apology for her sourness of the previous evening. 'I'm so glad I haven't missed you.'

'Haven't missed me?' he queried as they sat down.

'What time's your plane?'

'What would you like to do today?' he countered before she could blink.

'You're staying?' she gasped, surprised, delighted and unable to hold either down.

'You—don't seem to mind too much?' he queried solemnly, and again Lysan heard warning bells. Pride demanded that he never knew of her feelings for him.

But, insisted that wilting part of her, there was no reason to hide that she liked him. 'You work too hard—a day's holiday will do you good.' Doubt, nerves that had knocked her self-confidence, had stabbed at her since she had started to fall in love with him, were there again. 'But you don't have to spend your free time with me, Dante,' she felt obliged to tell him. 'Since I took myself from under your roof, you don't have to feel responsible for me.'

He smiled, and she loved him. 'Would you deprive me of the company of one of the sparkiest women I know?' he enquired.

She had no idea what he meant by 'sparkiest', but it sounded like a compliment, even if it did have connotations that, unlike those extinct volcanoes out there, he never knew at what moment she might suddenly erupt.

'I'd love to share your day with you,' she laughed. Oh, how marvellous, wonderful; she didn't know what she'd done to deserve it, but she was going to spend a few more hours with him.

'So where would you like to go?'

Lysan put her head to one side to consider. She would like a look around Puerto Varas, but they could probably do that on foot in too short a while. She guessed the car Dante had was a hire car, and since the only other place she knew was where her train had pulled into yesterday and would afford her spending more time with him she enquired, 'Could we go to Puerto Montt?'

'If you're hoping to meet Gabina's cousin, I think it only fair to tell you that he is fat, bald and fifty.'

Her breath caught in amusement. 'So what's wrong with fat, bald and fifty?'

Dante stared at her mouth picking up at the corners and took in the laughter in her eyes. 'I...' he began, glanced away, spotted a waiter. 'What would you like for breakfast?'

Nothing, Lysan decided as she sat beside Dante on the drive to Puerto Montt, was going to spoil her day. She was with the man she was in love with, and she wanted a time of happy memories—was it too much to ask?

Dante drove efficiently and well and after a fairly short but pleasurable drive he parked the car in Puerto Montt. 'Shall we walk?'

'Love to,' she murmured, and did love it as they strolled more than walked along the seafront. And later, and for her benefit, she was sure, since she did not think he was particularly interested in markets, they strolled the mile or so to the small fishing port of Angelmó where Lysan looked her fill at the various handicrafts on display.

From there Dante escorted her to a seafood restaurant where she tackled the largest portion of salmon she had ever seen on one plate.

'I won't be able to eat for a week after that!' she exclaimed, having demolished most of it.

'Did you enjoy it?'

Oh, Dante, she thought, if you only knew. She was enjoying the whole of this short time with him so much—she never wanted it to end. But end it must—

but she was not going to think of that—not until later. 'Was I a pig?' she asked, loving the glint of humour in his eyes.

'As one swine to another...' he murmured, and, remembering how last night she had murmured 'Swine!' at him, she just had to burst out laughing.

It was around four in the afternoon by the time they had strolled past many and various moored boats and back to where Dante had left the car. But as Lysan got in, and Dante joined her and steered the vehicle back to Puerto Varas, so unhappy thoughts that her time with him would soon be over began to penetrate.

He parked the car at their hotel, but as they got out so Lysan began to feel sick inside. Was this where they would part? Was this where he said 'I'll collect my case from my room and get off'? She couldn't take it.

'I'm still full from lunch; I think I'll walk a bit. That white church with the red roof we passed a few minutes ago looked interesting.'

'Would you like company or do you want your own space?'

Own space? Her life would be a void when he was gone. 'I'd love your company,' she said honestly—and was rewarded by Dante placing a hand on her elbow and turning her about.

The church was further away than she had thought, and was closed when they got there, but none of it mattered. From there they walked downhill, through the town square, and across the road to stand by a rail and look at Lake Llanquihue.

Dante was standing close, their shoulders almost touching, and she was having trouble with her breathing again. 'What are the two volcanoes called; have you any idea?' she asked, needing to say something, anything.

'The one on the left, the cone-shaped one, is Osorno; the one on the right with its cone blasted is Calbuco,' he answered, and mentioned, as if it was by the way, 'We can take a drive that way tomorrow if you like.'

Blood pounded in her head. She could hardly believe it. He wasn't going! He was staying! He was *staying*! 'Anything you say,' she replied, her tone as casual as his. He was staying! He was jolly well *staying*! 'That Calbuco looks as though he's been knocked about a bit.'

'That's what molten lava will do for you,' Dante replied drlly.

Lysan joined him for dinner that evening, and found to her surprise that she was hungry. 'It must be because you tend to dine later here than we do at home,' she excused her appetite.

'Tell me about your home, Lysan?' he asked.

She looked at him; he seemed genuinely interested. 'Well, for a start, it's not as big as your home.' Gabina and Celso had their own apartments within his house besides other rooms into which she had never ventured. 'But it's still on the big side, I suppose.'

'Your—fiancé, he lives elsewhere?' Dante asked, his attention on the wine he was sampling.

'He has his own home. He's always lived there. When—' she broke off. She had forgotten all about Noel—and how she was going to have to hurt him. She wished Dante had never mentioned him.

'When?' Dante questioned, not so fully preoccupied with the wine as she had thought, apparently.

'I've forgotten what I was going to say.'

'You do not wish to talk of your fiancé?'

Oh, grief, his brow had come down. 'No!' she said bluntly.

'He is too—personal to you?'

Why couldn't he leave it alone? 'Of course he's personal to me!' Dammit, she was going to marry... Oh, Lord. No, she wasn't. Although as yet she was the only one who knew that. Somehow, she felt that she wanted to tell Dante that she was not going to marry Noel—but even though the two would never meet she felt she owed it to Noel to tell him first. 'Look, can we drop it?' she asked.

'Drop it?'

He knew what she meant. Any man who could ask her if she wanted her 'own space' must know her language and colloquialisms as his own.

'I prefer not to...'

'Not to talk of your fiancé while you are dining with another man?' he asked aggressively, his wineglass hitting the table with a thud.

Lysan stared at him in amazement. What had brought this on? 'Yes, if you like!' she snapped, her aggression coming out to meet his head-on.

'You prefer to have your men-friends in separate compartments?'

Damn him! For a start Dante wasn't a man-friend—well, not in the accepted sense. Nor, now, was Noel in that sense, though she hoped he would always be her friend. 'You sound more like an enemy than a friend!' she flared.

'So shoot me!' he snarled.

'Oh, for a gun!' she exploded, and suddenly found that her appetite had vanished. 'I wasn't as hungry as I thought I was,' she stated, and, placing her napkin down on the table, added, 'If you'll excuse me.'

He looked ready to give three hearty cheers. They stood up in unison. 'Goodnight, *señorita*,' he bade her icily.

The finality of that caused tears to sting her eyes. Without a word, she turned and left him. She reached her room barely knowing how she got there and wondered how, when she rarely ever cried, she was again close to howling her eyes out. Damn and blast him! So much for wanting a day of happy memories!

She showered and got into her nightdress and thumped down on her bed wishing she had thumped him. How dared he spoil it for her? Though... Suddenly she remembered how wonderful the rest of the day had been and every vestige of anger went from her.

Then the phone by her bed rang. 'Hello,' she said chokily.

'You're not crying?' demanded a voice she knew and loved and which had been arctic the last time she had heard it, but was now sounding very much concerned.

'Now why would I cry when you've phoned to apologise?'

'I knew I'd be the one in the wrong.' She could hear a trace of amusement in his voice and had never loved him more. 'You remember that "Anything you say" answer you made to my suggestion we take a drive tomorrow?'

'Yes,' she answered carefully, knowing she was going to howl for sure if he'd rung up to tell her he was cancelling it and that the only place he was driving to tomorrow was the airport.

'Does it still stand?'

He might still say, Tough, but she loved him enough to risk it. 'Yes,' she repeated, and found she was gripping the phone tightly as she waited, taut and tense, for him to say, Forget it, and that he liked his companions less volatile.

But, 'Good,' was what he answered, and, to make her

heart thunder, he added softly, *'Buenas noches, querida,'* and hung up.

'Buenas noches, querida' played back in her head for an age afterwards. She lay awake savouring the endearment, and at last contentedly closed her eyes. He did not love her, she knew that, but she would be with him tomorrow, and, since she felt sure he was not a man too free with his endearments, he must like her—perhaps quite a bit—mustn't he?

Saturday dawned with the sun struggling to get through a cloudy sky. Lysan looked out of her window at the lake and found the sun hitting the water through cloud was giving off a blinding light.

For countless minutes she stared, looked away and stared again. Then, this being another special day for her, she went and showered and washed her hair and gave full consideration to what she would wear.

She settled for a pair of white trousers and a smart shirt and, leaving her hair loose, she left her room. With a pounding heart she entered the dining room. Dante was not there!

Somehow she managed to keep a serene look on her face and went to the table she had used the previous morning. She was midway through toast and rosehip jam, with underlying anxiety that Dante had after all taken a plane to Santiago, when, her gaze flicking unconsciously to the doorway every thirty seconds, her anxiety quieted and her heart took up a singing lilt.

'I've had breakfast,' Dante remarked as he came over and sat down at her table, his eyes on her newly washed ash-blonde hair. 'But I'll have a cup of coffee if I may.'

'Couldn't sleep?' she questioned impishly, her heart laughing, joy in her soul.

'There's a wickedness about you, Lysan Hadley, a

man would do well to watch,' he told her mock-seriously.

He was teasing, and she loved him, and on that most friendly of notes her day began. It was bliss, pure and simple, to sit beside Dante as he steered the car round one side of Lake Llanquihue some thirty miles to a place called Ensenada. From there they drove for some way round part of the base of the huge volcano Osorno, when Dante stopped the car. 'We will walk a little,' he stated.

Once, she had objected to his bossy manner. Today, the sun had come out of hiding, and, while he was not exactly bossing her about, she felt she would not care a light if he did.

'Right,' she complied, and saw his lips twitch. Swine, wonderful swine.

The spot where he had chosen they should stretch their legs was in woodland with a river nearby. Her heartbeats fluttered when she felt Dante take hold of her arm as he began to guide her in the direction of the sound of rushing water.

'Where are we?' she asked. 'What river is that?' she wanted to know everything at once.

Dante looked down at her. 'You are a delight to be with,' he murmured as if he just could not help himself. He looked away, and while her heart raced so that she could barely breathe they went on. 'The river is the Río Petrohué,' he informed her matter-of-factly, and added as the sound of rushing water became a roar, 'We've arrived at the Petrohué falls.'

Lost in wonder, Lysan stared at the raging waters; blue water turned into spumey white froth as it charged down volcanic gulleys and hurled itself furiously at great volcanic rocks. And, raising her eyes, there, majestically overseeing everywhere beneath, was the snow-clad giant cone-shaped Osorno.

'Did you ever...?' she began in awe—and discovered that there was still more to come when, back in the car, Dante drove to where he had hired a vessel to take them the length of Lago Todos los Santos.

Spellbound, gasping at the beauty of everything around her, at the fact that Dante must have been up early in order to get his arrangements made for the day, she turned to him, her eyes shining with pleasure.

'Thank you, Dante,' she just had to tell him.

He looked down into her upturned face. 'I couldn't let you leave Chile without showing you the lake that matches your eyes,' he replied, and as her mouth fell open he said, 'This lake is also known as Lago Esmeralda—emerald.'

Lysan knew at that point that she was in danger of falling apart. She looked away from him—to the lake, which was indeed the colour of emerald. She ran her tongue along her top lip, a breath of sound escaping as she concentrated hard on seeing that which was around her.

As hard as she concentrated on the high, forested mountains they travelled between, past small islands, past languid waterfalls and snow-topped peaks, she was not, however, able to forget the man by her side. Nor, she realised, did she want to. Dante was a part of all this—she wanted all this to remember.

They made it to Peulla at one end of the lake for lunch, and she walked with Dante the short distance to a hotel.

Inside the hotel she halted. 'I must look a wreck,' she remarked, intending to go in search of somewhere to comb out the breeze and spray tangles in her hair.

Dante halted too, and looked down at her, his eyes raking her face, her hair. 'You look fabulous and you know it,' he replied.

She was mesmerised. 'Er—I—um—know,' she lied, and got her breath back to grin, 'I just wanted to hear you say it.' Some exclamation in Spanish broke from him. Then, to cause her heart to thud against her ribs, his head came down. Gently he saluted her cheek with his lips. Lysan tried to speak, but could not—not until Dante straightened away from her. 'I'll—go and find the ladies' room,' she mumbled as offhandedly as she could.

She spent some time in the ladies' room. She needed that time. Her hands were trembling as she washed them and brushed the tangles out of her hair. She renewed her lipstick, and all the while gave herself the sternest lecture on how a few complimentary remarks and a kiss on the cheek meant absolutely nothing more than, as she had previously thought, Dante must like her.

Lysan had herself under control when she joined him. 'This is a lovely spot,' she offered happily, and over the next two hours at Peulla spent more time in enchantment. She was vaguely aware of drinking tomato soup, of eating chicken and rice, but otherwise her whole attention was given up to just how charming Dante could be—without trying.

They chatted about everything and anything and after their meal, with Dante's hand on her arm to guide her, they strolled about for half an hour.

Nor was her enchantment over when they returned to the vessel Dante had hired. For not only did she still have his wonderful company, but there was all that spectacular scenery to be seen again on the way back.

It was late afternoon when they reached Puerto Varas and Lysan was still not any wiser as to when Dante

would fly back to Santiago, be it that evening, or tomorrow, Sunday. For certain he would want to be at
work on Monday after his long weekend away.

There was a sick feeling inside her as they entered
their hotel, and she braced herself should this be the
moment when he told her he would just go up to his
room for his case and then be off.

But he did not. Though she was still anxious when he
collected both their room keys and walked with her up
the stairs to her room.

'Thank you for a beautiful day,' she said sincerely as
he inserted the key into her door, opened it, gave her the
key and stood back to allow her to enter.

She looked up into his blue eyes, he looked back, held
her glance for long, long seconds, and then broke the
spell she suddenly seemed to be under. 'It was good for
me too,' he murmured. 'Thank you, Lysan.' With that
he turned abruptly away and went to his own room.

Lysan quickly entered her room and closed the door.
Had she imagined it, or had there been tension in Dante
just then? She could not properly decide. But, since he
had said nothing about leaving, her hopes rose again
that, for all he had said nothing about meeting her for
dinner, there might be a good chance she would see him
again later.

Deciding to take a shower, she went into the bathroom, and decided too that her hair needed shampooing
again. After towelling herself dry she shrugged into her
light towelling robe and went to the dressing table.

She was busy at work with the hairdryer when she
noticed she had caught the sun a little, and was acquiring
a faint tan. And as she dried the moisture from her hair
she noticed that her hair looked a shade lighter than its
natural ash-blonde colour. In fact, she looked well and

healthy, and it was obvious that living in Chile suited her.

Her hair was dry and she had just combed it into some sort of order when a knock sounded on her door. Her heart sank; if it was Dante on the other side calling to say he was just on his way to the airport—and good-bye—she just didn't know how she could take it.

The knock came again and she knew that take it she must. She tightened her robe around her and with her insides churning she went to see who was there.

It was Dante but, joy of joys, not with his luggage. Holding several coat-hangers aloft, he advised good-humouredly, 'Your laundry, Madam. It got delivered to my room.'

'Oh, thanks!' She went to take it from him but there was a clash of fingers and coat-hanger and to prevent a pair of trousers sliding off a hanger Dante took matters into his own hands by stepping into her room and hanging her various garments on the outside of her wardrobe.

She went with him back to the door, and loved him totally when he looked at her and after a pause remarked lightly, 'Don't I get a tip?'

She laughed, tilted back her head and laughed a tinkle of a sound in pure pleasure, relief rushing in that he was not leaving, not yet. 'Well, I don't usually,' she said impishly, 'but since it's you...' And, forgetful for the moment of that other time she had kissed his cheek, remembering only how Dante had that day kissed her cheek, she took a step forward, stretched up, and placed her lips against his skin.

Electricity shot through her from the contact. She knew she should move away, but seemed powerless to. Then Dante was moving. He stretched out a hand and held her arm, whether to move her that bit away she could not tell. But suddenly that hold on her arm tightened, and as she stared at him, unable to look away, so with his other hand he closed the door, then slowly he drew her closer.

Gently then he kissed her, a light, if lingering, kiss. Then he gathered her more fully into his arms. 'You smell wonderful,' he breathed, burying his face in her hair.

'I've—er—just showered,' she answered, and wanted to groan at how gauche that sounded.

'That makes two of us.' She could hear the smile in his voice, and didn't feel gauche any more.

She felt his kiss to her hair, then felt his lips at her throat, kissing and caressing, and her arms went around him. I love you, she wanted to tell him, but retained enough awareness not to. Then Dante's mouth had found hers again, and as she responded, clutching onto him, so his kiss became seeking, finding, wanting.

'Oh, Dante!' she cried as his lips left hers.

He said something tender in Spanish. It sounded wonderful. 'You're irresistible,' he groaned, and kissed her again.

She knew the feeling, and clung onto him, a fire starting to rage in her as his hands caressed her back. Her hands roved his back too, all muscle, all male.

He kissed her again, and pressed to get closer to her. It was what she wanted. She leaned into him, heard him groan, and then was kissed with a rising passion that fired a rising passion in her.

With her safely secured in the harbour of one arm, Dante caressed her, his caressing, seeking fingers moving to capture her full, throbbing breast. 'I've—er—got nothing on,' she thought she should mention.

'I know,' he responded. '*Querida*, I know.'

'Oh,' she murmured, and as his fingers tormented the hardened peak of her breast he had created so the flame of passion inside her started to burn out of control.

Again both his arms came around her, and again he fanned the fires within her to a roar. His hands caressed down her back to her legs, and he pulled her against him. A sound of wanting left him and Lysan choked his name—'Dante!'—wanting him as she now knew he wanted her.

She had thought she would deny him nothing; nor would she. But when she felt his fingers at the tie of her robe so a shyness she had not expected was suddenly there to cause her to hesitate.

She took her arms from around him, and quickly stayed his hands. He halted immediately, and looked down into her face. But as she looked up at him so Lysan could see nothing in his darkened blue gaze to disturb her. 'No?' he queried, and there was even a hint of teasing in the question.

'No—I mean yes—that is...' she quickly went to qualify, was swamped again by shyness at this new territory she found herself in, but bravely told him, 'I didn't expect to be shy—but I am.'

'Lysan,' he murmured her name, and kissed her.

'You c-can undo it if you like,' she grabbed hold of all her courage to invite.

'There's no rush,' he breathed, and traced kisses down her throat, moving her robe to one side so that he could kiss her right breast, capture its tip inside his mouth and drive her insane with desire as his tongue teased, tantalised and moulded its throbbing crown.

She pressed her body to him, wanting, ready then to be his completely. She felt his hands once more at the tie belt of her robe and this time had not the smallest objection to make. She had to be his; if he needed help with the double knot of her belt, she would willingly help.

But he needed no help, and suddenly her robe was undone. She swallowed hard as his hands came beneath the folds of her only clothing and went round her and slowly he caressed from her back to her front, capturing with warm, intimate hands the silky, swollen globes of her breasts.

'Dante!' she cried his name in longing, and was thrilled when he shrugged out of his shirt and she felt his hair-roughened, manly chest against her. Enraptured, she pressed her naked breasts against him, moving against him the better to feel him.

She heard a hoarse kind of sound escape from Dante. Then his hands were on the shoulders of her robe, and, his mouth against hers, he moved the material from her. She clutched onto him as her robe fell to the ground. Clutched hard.

'I want to look at you,' he breathed, but she wasn't ready for that yet, and pressed close up to him. He stilled, his body quiet. She grew afraid that she had put him off. 'Are you still shy?' he queried quietly.

'N-no,' she lied, not wanting to put him off. She loved him; it was right that he should love her this way. Bravely she put some daylight between their bodies— and Dante looked down, gazing at her breasts, her flat belly, travelling the long length of her legs, and back up to her creamy breasts. Tenderly then he kissed first one breast, and then the other.

'Oh, *querida*, my little darling,' he breathed. 'You're so beautiful.'

'Am—I?'

'Don't you know? Don't you know you have a most exquisite body?'

'I'm—er—glad,' she answered shyly, and was glad that he thought her body exquisite—and didn't know where she was when, pulling her close with one hand, Dante removed his trousers with the other.

'My love,' he breathed tenderly, and she was not thinking but feeling when, unhurriedly taking her over to her bed, he moved her to lay her down and lay down with her.

And it was heaven to feel his legs naked with hers, to have his long, sensitive fingers caress over her body, over her breast, her waist, her hips, belly and thighs.

She moaned in pleasure as gently he caressed her silky thighs. He pleasured her so much, she just had to ask, 'C-can I do something?'

'Of course, little Lysan,' he breathed. 'Anything. What?' he asked in turn, caressing her naked behind, tormenting her with longing.

'I—don't know,' she murmured, and shyly confessed, 'You pleasure me so. I want to pleasure you, but I don't know what—er—pleases a man.'

His hand on her curvaceous skin stilled, then moved to the side of her face. And his gaze was fixed on her face when, very carefully, very quietly, he questioned, 'You don't know?'

'I'm sorry—no.'

Looking at him, she saw him swallow—hard. Then it seemed to her as if he must be going back over her shyness when he had first wanted to see her uncovered body, as if he was recalling her shyness now, and, perhaps, her inexperienced reactions—ardent though she had thought they had been—to his lovemaking. She saw a muscle jerk in his temple, and suddenly, a raw note there in his voice, he was asking, 'Are you telling me that you have—never been with a man? That you are— a virgin?'

She knew, from his tone, from the almost frozen stillness of him, that something was wrong. 'Don't be cross about it,' she pleaded.

'Cross?' His frozen immobility cracked. 'You mean— you *are*!' he exploded—and as if suddenly shot he rapidly broke from her, and while she was still trying to comprehend what was happening he was off the bed and getting into his trousers, a torrent of furious Spanish leaving him—and leaving her not needing much imagination to guess that he was roundly cursing about something.

'What did I do wrong?' she asked, desperate to know, desperate to have him back with her, to help her cope with this raging need in her he had stirred.

'What did you do *wrong*?' he barked. 'Look at you!' She looked down. Oh, God, she was as naked as the day she was born—which hadn't mattered when they were like-minded, but now, all too obviously, they were no longer like-minded. 'Look at you—begging to be made love to!'

Swiftly she leapt off the bed, searching frantically for her robe. Dante found it first and tossed it unceremoniously at her, and while she struggled into it he got into his shirt and shoes.

But she was starting to get angry too. Begging to be made love to! How dared he? '*You* kissed *me*!' she flared.

'Did I?' he challenged.

'Oh, go to hell!' she erupted. 'Mine was a peck. You're the one who took it further!'

'And you objected?' Misbegotten swine! He'd got her

there! 'You're the one who's engaged to be married, not me!' he snarled.

'You didn't care about that a couple of minutes ago!'

'Two minutes ago I wasn't even remembering you were promised elsewhere!' he retorted curtly.

'I'm not a parcel!' she raged, her green eyes flashing with fury.

'But you *are* a virgin,' he reminded her, and added cuttingly, 'I suggest, *señorita*, that you save your virginity for the man you are promised to.'

With that, he turned to the door and, while she was searching round for something suitably heavy to throw at him, he opened it and went out.

The unspeakable brute! The outrageous fiend! Never, ever had she been so furious, so incensed, nor so utterly, utterly confused. Making love with Dante had seemed so right, no blame to be levelled anywhere. Yet he blamed her.

Minutes later she realised that she had felt blameless because what she had felt was love. Dante, clearly, was able to put blame onto her because there had been no love in his heart for her when he had been making love to her.

Lysan forgot all about dinner and only when, nearing midnight, she climbed into bed did she realise that the fact that Dante had not contacted her about going for a meal showed that for all he cared she could starve.

From having spent such a wonderful day, Lysan spent a most miserable, unhappy night. She should have realised, she supposed, that reality would crash into her enchanted world at some time.

CHAPTER SEVEN

THE night seemed endless but at last dawn filtered through the night sky. Lysan had always been an early riser but for once she was in no hurry to greet the day.

Eventually she got up and showered and dressed and, knowing that Dante would already have breakfasted— and if he hadn't that he would prefer not to have to sit at her table—she took herself off for a walk. Who wanted breakfast anyway?

For over an hour Lysan went up streets, down streets, took a path round the lake, her head so dominated by thoughts of Dante that she could not have said what she saw on her walk. She did not question whether Dante would leave Puerto Varas today. She knew it for a fact. In all probability he had gone already.

With no idea of the time, Lysan finally returned to her hotel, when, approaching the reception desk, about to ask for her key, a voice, a very English voice, cried her name.

'Lysan!'

She spun round, recognized Noel, but just could not believe it! *'Noel!'* she exclaimed, and moved at the same time that he dropped his case and flight bag and charged forward to grab her in a bear hug. 'What are you doing here?' she gasped as they kissed briefly in greeting, and she drew back to smile in amazement to see him there— when he should be in England!

She did not immediately receive an answer because

just at that moment, to her astonishment, someone charged up and pulled them apart. Startled, she recognised Dante. A furious Dante—who looked about to flatten Noel!

'Is this man annoying you, *señorita*?' he clipped, his eyes almost black with the intensity of his rage.

Now was not the time to hang back if she did not wish to see Noel measuring his length in the hotel foyer. 'This is Noel—Noel Whitmore—my fiancé!' she stated in a rush, her heartbeats thundering to see Dante again. She did not like that '*señorita*', though, nor did she care for the way, his rage coming off the boil, he favoured her with a distant expression. How dared he look like that when last night they had lain as close together as any couple could in a prelude to total lovemaking? 'Noel's here to—safeguard me now,' she smiled distantly as pride insisted, and even as her heart ached that she had as good as told Dante she needed nothing from him now or ever Noel was stretching out a hand to shake hands with him.

'You must be Dante Viveros!' Noel exclaimed. 'I rang your home when I hit Santiago yesterday. Good job you'd phoned through to tell them where you were staying, should business demand.'

Dante favoured her with a hostile look, but no longer looked as if he was about to shatter Noel's jaw; he then turned to Noel—and proceeded to ignore her totally.

'My apologies for rough-handling you a moment ago,' he addressed Noel as the two shook hands. 'Your fiancée forgot to tell me you were expected. I had no idea who you were.'

'Think nothing of it,' Noel assured him. 'Actually, I didn't let Lysan know I was coming—I rather decided on the spur of the moment. I—er—need to book a room and dump my case. Perhaps we can lunch—'

'I'm leaving for Santiago in a few minutes,' Dante cut in affably, and as Lysan's spirits suddenly hit the floor he invited, 'Will you have time to take a look around my vineyards before you return to England?'

'I'm only here for a few days. A long way to come for such a short time but I thought I'd have a few days off, and travel back to England with Lysan next Wednesday.'

'Another time, perhaps,' Dante replied smoothly, and, as they were quite close to the desk, he said something in Spanish to the receptionist, turned back to say, 'They have a room available for you,' and, shaking hands with him, he turned from him and while Noel looked to the receptionist Dante stared unsmiling at Lysan. Her heart pounded—this was the end, she knew it. He stared at her for maybe another second longer, then, without a word or so much as a nod, he moved from her and strode towards the stairs.

Lysan turned away. If he looked back, which he wouldn't, she did not want to be caught watching him. She went to stand close to Noel; he stretched out an arm and put it round her shoulders. Momentarily her heart lifted when she recalled how Dante had broken Noel's hold on her not so long ago. But any notion that he might have been upset to see her in another man's arms was short-lived. Her father had faxed Dante that she was arriving in his country. In Dante's book that meant 'Will you look after her?' which in turn meant that Dante had taken her as being his responsibility. Which was part of why he was so furious that he had come close to taking her virginity last night—

She blanked her mind off; she didn't want to think about it—oh, how glad she was that she had told Dante that she was under Noel's safekeeping now! Not that he'd known Noel from Adam when he'd come across him with his arms around her—which was why, his sense of responsibility out in full force, he had looked ready to separate Noel from his breath.

'I'm on the second floor. Coming up with me?' Noel asked as he turned away from the desk. He looked round, spotted a lift, and they went over to it. And as they went up in the lift he said, 'It was good of Dante Viveros to give up his spare time to bring you here.'

'He didn't bring me. I came on my own, by train. He came later when—'

'Your mother said he seemed to have a great sense of responsibility.' Lysan was starting to hate that word. Nor did she wish to talk about it.

Noel's room was pleasant, but did not look out over the lake as hers did. She came back from the window to find he was watching her. 'Aren't you going to unpack?' she asked, feeling edgy, sensing Noel had something on his mind.

'In a minute.'

'How are Mum and Dad?'

'Fine. They send their love.'

'Good. Thanks. And Todd?'

'Same as ever, though he looks a wee bit serious with his latest,' Noel answered, and, coming over to her, he pulled her into his arms. 'Talking of serious, love, I don't think, regardless of what your mother says, that I want to wait any longer.' His arms weren't right. As a brother they were right. But, as a lover—she wanted Dante's arms. 'I think we should be married straight away,' Noel added, pulling her closer, his head coming nearer.

She couldn't. She twisted out of his hold. 'I—c-can't, Noel,' she said sorrowfully, and went to stand by the window again.

'You can't—what?'

She wanted to weep. He was dear to her and there was no way she could say what she had to without hurting him. 'I can't marry you, Noel,' she blurted out on a moment of courage.

'Can't?' He looked winded.

'I'm sorry,' she said softly, 'sorry' such a dreadfully inadequate word.

'Dammit, I knew there was something wrong! I've known it ever since I tried to get you between the sheets and you told me to cut it out. I've tried to believe that everything was OK between us. But it's been niggling away at me, so much so that I had to come and see you.'

'Oh, Noel,' she mourned. 'You're such a super person. But...' she stopped; there was nothing more to add.

'But you don't love me?' he took up.

'Not in that way. I love you; of course I do. I hope you'll always be a part of my life. But I just don't love you in the—marrying way,' she ended, feeling close to tears.

'If you say you love me like a sister I'll hit you,' he threatened.

'Oh, Noel.' She had never felt so much love for him than at just that moment. 'I—can't marry you and I'm sorry if I'm hurting you, but I just can't.'

Now, she knew, she could take off her engagement ring. Before she had told him it had not seemed right.

She took it off, but Noel saw what she was doing. 'Put it back on! Please.'

'I can't, Noel,' she told him honestly.

He eyed her steadily for long, silent moments, but in the end knew her well enough to know that she would not put it back on her engagement finger ever again. 'Then keep it—I don't want it.'

She couldn't keep it. It had belonged to his mother. It belonged in his family. He would marry one day; his wife should wear it. And, since she would never be his wife, Lysan had to hand it back. 'Please take it, Noel.' She walked towards him, stretching out her hand.

At last he took the ring from her. And for a while he stood there looking at it. Then, as a thought suddenly seemed to occur to him, he looked up. 'There's no one else, is there?'

It would have been easy to lie. Nothing was going to come of her love for Dante, but Noel was essentially decent; she owed him honesty. She moved back to the window and stood staring out, not really seeing, until all of a sudden she realised she was looking down into a rear garaging area and that Dante had just come out, and was throwing his case into the boot of the hire car.

'Is there someone else?' Noel asked, rephrasing his question.

As if knowing someone was watching him, Dante looked up—and saw her. Even from there she could see he was hostile. 'It doesn't affect us—it never did,' she answered.

'Then there is someone?' To move now, to make any sort of jerky movement, would make Dante aware that she was affected in some small way by his hostility.

He slammed the boot shut, favoured her with a look

that said, My God, last night you were ready to jump into bed with me, this morning you're in your boyfriend's room and he's the one about to get lucky, and, with no more sign of recognition than that, he slammed into the vehicle and roared out of the car-parking area as if he couldn't get away from her fast enough.

Lysan swallowed hard and turned back from the window. 'He doesn't want to know,' she told Noel, and could have wept at the truth of that.

'It's not that creep you used to go out with before me, is it? Paul something or other?'

Lysan had no idea who he meant. But, while honesty ruled that she should not duck the question when asked was there someone else, she just could not tell him who it was that she did love. It was much, much too personal for that.

'No, and please don't ask,' she replied, nothing more to be said on the subject as far as she could see. 'Can I help you unpack?' she asked.

'It hardly seems worthwhile unpacking at all now,' Noel grumbled.

'That sounds more like you.'

'What?'

'You're going into a sulk.'

'Sisterly candour I can do without,' he grumbled. 'And, dammit, I've got something to sulk about!'

'Oh, Noel, I'm so sorry. I do love you, but not in that way.'

She was still of the view, now she knew what 'that way' was, that perhaps Noel did not truly love her in 'that way' either, when he threw her a much miffed look but deigned to toss his case key at her. 'You can start doing penance by unpacking anyway.' But his mood had lightened a little, and, by her reckoning, to do all of his unpacking was the least she could do.

They spent the rest of the day in Puerto Varas. But standing by the rail after dinner and gazing over Lago Llanquihue with Noel was nothing like standing at the rail and looking over the lake with Dante. And her heart ached, and she didn't think she could take it.

'It's getting a little chilly,' she said of the wonderfully warm evening. 'Shall we go in?'

It was her suggestion too the next day that they return to Santiago. 'You don't fancy showing me Puerto Montt?'

She'd been to Puerto Montt with Dante. She wanted— while at the same time did not want—to return to England where she could go to places that she had not been to with Dante. Places where the memory of that time with him would not dominate everything.

'Christmas is nearly here. The airports will be busy and we could have a problem getting a plane to Santiago, not to mention problems getting a couple of hotel rooms, if we don't go now.'

By good fortune they managed to not only get a flight to Santiago that day but to also book in for two nights at the hotel where Lysan had originally arranged to stay.

It hardly seemed possible that in so short a time so much had happened; that she should have fallen in love with not only Dante but his country too. She sighed. She did not want to leave. But, the day after tomorrow, leave she would.

'What shall we do tomorrow?' Noel asked as they sat at dinner in their hotel that night.

'Shopping?' she suggested, familiar with quite a few of the shops now, thanks to Gabina, and suspecting that

Noel might still have some of his Christmas-present list outstanding.

'Stuff that. Though you can finish mine off for me when we get home if you like,' he replied.

'Thanks,' she answered. If memory served, she'd had to hunt up something for his secretary for him at the last minute last year.

'You're welcome. Tomorrow I thought we might hire a car and take a look at Viña del Mar. The chap on Reception says it's well worth a visit.'

Lysan's heart sank. She had been to Viña del Mar with Dante; they'd had a wonderful day. Well, she had. That night he had kissed her... 'Sounds good,' she told Noel; it wasn't his fault that he wasn't Dante. And, poor love, he'd come all this way to see her because it was eating at him that things weren't right between them. And, for his pains, she'd broken their engagement. But, given he'd dropped his lip a bit and had a little sulk, he'd been extremely good about it.

It was one thing telling herself she was being selfish and that Noel deserved to find something akin to a holiday on this trip, Lysan considered the next day. But it was quite another to be in Viña del Mar and see some of the same things she had seen with Dante with a man she did not love in the same way.

She and Dante had held hands, she recalled—well, he had held hers, and she had not objected. She wished he were there now holding her hand. Even with Noel by her side she felt lost, alone. She tried to buck up. It wasn't fair to Noel. He'd done nothing wrong.

They sat down to lunch. She had lunched in Viña del Mar with Dante. After that lunch Dante had kissed her cheek. Oh, God, when did it start to get better?

'Have you bought your secretary her Christmas present yet?' she erupted into sudden conversation, which fortunately Noel was too engrossed in his pudding to be surprised at.

'As a matter of fact...' he began loftily.

'You haven't!' she accused.

'So first thing on Thursday you can—'

'Hang on. We won't hit Heathrow until about nine on Thursday morning. I'll need to get home and...' her voice faded. She did not want to go home! She wanted to stay, to stay. Oh, how she wanted to stay. How could she possibly leave?

'So, OK, make it Friday,' Noel said easily, and finished the rest of his pudding.

Shortly afterwards they left the restaurant and she again fought a battle against her inner unhappiness, against this new and overwhelming urge not to take that plane tomorrow.

'Let's take another look at the Pacific,' Noel suggested, and her heart sank.

'Let's,' she agreed, wanting her memories undisturbed. She had come this way with Dante. Tears stung when winging in came the memory of seeing that gorgeous baby seal. She had thought she had embarrassed Dante by being excited to see the lovely creature—but Dante had assured her that her innocent pleasure delighted him...and she thought he had kissed the top of her head...

'I think I've left my wallet back at that restaurant,' Noel cut into her thoughts.

'Twerp,' she becalled him affectionately as they turned about.

His wallet was safe at the restaurant, and they did not

go back to look at the Pacific, and that pleased Lysan. Crazy though she knew it to be, she did not want to see a seal with Noel. She regarded a seal to be precious to her and Dante.

There was no sense in love, she reflected when late that night, barring last-minute items, she completed her packing. She had not asked to fall in love with Dante, but she had, and it had turned her world upside down. She should be looking forward to going home tomorrow, but she was not. As idiotic as it was, for Dante didn't care one way or the other, to leave seemed to make parting from him even more final than it was.

Striving hard to cheer up, she went to bed, to lie there going over and over every moment she had spent with him. But even though the end result of her knowing him was her feeling bereft she could not wish that she had never met him. She had laughed with him, loved with him—loved and, she recalled, hated him. Hated him when in his cold, jealous moments he had…

Abruptly her thoughts ceased. She sat up in bed, and felt her face drain of colour. *Jealous!* When jealous? When had Dante ever been jealous?

Slowly, painstakingly, she went over again her every moment spent with him. Had he been jealous that evening, in this very city, after they'd spent the day in Viña del Mar and he'd brought her back to Santiago for dinner? Of course he hadn't been jealous, common sense asserted—but he had come over all sharp and cantankerous when he'd asked her about her men-friends. He'd apologised afterwards, had kissed her…

Lysan's thoughts drifted off again as she remembered his kisses. She pushed the memory from her. This was too important to be side-tracked. She got out of bed and paced up and down as she endeavoured to recall every word, look and nuance. She was mistaken, she realised. It was just wishful thinking; it had to be. For Dante to be even the smallest particle jealous would have to mean that he loved her just a tiny bit, wouldn't it?

After an impossible night Lysan was up early the next morning. Noel wanted to leave around ten to be in good time at the airport. With leaden spirits she went down to breakfast, saw nothing of Noel, and, having fancied nothing more than a glass of orange juice, she went to pay her hotel bill.

She was waiting for the cashier to finish dealing with someone else, however, when she recalled Dante's fury on Sunday when he had unceremoniously pulled her and Noel apart. 'Is this man annoying you, *señorita*?' he had asked. Only then did it occur to her to think that odd. Dante was a highly intelligent man. Was it likely he would think she would be in the arms of a perfect stranger, someone who was annoying her, without kicking up some sort of a fuss?

Swiftly she turned from the cashier's desk, to find the male at the receptionist desk had been watching her. 'I was leaving today, but I've changed my mind. Is it possible for me to keep my room for a little while longer?' she heard her voice ask.

'But of course, Señorita Hadley,' he said at once, not needing to check, giving her the impression that, for her, anything, as he beamed a smile at her.

'*Gracias,*' she smiled, and, not knowing quite where she was any more, but because he had earned it, added, '*Muchas gracias, señor,*' smiled—and went in search of Noel.

'You're joking!' Noel exclaimed when, taking the seat

next to him as he ate his breakfast, she told him she was extending her holiday.

'I was never more serious,' she replied, barely knowing what she intended to do, other than it seemed vital that she remain.

'But why? You've had two and a half weeks of sunshine.'

'So what's wrong with me wanting more?'

According to Noel there was a lot wrong with her wanting more but after five or so minutes of trying to convince her, all without success, he finally, if reluctantly, accepted that she would not be flying back to England with him.

'Shall I stay with you?' he asked. But before she could form a reply he said, 'Oh, damn, I can't. I've an important meeting on Friday! You'll be able to make it home for Christmas?' he queried.

'I—don't think I'll be able to.'

'But you've never been away from home for Christmas before! Your folks aren't going to like it.' And, as a sudden thought struck him, he said, "Strewth, Liz, you're not going to let me be the one to break it to them, are you?'

Oh, Lord, she hadn't thought of that. Her head was so full of Dante, she had not thought how her parents would feel that she would not be home for this special festive time. She almost changed her mind about staying—but found that she could not.

'Coward. I'll give Mum a ring.'

She went to the airport with him to see him off. 'Don't do anything I wouldn't do,' Noel bade her, putting an arm round her as she walked with him as far as the control point would allow.

'There's no answer to that,' she replied, looking up at him with a smile. 'Happy landings!' she bade him when a minute or so later he gave her a hug and a kiss good-bye.

'Don't forget to ring your mother!'

Still far from certain that she had done the right thing, but feeling compelled to stay, Lysan took a taxi back to her hotel and, up in her room, reached for the phone.

'Where are you phoning from?' her mother asked as soon as Lysan got through. And, clearly having famil-iarised herself with her take-off time, she answered her own question. 'You must be at the airport.'

'Actually, Mum, I'm not. Noel is; I've just left him. But...'

'What on earth's going on?' her mother was sounding quite alarmed.

'Nothing at all for you to worry about,' Lysan told her quickly. 'Er—Noel and I have broken our engage-ment, but it's—'

'You've broken your engagement?' her mother ech-oed.

'That's right. Noel's coming home, but I've decided to stay on here for a little extra holiday.'

'You're all right?' her mother questioned promptly.

'I'm fine. So's Noel too, I think. He'll stay with you for Christmas, won't he?'

'Of course he will,' her mother answered without hes-itation. 'But what happened between you?' she wanted to know. But as realisation suddenly struck she asked, 'Are you saying that you won't be home for Christmas?'

Lysan spent the next few minutes assuring her parent that she would be fine, that she wouldn't be lonely, and that neither parent had cause for a moment's worry on her account. 'I'll make it for New Year,' she promised.

'I should jolly well hope so,' her mother said firmly, striving to get adjusted to the fact that part of her family would be missing at Christmas. 'How did all this come about, you and Noel? I thought the pair of you were fine together?'

'It's a long story—well, perhaps it isn't. But anyhow I'm to blame, not Noel. I just know I don't want to marry him, Mum. I—' she broke off. 'Do you mind so very much? Have I let you down? I know you and Dad would like me to marry Noel, but—'

'Forget that nonsense,' her mother cut in briskly, but her voice softened as she added, 'Your father and I would mind very much, Lysan, if you married Noel to please anyone but yourself.' And, coming to terms a little that she would not have her daughter home at Christmas, she said, 'By the sound of it, you've been through an emotional time,' and, so understanding, Lysan felt moved to tears, she advised gently, 'Take a few more days and build up your emotional strength. We'll see you for New Year.'

'Oh, Mum,' Lysan mumbled weakly. She had a fair idea that her mother thought, because Noel, without any family now, would be spending Christmas with them, that it would be less embarrassing all round if she stayed away and gave them all time to get used to the fact that she and Noel were no longer engaged. She felt guilty, but could not just then tell her otherwise. 'My Christmas presents for everyone are in the bottom of my wardrobe,' she weathered her feelings of guilt to get down to practicalities.

'I know. Your red skirt came back from the cleaners; I found them when I went to put it away.'

They chatted for about two minutes more, but just as they were saying goodbye Lysan suddenly started to panic. 'Oh, Mum, will you get Dad to promise something?'

'Sounds serious!'

'It is rather—and important to me.'

'Go on.'

'Well, you know Dad sent a fax to Dante Viveros?'

'You're not in his home any longer?'

'Grief, no!' Lysan attempted a light laugh. 'He was so good, and showed me no end of places. But I should be dreadfully embarrassed if Dad sent another fax, or phoned,' she covered for good measure, 'when he knows I'm on my own again.'

'You think it would be an imposition if Mr Viveros was made to feel responsible for you again?'

'Don't you?'

'Perhaps you're right.'

'You'll get Dad to promise?'

'Leave it to me.'

Lysan sat staring into space for a long while after she had finished speaking to her mother. She wished she could have confided in her completely but her love for Dante, her hopes and fears were much too close to her heart to confide.

While she knew what her fears were, however—that she had acted like a complete idiot in not taking that flight—she was not so clear about her hopes and what she was going to do about them. If Dante had been a mite jealous—and, while she could not get that notion out of her head, the idea was starting to seem more and more absurd the longer she thought about it—then she was hopeful that that might mean he loved her a little. But, to cause her to become even more unsettled, Dante was a Chilean; what if a tinge of jealousy was all part of his Latin temperament? Might it not then be possible for him to experience a brief surge of jealousy without his affections being involved?

Feeling suddenly impatient with herself, Lysan got up and went out into the warm sunshine. Whether Dante had any regard for her or not was neither here nor there. So far as he was aware she had flown back to England today. She could hardly ring him up and tell him, 'By the way—I'm still here!' If the hostile way he had looked at her last time she had seen him was anything to go by, she'd be lucky if he didn't put the phone down on her, much less question, 'So what?'

Without any real idea of where she was walking, Lysan suddenly realised she was in an area where she had shopped with Gabina. Instinctively, not wanting to bump into Dante's sister-in-law, Lysan turned, intending to hurry away, when she hesitated. All at once she was recalling that last time she had seen Dante was when she had been looking out of Noel's hotel bedroom window! Oh, grief! She remembered thinking then that his hostility stemmed from a belief that she was so eager to get rid of her virginity that she'd gone from lying with him to Noel's room—had Dante's hostility stemmed from jealousy?

Realising she was going round in circles, she spotted a café where she and Gabina had sometimes paused for a coffee. Lysan went in and ordered a coffee. From not wanting to see Gabina, Lysan started to think that, if

Gabina happened to come that way, well and good—she might be able to ask, casually, after Dante.

Lysan did not see Gabina. Nor did Gabina come by the café the next day. And Lysan started to grow annoyed with herself. She was being ridiculous. Why didn't she just book a flight and go home?

But, somehow, she couldn't. There were forces at work within her, forces that overrode logic, forces which insisted she stay, those forces so strong, she could not leave.

Each day she went and sat in the café while people bustled about with their Christmas shopping. And then it was Christmas Eve, and she had still not caught so much as a glimpse of Dante's sister-in-law, and Lysan hit rock-bottom.

It was then that she realised that she was being totally ridiculous—and started to grow angry with herself. She had no appetite for dinner, nor did she wish to go down to the hotel's dining room where she suspected parties might be going on as everyone celebrated the festive season—but this had to stop. First thing tomorrow she was going to see about catching a plane out of Santiago. She was going home!

Dante Viveros didn't care a fig for her; she must accept that. Damn him, damn him to hell for doing this to her, for making her this—this—non-person.

She still could not face going down to the dining room where a party atmosphere was in full swing, but, determined to eat something—was she so pathetic as to starve through love? Like blazes she was—there was always Room Service.

Lysan glanced to the phone—and as every scrap of anger evaporated so she knew that love had weakened her to such an extent that she could not sustain anger for more than a few minutes. She wanted to use that phone, not to dial Room Service but to dial Dante's home.

This *is* pathetic, she told herself—and found that she was going to her bag and taking out the slip of paper her father had given her with Dante's phone number. She thought hard for some minutes, then she picked up the phone. She did not dial Room Service.

What was more natural than that she should ring Gabina on Christmas Eve and wish her a merry Christmas? The number she had dialled started to ring out. Lysan was glad the number was not engaged; she didn't think she would have had the nerve to try again. It was taking her all her time to hang onto the phone now. She would let Gabina think she was phoning from England, ask after everyone... What if it was not Gabina who answered the phone, but Dante himself?

Lysan almost put the phone down there and then, but suddenly she remembered Ondina Alvarez and she gasped aloud, 'Oh, no!' How on earth had she been able to leave that dark-eyed, striking-looking woman out of her calculations? Good grief—Dante was probably out with her somewhere at this very minute!

Jealous! Suddenly it seemed totally ludicrous that Dante might know so much as a second's jealousy where she was concerned. The only jealousy around was that dreadful monster that was making her feel sick inside just to think of Dante with Ondina.

On that instant she went to slam the phone down. But, at that same instant, and to prove that while he might be with Ondina he was not out somewhere with her, the phone was answered and she heard Dante's voice—and the phone stayed glued to her hand. She just could not put the phone down—she seemed paralysed to move, or even speak.

'*Alo?*' His voice came a second time, his 'Hello?' sounding impatient.

'I—er—thought...' Lysan began croakily, but could go no further.

'*Lysan!*' Her name sounded clipped, taut, on his tongue. But the fact that he had at once recognised who was on the other end of the phone meant she could not just hang up—not if she didn't want him to think her a touch strange.

'I—um—thought Gabina might be there,' she managed to string together.

'Gabina and Celso have returned to their own home,' he informed her—which made no sense at all, because they lived there, with him, didn't they?

But, 'Oh,' was all she could think of to say. 'Er—thank you,' she added, and realised that that was it, and that she must put the phone down.

'You wanted Gabina for something in particular?' Dante asked before she could follow that thought through.

'Er—not really,' she replied, so churned up inside to be actually talking to Dante that all thought to say she had rung up to wish her a merry Christmas went from her. She even forgot for the moment that it was Christmas and that the shops stood to be closed when she invented, 'I just thought that, if she was shopping in town, we might meet up for a cup of coffee.'

A deathly silence met her words so that for a few seconds she thought Dante had gone. But he was still there, and she could have groaned aloud at her stupidity when, very quietly, he asked, 'Where are you, Lysan?'

Oh, Lord, so much for her going to pretend she was phoning from England. There was nothing for it but to confess, 'Um—in Santiago, actually.'

'You're in *Santiago*?' He seemed astonished. Which well he might, she realised; she was supposed to have left last Wednesday.

'That's right,' she said brightly.

'Have you been to England and come back again?' he questioned, which she thought was rather odd—though no odder than her calling him out of the blue from Santiago when she should be thousands of miles away, she supposed. 'Is your fiancé with you?' he questioned when she did not answer.

She thought a hint of chill had entered his voice—it had a matching effect on her. 'Noel went back to England last Wednesday,' she replied coolly.

There was a long pause. 'You—didn't think to go with him?'

Well, that was one way to say 'I wish you had', she supposed. 'I told you, I like it here,' she replied flippantly. 'Have a nice Christmas, Dante,' she added quickly, and, while she could, she hurriedly put the phone down.

Oh, what an idiot she was! What a fool! Oh, how she wished she had never made that phone call. Tears sprang to her eyes as again she heard his 'You—didn't think to go with him?' Brute, she was getting out of here!

Any notion of sending down to Room Service for something to eat was forgotten. If she'd had no appetite before, the mere thought of eating now choked her. She went and stood under the shower, wiping away the stray uncontrollable tear that mingled with the shower water. Love was said to be wonderful—why had no one warned her it could be like this?

After her shower she blew her nose, wrapped a towel around her wet hair and pulled on her robe—and got out her suitcase. Lysan tried to keep herself occupied, tried not to think about Dante, and tried to keep her mind on her packing.

She came across the gift Gabina had given her and knew that Gabina would be opening her own gift—at midnight, she'd said. Perhaps I'll open mine then, she mused—it was for certain she would not be asleep.

With her case packed, her passport checked, Lysan toyed with the idea of phoning the airline that evening. Any plane would do providing it was heading in the general direction of England.

That idea, however, became temporarily mislaid when her thoughts settled on Dante once more. Pig, devil, toad—she loved him!

How long she sat there trying to drum up hate for him only to find that, no matter what, she still loved him Lysan had no idea. But suddenly she was brought away from her thoughts when there was a knock at her door.

Since she had not ordered anything from Room Service, and had no laundry outstanding... Visions of Dante coming to her room in Puerto Varas with her wrongly delivered laundry momentarily blinded her— she pushed such memories away, opened her door—and nearly dropped with shock.

'Dante!' she gasped. 'What are—?'

'*Buenas tardes*, Lysan,' he cut in smoothly, his eyes on her scrubbed face and towel-wrapped head.

He looks tired, she thought, all false hate draining

from her. Suddenly she became aware of how she must look and her hand went up self-consciously to the towel wrapped around her head. 'As you can see I'm dressed to receive visitors,' she trotted out in an attempt at lightness—and felt colour flame to her face. Oh, God, she'd been in a robe and nothing else the last time he'd come knocking on her door.

But Dante must have seen the sudden surge of colour to her face, for, 'Save your blushes, little one,' he murmured quite kindly, 'I took your comment the way it was meant.'

'Yes, well, I...' she floundered lamely, and started to get angry at the pathetic mess he could so easily make her. 'It's—pleasant to see you again, Dante.' Pleasant! Ye gods! 'But I've just finished packing, and I'm getting ready to leave,' she asserted herself, 'and...'

'You're leaving?'

'In the morning,' she replied without hesitation.

'Then you'll allow me to take you to dinner on your last night in my country, I hope?' he, with an equal lack of hesitation, batted back at her.

Had she been going to eat, she would have already eaten by now. But, had she eaten, as weakness to have just a little more time with him invaded, then she knew this would have been her night for eating two dinners.

'If you don't mind waiting while I—er—pretty myself up.'

'That should take you about ten seconds,' he replied suavely. Oh, Dante, you'll be the death of me, she thought as his charm sent her heartbeats racing. 'I'll wait for you in the downstairs lobby,' he added, and, with one last look at her, took a step back.

Lysan closed the door and in the next fifteen minutes

charged round in her efforts to make herself look totally different from the scrubbed woman Dante had just parted from.

Five minutes after that, her hair for once behaving itself, Lysan, sending up thanks for 'crease-free', stepped from her room and into the lift. She wore a long flared red skirt that parted in several twelve-inch slits from the hem and was matched by a short-sleeved, round-necked top. She'd left her hair loose.

Dante saw her the moment she left the lift, and her heart pounded as he came over to her. She could hardly believe this was happening, this marvellous, marvellous chance to spend just a few more hours in his company!

He reached her; she smiled up at him. 'As beautiful as ever,' he said, and she sailed out of the hotel with him, her feet barely touching the ground. Only when she was sitting beside him in his car did she realise that they were not going to dine in her hotel as she had imagined. It seemed a bit pointless to mention it now.

Dante steered into the traffic, but suddenly another car, with some reckless driver at the wheel, came at them from nowhere. Lysan forgot everything for a moment and braced herself for the crash. Then discovered that Dante had superb reflexes. Before the other car could hit them he had spun the wheel, braked, while his right arm shot out across her to protect her.

'Are you all right, Lysan?' Dante asked, the other driver roaring away to the sound of other drivers' car horns.

'Thank goodness for your seat belt laws,' she commented lightly, and found she had instinctively clutched at the arm across her. She saw him glance down, and feeling self-conscious suddenly, she let go of his arm.

'I'm all right—fine,' she mumbled, and only then noticed that Dante appeared quite shaken. 'Honestly,' she
smiled, realising that but for his split-second reaction,
they would be sitting in a heap of crumpled metal by
now.

Dante took his arm from in front of her, but as he
started to move forward again he seemed to alter direction. Since, however, she had no idea which restaurant
he was making for, she put the thought that he had suddenly switched direction from her.

The notion returned about ten minutes later, though,
when she realised that they were leaving the hectic
Christmas Eve hubbub of Santiago traffic—and were
heading out on a route she had travelled many times with
Gabina!

Her mouth went dry. I'm mistaken, she denied her
instincts. Yet the further they travelled, the more the
feeling persisted. And if Dante had been shaken a little
earlier, then a short while later it was her turn to be
shaken. Because, unable to deny what her intelligence
was telling her any longer, she suddenly knew, with certainty, that Dante was taking her to neither restaurant
nor hotel to dine—but was taking her to nowhere but
his home!

CHAPTER EIGHT

DANTE had seemed not to want to talk on the drive, and Lysan discovered she was feeling very like-minded. Had she felt in any way in control, though, she might well have said something to him to the effect that she had not realised he meant to take her to his home to dinner.

But she did not, and the moment passed when she might have made some reference to the fact she had recognised the route. Then she had no comment to make because she found that to go to his home was what she wanted, was a bonus, an unsought but wonderful bonus. She had so loved it there and was greedy to have this one last opportunity to be there again. To have this memory to hoard, to keep.

The house seemed oddly quiet when they left the car and Dante, switching on lights as they went, escorted her along the hall and into the *sala*. But, as well as recollecting that Dante had said something strange about Gabina and Celso having returned to their own home, Lysan was marvelling that, when a few hours ago she'd been at her lowest ebb, she was here at all.

'Would you take a seat?' Dante suggested, his words slightly clipped, as if he was a mite tense about something, Lysan thought. Then realised that because she felt all of a flutter inside it was most likely she who was tense, not him. To take a seat seemed a good idea. 'Traditionally, we have a large meal on Christmas Eve,' Dante went on conversationally, paused for a moment

153

or two, and then added slowly, 'But I have given Emilia and the rest of the staff a few days' holiday.'

'I—see,' she murmured, while owning to be a pinch confused. He had invited her to dinner—but had no cook? Perhaps Emilia had left something cold.

'I thought we might, later maybe, go to the kitchen and cook something for ourselves,' he suggested.

Later! It was gone eleven now! He *did* know she had a plane to catch in the morning. 'Er—sounds—fun,' she agreed, realising as he went over to the drinks table that she was, for the first time ever, in his home with him alone.

Feeling a little dazed by that lovely thought, she looked over to him, her breath catching to see that Dante was not pouring out pre-cooking drinks as she had thought was his intention, but had turned and was look-ing at her so seriously that she knew he had something on his mind. It worried her. She wanted to say some-thing, anything, to relieve the build-up of tension she knew this time she was not imagining, but was there emanating from him.

But her throat locked as Dante came back to her and looked down at her. Then, very quietly, 'Where is your engagement ring, Lysan?' he asked.

Oh, grief, he sounded as serious as he looked. She wanted, quite desperately, to tell him that she had given it back to Noel because she knew that she could not marry him. But nerves were starting to bite, and she grew fearful that Dante might guess that only from find-ing out that she loved *him* had she discovered why Noel was not the man for her.

'You—um—noticed?' she asked lightly.

The serious look stayed with him. 'On the way,' he nodded. 'In the car. You put your hand on my arm.'

'Oh, yes,' she mumbled. 'We nearly had an accident and I…' her voice faded. He had looked shaken. Had he been shaken, not from the near accident, but because he had noticed her ringless engagement finger? Don't be idiotic, snorted her brain—but the idea wouldn't go away.

And he was clearly wanting an answer for he insisted, 'Where is it?'

Lysan swallowed; if he was so intent on being answered, did that mean her answer was a jot important to him? Her insides grew all of a tremble, and she knew at that moment that if the notion she had dismissed as nonsense was true and he had been just a tiniest bit jealous, and did have a trace of caring for her, then now was not the time to be evasive, or to lie to him.

'Actually, it's—um—back in England.'

She saw a pulse start to pound in his temple. 'Your fiancé took it back to England when he left last Wednesday?'

'Yes,' she admitted.

'There was nothing wrong with it? It was neither too big nor too small?' he questioned, and that pounding in his temple worried her. His voice was taut, as if it, and he, might break at any second.

'There was nothing wrong with it,' she stated quickly in her alarm, and added, because she simply had to, 'I gave it to Noel to take with him because I was no longer entitled to wear it.'

'Your engagement is broken?' he questioned, no let-up in the tension. 'You are no longer to marry this man?'

'It's—important to you, Dante?' she had to ask, her own voice sounding taut in her ears.

'*Tell me!*' he demanded forcefully.

'Well, if you put it like that,' she struggled, 'yes, my engagement is broken, and no, I shall not marry Noel.'

His tension seemed to visibly ease, but hers increased tenfold when, 'Are you in love with me?' he asked.

'Oh, come on!' she exclaimed.

'It's impossible?' He was looking tense again yet defeated somehow.

'*You're* impossible!' she flew.

He studied her, thought about it as he endeavoured to comprehend her meaning. 'You're right,' he agreed at length. 'Forgive me, Lysan, this is all so new to me that I'm forgetting that perhaps I should tell you how things are with me first, before I ask you that very important question.'

Oh, help, this sounded so serious, so wonderfully, wonderfully serious. Yet, even though there was a large hint there that maybe the way things were with him meant he cared a little, Lysan was still so unsure that, in the interests of her pride afterwards if she was deluding herself, she could answer no more than, 'Perhaps you should.'

'You no longer love this man you were betrothed to?' he seemed to want that out of the way first.

'I do love Noel,' she began, and heard Dante's sharp intake of breath as he turned abruptly away from her. Panicking, she leaned forward and caught hold of his hand. 'I'm telling it all wrong. I don't love him that way... Oh...' she sighed in agitated frustration. 'I'm new to all this too!' she muttered jerkily.

Dante turned; she let go his hand. 'You're new to it?

But—you've been engaged?' Oh, hell, this was going all wrong, she stared up at him, unaware that her eyes mirrored her feelings until he said quietly, 'Don't look so sad.' And, to cause her heart to drum against her ribs, he came and seated himself beside her on the couch, and, turning to her, suggested softly, and with far more patience than she had expected, 'Tell me of this way you love him, this way you do not, and how you agreed to be his wife—but no longer wear his ring.'

She looked at Dante, his nearness not helping her very much with coherent thought. Then there seemed to be such a look of wanting to understand in his blue eyes that she found she wanted to explain if she could. She had no wish to be disloyal to Noel and hoped, although he would never know, that Noel would not have seen it in that light. But Dante was important to her—more important than anyone.

'I—er— Well, to begin with, I've known Noel all my life. We grew up together.'

'He lives quite close to you?'

'In the same village. It seems now that either Todd and I—you remember Todd, my brother?'

'I remember him.'

'Well, as we were growing up, and later, it seemed that either we were round at Noel's house or he was round at ours.'

'You grew up as friends?'

'Yes,' she agreed. 'Anyhow, after school, I went around with other friends—Todd and Noel are a bit older than me. Though I still seemed to see as much of Noel and his family. Then at the end of last August Noel's parents were killed in a flying accident and we were all dreadfully upset, particularly Noel, of course, and…' she hesitated.

'I wish to know it all, Lysan,' Dante said quietly. 'I need to understand.' He did not say why he needed to understand, but that he owned to needing anything from her gave her the spur she in turn needed to continue.

'Well, it was after his parents' funeral. We were all over at his house, when I found Noel alone, and—and everything much too much for him. I couldn't bear that he was so distressed, so I went and gave him a cuddle…'

'What a lovely woman you are,' Dante murmured, which set her heart hammering again, and quite made her lose track of what she was saying until, plainly not wanting her to stop there, Dante prompted, 'So you went and gave him a cuddle.'

She took a shaky breath, opened her mouth, paused. 'Yes,' she said. 'Then I said something about… No, he said something about having no one—he has no other family,' she put in, 'and I told him he was part of our family, which, of course, despite there being no blood tie, he is. Er—am I rambling?' she questioned, ready to shut up the moment he said the word.

'You are telling me what I have asked to know,' Dante replied, his blue eyes intent on hers, 'but you haven't finished yet.'

'You really do want a blow-by-blow account!'

'Please,' he replied—just the one word, but, as a hint of a smile appeared on his mouth with it, she could not hold back.

'Well, I was just about to take my arms from him—I think I must have judged he was feeling a little better—I'm not really sure. In fact, it all seems a bit confused from then on, because the next thing I knew Noel was talking about us being married soon, and then my father walked into the room and Noel was telling him that we were going to be married, and what with Noel being so distressed and everything it didn't seem right just then for me to say that we weren't.'

An exclamation in Spanish left Dante. 'That is how you became engaged?' he reverted to English to ask.

'I—' She broke off. What could she say? 'Yes,' she answered, but went hurriedly on. 'I wasn't really so averse to the idea when I got used to it. Well, not then,' she qualified, and was in panic again lest Dante ask her what, or more particularly who, had made her change her mind. With yet more speed, she rushed on, 'Only when one day he got a bit...' Aghast, she stopped. 'I can't. It's not right. I...'

'You can.' Dante took hold of both her hands. '*Querida*, for me?' he asked.

'If you're playing with me, I'll kill you,' she threatened, and loved him so when he laughed.

'There are so many facets to your nature—and I love them all,' he smiled.

Did he say that? Her heart pounded. Did he just say that? Lysan started to calm down when she realised he had merely said that he loved her nature—that did not necessarily mean that he loved *her*. But it was enough to give her the encouragement she needed. Enough to have her forcing her way through that barrier of love and loyalty to Noel, and the barrier of shyness with Dante.

'Well, if you put it like that.' Her voice was husky. She gave a little cough to clear it. 'Well, Noel and I, we—er—were never—um—passionate with one another.'

Again she hesitated, and was again prompted. 'This, my dear, I have learned,' Dante commented seriously.

She felt her face go a hint pink as she realised he was talking of the passion they themselves had shared, and his discovery that she had never been *that* passionate with any man before.

'Yes, well, then one night Noel did—um—try—attempt...' her voice faded.

'He wanted to make love to you?' Dante questioned sternly, and at the glint that entered his eyes she wanted it all said quickly.

'Yes, but the idea alarmed me.'

'He frightened you?' Dante asked angrily.

'No,' she denied, and added with a trace of a smile, 'I told you, I've known Noel all my life; I've always been—comfortable with him—well, until then,' she qualified. 'And that was what was wrong. I didn't want to make love with him. The whole idea—embarrassed me.'

'Embarrassed you?' he questioned, his blue eyes showing his surprise.

Lysan snatched her hands from his clasp and turned her head away. 'Yes, embarrassed me!' she said shortly. 'Then I thought I must be frigid...'

'You—frigid!' Dante exclaimed, and Lysan shot to her feet.

'Yes, me—frigid!' she agreed tautly, and, feeling a fool, she snapped, 'I think you should take me back to my hotel now!'

She heard him move and did not need the weakness that invaded when he came and caught hold of her shoulders and gently turned her around to face him.

'I think, my dear Lysan,' he murmured, a hand coming beneath her chin, tilting her head up so he should see into her nervous green eyes, 'that we both feel as if we're walking on the edge of a precipice. I,' he confessed, 'am as jumpy as you, but nothing will be resolved between us if I let you go back to your hotel now. And I hope you'll agree that there *is* something to be resolved between us.'

She owed him honesty, she owed herself honesty, Lysan well knew. But with the touch of his hands on her shoulders, not to mention his nearness, that steady, not-to-be-deterred look in his eyes, her feeling of wanting to run mingled with a feeling of wanting to stay. She felt his grip on her shoulders firm—almost as if he feared she might make a bolt for it.

'I—um—' she murmured, and knew that if she was going to think at all clearly she had better put some space between them.

She moved, and, confirming that she agreed that there was something to be resolved between them, she went back over to the couch and sat down again. So much for any notion to put some space between them, though, because Dante came and sat beside her.

'I don't think I—' she broke off, nerves biting, and tried again. 'I've—um—I told you I don't love Noel— in the way I should—to be thinking of marrying him, I mean. But…'

'But now you feel that, although you still love this man in some way, but have broken your engagement, it is up to me to tell you of the emotions that have warred in me since that first moment I saw you.'

Her mouth fell open, and she turned in her seat, staring at him; her heart was beating crazily. 'I didn't mean—' she began, but broke off, uncertain, as his eyes fixed on her, what she did mean. 'Since *then*?' she asked. 'Since…'

'Since I first saw you when I dined with you, your father and Todd. You looked at me with those gorgeous green eyes, smiled at me with your wonderful mouth, and as I looked at you—beautiful, your hair a superb colour—I learned that you were engaged to be married.'

Lysan stared at him, remembering that moment as if it were yesterday. 'You went—all aloof on me,' she recalled softly.

He did not deny it. 'I was having to swallow the most unpalatable piece of news—that this woman who I felt so instantly at one with belonged to someone else—I had to concentrate my attention elsewhere.'

'Oh!' she murmured croakily—Dante had instantly felt at one with her! 'You—um—wrote to my father…'

'With you in mind, I confess.'

'You had me in mind when you wrote you'd be pleased to return my father's hospitality if one of us should visit your country?' she gasped.

Dante smiled, 'Dear Lysan, I couldn't get you out of my head. I'd returned to Chile—but you were every-where.'

'You were calling me!' she exclaimed in wonder.

'You came,' he replied, and went on to confess, 'I felt my heart would burst when I received that fax from your father saying you were on your way.'

Her heart felt much the same just then. This was all so incredible. 'Truly?' she exclaimed chokily.

'Oh, very truly. Such a joy came over me—I didn't know what to do first. You could not still be engaged to come without your fiancé, I thought. My next thought was that you must stay nowhere but here in my home.

But even while I was instructing Emilia to prepare a room for you I began to fear I know not what.'

'You—didn't know?'

'I knew that I was vulnerable, that you would be vulnerable too if I brought you into my home unchaperoned. Your father trusted me, otherwise he would never have contacted me—I telephoned my brother in some urgency, asking him to come and stay.'

'I'd always thought he and Gabina lived here.'

Dante shook his head. 'They have their own home a couple of hours' drive away. But, like the good family they are, they dropped everything to come—delaying only to arrange domestic matters and to pack suitcases—when I told Celso, for the first time in my life, of my great need. They arrived here an hour after you.'

'Well!' she exclaimed, feeling slightly shaken. All this had gone on—and she hadn't known a thing about it.

'All was very far from well,' Dante told her solemnly. 'The second thing I saw after catching sight of your lovely face at the airport was that you were still wearing an engagement ring.'

'That—upset you?'

'That is an understatement,' he replied, but smiled as he recalled, 'You were later very upset when you realised I was not taking you to your hotel.'

'I—um—should think so!' she smiled.

'It was my first taste of your spirited temper,' Dante teased.

'It—er—didn't put you off me?' she asked—and could scarcely breathe at his reply.

'Put me off? *Querida*, I fell more in love with you than ever,' he murmured softly.

Her eyes went wide. She felt pink tinge her cheeks.

Her breath caught, and on that gasp of breath she just had to croak, 'Do you know—what you've just said?'

His blue gaze was tender, gentle. 'Little one,' he stated lovingly, 'it is what I've wanted to tell you since the moment I saw you were no longer wearing an engagement ring.'

'That—you love me?' she wanted to hear it again before she could truly believe she had heard what she thought she had heard.

'I have loved you, Lysan, since that first moment I saw you,' Dante owned, and while with shining eyes she stared at him, her heart drumming loudly in her ears, he added, 'My darling, I have fallen deeper and deeper in love with you with every new part of you I have discovered.'

'You have?' she questioned huskily, hoping, if she was dreaming, never to awake.

'I fell in love with your beauty, soon found you had intelligence to go with it, and, when your plane landed in Santiago, I learned of your spirit, your laughter—that gurgle in your laughter has made me light-headed on too many occasions. I've loved your pride, your arrogance—'

'*My* arrogance?' she just had to cut in—and Dante laughed.

'Oh, you're so adorable! Is it any wonder that my own normally sane temperament went scattering the moment I met you?'

'Did it?' she could barely believe any of this.

'My temperament never seemed to be the same for two seconds together when you were around,' he admitted. And was never more serious when suddenly, taking a firm hold on her hands in her lap, he said, 'Am I still impossible, *querida*? Or can you tell me if I am right to believe, to hope, as I have in my less sane moments, that you have a little love for me?'

She looked at him and as he stared tensely back she felt that she had never loved him more than at that moment. 'Of course I love you,' she replied, a trifle shakily. 'How could I not?'

'Oh, Lysan, Lysan,' he cried her name—and gathered her into his arms, and just held her. 'Oh, my dear one, if only you knew the many, many times I have wanted to do nothing but hold you and hold you in my arms like this.'

'Have you?' she whispered.

'Oh, so many times,' he answered softly, and held her close up against his heart as if he would never let her go. Minute after wonderful minute ticked by, then Dante wrenched himself back to look into her face. 'Tell me again,' he commanded her.

'That I love you?'

'It's what I need to hear.'

'I love you so much, Dante Viveros,' she said softly. *'Querida!'* he breathed, and tenderly laid his mouth over hers. And, after some moments of placing gentle kisses over her face, he pulled back to look at her again, adoration in his look as he breathed, 'Oh, what a joy you are to me.'

'Am I?' she managed.

'Oh, yes,' he replied, and held her close for more long minutes, as if he sorely needed to hold her, to feel her in his arms, before he could go on. 'Do you remember that day in the wine cellars?' he asked when at last he drew back to look into her face again.

'I've forgotten nothing,' she smiled.

'Nor I!' He returned her smile, his eyes fixed on her face as he recalled, 'I just couldn't get over the way you stood there so cheerfully getting wet when the sprinkler system activated. It was your second day here,' he reminded her when she needed no reminding. 'You laughed, and a feeling of such love for you welled up in me, it was only with a great effort of will that I was able to stop myself taking a hold of you.'

'I remember it so well—something was happening to me too. Though I didn't recognise what it was then.'

'You were—affected by me then?' he demanded to know.

'I confess it,' she smiled. 'But later, in the dark, when I stumbled, you did put your arms around me...'

'And because I was haunted by that ring you wore I had to fight with everything in me to let you go.'

'Oh, darling!' she exclaimed in sudden understanding. 'Was that why you were so cold to me afterwards, because you were fighting...?'

Gently, he pulled back from her to look into her face. 'Always call me darling,' he breathed, and as his head came forward he kissed her. 'Forgive me if ever, for a moment, I hurt you,' he breathed, and tenderly kissed her once more.

Willingly, she returned his kisses. 'Now that I know you love me, I don't think you ever could,' she murmured, and Dante kissed her again, his arms around her tightening, the strength of his kiss deepening. Then, as a fire started to kick into life within Lysan, suddenly Dante pulled back.

She looked at him, her heart in her eyes, and he swallowed, hard. 'My life, my love, I want to make you mine with a fire that seems to burn constantly in me for you.

But I have discovered in me another need, a need that says you, and the protection of you, must come before anything I want.'

'Oh, I couldn't agree there,' she grinned, utterly enchanted.

Dante's eyes stayed on her, arrested by her impish grin. 'I have a feeling that my life will never be dull again,' he said slowly after a moment.

Her heart again picked up speed. Was Dante intimating that he envisaged some sort of future for them together? 'Er—it was dull—before?' she managed. 'I can't believe that.'

'Perhaps I should qualify that, after my return from England, my life was more despairing than dull. You were everywhere in my head, and I couldn't get you out of it. Work, which I'd always enjoyed, meant nothing any more. I decided I would not let this love I had for you ruin my life, and went out every evening for a week—only to return home bored beyond enduring, and in even deeper despair.'

'Oh, Dante!' she cried; he had suffered so and she had never known. She leaned forward, was about to place a sensitive kiss on his cheek, when suddenly, and with a sick feeling inside, she remembered.

'What is it?' Dante asked at once. 'The light has gone from your eyes—tell me quickly!' he commanded.

'Did Ondina Alvarez bore you beyond enduring?' She had not wanted to say that—she hadn't, she hadn't—but the words were said—and, worse, she suddenly felt a coldness creeping over her towards him that he had lied to her.

'You're jealous!' It was a triumphant cry, and not at all the sound of a man who had been found out lying.

'You think jealousy is your prerogative!' she retorted coolly.

'Oh, my darling, my darling,' Dante crooned. 'Some inner sense must have been warning me that I must clear away any worry and doubt you might have before I...' he halted; Lysan had stiffened in his arms. '*Querida*, don't be like this with me,' he murmured gently. 'It is natural that I should have had women-friends, is it not?'

'It's perfectly natural,' Lysan replied, not wanting to be the way she was, in fact hating the way she was being, but seeming to be unable to do anything about it.

'Understand me, my little love,' Dante said urgently. 'Before you, the affairs of my youth, before I learnt control, were always judicious, with no risk to anyone. Since then, I have always been equally circumspect. But, since you, since falling in love with you, there has been no one.'

And that made her furious. 'Don't *lie* to me!' she exploded, and would have dashed from the couch had not Dante been keeping a firm hold on her.

She had an idea that the exclamation that left him bordered on a swear word, but he was still not letting her go when he said, 'Hell, did I say you were volatile? Stop wriggling, woman, and listen to me.'

'Why should I?' she flared angrily.

'Because I love you to absolute distraction,' he roared. 'And, now that I know you love me, there is no way I'm prepared to let your petty jealousy come between us!'

'*Petty jealousy!*' she erupted. 'Once I knew I was in love with you nothing on God's earth would tempt me into any man's bed but yours. Yet, on only my second evening here—when you just wanted to hold me and

hold me,' she hurled back at him, 'you not only invite
your girlfriend to dinner but when you took her home
you stayed out *all night*! I know,' she charged on furiously, 'because I lay awake for hours listening for the
sound of your car returning.'

Dante looked totally and utterly stunned, as well he
might, she fumed. But then he burst out into delighted
laughter, and she could have boxed his ears.

'What's so funny?' she challenged hotly.

'You are, my lovely, wonderful little darling.' Had she
got it wrong? She couldn't have! 'Funny, loyal, and absolutely adorable little darling.'

'I'm not so short!' she sniffed, five feet nine in her
stockinged feet. 'So tell me about it,' she requested huff-
ily—but some of her fury was starting to go. She loved
him so.

'To begin with, Ondina Alvarez is an old friend,' he
stated.

'So what else is new?'

'Shut up, *querida*,' he instructed pleasantly, and went
on, 'We were at university together. We were friends—
only now do I realise—much like the relationship you
have with your ex-fiancé, though perhaps not as close.'
Lysan stared at him; was he saying that he regarded
Ondina as a sister? She didn't think so. Ondina was
much too good-looking for one thing. Though if she
thought about it she supposed Noel wasn't bad-looking
either. Perhaps the two should meet.

'She was all over you when she was here,' Lysan
burst out—hang that for a tale of a brotherly-sisterly
relationship.

Dante shrugged. 'It is her way. We hadn't seen each
other in months,' he stated, and broke off to confide, 'As

my only love, I can tell you that Ondina seems to have a fascination for falling for the wrong kind of man. Occasionally in the past I've been called upon to help in her recovery.' Somehow, Lysan could not imagine that. Though, if they'd been at university together, Ondina could, she allowed, be a bit like one of his male chums to him. 'But, to get back to you and me—us— my sweet hothead, I'd held you briefly in my arms that Monday—and knew, because of that engagement ring I kept catching sight of, that it mustn't happen again. For sanity's sake, I had to distance myself from you. It was then that I decided that, while wanting you nowhere but in my home, I must at the same time keep out of your way as much as possible—I then rang Ondina to come to dinner.'

Lysan remembered how, after that night, she had seen very little of him for almost a week. She wondered if she had been a little over-hasty. 'Er—' Thoughts of Ondina would still not let her go, though. 'Er—you took Ondina home; I heard your car start up,' she could not hold back from saying. 'Did you stay the night on her couch?'

'You would believe that?' he asked quietly.

Suddenly Lysan knew that she would. She took a shaky breath. 'If you told me it was so, yes, I'd believe it,' she murmured.

'You trust me that much?'

Lysan swallowed. 'Yes,' she replied, and knew ease from her heartache when gently, reverently, he tenderly laid his lips against hers.

'I didn't spend the night on her couch, Lysan,' he admitted.

She was determined this time to trust. 'You didn't?' she questioned as calmly as she was able.

'No. For the simple reason that it was not my car you heard start up—but Ondina's.'

'Ondina's?'

He nodded. 'Ondina drove herself here and drove herself back home again—I never left here.'

'You wretch!' Lysan exclaimed. 'I was awake for hours...'

'Kiss me,' he commanded, and as she willingly complied he took over, and her out-of-control emotions of a few minutes ago began to get out of control in another direction.

'Oh, Dante,' she sighed shakily when he broke a most wondrous kiss.

'Lysan,' he breathed hoarsely, seemed about to kiss her again, but then manfully pulled back to look deeply into her all-loving eyes. 'My heart, I love you so much. Nothing must hurt you, or make you know the pain of jealousy I have known all too well, ever again.'

'I'm sorry I was such a monster over Ondina, sorry that you've known the pain of jealousy too. But in all honesty,' she confessed, 'I've been barely aware myself of Noel's ring on my finger since I've been here—nor, in truth, of Noel.'

Dante looked at her steadily, 'Yet you were very close to tears when he phoned you from England.' Like her, he seemed to have forgotten nothing.

'That was because I suddenly knew why it was Noel's more—er—um—lover-like kisses embarrassed me. I didn't love him like a fiancé, I loved him like a brother.'

'You love him like a brother?'

Only then, at Dante's exclaimed question, his look of

relief, did Lysan realise that—handling his jealousy far better than she had handled hers—Dante had still been uncertain about the love she had for Noel.

'Oh, Dante, didn't I explain…? I'm sorry. I…'

'Go back to the part when you suddenly knew you loved him like a brother,' Dante suggested helpfully when she did not seem able to get started again. And Lysan laughed, loved him—and kissed him.

'You're wonderful,' she sighed.

'I never thought I'd hear you say that,' he smiled, but after a moment insisted, 'You were saying about your sisterly love…'

'Oh, yes. Well, it was only when I was on the phone talking to him that I realised why it was that I got cross when he got amorous…'

'You got cross?'

'I told him to "Cut that out!",' she replied, and Dante laughed, a free—free-from-pain, free-from-doubt—fantastic laugh.

'You, my darling, are the one who is wonderful,' he stated, and while she stared at him in bemused fashion he growled, 'Continue, woman.'

'I love you,' she said, simply because she couldn't help it, and as he pulled her closer, and kissed her, one hand tenderly going to the side of her throat, caressing, she was lost.

It was a minute or so later that Dante seemed to comprehend that they were more lying on the couch than sitting on it. 'You're going to have to stop doing that to me if we're going to get any dinner tonight,' he muttered deep in his throat.

It was her turn to laugh. 'It's your fault,' she accused

lovingly, and tried desperately hard, since Dante seemed to want all doubts and worries out of the way, to remember what they had been talking about. 'Anyhow,' she resumed as they sat a little straighter, 'you had kissed me by then. Er—I'd responded—so I knew I was not frigid as I'd feared.'

'I'll vouch for that,' he murmured wickedly, and she gurgled in delight, and looked like being kissed again.

'Anyway,' she started again, wanting it all said now, 'I knew at that moment, as I was speaking to Noel on the phone, that I was going to have to hurt him. That I loved him as a brother and nothing more. I knew I was going to have to break our engagement because I wasn't in love with him—I was in love—with you.'

'You knew then! Oh, *querida*—my darling,' he breathed, his expression changing as he remembered, 'And I wasn't very nice to you.'

'You were a pig,' she said cheerfully.

'Will you forgive me?'

'I like pigs,' she smiled.

'Did I not say you're adorable?' he breathed, and went on to gently probe, 'Did you know you were falling in love with me?'

'There were signs,' she laughed, but realised that, astonishingly, he needed reassuring, that he needed to know more of how it was with her. 'You, thoughts of you—for no reason I could understand, especially since I'd only met you the one time—kept coming into my head in England. After your letter to my father I started to get restless—and thought about you again.'

'Did you, my love?'

'Wretched man, you were calling me, and, once I arrived in Chile, even if I did object strongly that you had cancelled my hotel reservations, I felt nothing but joy the closer we got to your home.'

'Oh, I really must kiss you for that,' he murmured. And, drawing her close once more, promptly proceeded to turn her backbone to water. 'Are you going to tell me more?' he asked, looking deep into her eyes, when he at last drew back.

'If I could think straight after that, I might,' she answered huskily, loved him to pieces when he laughed in delight, and managed to recall, 'Normally, I regard myself as being a fairly unflustered person. But since knowing you my emotions have been in an uproar—I even hit you on one occasion I shall never forget.'

'Entirely my fault,' Dante swiftly took the blame. And, to her enchantment, he began to tell her a little of how it had been with him. 'I'd dined alone with you a couple of evenings before. The look of you that night, *querida*, seriously threatened my sanity.'

'Oh, how lovely,' she sighed. 'Er—we quarrelled,' she remembered.

'Why wouldn't we quarrel? You had the audacity to tell me you were leaving!'

'You afterwards made me laugh.'

'And you made me want to hold—and kiss you.'

Lysan swallowed. 'Oh, help,' she mumbled, and he laughed.

'And the next day I took you to Viña del Mar.'

'You asked Gabina to come with us.'

'A courtesy, no more. I'd seen Gabina earlier and she'd told me she was hoping you would go with her to meet her friend. She had arranged it the evening before.'

'So you knew in advance...'

'That she could not come? Of course,' he replied, going on, 'What a superb day that was for me.'

'Me too,' she confessed. 'I saw a baby seal and—' she broke off, not wanting him to think her an idiot.

'Oh, beautiful Lysan, you remembered!' he exclaimed, and, obviously not thinking her an idiot at all, he in fact looked very pleased.

'We—um—dined in Santiago,' she recalled.

'Simply because I never wanted that wonderful day to end,' he admitted.

'Honestly?'

'Truthfully, my dear love,' he said lovingly, adding, 'Only what did I do but spoil the whole wonderful day when jealousy raged through me when we spoke of your past lovers.'

'I—er—did add that I hadn't made a habit of sleeping around,' she put in.

'Wretched woman,' Dante borrowed her word. 'And I, on the drive home, told myself I was being ridiculous, that your past was your business, that before you knew me you had a right to take as many lovers as you wished. Then I remembered that there was no me, present or future, because you had a fiancé. And I started to get all knotted up inside again.'

His jealousy had been equally painful as hers, she realised. 'It's over now,' she said gently.

'Thank God for it,' he said on a heartfelt breath.

'Anyhow, you apologised for being a brute,' she smiled, trying to inject a light note, not wanting him ever to be unhappy again.

'And, in doing so, we kissed. And, before I could gain control of the situation, I was making love to you, and you were reciprocating—save for a shyness that should, had my brain been working, have given off signals that you were in no way as experienced as you would have had me believe.'

'Er—yes—well, anyway,' she said, unbelievably finding that she was a little shy still in this newish territory, 'you suddenly became aware of my engagement ring and from *"mi querida"* I was suddenly *"señorita"* again.'

'My love,' Dante breathed, and tenderly kissed her brow. 'My beautiful, shy Lysan. You have so much to forgive me for.'

'No, I haven't,' she denied.

'But yes,' he countered. 'Even though I spent a wakeful night thinking of you, vowing to never let my jealousy, my need for you conquer me again, the very next morning I was horrified to hear myself losing control and saying words in jealousy that I had never meant to say.'

'And—I hit you,' Lysan mourned.

'And I, once my fury had died, was afterwards not a bit surprised that you, my spirited lovely one, should have given me what I so deserved.'

'Which is why you invited Ondina to dinner that selfsame night?'

'You were jealous?'

'I was livid. I was sure you'd been to bed with her the Monday previous. How dared you bring her to the house when only last night, but for Noel's ring, you would have lain with me?'

'You're magnificent, do you know that?'

'Oh—shut up,' she whispered, her heart hammering. Then she laughed—and he joined in.

'Though in point of fact,' Dante took up as their laughter faded, 'thoughts of you had dominated me all day and, even though I'd deliberately asked Ondina to come, I was having a hard time keeping my eyes off you all evening. You were never lovelier in your black dress and I was having a desperate fight within myself. Forgive me, *querida*, but you had shown yourself willing—why should I not make you mine, and to hell with the consequences?'

'Is that why you flew down to Puerto Montt?'

'To make you mine? No, by then I'd got myself under control again. Though it was one hell of a bombshell to return home and find your letter waiting for me, without Gabina's confirmation that you had packed your cases and gone.'

'Gabina told you I'd gone by train to Puerto Montt?'

'And that she'd arranged for her good-looking cousin to meet you.'

'Good-looking? You said he was bald, fat and fifty!'

'I lied!'

Lysan burst out laughing. 'My stars, what have I fallen in love with? Were you very cross?' she thought to enquire.

'How *dare* she? was my first furious thought,' he owned.

'Oh, dear. You—um—still sounded a bit miffed when you met my train.'

'You were a little cross too, as I recall,' he murmured.

'I got over it and we had a lovely evening together. At least I did until you went all frosty when I lied and said I'd got a letter to write.'

'*You* lied?' he exclaimed in surprise. 'You didn't write to your fiancé—your ex-fiancé?' She shook her head. 'I thought you wrote to him every day?'

'I never wrote to him once.'

He stared in disbelief, then started to laugh. 'What
have *I* fallen in love with?' he tossed her question back
at her.

'Don't stop.'

'Never, ever,' he vowed, and held her close for long,
long minutes, then murmured to the top of her head, 'I
loved being with you in Puerto Varas.'

'It was wonderful,' she agreed. 'That day we took a
drive, went on the lake...'

'It was a time of wonderment for you too?'

'Enchantment,' she replied softly.

'Did you know I was running out of control a lot of
the time?'

'No—were you?' She moved her head to look at him.
'You kissed my cheek,' she recalled on a whisper.

'I could not help it. Nor could I help it when, back at
the hotel, I came to your room and you returned that
kiss. You stayed close a second too long—and I was
lost.'

'Oh, Dante,' she sighed, and as, suddenly, an imp of
mischief lit her eyes she teased, 'Not completely lost.'

'As close as I shall ever be,' he grinned. 'I break out
into a cold sweat each time I think of how close you
came to being mine before I discovered I was to be first
with you. I was barely thinking straight when I realised
I had been wrong to assume you had made love, complete love, with your fiancé. But, in remembering you
had a fiancé, I was also bombarded by thoughts that you
had a father too. A father who trusted me, a father who
expected me to look after you like the precious jewel
you are to him—that must be so, or why would he have
contacted me?'

'Grief!' she gasped.

'Grief, exactly,' Dante nodded. 'And while all that was racing through my brain I was still desiring you like crazy. What could I do?'

'You decided to blame me.'

'I'd discovered, *querida*, that I appeared to have a knack for making you angry. And so it seemed to me in those moments of over-charged emotion, when honour was fighting a losing battle with my screaming need, that to make you angry was my only option.'

'You certainly did that—I was furious.'

'You were wonderful.'

'Swine,' she sighed lovingly.

'I left while I could, but I still wasn't thinking straight—I didn't dare contact you about dinner. Then gradually, as the night wore on, I calmed down, and round about dawn...'

'You were sleepless too?'

'Not for the first time over you, my dear Lysan,' he admitted tenderly. 'But as dawn started to break the most breathtaking notions came into my head—and just refused to leave.'

'About me?'

'Of course about you,' he affirmed with a wry smile.

'Go on,' she urged, uncaring now that her love for him was on show as lovingly she stared at him.

'There was uproar in my head when I began to see, and believe, on thinking everything through as logically as I was able, that to be so ready and—forgive me— eager to give your innocence to me must mean that you could not possibly be in love with your fiancé. Did that then mean, since you were innocent and yet were willing to allow me to make you mine, that you were a little in love with me, perhaps?'

'What did you decide?'

'I was in a state of shock. My first thought was to come to your room with all speed to find out—my brain exercised caution. But the idea wouldn't go away and I decided that we would spend another lovely day together…'

'You intended we should spend the day together!' she exclaimed. 'You weren't leaving?'

'With the notion you might love me a little fixed firmly in my head, I wasn't going anywhere but with you until I'd found out more,' he replied, and went on ruefully, 'Which I did in no uncertain way when—after knocking on your door to find you weren't there and searching all over for you—I found you in the arms of another man, *and*,' he added, 'with nothing but love on your face.'

'Oh, I'm so sorry, darling,' she apologised at once. 'I didn't know Noel was coming to Chile, but I'd have been just as pleased to see him had he been my brother Todd. Did you guess he was Noel?'

'I was so blindingly outraged that you could so cheerfully be in someone else's arms after you had been in mine the evening before, that, so soon after my kisses, you should kiss another man—so blindingly jealous that for a few seconds I wasn't capable of thought—only action.'

'I thought you were going to hit Noel.'

'It was a close thing. Sense—a semblance of it, anyway—came to me in that moment that I separated the two of you. And it was then I realised that, while clearly I had been wrong to imagine you had any love for me, I was in the gravest danger of revealing how desperate I felt about you. Pride, my dear one, came to my aid, and somehow I managed to shake hands with Noel and found I was even inviting him to look around the vineyards.'

'Oh, I feel so dreadful about it, about hurting you,' Lysan cried, reaching up to kiss him.

'Always mend my wounds that way,' Dante teased, but was serious when he asked, 'Why did he come—was it just a spur-of-the-moment notion as he said? He couldn't keep his hands off you. Even while he was checking into the hotel he had his arm around you.'

'You saw?'

'I looked back. I had to have one last look at you before I went to throw my belongings into a suitcase and got out of there.'

'Oh, sweetheart, I can't bear it that you were so stewed up.'

'Now that I know that I'm the one you love, that I'm the one you'll marry, I—'

'Marry!' she exclaimed, and had a volley of rapid Spanish hit her ears before she could say another word.

Then Dante was taking a shaky breath and, reverting back to English, his expression never more serious, stern almost, 'You are going to marry me, Lysan?' he demanded tersely.

Now, she saw, was not the time to demur—not that she had any such intention. 'Well, yes, of course I am. But—er—' an impish light appeared in her eyes '—forgive my surprise, but this is the first time you've mentioned it.'

Dante looked totally shaken that he had somehow overlooked that very important question. Then he asked formally, 'Señorita Lysan Hadley, will you do me the very great honour of becoming my wife?'

Lysan did not hesitate. 'Yes, *señor*, I should be very pleased to be your wife,' she answered softly.

Gathering her to him, Dante kissed her eyes and her cheeks, and lastly her mouth, and for long seconds afterwards he cradled her to him, cherishing her. Then, as if trying to overcome some emotion that gripped him, he pulled back from her and, his tone mock-censorious, he began, 'So, as my fiancée now, do you wish to tell me why you drove me into yet another murderous rage by daring to stand at the window of another man's bedroom?'

'I've been in Noel's bedroom hundreds of times—' she began.

'Now I know that you really do think of him as a brother,' Dante interrupted, seeming much relieved.

'I'm glad,' she said simply. 'What convinced you?'

'Nobody could make a statement that she'd been in some other man's bedroom so guilelessly, so innocently, for it to mean any other than she thought of him in the same light as her blood brother.'

'Oh, really?' she smiled, and confided, 'When we were small and Noel stayed overnight he would bunk in with Todd. Then later my mother decided she might as well keep a room made up for him. I was always in and out of there. So when Noel suggested I went up to his room with him it just seemed perfectly natural to go with him. Anyhow, as you surmised, Chile was a long way for Noel to come on the spur of the moment.'

'Why did he come?' Dante asked quietly.

'He'd been feeling that things weren't right between us. It worried him so that he had to come. He said he thought we should be married straight away, and not wait.'

'And you said?'

'What I had to. I broke our engagement and then felt able to return his ring to him. Then I went and looked out of his bedroom window…'

'You did it then, as soon as he arrived?'

'I'd have done it sooner—only it wouldn't have been right to have phoned and told him.'

'Oh, my love,' Dante groaned. 'There was I, but for a fast car and the moment's will to put my foot down and get out of there, ready to commit murder when I saw you at his bedroom window. And there were you, all upset at what must have been painful for you to do.'

'I'll forgive you,' she grinned happily, and was soundly kissed. 'Wow!' she quietly exclaimed, very much subdued when she had her breath back.

'So what made you decide not to fly back with your ex-fiancé?' Dante asked, and promptly went on to astound her by adding, barely seeming to be aware of what he was saying, 'I went to the airport for one last look at—'

'You went to the airport to…!' she gasped.

'Punishment though it was, I felt compelled to go. Until one sight of you, both arms around each other, proved more than I could take. I left without coming over to say goodbye—and had a hell of a time of it—cancelling Christmas—until tonight when I answered the phone and heard, to my utter amazement, that you hadn't gone, that you were still in Santiago. What made you stay?'

'You did,' she replied simply. 'I've thought of barely anything else but you since Puerto Varas. How we were together, what we said, what we did, how you looked.' Dante's gentle expression said he'd been there. 'Then the night before I was due to leave, after the most miserable time of my life,' she inserted with a cheerful smile, 'I suddenly got it into my head that you might have been a tiny bit jealous that time we had dinner in Santiago when you asked me about my men-friends. I rejected the idea of you being jealous because for that to stand would have to mean that you cared a little, and you didn't. And yet...'

'And yet?' Dante prompted.

'I was waiting at the cashier's desk the next morning, waiting to settle my account prior to checking out and flying home, when I remembered your fury when you'd pulled Noel and me apart in the lobby. The next I knew I was asking the receptionist if I could extend my stay. Then I was telling Noel I wasn't going back with him.'

'Oh, my dear, how I wish you'd thought to pick up the phone to tell me,' he breathed tenderly, aware now of the torment she had been through.

'I couldn't. I still wasn't certain that I'd done the right thing in not going back to England. As it was I had to ring my mother to tell her that not only had I broken my engagement to Noel, but also that I wouldn't be home for Christmas, and—er—' she hesitated.

'No secrets, not now,' he prompted.

'It's not a secret,' she smiled. 'I just feel a little awkward, that's all, in—um—sharing with you that while I promised I'd be home to celebrate New Year with them I asked my mother to get my father's promise that he wouldn't send another fax to you.'

'You thought he might fax to tell me you were still here?'

'I was so mixed up then,' she owned. 'I don't think I'd have been able to take it if, in response to any fax from my father, you had contacted me out of a sense of duty.'

'So you let day after day go by before you did contact me.'

'Day after horrible day,' she admitted. 'I thought I might bump into Gabina on one of her shopping trips, when a casual enquiry might tell me how you were. But I didn't know until tonight she doesn't live here.'

'Thank God you didn't or you might never have phoned.'

'Oh!' Lysan gasped. 'I never thought of that.' Then she smiled. 'I'm so glad I didn't know, so glad I did ring.'

'No more than I,' he breathed. 'But you'd put the phone down, left me hanging on, before I'd got myself anywhere near together. Then there were so many ifs and whys buzzing around in my head. While it might have been quite natural for you to ring Gabina, you and I had almost been lovers, and had parted hostilely. Would you, with the enormous pride I'd seen in you, ring to speak to my sister-in-law purely because you were in need of a coffee?'

'You didn't think I would? Not for that simple reason?'

'I didn't get an answer to that before my brain was going rapidly on to ask why, when your fiancé had returned to England, you hadn't—as you were scheduled to do—gone too. I'd seen you both at the airport, smiling, happy with each other, so you must still be engaged. What was going on?'

'You decided to come and find out?'

'I've barely slept since the last time I saw you—felt I was going insane trying to get you out of my head.

And there you were, still in Santiago. I knew I wouldn't rest until I'd seen you.'

'You guessed which hotel I was in?'

'They confirmed it when I rang. I almost asked to be put through to you. Then I remembered you were going to marry someone else. I put down the phone—and before I realised what I was doing I was in my car driving to get you. And it was oh, so good to see you!'

'Oh, Dante!' she cried, and they wound their arms around each other and clung to each other in a choking, emotional moment.

Then, at last, Dante drew back a little. 'I thought I was going to have heart failure when I noticed you weren't wearing your engagement ring,' he revealed. 'I wasn't thinking then, but acting. I didn't dare to hope for too much—but I knew I couldn't go on any more without finding out if you, as I so fervently hoped, felt a little love for me.'

'A lot of love,' she admitted, and gently they kissed.

'Do you have to leave tomorrow?' he asked as he broke their kiss.

'Tomorrow?' she wasn't quite with him.

'Are your parents expecting you home on Boxing Day? You said you were leaving in the morning.'

'Ah,' she said.

'Ah?' he queried.

'I was leaving simply because I'd grown exasperated with this non-person I'd become—no appetite, little sleep—and Dante Viveros didn't love me. I'd decided to leave. But,' she smiled, 'I haven't got round to booking a flight yet.'

'We'll book a flight for two,' Dante took charge. 'You've promised your mother you'll be home for New

Year—but even if I didn't need to speak to your father about our marriage by no chance would I let you go alone.'

'This all sounds too wonderful!' she sighed.

'There's a small problem in that we'll have to tell Noel Whitmore that you are soon to be my wife, but we'll do that as sensitively as possible.'

'Are you always this well organised?'

'Bossy, I think you once called it!' he grinned, and she laughed, and he paused to kiss her before he moved to stand and brought her to her feet with him; and, with his arms still about her, 'My darling,' he said softly, 'much as I want to take you to my bed, to lie with you in my arms through the night hours, I am mindful that I have to present myself to your father as a man of honour if I'm to be allowed to take you from your home, from your own country, to live with me.'

'Did I ever tell you how much I love it here?' she smiled.

'I'm so very, very glad,' he answered softly, and after a minute resumed, 'So, since I am fighting with everything I have not to hold you in my arms through this night, but in order not to deprive myself of your company through this first night of our love together, I propose we drive back to Santiago for your luggage, find somewhere where we can eat—and then drive together through the night to my parents' home.'

'You—want to go to your parents' home?'

'I want *us* to go to my parents'. I want to introduce them to this wonderful woman who will shortly be their daughter-in-law.'

'Oh, Dante, that sounds fantastic.' She was still trying to take in all that had happened, that had marvellously happened, and was still happening, when Dante, prior to making a start on the arrangements he had outlined, glanced at his watch.

'It's midnight!' he announced, and suddenly seemed to remember something for he quickly put his hand in his trouser pocket and pulled out a small, gift-wrapped parcel. 'For you, *mi novia*.' Startled, she took it from him and removed the outer wrapping. It revealed a jeweller's box. Large-eyed, she looked from the box to Dante. 'Open it,' he instructed her softly.

She took her eyes from him to do as he bid—and a gasp of astonishment broke from her. And a split second after that sharp tears stung her eyes. Clearly Dante must have had his gift made especially for no one but her.

'Oh, darling!' she cried, and gazed in wonder at the brooch made from lapis lazuli. It was in the shape of a baby seal. The lapis lazuli was a beautiful deep blue, but, in exquisite contrast, the large eyes of the baby seal were emeralds. 'Oh,' she gasped, 'you remembered!'

'I shall never forget.'

'I...' she couldn't get over it. She swallowed hard. Dante had had this specially made for her! He might never have given it to her, she knew that. But that he had had the brooch specially designed, specially made, in memory of that lovely day they had shared at Viña del Mar, was overwhelming. Here was proof, if proof she needed, that Dante did indeed love her. She felt on the brink of tears and was suddenly fearful that she might cry all over him—and so struggled to conquer her emotions. 'I—um—don't have a gift for you,' she murmured chokily.

'You *are* my gift,' he breathed. 'One I shall cherish for ever.' And, as she raised her face to be kissed, 'Happy Christmas, *querida*,' he bade her tenderly.

Michelle Reid

Jane Porter

Susan Stephens

One
Christmas
Night

On sale 3rd December 2004

*Available at most branches of WHSmith, Tesco, ASDA, Martins,
Borders, Eason, Sainsbury's and all good paperback bookshops.*

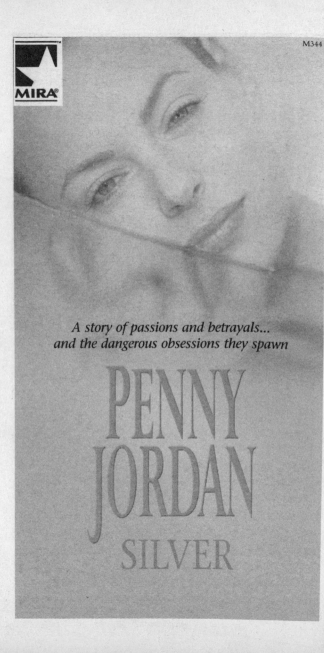

*A story of passions and betrayals...
and the dangerous obsessions they spawn*

PENNY
JORDAN
SILVER

M398

Published 17th December 2004

TESS GERRITSEN

BARBARA DELINSKY

Two emotionally compelling novels by international
bestselling authors in one special volume

Family Passions

MIRA®

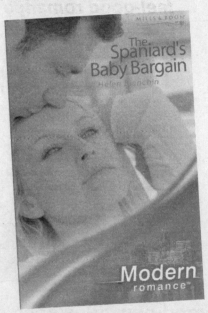

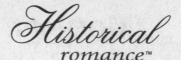

▼SILHOUETTE®

Life, love and family.

SPECIAL EDITION

THE ONE & ONLY
Laurie Paige

▼SILHOUETTE®

SuperROMANCE™

Right place, wrong time

Judith Arnold

Enjoy the drama, explore the emotions, experience the relationship.

❤ SILHOUETTE

Desire 2 in 1

Passionate, dramatic love stories

BEAUTY AND
THE BABY
Marie Ferrarella

SOCIAL GRACES
Dixie Browning